Geoff Nelder
Oct 2017

ARIA:

RETURNING LEFT LUGGAGE

Book Two
of
The ARIA Trilogy

Geoff Nelder

Vicious Circles are our speciality.

D1438423

ARIA: Returning Left Luggage

ISBN: 978-0-9574726-5-5
Paperback version
© 2013 by Geoff Nelder

Published in the United Kingdom by LL-Publications 2013
www.ll-publications.com
57 Blair Avenue
Hurlford
Scotland
KA1 5AZ

Edited by Billye Johnson
Proofreading by Janet Schelke
Book layout and typesetting by jimandzetta.com
Cover art and design by Andy Bigwood© 2013
http://topaz172.deviantart.com
Printed in the UK and the USA

Praise for

ARIA:
Left Luggage
Geoff Nelder

"*ARIA: Left Luggage* is a well-written novel with the pace and suspense of a video game...In typical Nelder style, there is black humour throughout the book, with more than a hint of camp as the virus progresses, and lots of fun as the plot unfolds."

Magdalena Ball, *The Compulsive Reader*

"*ARIA: Left Luggage* is a highly enjoyable book. A highly accessible sci-fi book. Something that you can read in bed before sleep without your head hurting and eyes crossing as you try to grasp some out there concept."

Katy O'Dowd, The British Fantasy Society

"Geoff Nelder inhabits Science Fiction the way other people inhabit their clothes."

—Jon Courtenay Grimwood

"ARIA has an intriguing premise, and is written in a very accessible style."

—Mike Resnick

Robert J. Sawyer calls ARIA a "fascinating project."

"Geoff Nelder's ARIA has the right stuff. He makes us ask the most important question in science fiction—the one about the true limits of personal responsibility."

—Brad Linaweaver

Dedication

To my wife who said with my writing, I might as well carry on; to son, Robert, who corrects me when necessary; daughter Eleanor who hugs at any excuse; and her son Oliver (4) who knows I like the kind of books that are full of words. Rob's Amy (3) too, whose life is full of pictures. My other grandkids too, Liddie-Ann, Nathan, and Charlotte whose magical lives fill me with the inspiration to write.

My memories, without which ARIA would be more true than I'd wish for.

ACKNOWLEDGEMENTS

Again, thanks to the British Science Fiction Association and their Orbiter critique group for reading every word and offering improvements. In particular, Mark Iles, Chris Riley, James Odell, and James Steel. Andy Bigwood – award-winning artist has again come up trumps with a superb cover. Kim McDougall created an intriguing, arty video trailer for ARIA. Extra tea and biscuits go for the morale-boosting encouragement from Terry Jackman; The Esoteric Bibliphilia Society (TEBS), who are the Chester Science Fiction and Fantasy Book Group, and the Chester Library SFF Book Group; Steve Upham of Screaming Dreams; the staff at the Bluecoat Books shop in Chester; Trevor Taylor, my school mate; Brian Withecombe, my legal adviser and fellow novelist; Les Floyd, self-awareness guru, blogger, and twitter extraordinaire; Dave Haslett of Ideas4writers; all the wise thousands who voted for ARIA in the P&E Readers' Poll; and with no superlatives too much to Billye Johnson, Zetta and Jim Brown of LL-Publications.

Foreword

Many readers of the first book in this ARIA trilogy have urged me to rush this sequel out into the world. Fear not, each sentence has been agonised over in Returning Left Luggage. I considered Left Luggage to be a stand-alone in that it ends with an upbeat message of hope, in spite of the demise of virtually everyone on Earth. However, I had piqued too much interest in how it all happened. Who are the aliens that left the cases to be found? What were their motives and how have the aliens changed planet Earth? How dare they? Was retribution an option? My urge to create aliens that are as non-human (yet not necessarily inhuman) as feasible and to follow the mad Dr Antonio's antics, along with the menial Manuel and other favourite characters, have resulted in this sequel being as intriguing to write as Left Luggage.

ARIA: Left Luggage was nominated by a reader for best science fiction novel of 2012 in the Preditors & Editors contest. It came first out of 85 novels! It remains the only work of fiction involving infectious amnesia.

ENCAPSULATION OF BOOK ONE
ARIA: Left Luggage

In *Left Luggage,* an innocent-looking silvery case discovered on the International Space Station, when opened on Earth, released a virus causing an infectious amnesia with no one immune. People lost their memory at the rate of one year per week, forgetting how to do their jobs, where they lived, and some woke up next to strangers. By the end of ten weeks, most children had forgotten how to read, write, and speak. Many of them die, as do many dependent on medication no longer made. By the end of two years, everyone will have forgotten themselves to death. Ryder Nape realized the danger, and with a few friends who isolated themselves in a university rural field centre, after meeting with the uninfected ISS astronauts, flew to Rarotonga in the mid-Pacific.

A second case released ARIA-2. Astronaut Dr. Antonio, after exposure to the contents, became an enhanced human but killed colleagues in a moment of madness. ARIA-2 halted the memory loss from ARIA and, although too late for most, became a treasured object of hope for the survivors.

CHAPTER 1

June 16th 2016, Rarotonga, one year and two months since ARIA arrived. Most people on the planet have lost over 60 years of their memory. Isolated areas such as the Pacific islands have been infected later and have lost fewer years.

RYDER FOUGHT THE URGE TO YELL. He let Jena do it instead. She had that American knack of shouting so well. He watched her draw in a deep breath to let out a long, loud, "No."

"Here we go," Ryder said to Abdul, sitting beside him at the polished mahogany table in the conference room of the tropical island's yacht club.

Looking past Jena and the six others around the table, Ryder could see through the large glass windows to the ocean beyond. For him, the acerbic words in the meeting became suspended while his soul squeezed between the glass atoms to splash in the azure ocean. After the months of self-imposed isolation in a wet Welsh valley, Rarotonga was a holiday. Escaping dangerous mainland Britain, some of his group were content with being absorbed into island life. They were slapping on sun block instead of thermal underwear, digesting fresh tropical fruit instead of tinned food, and enjoying security in the knowledge that any wanderers on the island were not carrying the Alien Retrograde Infectious Amnesia virus everyone called ARIA. But all that could change if the wrong decision was made in the next few moments.

Yelling at each other vibrated the large window. Ryder pushed his chair back and walked over to it, knowing all the arguments raging around him.

Two walls of the large room displayed inspiring photographs of the owners' yachts in full billowing sail, as if they tried to take the room out of this existence. His vision was drawn through and beyond the glass. The clubhouse perched on a bluff. A winding path, lined with aloe and palm trees, led down to the bay where yachts bobbed with skeletal masts. Above them, a ragged lace of cirrus clouds lingered, making a welcome change to the usual monotonous blue sky. He revelled in the absence of overcast grey Welsh clouds.

A notice beside the window said the horizon was 20.26 miles

away. Even with binoculars, he couldn't detect the flotilla of strangers heading towards them.

The incoming caused the cacophony in the room. Three vessels had been detected by satellites, reprogrammed for this task by Jena and Abdul. The data, routed through the International Space Station, told them one was the size of a car ferry, the others were large, motorised sailing ships. Presumably to save fuel, they all headed towards Rarotonga at unassisted sailing speed, which gave the islanders a couple of days to decide on the style of reception.

They had options: coast guard gunboats and a couple of armed helicopters. Ryder shook his head as he gazed at the idyllic scenery and calm sea. In all the six months since they landed the Boeing cargo plane, they had not needed to defend the island from ARIA-infected intruders.

Refocusing his eyes and brain, he saw islanders dawdle-cycling along the coast road. Life on the island carried on as if no global catastrophe had occurred. Ryder shuddered at his knowledge of chaos in the rest of the world. He and his small group had managed to start the spread of an ARIA antidote in North Wales and Canada, but there were many unknowns about its effectiveness and diffusion. The breakdown of society, including transportation, would have slowed it down so much that it might not have spread. And the antidote didn't give back lost memories: all they knew was that one person with ARIA, after being exposed to ARIA-2, stopped losing his memory. An experimental sample of one. He heated with frustration.

Ryder cooled his forehead on the glass window. The palm trees and ocean blurred out of focus as he thought of his friend Manuel. They were colleagues on the opposite sides of the Atlantic. Manuel had caught ARIA while working for NASA, but Ryder managed to get him exposed to ARIA-2 in Calgary. He should be in an enclave of people with halted amnesia, but most of the under sixties would have no memories left, dead or dying from starvation or disease. Sadly, sixty-five-year-olds would only possess the memories of five-year-olds.

Ryder banged his head on the window. Everyone in the room stopped talking and stared at him.

"Antonio, the bastard," he yelled.

Jena rose, walked over to him and pulled him from the window. "You're making an ass of yourself, Ryder."

"We left Manuel and Julia in Calgary in the hands of that murdering freak."

"Leave it. There's no point fretting over things we have no control. We'll keep trying to raise him on our satellite link. Now, we've got to convince these softies to blow the intruders out of the water before we catch ARIA."

Ryder returned to his place at the table. "We have to be strong. Yes, they might be infection-free travellers hoping for refuge but that has to be proven beyond any doubt, or we'll all lose our marbles."

Dominiq Massey, the self-acclaimed leader of the island, waved an angry finger at Ryder. "We know billions are dead or dying, which is all the more reason for preserving the remaining few, not obliterating them. We'll let them dock on Karinga, four miles away, until we know they are ARIA free."

"That's no fucking good," shouted Ryder. He should have been shocked at himself. A year ago, he never swore. Hardly raised his voice. Everyone had hardened. A survival instinct. "It's too risky trying to guard them twenty-four seven."

Dominiq stood. A tall, blond New Zealander, he managed to shadow a significant portion of his side of the table. A clichéd posture but it worked. "Ryder, how can those people have bloody ARIA? Unless they are all geriatrics, they would have forgotten how to sail, let alone organise themselves? They must be free, like us."

"Rubbish. I agree they can't be escapees from an old-folks' home or they wouldn't manage the heavy manual sailing work. But they might be from an island like this and only caught ARIA a few weeks ago."

"And caught it by letting infected boat people land on their island, like you want us to do," Jena said, teasing a pencil into her jet-black hair, surprising Ryder by her support. Although they were lovers, she delighted in humiliating him.

The biologist, Teresa, Ryder's ex-fiancée, leaning against the doorjamb, said, "They might have ARIA-2. So they might have lost some memory, depending when they caught the first amnesia adenovirus, but exposure to someone with ARIA-2, a kind of jamming neo-virus, means they can remember the older and new things, with just the gap missing in the middle."

"That wouldn't be a problem," Dominiq said. "It doesn't seem likely that an antidote to ARIA could harm us. Let them come."

Ryder banged the table. "We don't have a clue what the side effects might be of ARIA-2. We know that our astronaut doctor, Antonio, turned into a raving psychopath when he was exposed to it."

"Another example of one," Jena said, making Ryder groan as the frank speaking of his girlfriend undermined him. "He was exposed to the case itself, and to Brian, who'd caught the original virus by personal contact. And Antonio was always a fringe lunatic."

"In your opinion," said Abdul, who was Jena's assistant engineer in space and knew Antonio as a colleague.

Ryder smiled. "Thank you, Abdul. And that's the point. We have no concrete facts. The only certainty is that if we stop them arriving, we cannot catch anything from them." He looked over at Dominiq's wife, Nessa. He knew she was as naïve as a cactus in the Arctic and twice as prickly.

Sure enough, she glared at Ryder. Her hands so tightly clenched, her pencil snapped, as did her voice. "You want to kill people just because they are sailing towards us."

"No. I want to make sure they don't come near us."

"By killing them."

"Not if we use radio and loudspeakers from our coast guard helicopters and gunboat to warn them off."

Dominiq put his hand on Nessa's arm and said, "Do you mean you wouldn't kill them if they moved off to another island?"

"As long as it was at least two hundred miles away to give us time to react to our satellite alert system."

"That's absurd," Nessa said. "Suppose they don't have radio, or some idiot is in charge of three boatloads of innocents? Are you going to sink them?" She pointed a finger at Ryder.

"If that's what it takes for our survival. There's no value in being pious but dead." He was overheating again.

Nessa stood and shouted. "Oh yes, there is. I couldn't live with myself if we killed innocents just in case they were infectious."

"We all have a hell of a time living with you now." Ryder at once regretted losing his patience, and not just because of the multiple intakes of breath. "I'd rather live with the guilt and live. At Anafon, we had to make similar—"

"Spare me the idyllic life in the Welsh valley," Dominiq said. "We've heard it to saturation point. This is Rarotonga, and I'm in charge here."

Ryder spread his arms. "Life is comfortable and sustainable here. But this is the first real crisis you've had to face, and you need to be strong."

Nessa used her sleeve to dab at her reddening eyes. "We should have shot your damn plane down in case you had ARIA."

Dominiq put an arm round her shoulders then turned to Ryder. "You've had more experience coping with interlopers than us."

Jena shook her head. "But you must have had other boats come close over the last year? What did you do then?"

"When they replied on the radio," Chad said, the island's coast guard captain, "It was easy to tell if they had ARIA."

"And?" asked Ryder.

"If they did, we told them they couldn't land, so they went away."

"How do you know they stayed away?" asked Abdul. "And not sneak back at night?"

"We kept radar watch and patrolled for a week."

"Let's forget the possibility they are here then, because I guess we'd know by now," Abdul said. "But how many have you let in?"

Chad looked at a clipboard. "Four motor launches from Fiji."

"How did you know they were clean?" Teresa said.

"I am ashamed to say, we kinda took their word for it. But I did send my sergeant out to check them out before we let them dock."

"Oh well, that's all right then." Teresa shared glances with Ryder.

"You got away with that one, obviously," Ryder said. "But if just one of those people had ARIA, you would all have lost your ability to prepare food, keep power and machines going. Anyone under thirty wouldn't be able to have this conversation."

"There's a big difference now," Teresa said. "We now have the second case."

Residual muttering was silenced. Ryder groaned and glared at her. "Let us suppose we send the ARIA-2 case out to them–lowered it from the helicopter, for instance."

"No harm in trying."

"There might be a lot of harm in trying. Why can't you see that?"

"Oh, come on, Ryder. What could go wrong?"

"They might not return the case or not close it when they return it. Not returning it would eliminate future research. Returning it open with the virus-source exposed would compromise our safety." Ryder saw Teresa's mouth twitch as she accepted his arguments. At least for now. He continued. "We urgently need to warn them off. I'm afraid we have to be inhospitable."

Chad stood. "All right, I'm convinced. I think we all were. It's just a hell of a situation and needed it hammered out. I'll start sending radio hellos to the flotilla."

"No," Ryder said.

"Here we go," Nessa said. "You want to send a missile, blast the poor devils out of the water before they can put their case."

Chad leaned over and whispered to her, "We don't have missiles."

"Not at all," Ryder said. "We'll attempt to find out who they are and medical status, but not from here. Their comms system might be like ours and have auto-signal-position detection. We approach from an oblique direction with a helicopter. Then use radio. If no response, we use the loud speaker."

"Excuse me," Chad said. "How the hell do they answer so the

chopper can hear?" He looked around, pleased to score a point.

"We hail them to stop or we open fire," Abdul said, warming to the coming fray.

"Sailing boats can't just brake," Dominiq said.

"Instruct them to turn right," Abdul said, his face heating with frustration. "What do you say, Ryder?"

"We sort the details, but if we talk all day, they'll be staggering up the slipway and that will be it."

CHAPTER 2

FORTY MINUTES LATER, Ryder strained to see the boats on the horizon. The early afternoon sun had climbed too high to be a problem, but a cool ocean current condensed moisture out of the warm, overlying air, creating a low mist. Although the intruding flotilla approached from the southwest, the island's two helicopters travelled north then a wide westerly arc to approach them from the west. The island's coast guard gunboat, *Solar Sprint,* had surged on a similar route with a smaller radius. Ryder guessed that if the intruder's radar was being used, it wouldn't see the islander's boat until the choppers were visible.

Both helicopters and the cutter carried experienced combat crew. Ryder wore an ironic smile at the thought of the island's occupational structure being virtually unchanged except that no pay seeped into the defunct bank accounts. Luckily, the self-sufficiency in food, water and energy became supplemented with a post-crisis economy. Entertainment, maintenance, and service paid for on a bartering mechanism and exchange of precious goods, although the definition of precious was going through a metamorphism.

"Hey, Jena." Ryder yelled into his mike to overcome engine noise and the juddering of the rotors. "How's the cruise? Over."

"Hi, Ryder, it's Abdul. I think Jena is sunbathing on the bow deck, flirting with that good-looking hunk from Tonga. Over."

"I feel sorry for him." Ryder laughed, glad to have some light relief. "You're twelve miles from their lead boat. Sail another ten degrees to starboard. Over."

"Fine. You are going to hang around for us, as planned? Over."

"Yes. Their radar is already pinging us, but it doesn't mean anyone is glued to their screens or aware of the significance. We have our anti-missile decoy flares ready. We're trying radio contact. I'd feel happier with Jena's brain in addition to yours. Over."

"I heard that. Is that all you want me for? If that is the case, we are over. Over."

"Overly dramatic as usual. We've been listening through all the usual emergency and main radio frequencies and got zilch. We're transmitting... now. They should see us, even if they can't see you. Okay? Over."

"Whatever, over."

Ryder shook his head at Jena's unhelpful attitude and switched to a recording that repeatedly transmitted their entry-examination message to the flotilla ten miles ahead.

"Calling the three ships at twenty-one south, one-sixty west, heading on a bearing sixty degrees east. This is a security alert from aircraft carrier *USS Ronald Reagan*. You must stop or head full to starboard to circle. Failure to comply will lead to your destruction."

Ryder turned to Bat Malise, the pilot. "I suppose a two-mile radius should make us safe from their weapons?"

"The range of my guns is five miles. My vessel-ID finder tells me that boat is the *Viking Moon*, an island-hopping ferry based in Samoa. No built-in weapons, so small arms. Even so, I want to keep three miles away."

"Where is Samoa?"

"Fifteen hundred miles northwest, so they haven't come directly from there. I'm going to circle to have the sun behind us, in case they're armed. I'm telling Tilley to fly back and forth in front of them." Bat's worry lines smoothed as he settled into action-man mode.

Ryder leaned on a chart. "Remember our plan: the coast guard boat in front of them, and the two choppers either side. No response yet. Perhaps their radio is out of action or their memory of its use is."

"Someone knows how to move that ferry. It has twin-engines, electronic navigation, electrics. I can figure that someone in his early seventies still knows enough to sail her."

"Bat, the radio seems to be out. Someone with their full faculties would be able to work it, given that they knew which button started a simple engine, which automatically keeps the electrics charged up."

"The navigation, though, Ryder. How are they doing that if they have kids' memories?"

Ryder's eyes tired using the binoculars. "Anyone can look at a map, put a compass on it and keep in that direction. And they might have got lost since they are not coming directly from Samoa. Worrying me more is if they're aiming at our island rather than drifting aimlessly."

"You mean they know we have a community. Maybe they are hoping for medical help or an antidote."

Ryder rubbed his eyes. "Our medical staff is still investigating what can be done with the second case. It won't open except by an unprotected human nearby."

"Now's the chance, Ryder."

"So, Bat, you're in the 'let's invite trouble in' group? 'Cos that's what would happen. We've been waiting for a single ARIA-infected person to arrive, not a hundred or so. This could be the end of us unless we deter them decisively. Understand?"

"I've heard the arguments, and dammit, you could be right. How long do we keep broadcasting the radio message before we try the loudspeaker? You realize we have to get real close for them to hear that?" Bat looked as scared as he should be, flying a sitting duck.

"Until our boat is within gun range. We need *Viking Moon* to know we have an armed *Solar Sprint* bearing down on them. Looks like another fifteen minutes."

Ryder watched a scurry of activity on the *Viking Moon*. Initially, the adults running around on the creamy white decks might have been seeking cover and readying weapons for action. But after a few disbelieving moments, he would have sworn they were playing a child's tag game. He waltzed the binoculars' image over the undulating blue water. Too white into the sun, but he adjusted filters to see a pale blue ocean with a few white beads, to the sailboats. Their motion made surety difficult, but he convinced himself that the few lounging on deck meant nothing threatening was happening. Blurred seagulls spoilt his view, making him rest his eyes. "They might as well be out for a Sunday fishing trip, Bat. They must hear us, the first helicopters roaring out of the sky for a year or so, yet..."

"Not if they've lost their memory, in which case, they'll think it's normal to see us. Damn. Hey, Ryder, that boat of theirs is based in Samoa, are you transmitting in Samoan as well as English?"

"No, but we have some leaflets to drop on them that are."

Bat looked at him with narrowed eyes. "I'm impressed. But no way am I hovering over that boat while it's full of crazies."

"How else can we get the paper warning to them? Make paper airplanes? We'll wait for the coast guard boat. Point us over to the northeast, Bat."

With the sun behind him, he might have been looking at a different ocean. It appeared as a deeper blue, almost ink-black directly below them. Even without the binoculars, he could see the sun glint from the *Solar Sprint's* bridge and the dazzle of white bow spray. He drew satisfaction at the neat, straight line of their course. It showed forceful determination, although the *Viking Moon* wouldn't have noticed.

"They must be in range now, Bat. The incomers have not responded to radio, so let me drop a few leaflets. Looking at the antics on board, they are not paying any attention to us."

"Okay, but I'm dropping anti-missile flares as soon as I get within a half mile."

"Good idea, Bat. Then the leaflets will be ashes. Don't we have that chaff silver paper stuff?"

"Forgot to load it."

Bat took the helicopter in from the south. The blazing equatorial sun should make them invisible if anyone was bothered enough by their noise to look up. He slowed when they reached the two sailing yachts. Ryder dropped his first batch. Before they fluttered in great whirlpools from the blade downdrafts, they were over the *Viking Moon* for the next batch. As soon as the mobile library made its delivery, Bat turned to starboard and headed back for the sun.

"I forgot about the downdraft," Ryder confessed. "Out of a thousand leaflets telling them to stop or circle to starboard, I hope one reached a helmsman."

A few minutes later, the intruding flotilla continued their course.

Jena's voice crackled over the radio. "While you've been bombing them with paper, Ryder, we've laid out real mines behind us. If they continue for Rarotonga, they'll be blown to bits. Over."

"Right. If anyone is listening, that news should make them veer off course. I'm trying the chopper's loudspeaker now. Out."

"Bat, hover just in front of their bridge and turn that damn afterburner off to reduce noise."

"I don't like it. An automatic could pepper us so close, and we reduce our acceleration potential."

"I'm prepared to blow them out of the water but not before giving them a chance to listen and react. Which way is the wind blowing? Oh, it doesn't matter with us making our own wind. Here goes.

"Coast guard to *Viking Moon*. You are heading into a minefield. Cut your engines and turn to starboard–your right–and await instructions."

He repeated the warning three times before the *Viking Moon* slowed. The two yachts furled their sails, drifting now, and lagging behind their larger mother ship.

"That's good," Bat said, sounding relieved. But then, the two yachts started their motors and caught up with the *Viking Moon*.

"What the hell's going on?" shouted Bat.

"Looks like they're attaching lines, so they can move faster."

"That's good then, if they turn south or west. Damn it, Ryder, look. They're accelerating straight at our boat."

"Ryder here. Come in, Jena, go to starboard as fast as you—"

"We've seen them. Did you tell them about the mines? Over."

"Of course I fucking well did, and they must see them, they're obvious from here. Brilliant yellow–what sort of camouflage is that? Over."

"Your idea, Ryder, dear, to use mines as a deterrent rather than as a weapon. Anyway, there are some in between that look like normal Pacific flotsam. Over."

"Well it looks like our interlopers are on a suicide mission. Get out of the way."

"Over. You're supposed to say, 'over'."

"Fucking over."

Ryder puzzled over the *Viking Moon's* intentions while watching their *Solar Sprint* carve a graceful white crescent, behind a curtain of droplets.

Lilley, in the other helicopter to the east of the action, gushed with excitement. "Looks like people with rifles on the ferry's bow. Just seen a flash. Firing my flares in case they have heat-seekers. Over."

Bat set off a multi-flare too.

"They aren't firing at the choppers, or us," Jena said. "Not yet. They're firing at the mines. Ah, now they are firing at us, but unless they've a missile launcher, they aren't going to hi—whoa! They *have* sent a missile. Abdul's set off a flare to our stern, but it'll be too late. Chad is pointing our bow at it and told his crew to open fire at the missile."

"I see it, luckily they're inexpert and it's missed. Bat, open fire on their bridge. Lilley, open fire on their missile launcher if you can spot them," Ryder said, keeping his cool. He knew he had the superior firepower and manoeuvrability unless the ferry opened its deck hatches to reveal Howitzers. "Okay, Jena, get Chad to fire your gun to send a warning shot over their bow so their bridge can see it. Over."

He saw the orange muzzle-flash followed by a splash on this side of the *Viking Moon*. Perfect shot. That would make them reassess their situation, decelerate, or stop.

Jena spoke again. "Ryder, they're turning to port, towards us, and we can see idiots on board preparing to launch another missile. We're going to fire at them, orders or not."

"Okay. Tilley, rake their deck with your guns while we shoot at their tiller and props without hitting the yachts. Wonder if that's why they hauled them in so close? Over."

The next few minutes caused temporary deafness to every human and seagull in the area. In spite of hot metal splintering the ferry's deck, which must be slippery with blood, the morons continued firing with short arms fire and rifles at all three of them.

Ryder kept the helicopters just over half a mile from the flotilla, out of range of most modern hand weapons but within easy range of their own. Small fires built up on the ship's deck, but it ploughed on, changing course as if to ram the *Solar Sprint*.

Bat fired short bursts of his heavy machine gun at the waterline stern to no effect.

"Do you want us sunk, Ryder, you bastard?" shouted Jena.

"You have permission to sink them. Everyone shoot at their waterline. Over." The chopper blade cacophony masked the additional noise of the coast guard's main gun, but he knew those on the boats would hear it.

"Got their tiller," Bat said, grinning as they saw it come apart from the stern and splash in the sea. "But don't go ordering a cease fire yet. I expect these ferries, minus a tiller, will have some manoeuvring ability with their screws."

Ryder gave him a look as if to say: Why did you bother to spend so much time and ammunition obliterating a superfluous tiller? He became distracted by the radio.

"Ryder, this is Jena. I think we have holed the ferry below the waterline. It's listing. Over."

"I confirm that she's listing towards the north," Lilley said. "Another thing, our fuel is low. Five more minutes and we have to head back. Over."

Ryder tapped Bat's shoulder, but before he could ask...

"We have enough for another forty minutes. Both choppers started with full tanks, so—"

"Ryder to Lilley, head back now—don't bother with a zigzag course. Go straight there. You might have been hit. Out."

RYDER WATCHED LILLEY'S HELICOPTER head off to the northeast, straight back home.

"They're sinking. Now what? Over," Chad said.

"We keep away, of course."

"Let all those people drown? You're a cold bastard."

"Chad, I'm as gutted as you. I suppose you'd use your big heart and one brain cell to take as many as you could back to the island. Then what? Over."

Silence.

"It's all right, Ryder," Jena said. "He's a grade one asshole. We're moving away in case any of them think we are close enough. And I'm not going to keep saying this 'over' crap."

"Looks like they are being taken on board the two sailing boats," Bat said. "We're going to have to head back too, Ryder. Fuel."

"Did you hear that, Jena? We'll hang around another few minutes. I'd like to know that they're heading away from our island before you go back. Over."

"Yeah. So while you fly off to a cup of tea, you want us to hang around in the line of fire. Hey, the *Viking Moon* is about gone, but one of the yachts is heading for us. Chuck is firing our biggest gun at them. I'm not taking any chances with no air support. Over."

"Jena. We need you to see the buggers sail away. Over."

"You got satellite surveillance for that. We're coming back too after we plant a few more mines."

"No. If they head north, I need you to sink them."

A year ago, Ryder could not imagine he'd ever give such a grotesque order. Nor that anyone would have taken any notice of him. He might not have ARIA, but his personality had morphed in response to the changing planet around him. He liked it, but knew the old Ryder's soft centre simmered beneath his toughening exterior.

CHAPTER 3

Bryce Massey on one of the yachts, Second Mortgage III *is thirty-eight years old but with the memory of a boy aged sixteen. He was an anthropology lecturer at Darwin University before being infected, after which, he joined a group of desperate ARIA infected who had heard rumours of a cure on one of the Cook Islands.*

THROUGH BLACK SMOKE, all I see of the *Viking Moon* are splashes where our people scream while jumping overboard.

I turn to find Cap'n calling to me from the wheel. I could tell he was Cap'n because of his labelled baseball cap. The four others of us on board the *Second Mortgage III* have name badges or we wouldn't know each day who our fellow refugees are. "Fucking cast off, Bryce, or we'll sink with the *Moon*."

He has a point. I go forward to undo the towrope. He shouldn't swear at me, I'm no sailor. The swimmers get closer, so I guess Cap'n intends to use us as a lifeboat. I can't remember how many are on the *Viking Moon*. I look where the helicopter stays flickering in the sun. Its shadow must be on me.

"Bryce, come here, now." Benita calls me from a hatch, opened just enough for me to see her black wavy hair and come-to-bed dark eyes tugging me into her lair. Her coffee skin glistens. People either go insane with screaming fits when they wake next to complete strangers–in which case, they don't last long—or they're like us, block out the bad stuff and live day to day. This shooting and sinking situation should freak me out, but I'm detached, and now, Benita wants her distractions.

"Can't. No time. We're about to take on survivors from *Viking Moon*." I should say that we'll be noticed and that she's already made me ravage her this morning. Didn't she? I think she's desperate to have a baby as part of her own survival strategy. I don't know why she picks on me. We're not an item as far as I know. Hey, maybe she has a dip from all the men on here.

"We might not have a chance later. Come on, Bryce. I'll come and get you."

"No, you've no clothes on." I could see her opening the hatch further. "All right, I'm on my way."

Benita treats me to the sight of her naked back wiggling as she runs to her bunk in the small cabin. Hormones make up for memory lapses. Benita is a complete pleasure-seeker. I'm not, just trying to get by: keeping notes, losing them, but aiming for survival.

I woke up this morning thinking I'm in my bed. I'm sixteen and throw up because I have a dead serious mathematics NTCE exam at Darwin High School. Only, I'm swaying, sick to my stomach, on a frigging boat, with a NoteCom on a string around my neck. A scratchy beard I never had before and bigger, also-scratchy balls. The notebook tells me I'm an ant-hra-pologist. What the hell's that?

"Bryce," Benita squeals, resting her elbows on the bunk so her arse waves in the air. "Shall I call Prentice instead?"

I cancel the on-deck shouting chaos by shutting the hatch behind me. Unbuckled trousers crumple to the floor as my body lunges to Benita's behind. Energetically, we fight the rhythm of boat and sea to optimise our action.

My eyes close with the rapture and I have to force them open again. It might not be everyday I have such an erotic view, framed by my worn hands either side of an exquisite backbone. I cannot rely on memory to relive such a moment. This is all about the here and now. I wonder if we're married.

Cap'n calls my name, but way off in another world. Senses and floor reel.

Again he yells, "Bryce, you fucking layabout!" He's getting closer, but so am I. Another wave and the surge.

Benita moans a "Not yet" at me as the cabin door implodes.

"For Pete's sake, yer rabbits. Get out here and help these half-drowned buggers trying to climb aboard."

EIGHT MAKE IT TO OUR BOAT. Cap'n tells Prentice to steer away from the *Viking Moon* in case we get sucked under and to let the pirates attacking us think we won't go after them.

"How do you know they're pirates?" Benita asks him.

"They attacked us, didn't they?"

I protest. "They shouted they were coast guard, and they have coast guard choppers and a coast guard boat."

Cap'n shakes his scraggy grey beard at me. "Too trusting, ain't yer, Bryce?"

Benita and I share bewildered glances. The *Moon* survivors shiver but won't go below. They can't pull their eyes off their boat.

I'd most likely been on the *Viking Moon* when it was a car ferry. A floating shopping mall between Samoa, Indonesia and other places I struggle to recall. Now, just the—what's it called?—front section, sticks above the choppy waves. Funny how it's sinking in stages as if the sea going in is exploring rooms. Water taking its time in the games room to test out the machines, sampling the restaurant, rushing through the car decks—banging as floating vehicles hit the bulkheads—gurgling through the duty-free shops before slopping up the bow decks. Hey, I remember "bow."

A girl in a bright orange T-shirt next to me points and shrieks, "There's Carlos."

"Where?"

Benita sees him. "There's someone clinging to the rail."

We all stare as Carlos struggles to keep his feet on the impossible slope while grasping the side rail with one hand.

"Let go the Kalashnikov," shouts Cap'n, then for our benefit, "I'm surrounded by fucking idiots."

The girl who first spotted Carlos—I read her name badge, Orchid—turns to Cap'n. "Turn the boat to get to him."

"We can't, Orchid, the *Second Mortgage* is only a forty footer, we'd get sucked under when the *Moon* goes down."

Benita leans towards me. "What's a mortgage?"

"Search me."

"Later."

"What? Oh."

Orchid cries and points at Carlos again. "He was shot by the helicopter. There's blood on his shirt."

"Sorry, Orchid, we're not getting any closer," says Cap'n.

Before any of us can stop her, she's over the rail and in the water.

"Bryce, after her," orders Cap'n.

"Why me?" My left foot betrays me by climbing on the rail, but I look to Benita to see if she'd rather I stay.

"Go for it, hero."

Bugger. I give her my NoteCom.

At least the water is warm, and I know I can swim. But once my eyes reach sea level, they fail to locate Orchid. I look back to our boat to seek directions, but their swearing tells me they misconstrue my intentions, thinking I want to return. I do, but there's a morsel of decency left in my brain urging me to attempt a rescue. I have no choice but to swim towards the only dry bit left of the *Viking Moon* in the hope of catching up with Orchid en route.

It might be a mere hundred metres, but I seem to be getting no closer. I had Speedo trunks last time I remember swimming, now I am thrashing the brine in go-slow trousers. Riding the up-waves, I see Carlos pointing the weapon at the sky, looking for helicopters, while clinging to the rail.

"Carl—" My mouth fills with water faster than I can complete a word. Still no sign of Orchid. I throw myself at the sinking ship, and instead of escaping, I clamber up on the outside of the railings near Carlos.

"Throw the gun away, Carlos, before this tub gets wetter."

"Sod off."

"Do you know you're bleeding? Your back—"

"What's it to you? I dunno anyone no more and I couldn't give a shit."

"Let's get you to the boat."

"Yeah. Like how?"

"Cap'n will bring it closer." I duck as he waves the gun near my face.

"Why's he going away then?" Carlos fires a burst up in the air. "Hey, you fuckers. I'm over here. Oh, shit." He slips, and though I struggle over the rail, I fail to reach him before he slips past me into the water heading up the bow deck. I grab the muzzle of the gun to stem his sliding.

I burn my hands holding on, but his descent stops. "Come on, Carlos, pull yourself up." Where's my dad? He's real strong and would just yank Carlos up.

The ship shudders, giving up fresh air and heading for the submarine experience. Carlos, up to a minute ago careless with his life, now opens his mouth in horror. With my bare feet slipping, my left hand on the rail, and the right knuckle-white on the gun, I pull in desperation to haul up the disappearing Carlos. The gun lets off an explosion of bullets. In shock and self-preservation, my hand lets go and speeds to my right ear.

"Idiot, you've shot me."

But Carlos is out of sight under water. I don't know how badly I'm hurt. My hand is decorated with blood and I'm dizzy. Another sinking shudder reminds me to try swimming again. I see the *Second Mortgage* bobbing a little closer. Cap'n must have decided the *Moon* wasn't going to suck his boat down. Hello, they're all shouting at me and pointing to my left. No way can I hear what they're yelling above the gurgling and banging noises beneath me, but I see a patch of orange.

My dizziness worsens. I look again at my right hand, blood but no gory brain bits, but then I'd be dead wouldn't I? My mum would know what to do. She'd be telling me I was all right. Seems she was packing me off to school only yesterday.

I scramble over the shaking rail and fall rather than dive into the sea towards the orange. Mum, the seawater is making my ear more sore.

Again, once I'm at sea level, I cannot see Orchid. I splash out towards where I think she is. I guess the boat will be going towards her, so that'll help my guidance system.

A few mouthfuls of water later, I hear encouraging shouts from the boat. Or are they calling something else? My God, it sounds like "shark." Of course, it must be from my bleeding head. I thrash more energetically, but hey, isn't that the wrong thing to do? I revert to stealth.

A hillock of water raises my viewpoint, and I see Orchid. She is looking away from me to the boat for succour. I open my mouth to call, but the sea sees its chance and dives in. I stop swimming and splutter out a gob-full. My accompanying coughing brings Orchid, who hugs me. Not such a brilliant idea for a person to drape herself on wounded shark-bait, struggling to expel a lungful of briny while treading water. We sink. Phew! She seeks self-preservation by releasing me. While submersed, I take the opportunity to shark-spot. Nothing.

I surface and see Orchid overarm to *Second Mortgage*, which has closed in on us. Just to our left, a huge spout of water splashes upwards and rains down. Fearing it might be a whale or sharks fighting for the first bite, I swim with arms going like eggbeaters.

Moments later, hands pull me aboard amid screams. A crash is followed by a shadow enveloping me. Splinters fly in all directions, I see three stick in my left arm before a canvassed spar takes me back to the deck again. Wigwammed by the sail, I feel the yacht lurch clockwise. I pull out the splinters from my arm, knowing that I'll be leaking more blood. Again, my thoughts go to my mum. She'd be bathing my wounds and applying plasters while soothe-talking me.

"Bryce! Get the fuck from under there and take the wheel." Cap'n sounds cross. I'd better help out and crawl into sunlight and chaos. Screams and shouts as splashes burst from the sea.

"They're shooting at us, Cap'n."

"I would never have guessed. God knows why they're attacking us. It's not as if we want to take over their fucking island. Prentice is hurt, so take over from me at the wheel. All you have to do is steer away from the gunboat."

"I'm hurt too," I say to his back as he dashes below. As I grab the wheel and turn a test rotation, I hear the motor chug into life. The yacht accelerates. Not to speedboat velocity, but we'd overtake a jogger, were one to achieve the running-on-water trick.

I want to ask Cap'n where we're going. My reading of my notes tell me we have only one objective, but there are maniacs guarding it. Well-armed maniacs. I head the boat south, alongside the other yacht, the *Bow Wave*. But what's out there close enough before our food and water run out?

I see Cap'n with broken spars to throw over the side.

"Hey, Cap'n, I guess we'll head out this way till dark and then circle back?"

"Clever, Bryce. That's why you're second in command."

"I am?"

CHAPTER 4

June 20th 2016, Canada. Dr Antonio Menzies was the Italian doctor on the International Space Station when the case was found. At the Welsh field centre, he volunteered to be isolated and exposed to the opened second case. He behaved normally until he agreed to treat an ARIA-infected man in isolation with him. He turned into a murdering psychopath but with extras. He had instant recall of his memory, displayed minor telekinetic abilities, and was able to sense the tenor of some people's thoughts. Although badly wounded, he'd persuaded the besotted teenager, Megan, to smuggle him on the airplane out of Wales to the fuel stop in Canada. He disembarked there and moved in with Ryder's friend, Manuel.

MANUEL HAD TO ASK ANTONIO TO REPEAT HIS LAST SENTENCE. He and Julia might have stopped losing memory, but confusion slipped into the vacant memory cells.

"They are coming," Antonio said, showing most of his immaculate teeth.

"Who's coming?" Manuel nestled a mug of coffee, tapping a finger against the handle, and glanced at Julia, busying herself washing evening dinner plates, sublimating fear with domestic chores. In spite of their retrograde amnesia, they'd coped living in blissful ignorance together in this cabin in the White Lake forest before Antonio guested himself. His Mediterranean charm comforted them initially, along with the euphoria of being exposed to the second case with its ARIA-2, stemming the annihilation of their memories. But now, Manuel feared the Italian, without knowing why, apart from his gut feeling and the implicit threats.

He realized that Antonio was talking again.

"... *si*, the aliens, of course."

"What? How do you know? Is our Internet uplink to the ISS working now? And you were able to see the alien ship at Cassini moving. Right?"

Antonio laughed. "All these questions, Manuel. How many times do I tell you to trust me? I *feel* their arrival. Why don't you check the Internet yourself?"

Manuel waved his finger in the doctor's face. "Because you put a damn password on it."

"What? You haven't figured that out? Try Cassini. Oh, I suppose you have forgotten your Saturn astronomy. *Mi dispiace.*" An apology, but he continued grinning.

Manuel tugged at Julia's elbow on his way to the computer. Her tears dropped into the washing-up water. He put his arm around her waist and whispered. "If we can access the computer, we can get hold of Ryder and get advice on how to rid ourselves of that bastard."

"It's not possible. Look how he wakes up when we sneak up on him, with or without a steak knife. He's right when he says he has enhanced powers. Gives me the creeps. Why us, Manny? Why is he hanging around us? He gets his kicks when he goes into Banff and comes back with blood on his shoes."

"I suppose we're his link to Ryder and the remaining crewmembers of the ISS. Come on, Let's see if he really has given us the password."

Manuel stared unbelieving at the acceptance icon with its big smiley face. "Shall we contact Ryder first or go for the link to the telescope pointing at where the alien ship was last seen? How do I do that? I've forgotten."

"Says on the notes, there's an icon on the start-up screen for everything we need. Yes, there, 'alien-watch'–what a name."

"At least the link to Hubble seems to be live. Hey, there's Saturn. The seek software's kicking in, and there it is."

They stared at a brown, fuzzy ball with Saturn behind it. Data scrolled down the right of the screen. Neither of them could remember the acronyms, but there was one line that stayed on screen. Slowly scrolling, it told them that the alien ship was on an intercept course with the ISS and expected to arrive in five days. For several rapid-pulse moments, Julia joined Manuel in silent shock.

"Let's click on the icon to contact Ryder," Manuel said. "Though I expect he already knows about the alien ship."

A white spot expanded on the screen to reveal a lime-green office.

"Hey, there's someone with their back to the computer. Is it Teresa?" Manuel said.

"How do we get whoever it is to turn round?" But Julia answered her own question by shouting "Teatime!" into the mike.

In the Pacific island lab, Teresa turned at the interruption.

"Well look who it is. Hi, you two. We thought you'd joined the bears in hibernation."

"Hi, Teresa," Julia said. "We weren't allowed the password to the computer by you-know-who. But he's let us in now that the aliens are on their way to Earth."

"Shush." Manuel looked around him, his finger on his lips. Then he realized Teresa would have seen him. "Hah, you must think we've regressed to childhood games."

"You've no need to explain. We've had experience of Antonio in Wales. What's the egomaniac been doing to you?"

"Never mind us, how are you?" Manuel didn't want to worry Teresa with their weird existence in Canada, where having a relaxed or fraught day depended solely on Antonio's manic moods.

Teresa smiled then launched into rapid speech as if eager to chat to new faces. "Apart from having to ward off probable infected strangers, we're having a ball. Okay, Gustav—my techie from back in England—and others are working their socks off trying to extract whatever viral particles might be in the second case and analysing them. But for the rest, it's like being on a long vacation. You both look well. Hope you don't mind me asking how your memory is since being exposed to the second suitcase?"

"We've lost over twenty years of memory, Teresa," Julia said. "But we have childhood and recent memories as if normal. It's like having to go back to school, relearning long words, how to drive."

"Oh, he lets you out?"

"We go foraging and on jobs, but one of us has to stay here with him."

"Hostage?"

"You got it. But the other people we see in Banff aren't so lucky. Most must have been re-infected by Antonio, one of us, or by each other by now, yet they look grim."

"Sorry, I don't get it," Teresa said. "Why aren't they recovering like you two? How do you mean, grim?"

"No spark. Not zombies but heads hanging. You know there are no children or teens anywhere?"

"I'm not surprised. They'd have lost all their memory. Pure genetics and instinct with no language isn't enough, especially with no food production or health services. Are the survivors dangerous?"

"We avoid them. Most are in groups; unkempt, skinny, looking confused and distressed."

"What does Antonio say?"

Manuel replaced Julia at the computer. "Not much, except that he's training a group in Winnipeg."

"Training? What for? Survival skills?"

Manuel cringed as he was pushed to one side.

"I thought I heard a familiar voice. *Buongiorno*," Antonio said, sticking his grinning head in front of the camera. "They're coming for you. All of you."

"Really?" Teresa said, keeping remarkably cool in the face of the maniac who killed half the people in their North Wales hideaway six months before.

Manuel groaned. It wasn't as if Antonio had harmed them, but his stomach jitterbugged except when the doctor went off in the Buick, for days at a time. He wasn't the least bit bothered where Antonio went–please, somewhere dangerous from where he might not return–but Julia used to interrogate him fearlessly. Even through his clowning obfuscation, Manuel worked out that Antonio had visited ARIA-infected people in nearby towns. Maybe contact with his ARIA-2 exhalations stemmed their memory loss, but Manuel suspected a more sinister purpose.

"Have you been thinking of me, Teresa? Or do you devote all your energy to snipe at Ryder and Jena? Ha."

"I've moved on, Antonio, but I see you haven't. What are you doing with so much time on your hands?"

"Preparation. *I miei amici,* the Zadokians are on their way. I know what to do for them. Your idyllic life is about to plunge into an abyss, and there's nothing you can do about it."

Manuel pushed in front of Antonio. "Watch for them, Teresa, he's a nutter, but—"

The screen snowed.

CHAPTER 5

TERESA TWEAKED THE CONSOLE, but it didn't retrieve the link. She smiled satisfaction at the discovery of Manuel and Julia and their apparent good health even if under stress. What were they on about with the aliens coming back? She prodded the touchscreen at the shortcut for incoming objects from Saturn.

The screen blackened. No, tiny spots flickered where they shouldn't. There must be a way to zoom in or to see which of those pinpricks was an invader. If only she'd paid attention when Ryder showed her how to use the Hubble software. Slumped in her swivel chair, she recalled that moment. Jena, who'd stolen Ryder's affection from her by overwhelming his staid Britishness with her brash American sexuality. Ryder and Jena wriggled their giggles while Teresa seethed. Even though Teresa knew her intimate relationship with Ryder had passed into memory, nausea struck when she saw that hussy pawing him.

"Hey, Teresa," called Abdul, as he banged through the door. "Is that Hubble on the wall?"

"Yeah, Antonio says the alien ship is on its way, but I can't see it. Come and pray to Allah, or whoever, and help me."

"Hah, look. There's a motion detection module. Just tap your manicure on that purple spot in the menu."

Dizziness hit Teresa as the wall-sized image swirled before settling with one circled dot in the centre.

"Doesn't look too scary," she said.

"I'm afraid that doesn't mean we don't have to be scared. And it's heading our way."

"I think we've got them all wrong, Abdul."

He blinked at her. "You've not joined up with the islanders, who believe the aliens are misunderstood benefactors?"

"They might be. We've had no overtly threatening messages–no messages at all."

Abdul raised a winning finger. "In that case, why do they feel the need to camouflage their ship? Look, it's a fuzzy ball. Possibly beneath whatever shield they use, we would see armaments. Go on, let's fill the wall with that image and add X-ray, infrared, micro-radar–everything."

Teresa hit the zoom. They looked at it in silence for a full minute.

Abdul laughed. "It's not camouflage at all. Their ship really is a giant brown fur ball."

"I don't suppose it's because the aliens are little furry balls too."

"Teresa," he said, with a condescending hand on her shoulder. "You think they're harmless because they look cuddly?"

"Okay, smarty pants, what do they want?"

"It's easy to deduce. They wanted a habitable planet with no hostile, indigenous occupants, but they didn't want to damage the environment."

"Yeah, let's not count billions of decaying bodies as pollution."

Abdul ignored her. "They didn't want long-lasting nuclear fall-out or chemical residue. Which adds up to an imminent alien physical presence. Smacks of colonization to me."

"Suppose they're not after somewhere to live but something to take home. Earth might have a mineral common to us but rare to them."

"Unlikely. The Periodic Table on Earth is no doubt the same on every planet."

"But new elements get discovered," Teresa said, "although, I admit, they have ultra-short life spans. Maybe we have a common element like aluminium that is rare on their planet."

"No. Even if aluminium was rare on planet alien, we know it's one of the most common minerals in our solar system. It would be easier for them to grab a few asteroids from the Oort belt beyond Pluto and sneak off with them. Why risk a disastrous planetary war over something they could pinch without us noticing?"

"Abdul, again, you're missing my point. We don't know for sure that the asteroids and other planets consist of the same proportions of elements as Earth. All the solar system bodies would have formed at different distances from the sun and its radiation. Some are still tectonically active, while others are frozen. Different minerals are bound to be more prominent on Earth than elsewhere."

"Fair enough. What elements are on their shopping list?"

CHAPTER 6

ANTONIO LAUGHED CONTEMPTUOUSLY at the remnants of humanity that existed in Winnipeg. Although their memories had stopped regressing because of contact with him, most had the feeble memories of four-year-olds. They could hardly speak, traumatised, confused, and barely able to carry out his instructions to burn the dead and dying. Two days to drive the empty, eight-hundred highway miles, but his friends needed him here.

At least, he thought they were friends. He internalized a bond with the alien mindset, even though he hadn't met them. Something in the engineered virus must have induced a synaptic-neuron configuration in part of his brain, allowing him to participate in their aspirations. He looked up at a patch of blue between the grey cumulus clouds. He experienced a greater magnetism to a species whose home was 8.6 light years away than to anyone on Earth. He wasn't stupid. He knew he might be self-delusional, but nagging doubts wafted away when he looked at what was left of Homo sapiens. His *supremazia* to their *idiozia*.

Without comprehending how he knew, Antonio had to organise a hundred people on the western outskirts of Winnipeg near the airport. Cruising the Buick round a large warehouse, he found them, hands in pockets, looking confused, not talking to each other. They had stopped losing their memory just in time, he thought, as he alighted; his approach making the mostly late middle-aged group stare at him. He'd picked those that should remember basic skills. He shook his head, trying to rid himself of the tinnitus yet knowing the buzzing contained alien information communicating in his head. These people must have had telepathic messages too. But for some reason, he was required to coordinate their construction activities.

He walked up to them, noting they had all brought toolboxes and knapsacks. Food? Possibly, though he presumed they had no sandwiches: no convenience foods. Antonio rarely ate these days, becoming emaciated. Anorexic Antonio. Hah. He nibbled the nuts, meat, home-baked whatevers that Julia prepared at the cabin but couldn't be bothered most of the time. An enhanced man on a mission. Fervour had become his nourishment.

Two women were in the group. All as thin as him. He wondered when cannibalism would creep in. *Errore*, a third woman cowered behind the other two, younger with more meat on her. They've been protecting and feeding her, probably a relative. In spite of their concealment, he could see a well-proportioned sexual *bella donna* with the mind of a four-year-old. He pushed his way to her.

"What's her name?"

The elder of the three women, wearing a quilted ankle-length black coat, stood firmly in front of the youngest, folded her arms and said, "She's not for you."

Antonio hit her hard on the side of the face.

She gasped and crumpled to her knees while the young one started crying.

"Her name?" he said, noting the healthy, shiny black hair, full lips and wet blue eyes.

"Carla," said a man.

Antonio looked straight at the younger woman's eyes. "Later, Carla."

He turned and saw that the crowd all looked away, sheep. He marched to the rear of the lorry that had brought some of the equipment that appeared on the end of the airport runway. He'd no idea how. He found a megaphone he knew was going to be there.

"Listen. I'm Boss. That is all you need to know about me. Some of you are One. You know who you are. The rest of you are Two. If you are unsure, then you are Two." He examined their faces to see if they understood. Their stares back told him nothing.

"Ones, gather six twos for a work gang. Come to me if you have a problem. Go."

The crowd shuffled in an apparent random Brownian motion. Wordlessly. Within minutes, there were distinct groups of seven people; moments later, two from each went to a large articulated lorry. It had started. The construction of the first alien dome had begun. Antonio took coffee from a silent woman standing behind a trestle table. He'd stopped being astonished at the mind control obliging these semi-sentient humans to perform out of character. He sipped while looking at a plan of the construction.

His medical training didn't help him grasp the technological ingenuity of the design, but in 2014, he'd been to the Sydney Telstra Stadium. A fourteen-storey high translucent dome, three hundred metres wide—enough to fit three Boeing 747's side by side. But, whereas the impressive structure needed over two thousand piles and a thousand workers for three years, this alien design needed no piles and only one hundred workers.

He smiled as he recalled an attempt by Manuel to interrogate him as surreptitiously as the old man could.

"Antonio, my friend, why do the aliens need domes?"

"As far as I understand, they are vast greenhouses."

"But they can choose whatever climate zone they like to grow whatever they want. Why go to the trouble of constructing complex structures?"

"They are not complex, Manuel. And the reason for greenhouses isn't just for warmth, but to control the quality of the air—not just for the plants."

Antonio laughed out loud as he recalled Manuel's shock at the thought that nowhere on Earth was the air clean enough for aliens. "Damn it, Antonio, if the air here is so fucking dirty, why don't they stay at home? And where the hell is their home?"

"Good questions. Their home world is a planet we know as Zadok, in the Sirius system nearly nine light years away. I can't pick up the name they have for it. In fact, I haven't a notion of their language at all. Maybe they use telepathy for all their personal communication. Like we use computers to transmit data between machines."

"And why the domes and need for cleaner air?"

"*Il amico mio*, think about it. Either Zadok is becoming too polluted for them—"

"I don't buy the notion that our atmosphere is so polluted they need to build domes."

"Maybe the domes are not just to grow plants and ensure air quality for Zadokians but to control movement."

"You mean they are bringing alien livestock too? I don't like the sound of that."

"Manuel, you want certainties when all I can give you are deductions."

He realized Manuel would think he was holding back, but he hadn't managed to find out anything for sure. Bursts of information, like computer data, would pour into his brain—often while he was asleep—but it was as if he was being used as a catalyst to get preparatory work done, rather than quenching his thirst for knowledge. He knew Manuel would tell Ryder. Antonio also knew he would have to do something about that irritating yet amusing little gang sooner or later.

Leaning against a sun-warmed brick wall, he sipped black coffee while admiring clusters of activity. Twelve groups had taken trailers of materials out to points on a large circle about two hundred metres across and were each gathered around a motorcar-sized white box. He expected special engineering, but nevertheless, he was impressed when tubes extended out of the boxes on the floor. Rising at an angle of forty-five degrees, shiny metallic tubes inched out like long telescopes.

He sauntered over to the nearest group to see how the tubes were supported. Nothing. They emerged, as if growing, out of the white boxes. The work gang ignored him as he placed his hand on top of the box. It was warm.

"It purrs like a contented cat," he said to the Number One of the group, to no reaction. "How is this box fixed? I can't see any cables, supports, bolts... nothing."

The Number One frowned then continued pressing irregular polygons on the side of the box. Antonio squatted to examine the shapes. They were indented by a couple of millimetres and the same mushroom white as the rest of the box. No wonder he'd missed it. There were no markings, but each shape was different in the number of sides and sizes. He hovered his hand over one shaped like a wave. Maybe it was the thrumming noises, but he thought he could sense emanations and lowered his hand to touch the wave shape. The Number One put his hand there instead, firmly preventing Antonio's hand from touching the box.

Antonio's reaction was to lash out, but he engaged the unfocussed eyes of the Number One and restrained himself. Just as well. These morons were programmed to press buttons, he wasn't. Somehow, these boxes had rooted themselves into the ground. They must have done in order to counter-balance the enormous weight of the spars going out to meet sixty metres in the air in the middle. Perhaps these telescopic spars were much lighter than they looked. If their engineering was as far ahead as their microbiology, he might as well have guessed a leap into his imagination and then some.

He turned to watch that Number One's crew, wondering what they needed to do if the box was pre-programmed to send the spars out into the sky. He knew he was wasting grey matter, but did the boxes get delivered by the aliens or were they also constructed by near-zombie humans? He'd hoped his special pseudo-telepathic abilities would help him, but they didn't. Occasionally, he'd be conscious enough to pick up nuances. Even with his ARIA-2-enhanced brain busying itself, he was hard pressed to figure out any words. Not surprising since the Zadokians didn't speak English, didn't speak. Period. That was his secret for now.

Even so, he had difficulty formulating ideas without using words. They must have a language even if it was not necessary to utter it out loud. Emotions such as fear and anger, along with physical needs such as sex and hunger, required no words. But Antonio couldn't think of a wordless way to work through an argument such as which Italian politician was the best orator.

In the meantime, he had an urge that needed no words. He knew that Carla was shepherded to the canteen building. Did they think he wouldn't have noticed?

The other women saw him first. Carla had her back to him, stirring a large pot over a bottle-gas stove. He smiled as they uselessly shuffled together to hide Carla, still oblivious, humming the tune of Georgie Porgie pudding and pie...

"Kissed the girls and made them cry," whispered Antonio.

Carla wore a beige nylon housecoat-overall that was too tight as it stretched over her round buttocks. She was voluptuous but not overweight, a woman who oozed sexual presence without effort or awareness. Maybe. His little Mussolini was aware. He sneaked up behind her, but before he could make contact, Carla's keeper stood between them. Under her mousy brown hair, with remnants of a long-forgotten perm, her thin face showed a thin-lipped defiance alongside the red hand mark.

Antonio was about to push her aside when he stopped, aghast. The woman had pulled aside her long quilted coat. He knew that in the freezing winters, such mobile bedcovers had their insulating uses, but they could equally hide a shotgun. The weapon she revealed was her breasts. He took a step back. A self-defensive reaction at the shock revelation. His rapid brain expected pendulous monstrosities, but the middle-aged woman must have had cantilevered implants. The breasts thrust at him like a pair of battleship guns. He missed most of her speech but the ending: "...take me instead."

He could have laughed at her but played a more cunning and cruel trick. "*Certamente*, go over to the restroom and take off the rest of your rags. I'll be along in *un momento*."

She pulled together her coat and scurried along. He imagined her being pleased with her ploy to protect Carla. As soon as her back was a few metres away, he took Carla's elbow and pulled her to the right and into the canteen, shutting the door behind them. He pushed her back to a table so she supported herself with her elbows, making her breasts stretch her housecoat even more.

"You're the real prize, aren't you, *dolcezza mia*?" he said, undoing her plastic buttons.

"What you doing?" She spoke childlike words but with the husky voice of an experienced whore. Not that he thought she was. Her milk-white breasts spilled out of her clothes, and in his excitement, he fumbled with more of her buttons.

"*Dio mio*, you are *magnifica*," he said, knowing it was a strange experience for him to give in to passion rather than logic, even alien logic. He mauled her breasts, squeezing nipples that hardened in seconds. His trousers threatened to sunder, so he removed his hands so he could unbuckle and unzip. He looked back at her face. A perplexing look but no fear.

She squirmed. Perspiration glistened on her perfect stomach, making a wet, salty bead dribble southwards under her still-buttoned waist. The remaining buttons flew off as he pulled apart her coat.

"Lean back more," he said, as she lifted her buttocks, letting him pull down her black underwear. The thought flitted through a synapse that maybe her hormones have kicked in no matter what her memory was telling her. She gasped when she saw his erection. It was possibly the first she remembered seeing.

He fought his immediacy and rubbed up against her. She started to gasp until he leaned forward and kissed her savagely, his tongue wrestling with hers. Her hips nudged into his. It was as if it was body over mind for her. A niggle developed in him. It was supposed to be his rape, his pleasure in the power. He lifted his face. The glazed look in her eyes and inane smile told him she was in ecstasy. *Che cosa?* This wasn't right. He pulled her hand away and put it on him, but it was too late, he was softening. He lifted up his head, squeezed shut his eyes, and let out an agonised cry.

CHAPTER 7

June 24th 2016, Rarotonga, one year and four months since ARIA
arrived. Most people would have lost over sixty years' memory. But
some isolated groups may have only been infected for a few months
or weeks. Those in North America and Northern Europe in contact
with people infected with ARIA-2 will have stopped losing memory.

RYDER FRETTED ABOUT THE LACK OF SECURITY around Rarotonga's
shores. On a large map he found in the Yacht Club's office, he took a
red pen and circled small inlets where insurgents could sneak in
under the 24-hour radar surveillance he'd bullied the coast guard to
monitor. He stood to take in the overall picture. Four red circles, like
ringworm, around the coastline. Not the main port of Avarua. To his
relief, Dominiq had agreed to a permanent watch there. Heat rose to
Ryder's face from the anxiety and frustration of being in the presence
of idiots who regarded the aliens, their domes, and ARIA as a
temporary situation. They were in denial because they hadn't
witnessed it themselves.

Teresa barged through the door, spilling some of the coffee she
carried for Ryder.

"Here, you don't deserve it." She put the mug on the
northernmost promontory of the map.

"Thanks." He saw that the mug showed Chopin with "Here's a
note I made earlier." He contemplated the unlikelihood of any more
composers on Earth. No more Beethoven, Mozart, McCartney. "Hey,
you've put a brown ring on my defence chart."

"Shoot me."

"Look, Teresa, forget about us and our past. Haven't you found a
man on this island that can keep up with you?"

"Don't worry about me, asshole."

Ryder looked up into her fiery-green eyes as if to say, "there's no
need."

"You know, Tess, I am truly sorry it didn't work out between you
and the mad Antonio."

"Who says it hasn't? You don't know everything." She stretched
up to her full five feet.

Ryder had to make her see sense. "Sorry to point out the bleeding obvious, but he's turned into a psychopathic killer since being exposed to ARIA-2, and he's on another continent with no handy airlines left."

"He was disturbed after the exposure, but he might be better now, and he knows how to fly planes." She stood, arms folded, triumphant. "Oh, Abdul says he has something to show you on the ISS Earth-watch monitors."

"Really? A large herd of feral horses in the Gobi? How can you call killing half our friends being disturbed? Antonio was a NASA doctor who was a hobbyist pilot of Cessnas over short hops. Not a genius airline pilot who can fly seven-five-sevens single-handed."

"No, something more crucial. Antonio and I have a bond. A much deeper love than the quick-fumble infatuation you and I had and which you have with Jena...until she wakes up."

"For all our sakes, including yours, I hope he doesn't come here. Why don't you find another doctor on the island?"

"You haven't heard, then?"

"Heard what? You've snared another man? Good luck to him."

"I didn't say that, and I'm sure your Jena will keep you informed. Abdul did say it was urgent. I suppose I'd better come too."

When they reached the communication room, they found Abdul waving them over to a large monitor.

"If that's you running here on the double, I'd hate to see you taking your time," he said. "Look at this infrared image from the Volga River basin in Russia; this one on the Tennessee; the Loire in France; the Yangtze in China."

"Are they nuclear warheads?" Ryder said.

"No. Nuclear power stations," Abdul said. "But good thinking. I'm running a correlation routine on known nuclear-arms caches now. Yes, they have a similar signature hit in the U.S., Pakistan, and the rest."

Teresa peered at the digital readout. "They're not hot enough to indicate detonations."

"I agree," Abdul said. "We are detecting one thousand degrees, not tens of thousands. Enough to melt the surface and seal in the facilities."

"Clever," Ryder said, nibbling a torn fingernail while his brain raced. "If the aliens are incapacitating potential strike capacity, are they hitting biological warfare plants too?"

"I don't think you've got it, Ryder," Teresa said. "They are not anticipating a counter strike. They are preparing the planet for themselves."

"Yes," Abdul said. "They are making safe the nasties we humans have left around in case they get contaminated. Remember the domes Manuel told us about? Our visitors need a cleaner planet than we can tolerate."

"Don't forget that many humans didn't want to tolerate those nasties either," Teresa said. "So, let's think what else they might be sealing up."

"How are they doing it?" Ryder said. "Has the ISS spotted orbiting alien stations?"

"No, but there are some hot spots appearing in non-nuclear, non-chemical, and biological sites. What do you think?" Abdul zoomed in on an aerial view of the Ganges delta, then the Mekong delta, Cairo, Shanghai, New Orleans, and Brussels.

"People. Or rather, bodies. They are places of high population densities."

"The callous swine," Ryder said. "So they are wiping out any possible pockets of survivors."

"Idiot," Teresa said, "they are cleaning up millions of putrefying bodies in areas where too many people have died for the old people to bury or burn. This is perfectly in line with the idea that the Zadokians don't want a polluted Earth to live in."

"Ah, even so, there will be plenty of people in their sixties, and older, with a spark left. This is awful. What sort of morality have these Zadokians?"

"Ryder, you have to stop putting human values into an alien species. We might be to them like ants are to us."

"That would explain a lot," Ryder said, "and puts your friend, Antonio, in a spot. They might have a rolled-up newspaper ready for him too."

"Keep laughing, Ryder," Teresa said, "while you can."

Laughing was the last thing on Ryder's mind. "Abdul, as far as we know, there are no aliens on the ground. They might somehow be mind-controlling people to build this dome thing in Canada with Antonio, but hopefully, we'd know if humans were being used as slave labour."

"You make too many assumptions. We can use the ISS along with the data Charlotte in Australia is sending us from spy satellites, but it would take a lot more time and computer power to analyse all the data."

"Perhaps the Zadokians are using lasers or something similar from orbit."

"Ryder, again, we do not have the ability for 360-degree look around twenty-four-seven from the ISS or anywhere else. Certainly, they could be buzzing the planet here and there, but it would be pure luck if we spotted them."

"How's Charlotte doing?"

"She's said little that's new since we arrived here, so I've not bothered you with updates. She reckons she is still on her own out there in Carnarvon. She rattles around in a big building. She has enough fuel to keep the generator going for another month or so, plenty of rations, and time to keep the surveillance work monitoring the orbiting satellites. Ryder, she keeps asking when we're going to get her."

Ryder rubbed his forehead. "You know we can't. To use a jet now would alert the Zadokians to us."

"You can't expect us not to give her some hope. She's scared stiff."

"I'll speak to Dominiq again about her plight, but she is only one of several difficult situations we have to deal with."

"I'm going to give you another one."

Ryder threw his hands up. His head had ached since Teresa had niggled him over Antonio, the alien action, then Charlotte. "I'll be back in a minute."

He opened a sliding glass door to the veranda overlooking the sea. Dead calm. No wonder so many liked to stare at that horizon. The sun's rays snuck through a cloud, allowing them to highlight the sea in horizontal swathes. The overhead deep blue paled to the difficult-to-find horizon. He had to narrow his eyes to spot where water met atmosphere. The scene delivered serenity to any troubled soul. Maybe it was the gentle curve to infinity stretching his mind. He took slow breaths and absorbed the expansive seascape, feeling his pulse decelerate.

"Ryder, you must come back in here. The aliens have landed in France." Abdul shook with excitement.

"How do we know?"

"There is an isolated group of non-ARIA students holed up at a Lyon University campus."

"Really? We knew there must be more than just Charlotte and us. Hang on, how long have you known?"

"Only a few days."

"Why haven't you told me before?" Ryder said, suspecting that Abdul might be colluding with Teresa or Dominiq to undermine him. But even as the thought materialised, he knew Abdul was too loyal to him. A realization reinforced by the broad smile on Abdul's face.

"You've been too busy, boss."

"Okay, but I'm not the first to know, am I?"

"You're right, but I needed to tell someone about the first contact with the French in order to verify they were genuine."

"Fair enough. Who?"

"Jena. There, you're happier now."

Ryder gave Abdul a slap on the back. "You're a tease. Now, this French group. You say they've met some aliens?"

"They claim to have seen them–they sent a digital picture. So come back to the comms room and see for yourself."

Images of little green men, purple blobs, and all the aliens in science fiction films flashed through Ryder's head as he rushed to the monitor. A copper-coloured, fuzzy, long-distance shot met him.

"Abdul, is this the best shot? It's no more than an upright, elongated fuzz-ball like their damned spaceship."

"Yes, but it's fuzzy because they were miles away and used a telephoto lens. Look, the wall near the Zadokian has no distinct edge. I've enhanced it as much as possible."

"And behind him is a bloody big dome, just like Manuel described in Canada."

"They originally lined up the photo to show us that when they got lucky with the alien. By the way, they think it's a robot."

"The way it moves?"

"The colour, Ryder. They assume it's metallic, bronze. Perhaps they've seen too many films."

Ryder laughed. "Don't tell them where we are, and use the backtracking scrambler when communicating with them."

"You sound just like Jena. She's certain they're genuine but told me to use the highest security in case it's the aliens tricking us."

"And you didn't need telling anyway."

"Correct. But there's more."

Ryder rubbed his forehead. "It's all happening today."

"Those nuclear power stations we saw were sealed? They saw it happen to one near them in the Rhône Valley."

"Did they see how it was done?"

"I received a confusing answer. Ask them yourself. They've only given me their first names: Bono, Françoise, and Elodie. They're due online again in an hour, hopefully with better pictures of the Zadokians, robots or whatever. May Allah protect them."

CHAPTER 8

June 25th 2016, Rhône Valley, forty miles south of Lyon, near the town of La Voulte.

THREE STUDENTS ALLOWED DAMP in the grass to soak into their denim clothes. Françoise smiled as she knew Bono's black leather jacket kept his upper body dry and his street cred high, if only his peers could have appreciated it. Françoise had selected this favourite teen night canoodling spot. It overlooked the Rhône a few miles north of Montelimar. Her main canoodler stayed back at the university campus. In any case, Victor favoured messing about on boats than being a dry-land commando.

Bono, scowling about his jacket acquiring mud and grass stains, complained to Françoise. "Are you sure? This is far more dangerous than before. We're a kilometre from that nuclear power station, which might go meltdown any moment."

"*Oui*, Bono, an hour ago, you said this nuke was decommissioned unlike the one they fried yesterday."

Elodie stopped chewing a strand of her blond hair. "It was me who said they might pick on these dormant nukes. After all, there's a lot of radioactive stuff behind those locked steel doors." She twiddled the damp strands of hair while she talked and then replaced it in her mouth. Still chewing, she smiled at Bono, whose black forehead glistened with worry.

"Don't worry, sweetie, I'm sure our Amazon Françoise will keep us safe."

"Keep silent and get right down," Françoise said, having spotted two people near the gates of the power station. "They're too old to be guards but with enough savvy to be dangerous. Bono, use that rifle on them if they get too close. Elodie, have that mpeg cam ready for when I give the signal, and pan from the power station to the sky. Bono, if those people go away, use your cam to keep a continuous sweep of the sky. Remember, Abdul asked us to look for any flying vehicles."

"Flying saucers," Bono said and then grinned.

"Any flying contraption would be a novelty these days. I'm setting up the NoteCom to upload the data to that ISS website Abdul gave us. No more chatting."

They watched the elderly couple look through boxes of rubbish. Françoise guessed they were looking for food. Hardly anyone under sixty was alive now. The infectious retrospective amnesia had reached France, like the rest of the world, within days of it infecting America. Once people forgot how to read and talk, any healthy individuals, relying on instinct, quickly starved. Typhoid, dysentery, and other epidemics were spread by impure water and bad food. She and a few others were on vacation at an isolated university campus in the French Alps. When the TV news and phone news told them there was a serious problem, many left, but a handful remained. She wondered whether they were really the lucky ones. Sooner or later, they would encounter an ARIA case when they took risky excursions for food or information.

Bono broke through her introspection, yet on the same wavelength. "Frankie, what's the chances of our new friends coming to pick us out of here?"

"Nice thinking, Bono, but they didn't say where they were and made no promises."

"*Merde*, they probably don't trust us."

Elodie unplugged her hair from her mouth again. "They must know we're not infected, and we're taking risks to gather information for them."

"True, but maybe they're on the other side of the planet and without transport. Anyway, helping them with information could be of help to us in the long run."

"We've been here hours," moaned Bono. "And those people have moved off. Let's raid that corner shop we saw on the way here and get back before it's too dark to see."

"We could use the lights on the car," Elodie said. "Oh no, I remember, the lights could alert others to us. All right, no need to say anything."

Françoise had been thinking the same. If they didn't head back soon, they would either have to risk using the car lights for the fifty-kilometres return trip or spend the night in a nearby house.

A high-pitched whistle interrupted her decision-making. It lasted three seconds and was followed by a muffled explosion. They all looked up and saw a red glow to the south, maybe twenty miles away.

"Here we go. Elodie, ready that camera. Bono, you use yours too."

"Are you sure we're at a safe distance?" Bono said.

"The one we came across yesterday only melted a kind of lid over the power station, the surrounding area was untouched." She was about to add that they should ready their eyeshades but another whistling grew louder. The abandoned power station less than two kilometres away started glowing. Françoise was terrified, she wet herself, and the beef stew she'd eaten an hour ago rose into her mouth. She glanced through wet eyes at them and saw Bono filming but with a grimace while Elodie was smiling. She shouted, but it took Françoise considerable effort to control her own emotions before she could hear Elodie's words.

"I got a clear picture of it, and a white line like a laser. Hey, I should be a news cameraman–woman."

A series of explosions came from the power station as buildings, pipes, vehicles, and storage containers melted.

The three squeezed themselves tight into the ground, crushing aromatic lavender leaves and sending insects scurrying for their lives. Françoise noticed that Elodie had buried her head in a sage plant but her hands held aloft her cam. On lifting her head just enough to view the screen on the cam, Françoise saw that they were not in danger. The aliens were *trés bien* at surgical destruction. She set up her NoteCom to receive the images and movie files via wireless from the cams and transmit the data to Abdul. Having done that, she gripped the other two on their tremulous shoulders as she stood to get a better view.

It was as if a giant saucepan lid had been rammed onto the power station and heated to cherry-red. The air shimmered above it, giving them a distorted view of the opposite valley side. Remarkably little smoke drifted from the cauterising process. Their nostrils wrinkled as smoke from the barbequed earth, metal, and bricks reached them. The explosions diminished, letting them hear the hissing as steam escaped, adding clouds to the smoke.

"What happened to that elderly couple?" Elodie asked.

Bono trained the zoom lens on his cam to the left of the power station where they last saw the couple. "I reckon they will have been far enough away not to get fried, unless they stopped for a coupling." He sniggered at the thought of geriatric *al fresco* coupling.

"Pervert," Elodie said, giggling. "Should we go and check on them?"

Françoise shook her head in negation but also despair. "Sweet Elodie, bursting with bonhomie, we have to resist rushing to the aid of those potential wounded people, because they have fucking amnesia! If we catch it, darling, we are only eighteen years old, which means that after fourteen weeks, we'd have the memory of four-year-olds. Is this sinking in?"

"Okay, and another month after that, we'd have the memory of a newly born and die of starvation. Sorry, I forgot." Her eyes moistened.

Bono gave Elodie a hug and said to Françoise, "Can we return home now, O Leader?"

"I'm not sure, Bono. I promised Abdul we'd get a better picture of that robot at the La Voulte dome."

"I thought you said they don't think it's a robot."

"We saw it with our own eyes. You saw its jerky movements."

Bono became agitated. "It would be cool if we could capture one. We could get Ricardo to reprogram it." His usual stony face collapsed into a grin—all the more comic with a missing front tooth.

Elodie lifted her face. "Unless it isn't a robot and infects us." She lifted a finger to Françoise.

"*Touché.*" The three of them smiled at each other.

AN HOUR LATER, Françoise once more dirtied her clothes, this time lying on the rough concrete ramp leading up to a bridge crossing the silent, careless waters of the Rhône. She'd never seen the fast river so clean. Although the paint factory here at La Voulte didn't disgorge its evil effluent into the river lately, she'd expected putrefying bodies to muddy the waters. She'd had to hold her nose as they drove through the village of St. Gervais. No dogs there to dispose of human remains. No humans to bury or cremate the dead.

They'd parked their Renault Megane Estate in amongst other abandoned cars so it didn't stand out. Being students, their vehicle hadn't had a wash, so it looked as grimy as the others.

In contrast to olfactory torture, the horizontal surveillance brought sweetness. She sniffed at a sage bush and reached for a welcome clutch of small wild strawberries. She turned to see Elodie being careful not to lay in nettles nor an old flaking cowpat.

"Psst! Ellie. There's some wild strawberries about."

The blonde flashed not-understanding blue eyes but then spotted the red fruit disappearing into Françoise's mouth. She started to rise in order to harvest her own dessert.

"Keep down, you idiot," cried Françoise, wishing she'd kept her exquisite discovery to herself.

"Hey! Have you seen them?" called Bono, kneeling up on the other side of the lane.

Françoise waved him down while shaking her head. They were on the east side of the river. The lane led across a bridge that used to double as a low-level hydroelectric power station. The alien dome was on the west side. She could just see its eggshell-like top above the trees a mile away. She used to swim in a pool over there, maybe at the same spot. She wondered if they'd built their dome over the pool complex, taking in the large grass surround. Why would they do that? Maybe they need to be in water for part of the day or guaranteeing a potable water supply.

She spat out a strawberry seed that had wedged in her teeth. They had to get a closer look. She levelled the binoculars at the bridge. No movement, and she didn't expect any. There were a few regularly spaced columns jutting out of the paving either side of the road, along the parapets. Useful for hiding behind. The road surface was light grey tarmac carpeted with debris. Mostly small rocks, bricks, wood, and an abandoned kid's bike; typical decoration for a society with forgetful citizens and absconded road cleaners. She played with the focus, determined to seek evidence.

She found it. A barely perceptible set of parallel tyre tracks in the grit on the bridge road. The edges of the tracks appeared sharp. The aliens, or their helpers, had transport and used this bridge. It didn't deny her intention to use it, but with mouse-looking-for-cat caution.

Bono disobeyed instructions and crab-crawled to her.

"Darkness is our friend. We must wait."

"You spaced out, idiot. We wouldn't see them either or anything else. And suppose they have infrared eyesight?"

Elodie called over. "Or radar like bats. Ultraviolet, X-rays…"

"Thanks, Madame Curie," Françoise said. "All the more reason to go in daylight when we have use of all our senses, even if ours don't match theirs."

Bono grunted as he flicked away a stone. "I dunno why we're risking our necks for people on the other side of the world."

"Because, numbskull, our survival depends on those with the alien suitcases knowing more about the domes and what's going on inside them. I can't detect any movement, so let's get across the bridge. Keep to the right, heads down. Bono, you first."

"I might have guessed," he said, looking over the parapet first. He ducked and jogged along.

Françoise followed him, hoping Bono wasn't going to break into a run, making it difficult to hide if seen. Elodie sauntered on in the rear.

"Keep up, Elodie," Françoise whispered as loud as she dared.

"My feet hurt."

"It'll be more than your feet if we get caught."

Halfway, a niche in the parapet provided a hiding place, ideal for three spies. Bono waited for the women to catch up.

Françoise caught up with him and leant against the creamy limestone wall. "You didn't have to go so fast. We shouldn't be so stretched out. Elodie…"

The smirk on Bono's face left him as they heard an engine. The bridge vibrated, agitating surface dust, as a deep growling announced the slow approach of a heavy truck.

Françoise and Bono squeezed themselves into the parapet niche, but Elodie strolled up the centre sucking a lollipop. Françoise remembered her discovering it that morning *en passant* a confectioner's shop.

"For Christ's sake, get down!" she screamed.

Bono laughed. "Where? This is the nearest cover, and that must be a spiced lolly 'cos she's spaced out."

Françoise groaned as she slumped. "Go get her. Maybe the driver hasn't seen her. I'll see how good a shot I am." She lay on her stomach, feeling small stones through her T-shirt, as she reached in her bag for the SIG-2012 pistol with an extended barrel for accurate targeting. Resting on her elbows, she flicked up a small digi-telescopic sight. It answered one query. A human drove the vehicle. So old, she could see his walnut face. Even supposing his memory loss had halted, he had the memories of a twenty year old. It accounted for his erratic and tortoise-speed driving.

"You'll not take him out with that popgun."

"Bono, I told you to get Elodie." Françoise turned to find the girl, fifty metres away, sitting in the middle of the road.

"I didn't vote for you to be leader. That's a military vehicle, the windshield might be bulletproof. What's the old duffer driving it for, anyway?"

"Maybe it's easier than walking. He must be at least eighty. But, Bono, suppose he is on a mission?"

"To find food for the wretched remainder of his family?"

"To scout around the locality for the aliens."

"Do you think they know about us?" Bono lost his perpetual grin.

"They must realize there might be groups like us. Oh well, here we go." She eyed through the scope and readied the pistol. The meandering vehicle inched towards them, now two hundred metres away.

"I told you. You'll never kill him."

"There's always more than one way to bring a man to his knees. Watch and learn."

She held her breath and squeezed the trigger. A noise like a slammed book accompanied a kick, but she recovered within two seconds and squeezed once more.

"I can't see you've hit anything. Let me have a go."

"Patience."

A few seconds later, the vehicle slewed to the left and collided with the wall. At least one of her bullets had penetrated the nearside front tyre.

"Hey, that's good work. What a shot. Now, he'll get out, and we can shoot him."

"Whatever for? He hasn't good enough eyes to see us properly. I bet he thinks he's got a puncture. My God, Bono, the poor man's ancient and has had the trauma of nursing his younger family members to their death."

"I guess we have to go back then."

"There's another bridge a mile upstream. Let's pick up bird-brain and keep to the side in case he sees us moving." On reaching Elodie, Françoise took the partly sucked red lolly and threw it over the parapet. "Give the fish a treat. Come on, Elodie, we have to get out of here."

Moaning, with eyes closed and frowning at the forced migration, Elodie struggled to her feet but was thrown back up the road, landing in a heap just as a shot echoed around them.

"Run!" shouted Bono, as he started a zigzag dash.

"What about Elodie?" she said but saw an ugly red hole in the girl's back. If she wasn't dead, she soon would be. Damn her conscience. She ran a few steps beyond Elodie before dropping and drawing her gun. The old man was in front of his vehicle struggling with the automatic weapon. After a few shots from Françoise, it didn't matter. He collapsed on top of it.

She went back to Elodie and turned her gently. Her glazed eyes, still open, saw nothing. Françoise turned to see Bono stop running. He waved his hands as if reading her mind by semaphore. Now that the old man is no more, maybe they could continue crossing this bridge. But Bono stayed where he was at the other end. Françoise shook her head wondering if he'd seen something else behind her at the truck. But nothing was there except one crashed vehicle and a human heap in the road. She stooped to retrieve Elodie's radio. Now, she needed to bawl out the idiot Bono.

"Bonehead, come on. We can cross here now the old man is... ah. I get it."

"About time, boss lady. He might not be dead, and even if he is, he might be infectious. Get your management derrière up this end."

She grimaced through his insubordination, and looking over her shoulder in case of any developments, hurried to his position. She hadn't time, yet, to grieve over her school friend.

AN HOUR LATER, they parked their estate car again, but after sneaking across the more northerly bridge. Bono reversed under a willow tree so that the car pointed back across the bridge for a quick getaway.

They shushed each other to listen. The lustre-cream dome peeped over poplar trees only half a mile to the south. A dog barked, making them jump, but they couldn't see it.

"Maybe a cyclist on the Autoroutes," Bono said with a nervous laugh. Françoise held up her hand in a request for more silence. A cool wind rustled the willow leaves, and a yellowed page from a newspaper hopscotched across white concrete southwards towards the dome.

"The Mistral," she whispered, acknowledging the forces of nature, ignoring man's plight. "Let's move closer. On foot."

An hour later, a laurel bush remained the only shelter between the two uninfected and the alien dome. At ten metres, through the translucent membrane, Françoise could see no detail inside the circus-tent-sized dome. Indistinct human-height shapes loomed up and away. She knew they had to take bolder action if they were to take worthwhile photographs for the scientists to analyse.

"I'm sorry to have to say, Bono, but..."

"We have to go inside?"

"Exactly." Françoise looked around on the sides as far as she could see, left and right, for tracks on the ground.

"It shouldn't take much to get in." Bono grinned as he flicked open a sharp blade, glinting in the late afternoon sun.

"I was thinking more of walking through a proper entrance."

"We would risk being seen, or worse, bumping into an infected human."

"True, but an improvised entrance might cause an unexpected gush of air at us if there is positive air pressure in there."

"So?"

"Idiot. I don't mean we might be blown away, but that ARIA spore, or whatever, near this side, would be blown at us. Anyway, suppose they have sensors, cameras, or other security devices? We would be announcing: 'hey look, dozy insurgents on their way in'."

"I get it. Walking in through a proper entrance is normal. We could pretend to be prisoner and guard. Me as guard."

"Of course, why didn't I think of that, Bono? After all, they must be taking in non-ARIA prisoners every day."

"Erm, actually, we are the only ones, and the rest of our group miles away. I think another plan is required."

"A diversion around the other side, so that the nearest entrance—look, I see one to our left—is deserted, temporarily."

"Yeah. I could set up an explosion. A makeshift fuse leading to a car petrol tank should do the trick."

"No need. A group is coming out. Cam now, Bono."

She swallowed, but her mouth was too dry. Cursing her poor preparation at leaving her water bottle behind, she fumbled in her bag for a stick of gum. She knew that the stress of possible infection disturbed her normally cool composure. Filling her with dread was the thought of losing her memory as fast as a year's worth every week. She was young, not like these geriatric survivors. Maybe the once-infected ARIA victims around here had stopped losing their memory or lost it slowly. Who knew for sure? She couldn't trust second-hand information from an island enclave somewhere, passing on observations from a Canadian group. They didn't know if the secondary or ARIA-2 people could pass on memory-problem infections to people like her. Her stomach heaved. In spite of the fact she didn't want to show weakness to Bono by throwing up, her eyes filled with tears at the thought of Elodie. As leader, Françoise admonished herself for not procuring flak jackets. Her control returned. The gun in her right hand offered some protection, and the car key in her left was ready for the fastest drive-off this region had seen all year.

"My God, it's an alien. Damn ugly," Bono said.

Françoise squinted through her gun's telescopic viewer. "Idiot, it's wearing a mask. An air filter? Maybe they're allergic to pollen."

"Or to lead. Put a hole in him, Fran."

"Clever. We'd have to kill all of them before being overpowered, killed, or infected. Then what? Put the alien in a mincer and feed it through the modem? You concentrate on getting close ups and leave the strategy to me."

"I've got good zoomed-in pics of orange man there. Now what?"

Françoise couldn't take her eyes off the human-like alien. It did, indeed, have a red tinge to the colour of his skin. Copper rather than orange. It stood under two metres tall, slim, short cropped hair, and now, it looked with its tiny black eyes straight at her.

"Down," she called and then shushed. After a second, Bono crouched beside her.

"Did you see his mouth?" he asked. "No bigger than those beady little eyes. But my head hurts."

"Mine too. Let's retreat. Carefully."

By the time they reached the Renault, their heads had stopped buzzing. Françoise looked quizzically at Bono, as if he knew what she suspected. The alien had sensed their presence, located them by superior hearing, smell, or something else.

them even if I don't remember sitting in a pool of sweat to take them. Hah.

I see a ragged white line in the dark. Now, if I strain, I see the lumpy outline of the island. This is going to be easy. I steer this little escape pod of a boat onto a beach. Oh, yes, cut the engine to let the mom—momentity? Its speed take us the rest of the way. Then, we sneak ashore. Fuck, I'll have to make sure Benita does all her yapping now, so she keeps quiet then. Gotta feeling that isn't gonna work.

There's something else to think about. I had it a minute ago, but now it's leaked out. That's not right, a thought isn't memory, is it? We should be able to hang on to a thought we've made. I speculate about all the things I must have known to pass all those degree exams and lecture and research stuff since. How much of it would come in handy now? Maybe nothing. What do I really need to know? The most important thing. For survival, it would be knowing what food and drink is safe. Knowing how to talk to get food and how to stop my head buzzing. It's worse when I think too much about what I'm supposed to be thinking. Can't stop doing that. Maybe the ones who give up easy, go loopy quicker. The sol—solliu—answer is going to be on that island. Has to be.

"Hi, Bryce. Hey, is that still your name?"

"It was a minute ago. Why? Have you lost yours?"

"Funny, but I couldn't remember the name of this boat. Anyway, you were talking to yourself up here. What were you saying?"

"Dunno. Can't remember. Damn." I increase the revs to get to that island quicker before I turn round for no reason.

CHAPTER 10

RYDER WOKE IN PAIN as his left rib sent shock waves through him. "Jena, when the bloody hell did you have your elbows sharpened?"

"When I needed to wake you in an emergency. They've found a boat, beached on the south side."

"No. What happened to the high-tech surveillance covering all the bays?"

"Too many screens, not enough eyes."

"You mean Captain Chad couldn't be bothered to enforce the rota."

Jena leant against the doorframe, looking at him with a here-we-go-again face.

"All right, it's no time for what ifs. But it is for what where?" He looked past her elbow at where her finger rested on the map. He knew there were only two populated towns. Avarua with around two thousand and Titikaveka, the next biggest but with a mere thirty sleepy households. The intruder, even if with half his marbles, knew to arrive at an easy approach, farthest from the most populated point. "How did he know?"

"Maybe he used to live here."

"Or someone here is helping him."

"Are you crazy? Just suppose a doting mother here, as a refugee from Australia, had a favourite nephew or cousin out there on a boat. How on Earth could she contact him?"

"Telecommunications via satellite worked for months on automatic while power fed it. Suppose that boat had left here before we arrived and increased security awareness. Now, it's back with extra people."

"Doesn't make sense, Ryder. If this hypothetical parent lived here, then by definition, they would be ARIA free. So inviting their infected offspring would send them and us down the drain."

"Logic doesn't come into it. Blood being slicker, you know."

"Thicker. Okay, you're right. Now, come on, you don't want to miss the meeting."

"What? We need to get in a chopper and cut that bastard off before he gets here. No time for discussing the chapel flower-arranging rota." Exasperated with the cavalier attitude to the islanders' security displayed by the majority of the staff, he knocked over a chair on the way to the door.

"And which way are you going?"

"To the helipad, where else?"

"Have you been on a crash pilot's course, Ryder? Let's see, you are a media expert and so–"

"Funny, but you are a pilot."

"I've not flown the Sea Hawk eighty, and night time over strange territory is not my idea of fun nocturnal activity, lover boy."

"Of course, I am a clod. I keep thinking you are Lara Croft meets Superwoman. Lead the way."

Out into the starlit, chilly night, they walked across glistening flagstones to the Yacht Club. In spite of his impatience, Ryder automatically slowed as his nostrils filled with the heady aromas of the droopy, flowered Brugmansia and the white stars of Jasmine. As Ryder heard Jena's flip-flops slapping the stones and his trainers squeaking, he looked at the Jasmine plants where hidden hoppers and crickets chirruped at them. At three in the morning that should be the only disturbance, but he looked at Jena as a wavering siren kicked in.

"Hey, Chad must have oiled that old air-raid siren from the museum, like I told him to."

"Naw," Jena had to shout. "He decided to use the one on the coast guard boat. At least people will wake and know to not let any strangers in their homes."

"But I said to put the siren on the peak so it could be heard all over the island. If it's at sea level–"

"Stop carping. At this time of night, it will be heard on the next island, if there's anybody there."

HE'D NOT BEEN IN THE CONFERENCE ROOM AT NIGHT. The bright neon light bounced reflections back from the huge windows. His usual escape ploy of standing at the window to watch the world outside would be unavailable to him this time. Sabotaged by optical physics, Ryder remained standing but leaned on the mahogany table and interrupted the cosy natterers. The island's leader, Dominiq, joked with his wife, Nessa, and Chad, the coast guard captain. The police chief slept, leaning grotesquely back in his chair.

"Why are you warming your butts in here when our biggest threat to date is zeroing in on us? Where's Bat Malise and Tilley, the chopper pilots. Get them out there."

Dominiq sat back in his chair as if to distance himself more from

Ryder. "I didn't think it was appropriate to send helicopters out over the jungle and mountains in the dark. We'll depend on the perimeter-fence sensors and patrols."

"Is this the fence with the Jeep-sized holes that were supposed to be repaired weeks ago?" Ryder's face heated. He glanced at Jena for support, but she was scrutinising the flickering brown eyes of Nessa.

"We'll have guards at those few odd places," Dominiq said. "And if you like, we'll send a squad to intercept by road."

Ryder was about to detonate again, but Jena grabbed his elbow and pulled him to the wall, whispering in his ear: "There's something fishy going on. Nessa and Dominiq are hiding something."

"Nessa? She hasn't said a word."

"She has, with her eyes." Jena looked at him and flicked her eyes back to the table.

"So, a man and his wife are communicating. It doesn't add up to a conspiracy, does it?"

"In this case, I think so."

"Okay, let's see." He walked back to the table with a more casual air. "Dom, let's see. I think we should send a squad or three in Humvees due south through to the mountain."

Dominiq laughed in short bursts followed dutifully by his wife, and then by Chad. The cacophony was added to by snores from the police chief.

Ryder rapped his knuckles on the mahogany. "What's so hysterical?"

"There is only one drivable road, and it circumnavigates the island," Chad said, stifling a snigger. "But, we'll send a Humvee in both directions." He picked up his phone and jabbed the buttons.

Jena grabbed Ryder's arm again. "We're wasting time, come on."

"Yes, go and leave it to us," shouted Dominiq. "But I'm not sure why we're bothering."

"Shush, Dom," hushed Nessa, but Ryder caught it.

"Excuse me. What is going on here?"

"Oh, come on, Ryder," sneered Dominiq. "Do you really think we can keep others out forever? There must be thousands of boats out there with desperate people hoping we have the cure. And maybe we have."

"You blithering idiot." Ryder lunged at Dominiq, but the table corner stopped him.

Jena grabbed his arm.

"Ryder's right. We don't know for sure that the second case fixes ARIA, and we don't know what would happen to us, who have not been exposed to either ARIA-1 or ARIA-2."

Dominiq laughed. "Your friend Manuel in Canada seems okay."

"But Antonio, who was like us and then exposed to the second case, went berserk, running amok like a psychopath, killing our friends."

Nessa looked shocked. "You don't seriously think we would go like that? We're far too civilised."

Ryder was shaking. "Remember, Antonio was a civilised doctor. Wake up, Nessa. And the rest of you. I am appalled that I'm having to go over this again." He threw a chair against a wall.

Jena grabbed both his arms this time.

"It's not their fault entirely. They've not seen what we've had to witness." She turned to Dominiq with furrowed brows. "Even idiots on this island know we have to keep ARIA away, or we'll all catch it and lose our memory and eventually our lives. Nothing like enough controlled testing has been done with the second case. Gustav and Teresa have only just finished testing the containment compartment."

"I know that, Jena, there's another agenda being played here."

"I agree. It's as if they want to commit suicide."

"Or, as if they know who it is sneaking in."

"Same thing. Unless... Hey, Dominiq, what do you know about this intruder? Do you have information that he is free of ARIA but were afraid we wouldn't let him in anyway?"

"We let you in, didn't we?"

"This is getting us nowhere," Ryder said. "Let's get Bat Malise and his Sea Hawk to cut across the island. We'll need some tough guys too."

"I'll call Gustav and Abdul while you drag Bat out of bed. We'll meet you at the chopper pad in ten."

IN THE DARK, Ryder stumbled on the uneven slabs, as he looked for the helicopter pilot's house. He'd been so hot, he could have powered a small village. Now, he could feel the heat in his face dissipating, energising the cool air around and attracting unwanted midges. Part of his annoyance was self-inflicted, because he'd allowed them to laugh at his geographical ignorance. He'd not lived anywhere with a perimeter road and no drivable lanes across. He knew the place was mountainous in the middle—an extinct volcanic range—but there were gaps. They were filled in with the lush tropical vegetation, swamps and loose rock. No funding here, nor need, to make a quick access diameter road. Even so, he bet that the intruder ran and scrambled straight across. He might have found a motorbike; there are plenty of them on the island. There might be several intruders. Fools. And yet, he still had a pang of sorrow for them. He didn't want to kill them, or anyone, but needed to tell them to keep away, in isolation while they assessed the situation. They might be reasoned with if they haven't lost too much memory. They couldn't be since they'd had enough initiative and survival skills to reach the island. So, they'd have teenage memory and ability. But he patted the Berretta in his belt.

The siren wailed, but Bat's house slept. Like a bat, Ryder thought, then revised the idea since bats flew around at night. He'd cooled to simmering by the time he rang the bell then rapped the wooden door panel before yelling up at an open window. A cat ran across his feet. The same one that bugged him most days.

The house gave up the dark, sending light streaks from the window slats across a lawn manicured so well, it looked like the extension of a fitted carpet.

A young woman's voice with a Welsh accent followed the light escaping out of the window. "Go away."

"Hang on," Ryder called, "is Bat up there with you, erm, Mrs Malise?"

"That'd be hilarious if you weren't battering the door and wailing that alarm thingey." She stuck her head out of the window, opened her mouth and disappeared.

"Megan? What are you doing in there?" Ryder was about to kick the door in when he remembered no one locked their doors, many had no locks. He rushed in and ran up the stairs two at a time. Megan stood at the top wearing a rugby shirt and a big smile.

"Hello, Ryder," she said. "Funny time to call."

He pushed past her to find Bat pulling on his jeans.

"She's only fourteen, for Christ's sake!"

"Actually, I'm fifteen."

"Going on twenty-five," Bat said with a silly smile.

Ryder struggled with the temptation to launch at Bat but needed his cooperation. "I know relationships like this are different on these islands, and now, with no law to speak of, but..."

"Oh, hello, Ryder," said an older woman coming out of the en suite bathroom. Ryder vaguely recognised her as Bat's fiancée.

"Have I blundered here? So, Megan wasn't in bed with..."

Megan smiled. "Not saying I wasn't, Ryder. Wanna join in?"

"I haven't got time for your games. Bat, we need to get airborne in a hurry. We have an intruder on the island over on the south side."

"So, that noise isn't part of my hangover? I can't fly in this condition, Ryder."

"I'm willing to take a chance. If we don't stop them, you might as well say goodbye to ever flying again in a few weeks. And Megan will be a gibbering wreck."

"No change there then," Bat said. Everyone except Ryder rocked with laughter.

Ryder realized this wasn't an alcoholic aftermath. Maybe he should give up on Bat and try Tilley Graver, their other pilot, but she was too fragile to be any use in making the right decision on firing the onboard weapons.

"All right, I'm not gonna get any sleep with that racket. Let's go."

"Before we leave, Bat, where would we pick up a megaphone, torches, and nets?"

"There's a megaphone connected to the chopper, a separate one may be in the depot, as will be torches, although they're not as powerful as the searchlights on the machine."

"We might have to leave the chopper and go some way on foot. I'm being prepared."

"I want to go," shouted Megan, running after them.

"No way, girl. Go back in. It could be dangerous," Ryder said.

"You know I'm resourceful and might think of stuff you don't."

"I'm not wasting time with a debate, Megan. Jena is rounding up more crew, and there's already squads going round the main road in both directions."

Ryder followed Bat around the side of his house where a Jeep waited. Bat jumped into the driving seat while Ryder spotted ropes and a torch in the back, which he grabbed. He didn't have time to worry about Bat's blood toxicity as his focus was entirely on stopping being thrown out of the vehicle at each sharp turn and jumps over curbs. He had to let the torch go in order to save his life.

"No need to kill ourselves, Bat," he yelled. "The others are probably not there yet."

"I always drive like this. Great, ain't it? Damn, I missed Coral Street in this dark." The Jeep gouged the gravel then reversed.

At the coast guard depot, Ryder carefully disembarked with his vision blurred and bones resonating from the ride. He reckoned he could've walked the journey in just the same time, considering the wrong turns, long shortcut, and the vibratory trauma. Bat had turned on the store's lights before staggering to the helicopter, enabling Ryder to rummage for essential accessories for their search and destroy... repel... detain... mission. Once his ears settled to normal, he heard the siren again. The dual sounds of helicopter and car engines drowned it. He found a handheld megaphone and another torch. Ideally, he'd have liked a gladiator's net, trident–extra long–

and tranquiliser darts with a telescopic lens viewfinder. He found a long stick then threw it away in disgust as he heard brakes.

Looking at his meagre haul and deciding that if they survived this encounter, they must organise a well equipped, fast-reaction squad, said, "It's about time you lot arrived."

"I came as fast as I could."

"Megan. For pity's sake. You know we can't take you."

"I'm smaller than you, so I can hide and get through small gaps. I'm more likely to be the intruder's memory age. And I want to be useful."

Ryder had to concede that the first two points made sense. The blasted girl knew how to work on his obsession to cover all possibilities.

"If I let you come, there will be conditions."

"I have to do exactly what you say. In my bag here, I have this useful communicator."

"Ah, good, a mobile phone charged and tuned to our island transmitter?"

"That would be good, but I meant this gun."

A year ago, Ryder would have blown up at her in an apoplectic outburst, but now it was: "Excellent. Don't let this intruder get near you, shoot to kill if he or she keeps coming at you and closer than twenty metres. You do know–"

"How to use this? Yes, most of us are in the gun club. Your idea."

"Oh, yes. Sorry, a necessary evil. Now, where the hell are the others?"

Bat called over that he'd had a message that Tilley was taking Teresa and Gustav in the other Sea Hawk in twenty minutes.

CHAPTER 11

ONCE RYDER AND MEGAN clambered aboard with their gear, including part of a large fishing net Megan found, Bat made the helicopter add to the night noises with the roar of the engine and headed 160-degrees in a direct line to the intruder's landing spot on the southeast.

Ryder was eager to get there. "Can we have the infrared monitor on? I want to see their boat to assess how many people we have to deal with, but we might spot them on the way."

"I can switch it on, but they can already hear us, so they'll be hidden in the trees. We'll be there in minutes. Let's hope they haven't brought any ground-to-air missiles."

"If they did, they wouldn't know how to use them," Ryder said with a soft smile.

"But if they did," Megan said, "it might show they don't have ARIA."

"True, but in that case, they'd have used their radio to call us to ensure we didn't attack them."

She had to shout over the noise. "Maybe. Ryder, you sometimes talk like you wanna eliminate all humans to make sure you make it."

"Really? I thought I was trying to protect all of us." He wondered if this was it. The last hour of *compos mentis* and not just for him. If anyone on the island became infected, then they *all* would, followed by obliteration unless ARIA-2 was an antidote. What a hell of a risk.

He studied the moving greyscale image on the screens. One displayed the forward camera at forty-five degrees, giving an oblique angle that might detect under-canopy warm bodies. The other showed the directly overhead view. Both were calibrated to show human heat as white, but goats and pigs showed the same brightness with the few cows a little darker. Ryder imagined the derision from the island's elders if he arrested a pig, after megaphoning it to stop and lie on the ground.

Bat settled the chopper near the beached motorboat. Ryder didn't want to waste time, so he sent Bat looking for tracks while he and Megan looked for clues.

"There's a woman," Megan said.

"Well done. How do you know? Is the toilet seat down?"

"Women's magazines–old but so's everyone's–mirror's been cleaned recently, and green makeup on a dirty towel."

"Green? So she's a redhead, or am I generalising? And why bother in a crisis?"

"Might not seem like a crisis if the woman has the memory and attitudes of a young teen. Could be black."

"Both? Assuming there was a man too, or two women."

"Difficult to say, except I doubt one teenaged person would make it to here without two brains unless she was damned clever, like me."

"You're a one-off." Ryder grinned and Megan smiled back.

Bat returned and pointed to the edge of the white beach where shrubbery guarded its edge and, incongruously, that of a rugby football pitch.

"We had a good team," he said, answering Ryder's raised eyebrow. "You wouldn't think it now with it being so overgrown, but this was a super pitch. We played the All-Blacks, you know."

"I might have guessed. What about our invaders?"

"There's trampled grass where two, maybe three, people have gone across the pitch towards the banana plantation on the other side."

"Towards the road, and if they crossed it, straight where we came from."

"Shall we go after them?" Megan had an eager face.

"No. We'll use the chopper to get in front. The squads coming by road can follow them."

"Pincer movement. Good tactic," Bat said.

"Only if it works. You get on the phone to let the others know, Megan, while Bat and I have one last look in the boat before taking off."

Ryder knew that Bat would pick up on clues he couldn't, and he did. The boat had a mini-GPS direction finder that had been detached, old-fashioned charts lay on the floor with *Viking Moon*'s logo.

"So they came from that flotilla we turned back a couple of weeks ago," said Bat. "Look, Rarotonga is ringed on this chart and the lat-long coordinates for it."

"There's also dozens of stick-it notes and bits of paper with scribbles. We haven't time to analyse them all. Probably trivial stuff, though I see the letters ARIA on this one, names too. Stuff some in pockets, and let's go to the centre of the island to cut them off."

Concentrating hard on the infrared displays, Ryder urged Bat to go against his racing tendencies and not exceed twenty miles per hour. Otherwise, they followed a straight-line route back towards Avarua.

Megan had to yell in Ryder's ear. "If I were them, I wouldn't come this way."

"Why not?"

"They can hear this racket on the next island. They must know we're searching for them. So why make it easy?"

"I'm hoping they aren't thinking that logically."

"They might have lost memory but not their intelligence."

"To an extent." Ryder had to turn his glowing grey face from the screen to converse clearer. "Losing vast amounts of memory must be disorientating and the worry will not be conducive to logical decisions. They, like most people on the run chased by helicopters, will run in their intended direction only faster. Or hide." A headache was knocking in his skull. He was so tired of making impossible decisions.

"There's one logical decision they've made." Megan maintained her teenage upbeat excitement.

"You mean coming here. Yes, but that also means they want contact in the hope of a cure. So why run away from us?"

"I'd be worried this is a search and destroy mission."

"So, you'd hide and approach stealthily. Well, that would spell disaster for us, so we're not giving them a choice."

Bat flew a zigzag at a thousand metres with no searchlight. Ryder was hoping that, even if the intruders heard them, they wouldn't be able to pinpoint them. The splotchy screen image drifted by in two dimensions, but it gave him an impression of the ground; whereas, looking out of the window only presented him with black and moonlit whites, rather like a cryptic crossword puzzle with no clues.

This time, it was Bat who became excited. "Spotted 'em!"

"But you can't see the infrared display and there's no white splodges," complained Ryder.

"I made out two people running over a ridge at two o'clock, a mile away. Shall I fly over and hail them to stop?"

"No. Let them think we've not seen them. Fly north and land a mile in front. Ah, by turning the oblique cam I can see them."

"Two," Megan said, confirming Bat's observation.

"Megan, phone Teresa and the others to give them this position on the map."

CHAPTER 12

I LET LOOSE A GRUNTED LAUGH as I crouch by a group of honey-scented lilies. My chortle was for remembering the rugby football field I ran across. It feels so good, my hair bristles now on the back of my neck. I haven't seen or done anything for ages that I can distinctly relate a memory to. On the other hand, I can't remember exactly why I can't remember everything else. Oh, yes, the–I check my NoteCom–ARIA. I laugh too at, erm,–Benita–who is looking for me.

"Brycie, where the fuck are you?"

"Stop making so much noise," I yell back, making us both giggle.

"I can't walk properly after being bounced up and down on that boat for months, years, whatever. My, that flower is so powerful, it should be bottled."

"I bet it is, was."

"The air is so thick with that sweet perfume, Bryce. You can swim in it. Umm."

I worry she'll slow us down. "Hey, don't lie down and sleep, you druggie. We have to cross this island to get to the town where the cure is."

"Oh, yeah. Which way? Hey, there's a road. We can catch a bus."

I smile at her simple thinking. "Good plan. You wait here for one. It might be a few years. Meanwhile, I'm sneaking off across the road and through that banana plantation. I must have been here as a kid, 'cos I know there's tracks right through the mountains. You have to keep that pinnacle rock to our left. Oh bugger!"

"What? Can you see their army coming?"

"No, Benita, but look at the sports field we just crossed. I thought the uncut grass was too long to show our path. I expect it's too late to untrample the grass."

"We could go back and create a load of false trails." Benita says this, employing a rare frown as the thinking intensity bites.

I praise her. "Hey, that's an impressive idea."

"I'm not just a pretty face."

"I didn't think you were."

"What? A pretty face?"

Is she trying to trip me up? I have enough trouble coping with my own disappearing brain, let alone fielding Benita's trick shots. Is she losing her memory faster and so sending her spinning down into childhood before me?

"We haven't time to go back now, let's get on. Try and keep up."

"S'all right. You keep going at your own speed. We're bound to get caught anyway."

A wicked thought is wheedling its way. If Benita is caught, maybe the islanders will believe she is on her own and not look for me. Or at least their searchers will be confused and split up.

"Tell you what, Benita. If we get separated, let's pretend the other one doesn't exist."

"That's not fair. You just want them to capture me to leave you alone."

"If I'm in front, they are more likely to see me first and so leave you alone instead."

"Oh, yeah. Don't you get tired being so clever, Brycie?" She catches me up and links arms. "Don't worry, I'm never going to let you go."

Damn.

She has to relinquish her grip once we start weaving our way through the banana plantation. Vague flashes of past living hit me. Playing hide and seek in here. It's become overgrown, bad odours of rotting fruit. The growers must have moved away. It's a dark, spooky forest with broad leaves as big as goblins towering over us. I turn to check and see she's keeping up. But I trip. No harm done. Actually, it's fun down here with the roots. A mouse scurries away. Hah, that would've made Benita scream. I turn on my back and see the stars framed by the huge leaves. Benita flops down beside me, panting.

"What game's this then?"

"Shush." I put my finger on her thick, wet lips.

"Hey, none of that—ah, I hear it too."

We hear the percussion before seeing a silhouetted helicopter pirouette over us before it flew onto the beach.

"Shall we go over to them?" Benita says, standing up.

I pull her back to the damp ground, but why not let her go? She would traipse through the long grass to the chopper and say, "Hi." Then, they would either shoot her or run away. Maybe they would be shocked into standstill. Or perhaps they wouldn't realize she is afflicted with ARIA and think she's an islander. If they haven't solved the ARIA-infection problem, then they'll become infected. But at least they'll be delayed. Unless. Unless what? Oh yes, unless she tells them about me. Then, they will know I'm not far away. Damn.

"Come on, Benita, we have to sneak off, fast."

"But, Brycie. They might be friends. I miss Tina and Janey from school. But wasn't it yesterday I saw them?"

Poor sod. I know the feeling. I don't think Benita reads her notes as much as she should.

"Listen up. The people here wanna kill us. Charging up to the nearest person, waving a Barbie doll, is not gonna get us cured. You hear me?"

She pouts but lets me grab her hand to jog through the rest of the banana plantation towards the mountain range northwards.

Not so clear now. Although it was gloomy in the plantation, the lines made it easy to navigate. I thought there should be a track up to the gap in the hills above, but I'm not going to waste time looking for it. Anyway, they might assume we'll use it. The ground has tussocks of grass and herbs. I must have just crushed a lemony herb.

"Hey, which one is that? It's lovely, let me," she squealed, while leaping around.

"For Christ's sake, stop it. The fragrance is lemon, but we'll be shit if they've dogs to track us."

"I hadn't thought of that. You don't really think they'll have dogs?"

"How should I know? They always do on TV."

She suffers in silence as I pull her through the undergrowth and gravel streambeds. I let her go when she complains too loudly. The going becomes tough uphill, and I wait on a big, flat rock for her to catch up.

"I'm tired."

"We can't stop. They could catch us so close to the beach."

"But we must be miles away by now."

I turn her to see the breakers two miles distant. But I'm surprised at the height we seem to be. I can't see Benita progressing much more up this steep slope, sliding back and tripping, bawling her displeasure. Narrowing my eyes, I try to see if there's a track. A gap in the black cloud allows a silvery moon to send its floodlight at the mountain. I see a way and thank the moon.

Benita has thrown herself on the ground once more. "Aren't you coming down away from the helicopter's searchlight."

I instinctively follow her into the prickly flora, thinking how my urging her to be more aware is working.

"Good thinking, Benita. But this time, it's the moon. Come on. The extra light might show us up more, but we have to take some chances, and I think I see an easier way up."

"I'm all for that. But what happens when we reach the town, Avalon?"

My God, she thinks we're in a King Arthur fantasy. "I think

someone in Avarua has a cure. At least that's what my NoteCom says, and it sent the location to the boat GPS. Someone here might be looking out for us. What is for sure is that without a cure, our memory disappears into when we wore nappies."

"Mummy will look after me, then."

"Sorry to tell you, but mummy ain't here. We gotta do this for ourselves or die."

"If you say so."

"You don't believe me? And can we walk while we talk?"

"I dunno what to believe, Bryce, and nor do you."

Tropical plants and trees clothe the mountain, filling the air with bird squawks, insect chirrups, drips from leaves and sweet aromas. But the steady uphilling robs us of spare oxygen for nattering. We have to stop whenever a seat-shaped slab of rock or fallen tree pull at our wobbling legs. Gasping, we admire the view of moonlit sea. I imagine we would have seen lights on the black islands a few miles out, but not now. Can't see the beach clearly either, nor the helicopter. It might have taken off again and circled around. Our ears have been too full of pounding blood to notice whirring engine noises. The view is awesome, but it can't lift us over the mountain. I fill myself with an image that if I were the islanders and came across us, a bullet would be the hello.

Another half hour and the track levels off between two peaks. I'm tempted to scramble up one to get an eyeful of the north of the island.

"Don't leave me, Bryce. I can't go up there, and I'm too scared to be on my own. I've seen snakes and spiders, you know."

"You think you have. Just shadows."

"Really? What's this then?" She throws something like a three-foot stick at me, but it is a real snake. I step back and laugh out of embarrassment.

"Benita, you're not normal, you. Why didn't you scream? You've scuppered your argument for not being left alone."

"Go up there then. Don't expect me to be here when you get back. You shouldn't aban—abandaid—leave me." Her arms are folded tight under her breasts like a scowling wife. This means that if I do go up the hill to get a better view, she'll hide, hoping I will worry about her. It would serve her right for me to then march off. But she'd call, and I'd have to waste time on a search just to keep the silly mare from making enough racket to let the searchers zoom in on us.

"Come on," I say, trampling on the moonlit track now weaving towards a clump of palm trees to the north.

She skips alongside. I think of telling her how daft she looks: a middle-aged woman acting like a kid, but maybe she's regressed more than I hope I have.

Just in front of the palm trees, a bright flash sends my knees buckling; my right hand grabs Benita to pull her down. But, ignorant of danger, she pulls back.

"Hey, Brycie. Hah, do you see it too? It's a motor scooter. We can drive the rest of the way."

It must have been its mirror reflecting moonlight. I'm too late to stop her galloping across the uneven ground towards the parked bike.

"Come back, Benita," I called, wasting my breath.

Those palm trees look so black. I have to follow the idiot girl-woman, but I haven't straightened up. She's trying to upright the abandoned scooter by the time I reach her. She's right, we could use it to get us to the town quicker, but at what noise cost?

I catch the saddle before the Lambretta falls on her, but it's muddy underfoot, and I can't hold it. She grabs at the handlebars in a fit of giggles and presses the horn. The stupid machine is still falling, all the worse because two idiot humans are trying to tame it. We are like a three-man mud-wrestling bout in a small-town circus. Both of us collapse into mud and laughter.

Once again, I lay on my back. I can see two full moons. One is in the western sky, which has blueness. The other moon lives in the scooter's mirror. Hello, it is eclipsed. I look to my left and see Benita lying, looking enraptured by the sky. If she isn't moving, then what's in the mirror? As I lever myself up on my elbow, a whooshing noise rushes up as a large fishing net covers us, and shouting from the palm trees tells me we can stop looking for the town.

Benita screams until I shush and tell her to remain lying. They might not know she's here—except for her screaming.

I kneel with my head making a tent pole with my fingers holding out the net. I see that it could easily be pulled off. Someone was lucky with throwing it. I could get out from under it without problems unless they put barbs on the edges. Looking through a diamond, I see three people maybe twenty metres away, spread out with torches and guns. One shot and all my efforts will be blown away. I can't blame them, I'm carrying a weapon worse than a gun. I wonder if they're open to negotiation. If there are no other ARIA carriers on the island, they might consider that Benita and I can be useful guinea pigs. Anything to keep the spark of life flickering.

"Okay, you got me."

CHAPTER 13

RYDER WAVED FOR BAT AND MEGAN TO STOP. "Megan, that was a brilliant idea to set up the scooter as a trap and place the net with a pull-rope to snare them."

"The benefits of a wayward childhood."

"You're not a child any more," Bat said. "What now, Ryder? You haven't detailed your plan."

"That's because he hasn't got one. His ears are more played than a kid's playground."

"Enough cheek," Ryder said. In spite of the difficult situation, he smiled at the way her sarcasm kept hitting home. And it wasn't fair. He'd planned and activated similar intrusion situations when they were holed up in North Wales. They'd shot intruders there, but only after warning them off. This situation was different. The two people they'd caught in the net might have full-blown ARIA, though only recently caught. They'd operated a boat at night, and up till now, evaded capture, so they must retain their early-skill memories. He pressed the megaphone button.

"You must stay there until further orders."

The man kneeling under the net shouted back: "I will. I understand you don't want to catch my ARIA."

"Hey, that's good," Megan said. "It means he's being sensible."

Bat grunted. "More likely, he's hoping we haven't spotted the other fucker on the ground."

"I agree," Ryder said, "and so it shows he can't be trusted."

Before Megan could protest, Bat lifted his rifle and aimed at the netted prisoner. His finger started the squeeze.

"No!" shouted Megan, who threw her gun at him. She missed, but so did Bat. The man had dived onto the other prisoner.

"Stop firing," yelled both Ryder and the prisoner.

Ryder glared at Bat, who stooped and picked up Megan's gun. "Want this back?"

Megan stomped over and grabbed it. Then, she went for the barrel of the rifle too, but Bat was ready for her and sidestepped to the right.

"Megan, come back here. Bat, continue to cover them, but *don't* fire unless I say so." Ryder realized that he had no real authority over Bat but sounding as if he had did the trick.

"Why did you fire at me?" cried the man in a quivering voice.

Ryder shouted then realized he had the megaphone and used it. "We know there are two of you."

"It's Benita. I didn't want her hurt."

"See?" Megan said to Bat.

In Bat's defence, Ryder told her that the prisoners will be more submissive after that scare, but he also knew they might be frightened enough to run off at their first opportunity. "Okay, we won't fire if you both stay where you are."

Megan didn't need the megaphone when she yelled. "What is your name, sir?"

"Sir?" Ryder said, "You're never that polite to me."

"Circumstances."

"I'm called Bryce."

Bat, keeping his rifle pointing in Bryce's direction, walked over to Ryder and Megan. All three stayed twenty-five metres from the couple. "He's admitted he's got ARIA. You're the one, Ryder, to go banging on about deterring people with it from reaching us. 'Harbingers of death' you said. Kill the infected ones if necessary, you said, 'cos there are thousands of us on the island, and the infected will die anyway."

"This is different," Ryder said, to Megan's obvious relief. She was always an enigma to him, and this was a good example. Her uncle, Brian, was killed after a fight with an ARIA-infected intruder at Anafon, North Wales. Ryder thought she'd want them all killed, but here she was oozing sympathy for these two strangers.

"How is it different? I'm all ears but only for a minute or two, or unless they move."

Ryder wasn't sure how to answer. He had it clear enough when Teresa pumped it into him. Something about antigens, pathogens, contra-indications from her viral extraction studies with Julia in Canada. Julia's own blood as an ARIA infected but ARIA-2 treated self-examined specimen. Both women were expert virologists, possibly the only ones left on the planet who knew what the vocabulary meant, let alone the biology. Then, there was the ARIA-2 case. The case was in containment here on the island, and Teresa with her techie, Gustav, worked hard towards preparing safe extracts but virtually nothing is known. This was because they had no ARIA-infected people to work with here. And now, two sat over there. How the hell could he nutshell that to Bat?

"You have to take my word for it."

"No way. I'm not risking my life on some half-baked plan. Tell me something definite or my trigger finger is going to stop this nonsense."

"We've done this before, haven't we, Megan?"

"You mean the isolation cave at Anafon? Have we got an isolation unit here?"

"There's lots of them," Ryder said, grinning.

"You mean," said Bat, "there's a lot of abandoned houses on the island. Sure, which one were you thinking of? I would be particularly edgy if I thought they were in one of those empty chalets on the outskirts of Avarua."

"So would I, but Teresa and I thought one of the villages on the opposite side of the island or even the next island is better. But, if we set them off again in their boat, there's no guarantee they wouldn't return."

"That's true of putting them on their own in a village on the south coast."

Megan, looked at her gun and wiped off a small, wet leaf. "We had cameras set up to watch the isolation cave."

Ryder brightened. "That's right. We have more gadgets here. We can electronically tag them."

Bat shook his head. "You're a sad git, Ryder. You could do what you like to them, but they will always be a danger. All the electronics left in this shrunken world is no use without an army of watchers and guards, which we couldn't maintain. Oh, just a minute, Ryder. I have a call."

Ryder watched him take out his phone. Was it the other helicopter asking for directions? Or had the radar surveillance spotted a flotilla heading towards Rarotonga having decoyed the island's defences with these two? Nothing would surprise him. He sneaked over to catch Bat's side of the conversation.

"... before the trees. If they make a break for it towards you, shoot to kill. In fact, if you get a clear shot, shoot them anyway."

"That's not the arrangement," Ryder called and made a grab for Bat's phone. The pilot laughed as he threw the phone to his other hand and into his pocket. Anger surging from his stomach, Ryder launched himself at Bat to stop him raising his rifle to signal any attack. Mid-flight, a loud, reverberating noise thundered overhead.

Sound waves pushing from above added to the pull of gravity from below to bring Ryder to an undignified landing among long tufts of grass. He watched the helicopter pass over him, the pair under the net, and on to the up-hilling squad now stopped. Ryder could hear the chopper's megaphone talking to the armed squad, but not the words.

Ryder expected to hear the megaphone again, but a small package was dropped, and the helicopter lifted up and away. Maybe Tilley had decided it was too risky to hover within small-firearms range of the unknown pair and dropped a written message instead. Ryder cursed letting Bat have the mobile phone.

Megan waved hers at him. "Teresa's on the phone for you."

Ryder ran over to hear Teresa already talking. "... dropping the ARIA-2 case in a moment."

"Hang on, Teresa, how do we know they won't damage it? Maybe they have a gun and just fire into it."

"It's the best chance we have of testing it. We don't want them dead. Do you?"

"We need to discuss this. Do risk assessments. For example, how far away should we be when they open the case? Last time–"

"No, Ryder. Back in the lab, we've gone as far as we can without testing the ARIA-2 case on live subjects. Bat and his cohorts are after a straight blood killing here. It's either they're dead or we have a once-only chance. If they damage the case, tough. What plans did you have for it?"

"None. Have you thought through what we're going to do with those two after they've been exposed to the case? Quarantine, for example?"

"Oops, they're signalling, no time for a chat. Out."

Megan elbowed Ryder and grinned. "They're going with my suggestion for isolating them at an Aroa beach house. It's been abandoned all year and monitored with cameras and guards. Trust me."

Ryder took in the information but had no time to react. With a mixture of horror, foreboding, and yet with the release inevitability brings, Ryder watched. Bryce knelt by the case, which opened when he placed his hand over the double-chevron emblem.

Ryder shivered when he saw the blue fluorescence reflected in the two scared faces.

CHAPTER 14

July 2nd 2016, Dr Antonio Menzies in Winnipeg near where the alien domes have been constructed.

ANTONIO HATED MORNINGS. Not true. He liked to spend pre-lunchtime in warm and drowsy blissfulness, letting Manuel and Julia brush away his night-before mess and prepare breakfast. He hated the chore of morning rituals: the ablutions, shaving, searching for clothes, and dressing. His clothes had to be immaculate, but he couldn't be bothered to clean and press them himself. He couldn't fathom whether Julia performed such duties out of feminine duty, afraid of the alternative consequences, or maybe his piercing mind control really worked. He wore a sly smile when he thought of the manual workers who constructed the alien domes. After a few days and the initial sexual fiasco, he only had to think of indulging himself with the younger women for it to happen or for food to be brought. But they were near zombies, under alien programming. Manuel and Julia were marginally more intelligent and independent. He wondered whether exposure to both ARIA and ARIA-2, although having the beneficial effect of stopping the memory loss, had a consequence: making their minds more susceptible to telepathic suggestion. He could test that to interesting and nasty limits, but he'd rather have the convenience of their company and housekeeping for the moment.

Simultaneously scratching his five-day beard and his hungry stomach, Antonio wandered into the kitchen. Empty of the stupid people, but their breakfast simmered. Correction, their lunch—his breakfast. Eggs fought for survival in their volcanic cauldron of a deep frying pan. He laughed at the irony that all eggs were now fresh, free-range and organic with no high prices. This was no Zucchini Frittata like his mama used to make for him in Turin, but it would do. The bread was home baked from supermarket flour. Grain hadn't been sown, and would not be for years, if ever.

Butter had long since gone rancid in the non-refrigerated stores. Their liquid odours added to the stomach-heaving cocktail of putrefied meats, and bacterial wildfire in dairy and other non-sealed products. After a year since the power failed, most of the mess had dehydrated or had been devoured and the odour dissipated. Pity, Antonio relished sniffing the sour odours. Another high. He drizzled extra virgin olive oil over the toast before adding all four eggs.

No doubt they had intended the meal for themselves, maybe shared with him, but he grinned at the expected despair on their faces.

Using a corner of the tablecloth to wipe the last yellow slick from his stubbled chin, he wondered where the two had gone. He scowled at the cold coffeemaker but didn't fill and switch it on. Maybe they were keeping out of his way. He'd told them it was the Big Day. The day of the aliens, the Zadokians would come to the domes here in Winnipeg. More likely, Manuel and Julia were hiding from him, scared of what he would make them do. Fools. He stood at the window of this usurped house and saw the pickup they used waiting on the drive. Beyond the long, unkempt lawns sloped a grey tarmac road down to the ravaged mall and the domes. Maybe they'd walked next door to filch remaindering food tins. *Banditi*. They would surely not forget the pan of eggs. It wasn't that he was worried, Zadok forbid, but he liked to be in the possession of all relevant facts. Like where the *merda* were they?

A noise inside the house startled him. Turning, he saw them emerge from their bedroom.

"Good day to you, Antonio," Manuel said, betraying his Texan drawl more than he used to. "Hah. Did we scare you? That's a good 'un."

"Course not. Why were you two in there? No. Don't answer that. *Dio mio*, at your age."

"Look at him, Julia, he's perturbed because he couldn't mind read where we were."

"Maybe it's because his too-logical brain wouldn't let him believe in love and pleasure going together."

"Is that what you call it? Two geriatrics testing bedsprings? More pain than pleasure, I bet."

"Manny, he's not far wrong, I am a bit sore."

"See?" Antonio was gloating to overcome his embarrassment and his inability to pick up or control their minds as he could others.

Julia kept a straight face to hide her mirth. "So, Manny, we should do it more often."

Antonio threw his hands up, signalling defeat.

"Hello, we've had burglars," Julia said. "Our lunch has disappeared. I'll do some more. Seconds, Antonio?"

He slumped on a chair at the table. As a doctor, he was intrigued why these two were not afraid of him. They used to be, and sometimes were, such as yesterday when he threw a rage along with a bottle of Tabasco at a window of a grocery store where the cigarettes had already been cleared out. But when not in outrage mode, he had less power over these two than he had weeks ago. "Familiarity breeds contempt," said Aesop. Perhaps he knew something about ARIA two thousand years ago. Allegedly, he was an ugly sod, a turnip, like an alien. Antonio's telepathic faculties, erratic and inexact such as they were, weakened with these two. Had he become too familiar with them? They'd have to watch out, that's all. He was on a mission, and they'd better not get in the way. He'd tolerate their misbehaviour, to a point, as long as they didn't interfere.

Antonio denied himself the possibility that his otherwise loneliness tolerated the presence of Julia and Manuel.

"I'm taking the pickup," he said, without giving them the opportunity to argue. That would piss them off. As the door closed, he heard Manuel call out: "That's okay, I'm working on an RV. It'll be ideal for camping vacations."

Surely, they weren't deliberately annoying him. Did they think he would get so bored of their inanity and apparent nonchalance and would leave them alone? That he would then let them return to their idyllic cabin in the Banff forest? No way. They were his link to that danger point in Ryder, the bum note in his music of the spheres. But he had to focus on the events of the day.

He might not always pick up on the wayward synaptic meanderings of Manuel and Julia, but reception of message-meanings from the aliens burst in. The strange buzzing in his head was like off-tune radio signals. Tinnitus but with a distantly controlled force behind them.

All those pre-ARIA years as a physician and it hadn't occurred to him that patients with horrendous tinnitus might have been able to tune in to aliens all along. As he drove, the only moving vehicle in the city, he played with the notion that maybe the Zads had been trying to communicate for decades or centuries without success. The messages manifesting themselves as a nuisance buzz in the head. That could be why ARIA had to be brought to Earth, to enable humans to be receptive. Had it gone wrong? Probably not. The near extinction of humans was wrong for them but right for the Zadokians. Maybe he'd find out today. How did he know they were arriving? Nothing specific, just a strong feeling.

The three domes were magnificent. From above, they would appear as three giant white billiard balls touching with a triangular gap in the middle. Giant cream igloos with translucent roofs and positive air pressure to keep them clean. They must consider Earth atmosphere to be too polluted, yet, ironically, it was cleaner now that industrial and domestic smoke sources had gone. Antonio wondered if that was an influential reason for eliminating humans: to cleanse the atmosphere for Zadokians to breathe. He'd be all right. No worries he'd be extinguished now he was partly one of them, but there was so much he needed to know.

He parked by the tunnel entrance of the largest football-stadium-sized dome. No one else around for miles, although there were plenty of abandoned vehicles. He wondered where the workers drifted off to. Probably back to their hovels, left to get on with scavenging food, too traumatised to have organised any survival plan to ensure food and energy supplies for the future.

No locks necessary, he pushed the swing doors and strolled into the plastic odour of the short tunnel and into the vast dome. Small, white buildings and air-filtering equipment lined the walls, otherwise it was empty. He crunch-walked the gravel floor to the centre and looked up. A hundred metres above his head, the dome's roof glistened. He saw clouds drift by in the light blue sky. A crow alighted on the apex but, skidding, changed its mind and squawked off.

The doctor opened his arms wide in this circus tent and echo-sounded with: "Antonio Menzies waits for you." Was he the ringmaster or the clown?

An urgent need to get out penetrated his brain, from there to every organ, and more importantly to his jogging muscles before his logic told him why. Once it kicked in, his reasoning told him not to overreact. After all, he couldn't have been trespassing, he'd managed the workers to construct these things. Surely he'd a right to be there? Perhaps they needed the dome to be free of people while they landed. But they couldn't land inside the dome unless the roof slid open. That wouldn't be sensible, all that clean air would be lost. Perhaps they could teleport inside the dome from some orbiting spacecraft like on Star Trek. But that was unlikely—realms of fantasy. Besides, Manuel had reports via Ryder of the aliens whizzing around in craft, obliterating the French nuclear power stations. By the time he'd thought of the objections to leaving "his" dome, he'd reached the outside of the tunnel entrance. His jog converted to a hands-in-pockets stroll as he reached the pickup and looked around. Nothing but the uneasy feeling something was about to happen.

He climbed into the driver's seat and called Manuel. Julia answered. "He's out back somewhere."

"Chasing squirrels or looking for gold?"

"Well, you mightn't like it, but he's trying to get the older Buick going again, as well as the RV." She was brilliant at ignoring Antonio's barbs.

"Get him back inside for the rest of the day."

"Listen, you can't tell us what to do any more, Antonio. If we want to go somewhere in a vehicle, then we will."

"No, I mean it isn't safe outside today."

"Why today all of a sudden? You sure you're not concocting a threat to stop Manuel and me from being able to travel?"

"Not at all. Look, I haven't time for discussion. The Zadokians are coming to the domes today. I can't guarantee your safety if they do a surveillance and find you two wandering about."

"That's sweet of you, thinking of us for a change. Are you worried we might queer your pitch if we see something too interesting?"

"No need to get cynical." Damn the woman, often too close to reality. "There's something else. Have you been checking the ISS and with Ryder or that Charlotte in the Australian satellite tracking station?"

"Hardly at all. The equipment isn't up to it here, why? Oh, of course, you are expecting our brain-boiling visitors to beam down. We'd have to go back to Banff unless we get lucky with a signal."

"Get Manuel in first, and then check if anything's been detected out there coming this way. I'm not bothered about what's happening in France."

"If I get through, I'll ask how that poor, lonely Charlotte is too. Shall I pass on your concern for her? Ah, we're losing a satellite–this will be the last contact without your Moraine Lake-boosted system."

It didn't matter. Just above the domes hovered a chrome, fuzzy ball, the size of a small house. Like the images of the Zadokian space ship they saw through Hubble over a year ago, there were no distinct lines or edges. Antonio wanted to adjust the focus, but it really was indistinct. He watched it drift downwards into the triangular well between the three domes.

He wondered what would happen if he walked into the dome for a closer look. Maybe it was locked or a force field would repel the curious. That would be it. Not an invisible wall, but forces inside his head stopping him from prying. After a few moments, he had an overwhelming need to sleep...

CHAPTER 15

TWENTY MINUTES LATER, he awoke, a wave of triumphal warmth swept through him. A feel-good tsunami forcing a rare smile, created a realization that the Zadokians were inviting him into the dome. A welcome introduction. Confident, but with latent hesitation, he opened the car door and looked across at the dome. It wasn't so empty. He could see dark shapes. More buildings had sprouted in there, cubic, mini-domes, and plants.

The plants must be for their food, Antonio thought, then deleted. They would not have gone to all the trouble of preparing this planet for a limited occupation or colonization if they couldn't feed themselves on the food available.

His warm head-buzz told him to cease his agonising prevarication. He punched the air with both fists and marched in.

Whatever he'd expected to see—aliens lining up boxes of supplies, reorganising the simplistic buildings or creating new ones—he was open-mouthed at the reality. Had he walked into an avant-garde botanical emporium or a horticultural laboratory? Why did they need these seed trays and pots with cyan-blue plants of different sizes? Maybe to grow essential foods. Maybe they supplied a trace element necessary in their diet or the air or they were of religious significance. He couldn't see any of the Zadokians. Had they gone back to their ship or in one of the buildings?

Antonio listened for voices, but the dome conveyed no organically derived sounds. He heard the dome resonate as the membrane rippled with the wind like a Mexican wave. It was as if he was in a giant eardrum. Then, he caught voices. Not heard as such but vibrating inside his head. They were talking about him, but although he could feel the sense, he couldn't decipher the words. There was hope and expectation in those thoughts. A chill ran up his spine as he started to appreciate the trust these aliens were putting into his ability. Of course, he had superior qualities to other humans, especially now. He'd even coined the term *enhuman*, meaning enhanced human, but it made him sound more arrogant than his former friends and colleagues liked to hear. The nomenclature, although realistic, distanced him from the humans who might yet be useful to him so he desisted. He'd had to compromise his behaviour even if not his attitude. He worried, however, over the apparent reliance of the aliens on any networking they'd assumed he'd built with the rest of humanity. He had a small influential network in Canada and remotely on through to Ryder and his untainted escapees, but how could they be helpful to the aliens? If anything, the opposite might be true.

He couldn't reason a conclusion without further data.

There, a door slid open in a pale lilac building fifty metres away. A solitary alien stood there looking at him. Wearing a loose grey tunic, he stood barely a metre and a half tall; very human except with light copper-coloured skin where it showed on his head and arms. Antonio sensed it was male with very short, fuzzy auburn hair, tiny, piercing black eyes, and a three-centimetre-wide closed mouth. Another, this time female, in a similar but darker tunic appeared at his shoulder. Antonio picked up a faint intonation in his head as if the second was urging the first to start the dialogue. He did, but no sounds waved across the fifty metres. Words formed in his head but unlike the feelings he'd had up to now. These were as if a speaker boomed between his ears.

We know you to be Antonio. What do you know of us?

Antonio staggered back several steps with his hands clapped to his ears. His head buzzed with the unexpected in-head amplification. He couldn't tell if he received actual words in his head or the concepts for which words are used as labels. More likely the latter unless the aliens had gone to Zadokian-English evening classes.

"*Cretino*! Turn down the volume, *per favore*." A moment later, he'd sufficiently recovered to realize his opening dialogue with Earth's first contact was to utter profanity. "Sorry, sorry. I should've realized you were going to use telepathy. I will adjust." He took a few more involuntary steps back assuming the force of their directed thoughts to him was proportional to the square of the distance between them.

You have a problem receiving?

Another crash landing inside his head, but as he was more prepared, he stood his ground. "Nothing I can't get used to. What do I call you?"

I know not the meaning?

"You call me Antonio, so what do I call you?"

I understand. You need a label. Call me Zad.

Antonio looked at the Zadokian who'd taken a few little steps closer and then at the one behind. Had the alien just made up his name from their planet's identity? Antonio tried to remember who'd named it. He was sure Julia found the name on a database of ancients. A high priest in David's time, a sealer of the Covenant. But that was after they'd been given the name. Curses, it must have been from his brain—receiving incoming data from the aliens. A translation of sounds in his head that he'd blurted out to Manuel, who'd told Julia, and so the godless planet of the aliens ironically became Earth's Old Testament high priestess. But the coincidence of the concatenation of Zadok to Zad for this one alien stretched credibility. If they were all clones or androids, he could have believed their nomenclature could be Zad-1, Zad-2 and on, but surely they weren't all going to be called Zad.

"Okay, hello, Zad. What's your friend called?"

I do not understand the meaning of "friend."

"Zad, what is the name of the other one behind you?" This was going to be harder than he expected. Communication was telepathic—at least one way—but it didn't help understanding. There was no transference of meaningful concepts in this cerebral interlocution, just the words zipping across the filtered air between different species. He had perceived thoughts that were fragments of notions in the last year. Whole sets of instructions popped into his head to build the domes, but now, he tried to analyse those commands. They were conceptual rather than individual words with no attempt at two-way conversation.

He looked at Zad, waiting for the name of the other alien.

Zad.

"No, Zad is *your* name. What is the name of the Zadokian standing behind you?"

It is Zad. I am Zad.

Antonio groaned. Either he'd made his request as clear as if he was talking under water, or all the *grottesco* aliens had the same name. Hello, another word message was getting through to him.

You should be using your mind for communication.

"That's easy for you to say." Antonio hadn't tried to use telepathy with the aliens out of fear of the unknown. Months ago, he was able to use low-level telekinesis and to project fear thoughts to people but only when he was in an excited state. The people he'd met since leaving the protected haven of North Wales were all ARIA infected, and increasingly ARIA-2-modified, so none were in full control of their minds. He hadn't needed to exchange thoughts. He projected fear and orders rather than individual words. These were the aliens responsible for ARIA, thousands of years in advance of humans. How could he stay in control of himself if he opened up mind channels? He had to give it a go.

Antonio projected, *Nod if you receive my thought words.*

There is no need.

Wow, that's amazing.

What is "wow?"

Antonio laughed at his success with a new skill. Maybe the Zadokians could only pick up specific thoughts he directed as words at them. They weren't picking up secondary thoughts they would need in learning a language to pick up the context of an unfamiliar word, and neither could he. He'd better not be too complacent. They might have telepathic abilities far beyond his probationary efforts.

The Zadokian behind the first Zad, directed a thought at Antonio.

Are you the only one?

Antonio instantly knew why the Zadokians didn't need individual names. It wasn't sound, because in his head, as in the air between them, they made no sounds, only concepts. But everyone had a different interpretation from everyone else on how a word or idea was defined. The difference might be miniscule, a degree of emphasis or stress, but it was like two people's definition of tree or cup or anger. All distinctive to the person emanating and projecting the thought. Nevertheless, he needed to label the aliens for his own simplicity. Zad-1, and now, Zad-2.

Conversely, Antonio didn't think he would have a problem projecting his own conversational thoughts to the right Zadokian, although others might receive them too. Telepathic eavesdropping. His thoughts would leak all over the place–public broadcasting–while lifelong telepaths would narrowcast their messages. He had to think about Zad-2's question. In what way did Zad-2 mean when she asked if he, Antonio, was the only one? The only human who could think for himself or who had not been exposed to ARIA-1 but had been to ARIA-2? The only one with apparent telepathic abilities? That could be tricky since he knew the drone-humans, who he organised to put the domes together, had received brain signals to congregate at this Winnipeg site and fine-tuned by him. The humans didn't use telepathy to communicate. Zad-2 probably meant to enquire if he, Antonio, was the only sane one able to communicate telepathically.

Having thought that through, Antonio had to conjecture the reasoning behind the question. If he revealed he was the sole human telepath, did that make him more vulnerable or more powerful? While synapses worked on that thought, Antonio mused on the notion that Zad-2 wasn't able to mine his mind for the answer. Or maybe she could, but it took too much effort. Perhaps she'd already analysed his mind and waited to see if Antonio gave the correct answer. A telepathic lie-detector Zadokian-style. He rejected that idea. After all, it had taken Antonio several minutes to interpret the probable answer let alone go through all his own neuron webs to find other memories and ideas that might have a bearing. Nevertheless, an answer was expected, and he mustn't weaken his situation. Non-committal would have been weak, but he hoped that to answer with a question showed perspicacity.

Why is it important for you to know?

Curiosity. We have not met humans who use telepathy at the other landing sites.

I expect there are others. Antonio harboured considerable fear of being isolated. On the other hand, he didn't want the Zadokians to treat him as an obstructionist—with possible fatal consequences. He'd rather them be fooled into considering him an ally with greedy motives. And maybe that wouldn't be far from reality. *Are there specific tasks you want me to do?*

Zad-1 exchanged thoughts with Zad-2 that Antonio couldn't pick up.

It would be advantageous to have human manual workers to start the planting before the prisoners arrive.

The word burst in Antonio's head like a grenade. Prisoners? Had he helped to build concentration camps for the human survivors? If so, which ones? There must be a million or so humans left alive. These cannot be the intended prisoners. The number of ARIA-infected persons who had been exposed to ARIA-2 was difficult to estimate, because by the time ARIA-2 arrived, communications were already out of action. For all he knew, the North Wales exposure in Conwy hadn't worked or the affected population stayed there. There were few Canadian ARIA-2 people. He only saw the few dozen that turned up for dome construction. Maybe, like Manuel and Julia, those whose memory loss had been halted by exposure to ARIA-2 were so relieved at their own salvation, they focussed on their own survival and resisted contact with others.

Ah, so that left those humans who, so far, had dodged the original ARIA. He knew of Ryder and his islanders, a tiny group in France, and one in Australia. There must be others living in mountainous valleys or other islands. Antonio's eyes glinted at the thought of Ryder and his arrogant bunch being rounded up by force and brought to the dome detention camp he'd built. He laughed out loud, then stopped short when the niggles arrived in his head. Why go to the trouble when all they had to do was drop another ARIA-1 "bomb" on the island or plant an infected person there? Perhaps they wanted to examine them as uninfected humans. Experimental laboratory specimens.

Hah. Like a demented gibbon, Antonio rocked and roared with

laughter. Two minutes later, his convulsions settled, enabling his eyes to open sufficiently to see the two Zadokians looking at him in astonishment. Maybe he should attempt to control the madness in him. *Va' Al Dia.* Hell, why should he? Hah.

Si, I'll round up some horticultural workers for you. What are the plants for?

The two aliens buzzed information between them while facing Antonio. It was a weird sensation to see conversation where the interlocutors do not need to look at each other. He generated the uneasy thought that they didn't want him to know the real answer. He assumed the plants contained unearthly ingredients essential for Zadokians to survive, and they didn't want it confirmed. It would be a weak point in their survival on this planet. He waited for their response to be beamed into his skull but nothing came. They returned into the cabin without answering his question.

Need to know, eh? I can do that too. But they didn't bite. Never mind, he had urgent information to gloat about to Ryder.

CHAPTER 16

THE ZADOKIANS COULD WAIT for their agricultural slave-labour force. Risky, but he had to show them he wasn't a slave. In any case, Antonio was hungry. He arrived back at the commandeered suburban house. The aroma of fresh bread and vegetable broth met his nose, bringing a salivating smile. Julia stirred a large pot while Manuel toasted thick slices of bread. He tried his new telepathic skills on them.

I've got incredible news, Julia. Are you getting this?

No reaction.

Manuel, Ryder is going to be taken prisoner and brought here by the aliens.

Nothing.

Julia continued looking into the pot while she spoke. "Grab a plate and bowl, Antonio. You've done nothing to earn this, but we're feeling generous."

"Yeah, we found an untouched store in the suburbs. It had steel shutters, but we used a JCB to break in a side wall. Hadn't had so much fun for ages." They both laughed. It was obvious they hadn't received Antonio's mind send. "Of course, it's only canned, bottled, and dried foods that are of any use. Now, we're okay for batteries, firelighters, matches—"

"Never mind the shopping list. How you two get excited with such domestic trivia. Hah. Just wait till you hear the news I have."

"Well," Manuel said, "we know you've been to the domes, so I guess you've met our new masters and have been put on their payroll. Are you Emperor Antonio now?" He shared a snigger with Julia.

"You may laugh, though why you are taking this situation so lightly confounds me. There is no hope of returning to your previous sad, little lives. Every time you go scavenging, you risk being attacked by feral dogs and other emboldened animals, including remaining crazed humans. There is nothing but uncertainty about what our new alien occupiers want with us."

"And that's why, my dear Antonio?" said a smiling Julia. "We've outlasted all our families and ninety percent of our friends."

"Assuming we are counting you as one," Manuel said. "So, we relish these few days, hours, and minutes for we know they are numbered."

"And, we have an escape plan," Julia said, winking at Manuel.

"Oh," Antonio said, "you two are so risible. This will be the loading up of an RV and returning to your cabin in Moraine Lake? Don't worry, I won't stop you. But your smiles will be wiped when I tell you my news. Um, should I upset you now or wait a few days?"

"How can you be any more disturbing than you already are, Antonio?" Manuel said.

"Those aliens, the Zadokians, are going to capture Ryder and those miserable wretches with him. They are going to incarcerate them in the domes where, no doubt, they will do devious experiments on them."

"You're a twisted bastard, Antonio," Julia said. "Did the aliens actually say they are using the domes as prisons? It doesn't make sense to me. Why bring people they consider as troublemakers right into their landing site?"

"There's a lot you don't understand."

"I think it's you that's misinterpreted whatever they've told you. What did they say?"

"They didn't say anything. Hah."

"There you go—"

"No, Julia, they don't use speech. We communicated with thought. That's beyond you, I'm afraid."

"Okay, I'll accept that, but did they say they are going to grab Ryder's group? You don't know where they are, do you? That must kill you. There might be thousands on that island. How are they transporting them? What about their food and provisions in the dome? You built it, could it accommodate that many?"

"*Ciò è il problema.* So many questions, and always trivial. Nothing of the fundamentals of life."

"You don't know? Once more, you are talking crap. Have some broth."

An annoyed Antonio ripped open his bread and dunked it in his bowl. He'd thought he'd won a victory this time, but it got turned, again. He must have them worried though, *certamente*. They nattered through the meal, but Antonio chose to be a silent witness, waiting for them to break.

Julia turned to Antonio. "Now you have communication with the aliens, have you come to any opinion as to their moral outlook?"

Antonio looked at her as if she talked a language he didn't know.

She persisted. "Come on. They've screwed a whole planet's attempt at civilisation, obliterated millions of lives in great suffering. What sort of minds can do that?"

"I think you're asking the wrong person, Julia," Manuel said.

"You're right, what would that jerk know about morals."

"I am sitting right here," Antonio said. "I was too busy getting my head round being able to make out what words they were projecting to me. What purpose would it have had for me to start interrogating them about the evil they did? That could have been the undoing of me and any future chance of human-Zadokian communication."

Manuel pointed his spoon at Antonio. "I couldn't have resisted pointing out that more is gained by friendship than swatting us like flies."

"But that isn't true, is it, Manuel? If they stayed in orbit and talked to our leaders, negotiations would have stretched on forever. Military antagonists would have sent up a few warheads. It could've been a lot worse. Ah, all right, it couldn't have gotten worse, but at least the Earth is clean."

"Which, you say is what they needed, so they've done what they needed to occupy the planet by removing its only intelligent, rightful owners."

"How do you know that? Suppose the Zadokians were here first and left some humans millions of years ago. They've come back to reclaim their world and needed to eliminate their failed experiment."

Manuel pointed his finger at Antonio. "You've been reading too much science fiction. Even if we were the result of an experiment, we are sentient people with emotions, and as such, should have been given much more consideration than a vivisectionist would in gassing a lobotomized rat."

"Speaking of rats," sneered Antonio, "when are you going to let slip to Ryder that he is next for caging?"

"If we are going to warn Ryder," Manuel said, "assuming you're not a hay truck without its steering wheel, we need to get back to Moraine Lake."

"We knew we couldn't bring all that satellite link and solar-power equipment," Julia said. She turned to Antonio. "You said they used telepathy, so did the words, or image of Ryder, or their island form in your huge brain?"

"I'll take the insults from both of you and throw them out of the window, because it is your inferiority that makes you hostile. *Si*, the Zadokians definitely used the word prisoners for the main purpose of the domes."

Julia laughed. "And from that you assume it's Ryder's band of survivors they are going to imprison?"

"Elementary logic. What other group have enough sense and ability to cause trouble?"

Manuel used the last chunk of bread to mop his bowl, and without looking up said, "Have you considered that they might be bringing their own prisoners?"

Antonio dropped his spoon. Why hadn't he thought of that? It was so apparent, it needed an idiot like Manuel to think of it. He realized Manuel had continued.

"... maybe Earth is the Zadokian's Australia. A planetary Botany Bay penal colony. My God, Antonio, what hellish crimes have those bastards done to be sent on such a journey, and presumably, one way?"

"I've no idea. My mind is boggling at the possibilities." But he didn't say how he relished meeting such extreme criminal minds. He had so much to share and learn. Now Antonio had the edge on news, he couldn't resist rubbing in some malevolent boasts. "You know, this year is turning out to be one of the best. It's been like a *magnifico* shag fest in the city. Amazing."

Julia butted in. "Antonio, most of the available women are pensioners. A harem of ancients."

"There are a few young ones from the mountains. Anyway, some of them want it, or at the least are indifferent. I'm doing humanity a favour, it will require repopulating."

Manuel licked his lips. "He has a point. Maybe I–"

"Oh no, you don't," Julia said. "We have no antibiotics, and God knows what infections are rife out there."

Manuel mumbled while Antonio merely looked at the ceiling. His mind flicked to the stash of medicines he'd secreted, but he knew that their effectiveness had already waned.

"Your perversity can't shock me," Julia continued, "but I am disturbed by the vision of hordes of little Antonios running amok."

"Like little ants," Manuel said, grinning at his joke.

"Why don't you two go back to your cabin and play lumberjacks?"

"I thought you relished my home cooking," Julia said.

"Don't give me that. I know the real reason you followed me to Winnipeg was to spy on me."

"Paranoid and tiresome. Manuel, we're going for a walk in the fresh, untainted air."

"We are? Oh right, we are."

CHAPTER 17

WINNIPEG SUBURBS HAD MORE LEAVES than usual heaped in drains, blocking them, resulting in floods. Ironically, ARIA had seen off the usual commercial pollution of cigarette packets, sweet wrappers, and paper but had replaced it with abandoned vehicles, fallen branches, overgrown lawns, verges, and weeds growing in sidewalks and drives. Although the russet leaves fell in autumn and it was now July, no one had cleared them, and fresh green leaves waited their turn in the abundant tree-lined avenues. Manuel noted the movement in some heaps of nature's debris as rats scrabbled for food. He patted the handgun he always carried outside when he heard dogs howling nearby. He saw fallen telephone cables and a crashed streetlamp, no doubt a victim of the harsh winter, and marvelled at how much of the human streetscape was being reclaimed by the planet after a year.

"What do we need to discuss away from the maniac's ears?"

"Not just his ears, Manuel. I'm not sure how much of our thoughts he can pick up when in close proximity. He's correct about us doing favours for Ryder by keeping an eye on him."

"Even so, I doubt the aliens are bothered in the slightest about Ryder's group. Their ability to blast those nuclear power stations and arms depots means they could obliterate Ryder's island any time—assuming they know where it is. My best guess is that the aliens are bringing their own prisoners here. My God, just think of that."

"I have been. Billions of decent humans have been killed to make way for Zadokian criminals, who could be murderers, torturers, rapists... or guilty of crimes more heinous than we've ever considered."

"Or they could be prisoners-of-war from other planets. Other aliens that they don't want on Zadok."

"Once cleaned in their damned domes. Julia, we have to tell Ryder about this development."

"I agree, but I don't want to return to Moraine Lake and leave Antonio here unobserved. We're picking up useful information. I still need to get a sample of alien skin, blood, urine, hair—anything for me and Teresa to work on."

On their stroll, they were constantly stepping over fallen twigs, around piles of windblown rubbish, and dog excrement. In spite of the intensity of the conversation, their ears worked hard to pick up any growling or scuffling that might indicate hungry or demented bears, dogs, coyotes, or escaped zoo animals.

Manuel undid another button on his shirt and rolled up his sleeves. "It's damned hot."

"What d'you expect in July? And look at you, wearing a vest and thick trousers. You'd be cooler if clean-shaven and with some of that mop chopped off." Julia poked him playfully in the ribs.

He went to grapple her when they heard a scuffling noise behind them.

"Fuck," Manuel said. "Move very slowly to that Dodge. Let's hope it's not locked." He pulled at Julia's elbow as he edged towards the pickup parked at a skew to the curb where it had been abandoned months before.

"You needn't worry, Manuel. Look."

He looked behind over to a beech hedge separating two brick-built houses. With huge, wet brown eyes, a black and white Friesian cow stared but wandered off, trespassing on lawns, while Manuel burst out laughing. Out of control, he fell back against the Dodge but stopped himself from falling by clutching the wing mirror. As he steadied himself, the radio aerial flicked his ear.

"That gives me an idea. We'll find and attempt milking the cow later, but look for a car with a satellite radiophone. Then, we can call Ryder through the relay system we have running at Moraine Lake and the ISS."

"I'm sure you'd know how to code it, but the vehicle batteries will have all given up their spark months ago."

"I know the feeling. I'll use some of the batteries we liberated from the store. Look for an automobile with a small VHF FM circular aerial. I'll go along to that showroom we saw yesterday."

"No need, there's one on that Ford over the road."

IN THEIR ROOM AN HOUR LATER, Manuel was able to send a simple text message to Ryder via the Ford's fancy-pants mobile radio transmitter, the system they had left running at their cabin, and the uplink to the ISS.

> Ryder from Manuel & Julia.
> Antonio telepaths with Zadokians.
> Discovered domes to be used for prisoners.
> Uncertain what prisoners.
> Returning to ML soon.
> Take care.

Within minutes, they received a reply from Teresa on Rarotonga.

> Good to hear from you.
> Essential acquire tissue sample
> before your return to ML.
> Teresa.

"That's not going to be a piece of cake," Manuel said. "We can't tell Antonio we want a lump of a Zadokian, and he's not going to bring one round for coffee."

"Without a tissue sample, we'll know zip about their biochemistry."

"What are we talking about? A biopsy sample or a fingernail, presuming they have any?"

"We'd learn a great deal from a few flakes of skin, piece of hair, a blood-stained cloth, saliva—usual DNA sample material sources. But if you could get hold of a biopsy sample, that would be great."

"Me?"

"If I said I was going to go into the dome and wrestle an alien for his blood, you would volunteer to go instead of me, so I just short-circuited the process."

"Very funny. So, I just go up to the dome, which seems to be unguarded, walk up to the first alien and say, 'Take me to your leader.'"

"I would kill to hear you say that, but I doubt they'd appreciate the irony. Luckily, I have another plan for us."

"Thank God."

"We go in as two of Antonio's human idiot workforce."

"Oh God."

"Sorry, but I can't think of any other way of sneaking us in or of getting our hands on an alien."

"But you agree that they don't guard the dome entrance. Why don't we creep in at night, chloroform a sleeping Zadokian, and bring him home?"

"We don't need a whole one, Manuel, but if we did, we don't know that they would succumb to the same anaesthetics as we do."

"I bet a blow to the head would do the job," he muttered, "Fine. But I've a terrible feeling there's something about being one of Antonio's workforce we're not taking into account."

Julia stood and walked to the door. She opened it slowly and looked around. "Just checking that big ears isn't listening. You're thinking we're not going to convince Antonio to let us join his merry gang."

"That might be it. Go on, you're going to tell me how he's going to be fooled."

"Not fooled. Manuel, his greatest weakness is his arrogance. I'm sure I can work on him such that he'll think it's his idea for us to go in."

"Too risky."

"Nonsense, and the sooner the better. Today, before the Zadokians get wise that there might be humans not under their spell."

"I'm sorry, Julia, I think we should sleep on this. Maybe plan it properly tomorrow or discuss it with Ryder."

"Oh, come on, Manuel, it's not like you to be so wet. Hey, I can hear him coming up the stairs."

"Don't you dare!" Manuel ran to put himself between Julia and the door.

"Manny, don't be absurd." She put her arms around him for a hug. When he wouldn't move, she tickled his ribs, making him convulse. As soon as he moved away from the door, she grabbed the handle and opened it to find Antonio standing there.

"*Ciao*. I was wondering whether the fracas was an emergency that needed my intervention," he said before grinning.

CHAPTER 18

NEXT DAY, Antonio led fourteen of the dome-construction workforce to the main dome. All he had to do was stand outside their apartment block and think their names with a "come to work" thought add-on. Their faces showed no emotion. It was like an old-age pensioner's trip to the museum—before they find the crate of ale. He'd warned Manuel and Julia to refrain from their idiotic smirking if they were to pretend to be robot-like locals.

He knew the two were up to some mischief but hadn't figured it out. He wasn't worried. There was nothing they could damage or undo. They were probably on a fact-finding tour for Ryder, but that was okay too, though he pretended it wasn't. He liked playing games with those two. He was bound to win in the long run. There remained a juicy possibility that Ryder would be rounded up. He would give his horde of gold he'd been filching to see Ryder and Jena in shackles. He'd find some very interesting means of having fun with a restrained Jena. Hah.

Another wave of joyous feeling swept through him with the thought of Manuel and Julia working all day. They might have thought they were going to skip inside and enjoy poking their long noses in all the buildings and corners, but he'd ensure they'd be up to their elbows in fertilizer.

If Manuel and Julia were shocked at the appearance of the bronze-coloured alien near the entrance, they did well to hide it. Antonio was impressed. He shot a thought at the Zadokian whose tunic was a paler shade of grey than Zad-1 and Zad-2.

Hello, Zad

The alien looked away from Antonio. *Be silent.*

His face flushed hot as the snub hit him. His arrogance led him to believe the communication breakthrough would lead to an amicable relationship. Well, he could be awkward too.

Sulking, he walked over to the prefabricated white building he'd used as an "office" during the last days of the construction. He'd brought in a fold-up chair from the portakabin outside, but it was in a heap by the door. A Zadokian stood at a new white shelf along a wall, operating a console with a small screen. Antonio wondered if they never used chairs. Pity, he spent a lot of time lounging in his when supposedly at work.

Out.

This time he argued. *I have bus—* He couldn't complete his thought as an invisible wall pushed him to the door. An antagonistic thought wall. He was furious, and yet, his wily side couldn't resist admiring such a weapon. He must learn to hone his own telepathic and telekinetic skills.

Even so, he was rejected. He stomped off to take his ire out on Manuel and Julia. He saw the workers preparing seed beds, planting and laying irrigation lines. Damn, he couldn't see his tormenting human couple.

A buzzing tinnitus hit him. He fell to his knees with the sudden pain. A red pulsating pain filled his head, throbbing beyond to his lungs, heart, and legs. His eyes tightly closed against the agony, but he was able to wonder if this was another metamorphic phase change. Hands on both elbows and armpits lifted him to his feet. Voices.

"Antonio, it's us," Manuel said. "You were having a fit. Through that clear ceiling, we've seen what looks like another ship landing. Come on, we're taking you to a side building out of the way."

Antonio's battered brain thought that made sense: the newly arriving ship was no doubt sending bursts of communications to that console in the dome building. Useful information if he could store it away for future reference. They must be using some extended telepathic signals as well as radio, if they used radio at all. The extra signal strength must have knocked his newbie head. They must have known it would, the *bastardi*.

He cranked open his eyes and saw heaped white plastic containers. Julia looked into his eyes.

"Get off me, woman."

"He's back to the Antonio we love to hate."

"What were you two doing, anyway? You should have been on slave-labour duty."

"That's the funny thing," Manuel said. "The other humans seem to be manipulated as if a Zadokian foreman is sending them instructions. But although we both have piercing tinnitus, we have free will, so to speak."

"I think it's because we were exposed to the ARIA-2 elements in the case when Ryder brought it to us at Calgary airport. These others caught the counter-infection from contact with people who we'd given it to. We must have some kind of immunity to the telepathic control."

"Your tinnitus is the signal," Antonio said. "I'm getting it too but amplified. My guess is the same signal is de-encrypted for the others of our species here so they know their instructions. Believe me, you'd be affected if you got near one of the Zadokians. You haven't told me why you are really here."

Manuel and Julia looked at each other then at Antonio, the door, and back; their eyes playing air tennis.

Julia took the plunge. "We need to know the nature of our adversary in terms of biology."

"Ah. Yesterday, I would have laughed, turned you over to them, and laughed more at the sight of you both squirming in agony clutching your heads."

"And now?"

"You want a blood sample? Hair? I'd pull one of the bastard's heads off for you. But there's a problem. If they get riled, they can push you away with a thought wave."

Julia looked at him as if she didn't believe him, while Manuel waved his hands in the air. "My God, that's a useful anti-personnel deflector. That's it then. We can't get a sample now, can we?"

Julia didn't give up so easily. "We don't have to grab one, do we? Anything from them will do for DNA and tissue analysis. Hey, Antonio, where are their toilets, we can get urine and faeces?"

"Good question. You've hit on something that has been niggling me for some days. I don't recall seeing any ablutions being built. We humans used the portaloos outside the dome. There are several new buildings over at the far end, nearest the landing area that might contain a washhouse facility."

"Might? Are you thinking they don't need to flush out bodily wastes?" Manuel said.

"That's not too far-fetched," Julia said. "Just because terrestrial creatures do, maybe they can internally recycle everything."

Antonio laughed. "More likely, they didn't want us to witness their personal facilities being constructed. They're shy. Hah."

"Let's go see," Manuel said.

"Okay, but surreptitiously," Julia said, with a rare nod of agreement from Antonio.

Keeping to the peripheral buildings and walking behind partition walls and piles of boxes as much as possible, they sneaked over, nearer to where the incoming ship vibrated the walls.

"Should we wait until after the landing?" asked Manuel.

Antonio shook his head. "There might be a hundred armed guards on that ship. There only seems to be a handful of the advance party here at present. It's now or never."

They could see an exit similar to the entrance, but it was to the triangular landing space between the three domes. Two Zadokians stood near it with what looked to Antonio like plastic short tubular guns in their hands.

"It doesn't look like they're expecting an avalanche of prisoners," Manuel said.

"I told you, don't underestimate their telekinesis ability. Those guns might just be like barcode scanners. Let's search these buildings for toilets. I could use one myself."

"I thought you went against the nearest wall," Julia said. Antonio knew she said such barbed comments in a feeble attempt to counteract his own sharper wit.

He doubted the two noticed that he'd arranged for them to enter each cabin-like building before him. Not that it was difficult. Manuel was too keen to discover lifestyle aspects of the aliens.

Manuel complained first. "Have you spotted that these anal-retentives leave nothing out on tables for a decent nosey-parker to look at? And have you observed that no two boxes are exactly the same shade of grey? Even the whites are slightly different."

"And," Antonio said, "I wouldn't be surprised if they can detect more differences in the shades than us."

"I know we use colour coding as an aid to categorising, but there must be a limit. Perhaps there are labels we can't see," Antonio said. "Remember the holographic symbols on the cases? Perhaps when a Zadokian goes near or thinks a code to a box, a label pops up."

"Or if the box has such a chip, or whatever, embedded, the alien just needs to think a query at it and the answer pops into its copper head." Manuel prodded a box, failing to find how it opened.

"There's something else about these secretive containers," said Julia. "There are no two boxes precisely the same size."

"Or shape," Antonio said. "Some are cubic, others rectangular prisms, although the difference might only be a millimetre."

"That makes no sense," Julia said.

"It helps with categorising the contents," Manuel said, eyeing along the edge of a box. "We often use letters, numbers and colours with shapes to store objects."

"But to manufacture individual containers all different would be grossly inefficient."

"You are too used to Earthly economics," Antonio said.

"Yes," Manuel said, "you need to think outside the box. Ha ha, did you hear what I said?" Groans told him they had. "Hey, Antonio, try thinking a command to open the box. Pick one and think 'Open Sesame.'"

"I see," Julia said, "that's not a bad idea, but suppose it works? All these boxes could have their current status monitored such that if one opens unaccountably, an alarm is triggered."

Ignoring her, Antonio focussed on the nearest box to him, a charcoal grey cube: *Open.*

"Damn you, Antonio," Julia said, as in two seconds the top of the box turned from opaque grey to transparent. "Now, does that merely mean we can see through the top, or that now there isn't one?"

Manuel joined the other two. All three heads looked down at a collection of fist-sized cuboid shapes that looked like blocks of red jelly.

"All we need now is a kettle and we can make trifle," Manuel said. "Or perhaps they can be eaten raw, like Turkish Delight."

"Always your stomach," Julia said. "They could be explosives."

Antonio put in his hand and plucked out the smallest. He held it in front of his open mouth, while looking at Julia's horrified face. He bit a corner and started chewing it.

"You prick. You could've killed us all."

"No. I could sense it was food."

"I hope it gives you the runs. You've no idea whether their food is compatible with our metabolism. It might make you more like them."

He grinned. "*Buon.*"

"Grief. But then, you have warped away from humanity."

Manuel brought over a long box, and winked at Antonio. It looked as if it could have held an alien rifle, but instead, there were four white tubes like those held by the aliens at the exit.

"Ah, this is more like it. Well done, Manuel. Weapons."

Julia took a backwards step. Manuel reached in and picked up one of the weapons.

"Hey, it's quite hefty. Weird. I'd say this one is heavier than all four when the lid was on. Um, I'm not sure which is the business end. And there's no trigger."

"Maybe you should give it to me," Antonio said.

"I get it," Manuel said. "You think into it to get a trigger. Or just point and think 'fire'. Is that it?"

"I might have to experiment. There's no mark to indicate what you call the business end."

"Better set it to stun," Manuel said. "Oh, sorry. I get carried away with Star Trek, but you might be able to think stun, just in case."

Antonio put it on the table with none of them lined up with its long axis. He looked at a spot on the wall and thought *Fire.* Nothing. "I'm thinking the word fire at it."

He picked it up, holding it in the same cautious orientation and tried again. *Fire.* Nothing.

Julia had been watching carefully. "Try thinking an effect you want it to have. It might not understand Earthly gun-related terms."

He looked again at the wall and thought: *Melt.*

"Whoa," shouted Manuel as the white wall developed a black singed hole with molten plastic dripping to the floor. As smoke drifted up to the ceiling, Antonio's nostrils pinched with the acrid odour of sulphur and burnt plastic. He looked through the dinner-plate sized hole and saw a black smudge on the next building a metre away.

Manuel held his nose, making his speech nasal. "You need to turn your thoughts down a notch next time. My God, I must learn to do that."

"That's not likely," Julia said.

"Useful to have me around for a while longer, eh?" Antonio said.

"I suppose so," Julia said, "for today. We might need a quick exit doorway, though these plastic walls are not much protection against an electric saw. What now? We're not going to go through all these boxes are we? We still need their toilet facilities, though I have a feeling we're wasting our time."

Manuel looked puzzled. "You mean you think there are no toilets. The Zadokians have no use for them? I'd have thought the need to dribble and wipe your bum was a universal requirement."

Antonio shook his head. "Julia meant that a lavatory facility here would be spotless. We need hair and spillages, like a typical human toilet, to get DNA samples from."

Manuel laughed. "Now we are beginning to know their mental capabilities. I wouldn't be surprised if they can think their shit away."

"Which leaves us with an unresolved problem," Julia said. "We should get away and think of another plan."

Antonio shook his head. "We should wait until the influx arrives from the ship and get away when the other humans have to leave. That reminds me to go check on them. You two better come with me; I can field thought questions from curious Zads."

"We could just burn ourselves an exit door to the outside from here," Manuel said.

"No, it's not in my interests to antagonise them." Antonio pushed open the door and then stopped. "There are dozens of Zadokians coming through from the ship. I have an idea. Julia, come here."

Julia came up alongside him. If these were prisoners or planet conquerors, their faces gave nothing away, with emotionless, dead, straight, small mouths and black beads for eyes. They wore identical close-fitting, all-in-one grey tunics. None sported blemishes, and yet, with differing hues of copper-red skin, slightly different heights, slimness, and a variety of short blond to orange hair, they had individuality.

"I can't believe what I am seeing," Julia said, quivering in a state of shock. "Actual, real-life aliens a few metres away from me. Tell me I'm dreaming. This whole year has been a nightmare." As tears dribbled down her cheeks, Manual went to comfort her.

Antonio said, "We have to keep it together. Save your angst and philosophical realism for back in the house."

Manuel stood, puffed out his chest, then relaxed, knowing he couldn't take Antonio on. "Take it easy, Antonio."

The Italian shrugged, as if none of this impinged on his sense of wonder. "Have you noticed that while all of them have what might be thumbs, some have three fingers while others have four?"

Julia was too overwhelmed to speak.

Antonio continued. "Now, have your sampling kit ready, Julia. I'm going to create a disturbance as we walk by this lot. I sense their newness means they won't be prepared to use mind control to repel a sudden human incursion." He held on to the alien weapon but hadn't decided how he was to use it.

"I don't like it, but I suppose it's our best chance."

The members of the workforce he'd organised were standing around fifty metres away, waiting for the order to go out and home. Antonio wasn't sure of the details of their tasks that day except it involved both horticulture and constructing more buildings. Probably the sleeping quarters for these incomers. He received a *leave now* message, and he'd passed it on to the workforce by thinking it to them as he had before. It must be part of the condition he'd developed. The aliens were obviously using him as a means of communication with a built-in control element. They couldn't have realized that the three of them had a larger element of self-will than they'd wish.

"Come alongside me, Manuel, we need to stick together," Antonio said. "We'll stroll down to the rest of my hapless work party you see down there. You'd think they would be curious at this group of aliens walking towards them. Come on, let's walk."

The three of them kept to the same slow pace as the alien prisoners with Manuel on Antonio's left. Once they reached the work party, some of the aliens continued walking between them while others walked around.

Antonio could hardly control his derision at the incongruous situation of aliens walking through a human work gang as if they were walking through woods. He looked at Julia and Manuel who were wide-eyed and worried, taking small uncertain steps as if they had blundered into a horror film.

He looked for a sampling opportunity. Antonio predicted the destination of the group as the newly constructed dorms. He could've shot an interrogative thought to the leading Zad but didn't want an alert wave rippling through them.

He gripped the alien rod in his right hand and looked for a gap through the throng to a blue barrel next to a building across the dome's expansive floor. It could be full of water, a volatile liquid, or nothing. He pointed one end of the weapon at it and thought: *burn and explode.*

Nothing happened. Perhaps it was too far away. Damn, he needed a distraction. He'd have to try something closer. He peered through the walking aliens at the rows of boxes with the green plants they'd worked on today. There was nothing that would make a dramatic attention grab. The barrel he'd aimed at belatedly exploded, sending steam and boiling water into the air accompanied by a booming blast. The previously imperturbable Zadokians all looked at the noise source, Antonio shoved Manuel hard so that he fell against the nearest alien. A piercing buzz detonated in Antonio's brain, but he followed Manuel and the alien such that all three fell.

"Quick, get out of here." Antonio urged Manuel and Julia, as well as the other humans. It wasn't that he felt obliged to look after them all, but they were useful cover. Julia had bumped into another Zadokian on her way.

Breathless, they reached the exit where two aliens stood as if nothing untoward had happened. Antonio shot thought instructions to the humans to make their way to their homes while he climbed into the Buick.

Julia was already in the front passenger seat putting a pinprick blood-sampler into a specimen bag.

"This might give us more data," Antonio said as he gave her a polybag.

She looked in disbelief at half a hand. Purple blood coated most of two fingers and part of a palm. "How, how on Earth..."

"I didn't know you had a knife," Manuel said.

"I told the alien rod to amputate. Not bad, eh?"

"That poor man," cried Julia through tears.

"He's not a man. Hey, you'd better get driving, Manuel, before they decide to follow us."

"But if he was a prisoner, he might have been against coming to Earth. Without adequate medical treatment, he might bleed to death."

"Cut the sentimental crap. He was an alien and so part of the race that is exterminating humans. If he died, what's one of them in payment for all of ours? Anyway, he's probably growing another one as we speak. Manuel, drive!"

CHAPTER 19

July 4th 2016, 10:00 hours, Rarotonga Communications lab. One year and five months since ARIA. Sixty-five years' lost memory for most. Apart from isolated communities, a few thousand in Canada and North Wales, where ARIA-2 stopped memory loss, there are only the elderly left, fending for themselves.

ABDUL YAWNED as he ran through the morning procedural tests on the communication link to the International Space Station. His head didn't enjoy being vibrated into a jelly by the nightlong helicopter surveillance of the two boat people making their way on foot to their quarantine house.

Two hours sleep. How did Ryder expect him to be efficient on two zeds short of a nap?

In the spacious room with him was one of the islanders who breathed strong garlic and whistled The Beatles' "When I'm Sixty-Four." Maybe he thought garlic would keep ARIA at bay.

He had to do something to stop the twentieth repetition. "Is that the monitor at Aroa?"

"Yeah, I'm setting up the links for the three cams that are already there and the radio link to this monitor setup."

"Are Bryce and Benita having a well-deserved lie in?"

"Who? Oh, those two. I dunno. The link isn't ready yet. Maybe in ten."

"You mean they could've wandered off without us knowing?"

"Yeah, they could've sneaked off without me knowing, but there are a couple of binoculars staring at them."

"Oh right, I might have guessed it was all under control. I heard in the helicopter that Dominiq has taken personal command of them."

"Yeah, weird that, don't you think?"

"You mean why is the island's nominal commander taking command of the most serious, life-threatening security breach we've had? I'm Abdul by the way."

"Baxter. I mean has Dominiq any military experience? He's political. Know what I mean?"

"Yes, but take Ryder. He's a university media man, but he's learnt real fast to make difficult decisions. I would've expected one of our military or security chiefs to take control of Bryce. I'm sure Dominiq used to be a colonel in the New Zealand army. Are you an islander, Baxter? You don't like one of the whites around here."

"I'm an abo, Abdul. You from Iraq?"

"Qatar, smaller and safer. Or rather, it used to be. I doubt there's anyone left alive there now. I heard that an ARIA-infected flight from Kennedy landed there."

"Sorry, Abdul, man. I've not heard from my folks near Alice. Back to Dominiq and what I think is strange."

"Hooray. Oops, sorry, Baxter, it's just that all my lights have blinked green, so to speak. Go on, what else is strange about Dominiq?"

"That boatman's name is Bryce Massey. Right?"

"I didn't know. And?"

"Dominiq's name is Massey, as, of course is Nessa's, his wife."

"Ah, and you don't think it's a coincidence, Baxter. All the islander's details must be databased. Hello, the proximity sensor on the ISS had an alert during the night, though it's clear now."

"As soon as my spy cameras are online, I'm checking the Masseys out. You know where Dominiq was when you were helicoptering last night?"

"I can't say I do. Um, I have a feeling something has happened on the International Space Station."

"He was with two of his friends, guarding a hole in the town's security fence."

"You're not suggesting he'd arranged for Bryce to come to this island, direct him through the hills to the hole in the fence–and then what? Surely he wouldn't risk his own and everyone's survival, even if you are right and Bryce is related."

"If Bryce is his relative, then he and Nessa would've been mental. They'd convince themselves Bryce didn't have ARIA or was immune."

"If you are right, Baxter, then Dominiq has to be removed as leader. We can't have untrustworthy people in charge. There's too much at stake. Speaking of which, I wonder what happened up there?"

"I see a moving shadow from the exterior cam."

"Where? Oh, you're talking about the surveillance on Bryce."

"Yeah. We're trying out a tagcam. Before you ask, Abdul, we asked the two of them to wear tags so we know where they are."

"Cunning. I wish I'd set up something like that on the ISS. There are motion sensors up there, that's how I know something moved outside. There are dozens of cams that could be activated."

"I'll help you with the programming if you like. It's probably not much different to what I've done here. What data have you for what triggered the proximity sensor?"

"Only the time it's activated."

"What could be out there to do that? Have you left someone to keep the kettle going?"

"It's possible a grabber has drifted loose or a fault in the sensor. Or it could be..." Abdul froze as horrible thoughts fought their way into his imagination.

Baxter, oblivious to Abdul's fear, continued, "We can do a diagnostics. Oh, you did that while you were waking up. All green. You must have exterior cams. Turn them on, let's have a gander. Hey, you all right, mate? You're sweating cobs."

Abdul shook so much, he was able to ignore Baxter's garlic breath. It took him so many wasted, precious seconds to look up the code for the nearest cam to where the proximity sensor was triggered that he tapped the slideshow option.

"Come on, come on," Abdul moaned to the screen. He noticed Baxter looking quizzically at him.

"What's the rush? You expecting your lottery numbers to show?"

"I am afraid of what I am about to see. Nothing on that one of the Science Power Module. Come on computer, show us the next."

"My God, Abdul, you are sweating like a pom on holiday. What are you expecting to see? Ah, I get it. You think those aliens have planted another case up there. Whoo-wee! Where was the first left?"

"In the struts of the starboard photovoltaic supports."

"And the second?"

"In much the same place. It should be on the screen in the fifth shot after this."

"I thought there was a roving remote control camera on the ISS. Is it non-functioning?"

"To conserve energy, we only keep the processor batteries charged. We would need to charge up the motor and other module batteries if we wanted to bring it back into operation."

Abdul tapped his fingers on the console as the two men waited for the slideshow to scroll by, revealing the sunlit or shadowed aluminium sides of the station. One image showed a portion of the Earth.

"Just look at that, Abdul. How could you ever get used to seeing that jewel?"

"Baxter, look at it now. You wouldn't know that a momentous twist in our fortunes has occurred."

"I suppose you'd have seen the specks of light from cities at night?"

"And sometimes the condensation trails from high-flying jets."

"Wouldn't the lights from Rarotonga be spotted now and so lead the aliens straight to us?"

"Ryder checked soon after we made this link. Apparently, our light leakage is too small to stand out unless they zoom in. We keep our street lights out for that reason."

"It seems odd for us to be sitting down here observing our planet as if we are in space. Ah, another camera view. Where's that?"

"It should be the Russian storage module. Nothing unusual in that shot." His worried fingers drummed to a crescendo on the plastic desktop.

The fifth image flickered in. At first, he couldn't see much because sunlight reflected too much.

"Struth man, tone down the brightness," Baxter said shielding his eyes.

Perspiring, Abdul tweaked the brightness and contrast to discover that the sun was reflecting off an object in the struts. "By Allah, there's another one. Go get Ryder."

"Hang on, the picture's buggered. Let's be sure."

Abdul zoomed in and locked onto the image before it slideshowed to the next. He copied it to image processing software on a large screen. They walked over to it but could see the same distinguishing features of a silvery handle-less suitcase before they reached the console. Wordlessly, Abdul played with the image. It wasn't perfect because of the reflected light but clear enough to tell they had more trouble brewing.

Baxter waved his stubby aboriginal finger at the image. "Maybe this and the other slideshow images were archived ones. This could be the first or second case."

Abdul didn't answer. He didn't need to once he zoomed in to show the holograph of three chevrons showing on the side.

"I better go get him," Baxter said.

"No need now, I've just sent this image to his NoteCom. He'll know I'm in here."

RYDER RAN INTO THE ROOM, tightening the cord on blue pyjamas, cursing Jena for walking in front, slowing him down.

"Ryder, we've only had three hours sleep, you look knackered. I had to stop you tripping. What's the point arriving a few seconds earlier but with a twisted ankle?"

"Okay, Mum. Abdul, where is this case? Not in orbit? When did it arrive? Any sign of the aliens there?"

"ISS, yes, overnight, no. Coffee?"

Jena laughed, though she was obviously as nervous at the news as anyone. "Never mind the barrage of questions, Abdul, he'll slow down in a minute. I'll get the coffee while you brief us."

"Sorry, Abdul, where on the ISS is the third case?"

"In the struts of the Russian UDM, not where the other two were discovered."

Ryder waved his hands apart. "Remember, I'm not an astronaut, Abdul."

"Sorry, the Universal Docking Module."

"Is anything docked there at the moment?"

Jena walked over with a tray of coffees. "The Russian Emergency Return Vehicle is docked there, so it might not be a coincidence they changed the location of the case."

"But, if they want us to have the case, why leave it where it is so damned difficult to recover? They could have delivered it here."

Abdul stirred his coffee. "I'll get on to Charlotte. She might have archived data from other satellites."

"Excellent idea," Ryder said, "it'll keep her in touch with us, remind her that we often have her in mind."

"Except that we don't, do we?" Jena said.

"Only because we've been so busy lately. Abdul, who else have you told about the case?"

"Just you."

Ryder tapped his NoteCom. "I suppose we'd better call an emergency meeting this afternoon."

Jena poked his arm. "I suppose that Teresa bitch has to be there?"

"She says the same about you."

"The bitch. But then, you and Dominiq don't exactly hit it off, do you?"

Abdul held up a finger. "That reminds me–"

"No time for reminiscences, Abdul," Ryder said. "Send the image and other relevant data to the Security Council members, along with the meeting time. Then get onto Charlotte."

"Technically, Jena is my line manager," Abdul said.

"Do as Ryder says, this time," Jena said, "and why can't you remember that I have sugar in my coffee? Anyway, maybe the aliens have a warped sense of historical humour. You know what today is?"

Abdul laughed. "Jena, you made your own coffee. Now, July fourth. Do you think the case might contain celebratory gifts to mark the occasion? In their misguided fashion?"

"Maybe not. But it crossed my mind that since the anniversary features heavily in archived TV footage, they might have attached a significance to it, not realizing it wasn't a global event."

"It must be a coincidence," Ryder said. He didn't want his friends to start going soft on the aliens, treating them like hapless benefactors that had gone terribly wrong.

RYDER HATED MEETINGS. He knew what action was needed, although his reasoning brain cell recalled that his mind had been changed by rational debate. Meetings with the island's pre-ARIA political leaders dragged on with endless talking about lampposts, dog mess, and late trash collections. In between the amendments to such motions, Ryder wanted decisions on security patrols, training in dealing with ARIA-infected insurgents, improving communication links, and disaster avoidance. It was as if because Rarotonga was the only safe haven left on Earth, the islanders had a need to pursue normality as a means of denying insanity. But having empathy with idiots didn't mean you have to behave idiotically.

Anxious for action, Ryder was the first to the Yacht Clubhouse's Board Room, with Jena following, wearing the smirk she used in anticipation of a fun shouting match. He took his favourite bargaining position, leaning on the huge plate glass window overlooking the bay. It meant he was taller than the rest.

Maggie, an ancient islander, waddled in pushing, or being supported by, a coffee trolley. Her face was so lined, it was impossible to tell if she smiled when Jena lunged at the huge homemade cookies and the rich coffee aroma.

"That's just what we needed, Maggie. You're priceless," Jena said, then to Ryder, "Here's Dominiq and Nessa, try and not be horrible."

"Oh, look, here comes Teresa. Try not to rip her nose off."

Ryder's ex-fiancée glared at Jena and then at Ryder before turning her back on them to fortify herself with coffee.

Dominiq tapped a fancy gavel fashioned from a brass boathook. "Can we get started, people? I have another meeting at three."

Ryder objected. "I thought the only other meeting today was the Rarotonga Rose Society. Ah."

Jena hid the growing smile with her hand as Nessa glared at Ryder.

Gasping, out of breath from his gallop from the photocopying room, Abdul opened the door.

"What's happened?" asked Dominiq.

"Nothing. I just wanted to get the better enhanced prints for the meeting."

"They're excellent," Ryder said, passing them around. "The three chevrons are much clearer. This is indeed a third case."

Dominiq stood then threw the prints back onto the table. "It has nothing to do with us any more. They can attach ten cases to the space station. We can't retrieve them. It's irrelevant. Meeting over. In fact..." He paused for effect. "I think we should consider contacting the aliens to make our peace with them. Show them we are not a threat, so they'll allow us to live out our diminished existence with minimal interference."

Ryder shook his fist. "We're being eliminated by an alien species who shows no respect for human life. They've not tried to communicate with us via radio or any normal means. And the use of the cases are like a cat teasing its prey, to test its capabilities, not to engage in conversation."

"So you don't think we should try negotiating?"

Ryder seethed with Dominiq's apparent indifference to their plight. He realized he was arm waving and shouting but couldn't stop himself. "Antonio is communicating with them, and look how much more a lunatic he's become. If the aliens wanted to negotiate, they could do it through him, but they've shown contempt at killing us and then using survivors as a slave workforce."

Abdul interrupted to calm them both. His smile was intended to placate and ooze understanding. "I'm sorry, Dominiq, but just as you wouldn't consider opening a dialogue with a nest of bees to persuade them to behave differently, the aliens might harbour the same attitude to us."

Dominiq turned again to leave. "There's no point in these discussions. You have no jurisdiction on this island, and your intransigence brings you no allies here. We also feel you should leave the third case alone."

"Sit down, Dominiq," Ryder said, as calm as his simmering emotions let him. "There are several issues to consider here. One of them is that you shouldn't rule out the possibility of us retrieving the case. More important is why is it there and would we want to retrieve it?"

Dominiq laughed. "I know we have enough fuel for our helicopters to do another two hundred miles, but I have a feeling even Bat won't try and get into orbit."

Nessa laughed, and to Ryder's annoyance, so did everyone else.

Bat, who'd been studying the picture as though mesmerised, was too tired from the overnight flying to participate.

Jena, still laughing, came to Ryder's rescue. "There is a possibility we could robotically retrieve the case if we wanted to. At a pinch, we might be able to service the airplane we arrived in, refuel in Calgary again and see if the *Marimar* is still sufficiently serviceable to take a skeleton crew to the ISS."

Bat shook his head. "I doubt if we have enough fuel for the Boeing to reach Canada, and from what I've heard from Abdul, the *Marimar* will be ransacked by now."

Jena hated having her ideas trashed before she could think them through. "It wouldn't be impossible for us to search other larger islands for fuel. There's no hurry."

"I agree," Ryder said. "I bet the aliens know there're no humans up there, and so, the case would have to be moved or opened without us."

Abdul clicked his fingers. "I've already initiated a program on the ISS to use power from the photovoltaic arrays to charge up the batteries on the remote camera, and the Russian Emergency Return Vehicle, which is close to the case."

"That's suspicious," said Bat. "As if they are making it easy for us."

"Hey, it won't be easy," Abdul said. "Controlling the remote cam to grab the case might not work at all."

"True, it didn't with the first two cases. A human needed to be close for the case to be moved."

"Yeah, right," said Bat. "Give me a Big-Man yard wrench, and I'll shift it."

"No, Bat," Jena said. "Maybe force would shift it, but we don't know what's in it. It could be delicate or explosive. Anyway, if you were there with a monster tool, it would be your presence not the tool that enabled it to move."

"It's irrelevant," Dominiq said, "we should leave it up there."

"It's clearly put there for us," Ryder said. "I admit I don't know why. Maybe we should ask Antonio what he knows."

"We can't trust him any more than we can trust the aliens," Jena said.

"I think it's possible Antonio can be trusted," Teresa said. "I know he went mental when he was the first to be exposed to the second case, but I think he might have normalised."

"You want to think that of your lover," Jena said.

"I'm trying to be logical," Teresa said. "Antonio's ability to communicate with the aliens might result in useful information."

Jena turned on her, raising her voice. "Equally, it could expose us to them. He's playing a double-bluff game with both sides. Or at the best, a confused individual who doesn't know who he is any more."

Abdul tried to cool the heated air. "Suppose the aliens are not aware of our limited situation. They might suppose we have a human presence on the ISS with an escape facility. Their planting the case up there could be such an indication and revealing their poor intelligence-gathering skills."

"More likely, it's a trap," Dominiq said, "on several levels. For instance, it could be a booby trap so that if we returned it here, it detonates and finishes us off for good."

Ryder maintained his composure. "I wasn't suggesting we bring it here. Maybe an uninhabited island where it could be opened remotely or by a volunteer."

"You mean like Antonio was such a volunteer?" Dominiq said. "Because the second case wouldn't open with non-human contact. Look what happened to him. You might go to a lot of trouble, compromising any future use of the ISS, and end up with a case on a deserted airfield that cannot be opened."

"If they just wanted to take the ISS away from us," Abdul said, "they could just blast it like they did the nuclear power stations."

"Manuel and Julia might be prepared to accept it," Teresa said. "I don't like the idea of putting them in more danger, but if the third case has a third stage of ARIA..."

"You are being naively optimistic," Jena said. "I suppose there is a chance it contains ARIA-3. Teresa, has the lost memory in ARIA-infected people completely erased? Or does it remain locked in neuron clusters? Weren't you, Julia, and Gustav working on cadaver brain sections in Canada?"

"Our results are inconclusive, which is why I haven't broadcast it, thank you. But you might be right. The lost memories have been short-circuited. It would be fantastic if there is an ARIA-3 that might regenerate the withered neurons and so restore lost memories."

"Before we get carried away by thinking the aliens are our saviours," Dominiq said, "it was they who planted ARIA and fooled gullible astronauts to bring it to Earth."

Abdul stood, knocking his chair backwards. "Hey! We were instructed by NASA to send it to Earth. Jena was against taking it out of orbit."

"Whatever. Because of the aliens, only a few Earth people are left alive. If ARIA-3 exists in that case, just a few geriatrics could benefit."

"We'd benefit too," Ryder said. "And so would any other isolated groups we've not had contact with."

"There's another trap if we go get it," Dominiq said. "They might not have a fix on where we are. So, if by some ridiculous miracle you are able to get to the *Miramar* and fly it to the space station, they might backtrack the route to here."

Nessa said, "Even by reacting to the existence of the third case, we show them we have enough capability to be working the space station."

"So?" Abdul said, "Are you suggesting that would make us a bigger threat and so they'd make more of an effort to annihilate us? I suppose it might. I've been accessing the ISS computer every day. We use it as a relay and server for our phones, and Internet for Charlotte, the French, Canadian, and other groups we think log in without leaving us calling cards. The Zadokians must be sophisticated enough to notice the ISS is in use."

"And they can't object too much," Ryder said, "or they would have blown it to bits."

"Not necessarily," Dominiq said. "Maybe they've been monitoring your usage, learning from it, about us. And now to lure you up there. The biggest trap is if we collect it, it demonstrates our intelligence and ingenuity. And so worthy of energy expenditure to eradicate."

"Well, I think that's an over-the-top negative interpretation," Ryder said. "And it ignores the possible benefits."

"At our precarious stage of existence," Dominiq said, "we should act on certainties. If we ignore the third case, they'll leave us alone, because as far as they know, we don't know it is there."

Ryder rapped his knuckles on the table, as if it helped. "Nonsense. They know we exist. Their technology is far more advanced than ours, so they will have picked up our ISS communications. If we ignore the case, they might take the offensive and bring it straight to us, right here on the island. By fetching it, we can decide where it goes."

"Listen, Ryder, you had your way with attacking the boat people and making us waste time with unnecessary security measures. We are *not* going to use up all our remaining aviation fuel, skilled pilots, and supplies to go on a joyride in space. Nor are we going to compromise our safety by going to Fiji or New Zealand looking for fuel."

"That's a no, then? Vote?"

"No point. The rest of the committee and the island will vote as I advise them. End of meeting." Dominiq left the print on the table and marched out followed by Nessa.

Bat looked ambivalent as he shrugged. "Sorry, man. He should know what he's doing. He was a colonel in the army."

"I bet all his roses are neat and tidy," Abdul said.

Bat leaned towards Ryder as he passed. "He doesn't like having his position threatened, but if you had another approach so that he could make out it was his idea all along, it might work."

Ryder patted him on the shoulder but waited until he was out of the room and the door closed before facing Abdul, who was grinning a secret. Teresa, who had her hands on hips, sported a here-we-go face, and Jena had trouble stopping herself laughing.

"What are you lot laughing at?"

Teresa's scowl broke as she too fought to stop smiling. "They know you too well."

"Yes," Abdul said, "we know we are going to do what we can to retrieve that case, but–"

Jena took over. "Is it because of the need, or to spite Dominiq?"

"What? Give me a break, I don't give a damn for that idiot. Come on, back to the comms room. We have some planning to do."

"And we can keep an eye on those islanders who are supposed to keep an eye on Bryce," Teresa said.

"That reminds me," Abdul said. "I presume you all know that Dominiq and Bryce share the same surname?"

"What?" Ryder turned from not caring for Dominiq to being very bothered.

"That would explain a few things," Jena said. "The way an ARIA victim could navigate here. I presume Dominiq had sent coordinates to Bryce's boat's nav system. Maybe a homing beacon. The hole in the security fence around Avarua and the insistence of not shooting Bryce."

"Pity you didn't mention it at the meeting, Abdul," Ryder said. "It might have ended differently. On the other hand, it would have muddied the issues. Even more reason to be vigilant on the monitoring setup."

CHAPTER 20

RYDER JOGGED ALONG THE CORRIDOR in his haste to start on the plan to retrieve the case. His mind raced faster than his feet. Should he ask the young French group to help? Make them the landing spot. They are exuberant and keen to be involved. Or should it go to Charlotte, Manuel, or to a nearby island out here? What could be in the case? Is it a test or a trap? With his mind dancing such a jig, he bumped into the armed guard outside the comms room.

"Sorry, I didn't expect anyone to be here."

"Orders from the Security Council. No one to go in," said the huge man in his crisp blue uniform and gripping his black MAG-7 sub-machine gun.

Ryder laughed and said, "I bet this is the first time you've worn that uniform for a year." He could smell the nauseous gun-oil as Sergeant Deal–as could be read above his pocket–whitened his knuckles on the trigger.

"Come on, Deal, let me pass."

"Sorry, Sir."

"I've work to do and that's our lab."

"Sorry, Sir."

"Do you want ID?"

"I know who you are, Mr Nape."

"Who says I can't go in?"

"The Security Council, Sir."

"Do you know I am a member of the Security Council?"

"No, Sir."

"Well I am, so let me pass." Ryder could feel his face heating up. But the guard now looked uncertain.

"Do you have papers to that effect, Sir?"

"Of course I fucking don't. No one has had formal paperwork for months."

"Then, I can't let you in, Sir."

"Who would you let in, Sergeant Deal?"

"My instructions are to let no one in, Sir."

"Not even Mr Massey?"

"I'm not at liberty to say, Sir."

"Who's in there now?"

"No one, Sir."

"But there has to be someone monitoring the security camera on the boat people who came last night."

"I don't know about that, Sir."

Ryder, exasperated, stomped back down the corridor and met Jena and Abdul carrying breakfasts. He turned them back to the canteen for a conference.

"THAT SETTLES IT," Jena said and slammed her fist on the table so hard Abdul's orange juice glass fell and he had to jump back to avoid wet shorts. "Dominiq doesn't want anyone monitoring his cousin, brother, or whoever."

"Or he doesn't want us retrieving case three," Teresa said, using a tablemat to divert an orange rivulet.

"Or both," Ryder said. "Course of action? We could tool ourselves up and outgun the guard."

"For how long?" Teresa said. "We can't guard a guard for more than a few hours, even if tied up. It makes more sense to persuade Dominiq to allow us to get on with our work."

"But I think he's more concerned with Bryce and letting him reach here," Abdul said. "Of course, we can easily set up an alternative monitoring of Bryce. The radio signal can be picked up anywhere on the island. Damn, unless it's been encrypted. But I can hack through."

"That's urgent," Ryder said. "But I don't want you spending too much time monitoring once you have it set up. Get others you've become pally with, preferably some who aren't falling over themselves to lick Dominiq's shoes."

"More than you'd think. I've been hanging out with a group of computer nuts in the IT lab of a school on West Street. If I go now, the monitoring will be on track in an hour. I can access the ISS from there too, but I must get my memory stick from the lab here for the codes."

Ryder stroked his chin. There was a fire escape into the forbidden lab. It would mean a noisy, forced entry from the outside, as would lifting the red pantiles to get through the roof. More than the logistics of breaking into what he sensed was their lab, he was perturbed by the sudden eviction. The insult of the lockout simmered in himself rather than annoyance at Dominiq's childish behaviour. His neck throbbed with surging blood. He realized he'd been stroking his chin for several minutes. One of these two women would recognise the symptoms. He raised his eyes and saw Teresa smirk. The bitch. Before Jena dropped out of orbit into his life, Teresa had lived with him for too long, picking up too many of his auto-responsive quirks.

He flicked his eyes to Jena. Instead of looking at him, she glowered at Teresa. Jena had more brains than the whole of NASA, so it was possible she'd seen, interpreted and double-took his unease but targeted Teresa to pre-empt any takeover.

These relationship manoeuvrings did his head in, although they had their amusing dimensions.

"Maybe we should have made Abdul wait," Teresa said. "Do you know where in the lab is his memory stick?"

"Not exactly, but it's jet black with the Islam silver star and crescent," Ryder said, wondering what plan Teresa had in mind. It didn't take long for her to reveal it.

"One of us distracts the guard, and it doesn't take a genius who is most like a tart to do that."

Ryder groaned but Jena laughed. "Give a dog a bad name, I might as well live up to it."

Breathing easily again, Ryder wondered if the guard was immune to girls, and if so, whether he was attractive to gays. Shaking his head at that thought, he also tried to think ahead of the possibility of the guard having locked the lab door. He'd not known it to be locked since he'd arrived. Until now, personal and property security hadn't been an issue on this island. To his amazement, Teresa and Jena appeared to be cooperating. Blond hair mingled with black like liquorice allsorts. Then, they sprang apart like fighting tigers, but only for Jena to jog down the canteen to the opposite door.

"She needs to appear at the other end of the corridor."

"I get it. Jena will lure him away, and while his back is turned, we sneak up, in, and hey, presto." Ryder said. "What I don't understand is why the guard is being so fastidious. You'd think he'd be at home with his wife, kids, parents, not uniformed up as if the world's not in a febrile state. You'll be telling me he's getting paid too. Wasn't it New Zealand dollars on this island?"

Teresa stood. She stepped over a puddle of orange juice. "It still is. Haven't you considered that some people cope with a crisis by working hard at what used to be normal? And you are so with your nose in the air that the domestic situation here has passed you by. The island council decided to continue using the dollar for payments of local services and goods for the time being."

"But how does the shop get its merchandise? Is there a secret Wal-Mart delivery submarine, followed by Harrod's food drops by parachute?"

"The main convenience store here on Avarua was given the go-ahead to close the other shops around the island and collect all the goods. Tinned, bottled, and dried foods have been systematically collected from empty homes. A lot of people are growing food crops in kitchen gardens, plantations and orchards, then sending their surplus to the shop in exchange for dollars or goods. Maybe you should get out more, Ryder. Anyway, Jena will need help, so I'm following her on down."

Left on his own, Ryder marvelled at the way adversity brought opponents together. He snuck into the kitchen and picked out a steel meat tenderiser for window breaking should the need arise. He jogged silently back to the lab corridor but stayed on the corner, out of sight of the guard. He peeked to check on progress. The guard stood impassively, ten metres away, staring out of the windowed wall in front of him overlooking the harbour. Plenty to see out there, good.

He saw Jena in the shortest dress he'd seen, sauntering up from the other end of the corridor. Of course, it was her T-shirt with her jeans left in the other corridor. My God, she was hot, and so was his face. The stony guard hadn't noticed.

She called to him at five metres distance. "Excuse me, soldier blue, have you a light?"

At last, his head turned, and he was hooked. His weapon slipped. He grabbed it as he fumbled in his pocket for a lighter, stuttering affirmatives. The helpless Sergeant Deal probably hadn't seen anyone like Jena on heat. Ryder tiptoed up the corridor slowly, fast, then slow again as he thought the guard sensed his approach.

Jena took a step to an open window and leaned out just enough for her "dress" to ride halfway up her buttocks.

The guard looked as if he was having an apoplectic fit as he fumbled with the lighter.

Jena turned again, smiled at the guard then glowered at Ryder, who too, had his activity on hold while admiring the view.

Recovering, he pushed at the lab door, which opened. A small laugh of surprise escaped. He ran to the ISS monitor bench and grabbed Abdul's memory stick and slipped it into his pocket. He wondered what else might be useful. He saw a bulky file of ISS code printouts, so he grabbed that and returned to the closed door.

Through the glass, he could see Jena, hand on hip, laughing as the guard puffed on a spliff. What? He didn't know Jena carried drugs again. He'd have to have words with her. Interrogate her, in that outfit.

He gently pushed the door and slipped out, turned and tiptoed back down the corridor.

"Hey! Where did you come from?" The shout from the guard froze Ryder as he imagined the muzzle of the MAG-7 pointed at his back.

"Smoking drugs on duty, soldier?" shouted Teresa, dressed in a military uniform and marching down the corridor.

The guard dropped the spliff and yammered incoherently while Ryder's mouth fell in astonishment at, and admiration of, the repertory theatrics of the two women. He turned and marched before accelerating to a run.

CHAPTER 21

RYDER BLINKED at the sophisticated array of equipment when he stood in the entrance of the school IT lab. "Hey, Abdul, a present for you."

Abdul eagerly received the codes and memory stick, grinning as if his birthday had come early. "Look, Ryder." He pointed at a couple of young women who were dabbing at a large touch screen showing Bryce and Benita still in their quarantine.

"Ah, no wonder you wanted to transfer over here." Ryder lowered his voice. "Are you sleeping with both simultaneously?"

Abdul had a look of mock surprise. "Shush. I don't want Jasmine to overhear." He pointed at another young woman at a console in another corner.

"Good grief, Abdul, how come you never look tired?"

"Since I became a vegan, you should try it."

"Maybe. I hate to ask this, but have you a back up for this backup facility?"

"Don't worry, I have already arranged so we can monitor those two in quarantine on our NoteComs. Can't do that so easily for the ISS. We can for comms but not control. The remote cam-and-grab isn't fully charged yet, nor the Return Vehicle. Just as well, because you haven't told me the landing site."

"That's 'cos we haven't discussed it yet. Island democracy has failed us, so we'd better decide between us."

Jena caught up with their conversation. "I don't think you can count this island in the realm of democracy. More like autocracy: being ruled by one person."

"He's got Nessa, so isn't that a biarchy?"

"Okay. Abdul, where do you think it should go?"

"To Manuel, so Julia can work on the case, and you never know, Antonio might get killed by ARIA-3."

"I think it should go to the French group in the Rhône Valley. Antonio doesn't know we know them, so he can't tip off the aliens."

"Ah," Abdul said.

"You're not telling me Antonio knows about them?"

"I'm not sure. I have a feeling Manuel might have told him. After all, we passed on the information that the aliens were eliminating the nuclear power stations there and how."

"Even so," Ryder continued, "the French are young, intelligent, keen, and isolated."

Jena frowned. "Hang on, they're all arts students. How are they going to know how to handle the case safely? They'll spray it with gold paint and put it in an exhibition."

"There's another reason I'd rather it not go to Manuel and Julia."

"He means—" Abdul said.

"I know what he means. It might not be another ARIA virus. It could be explosives. The aliens figuring that it would be their most clever and active human troublemakers who'd be able to recover the case. Let them take it to their base and boom! Everywhere for a hundred-mile radius disappears."

"They wouldn't want a nuke to pollute the atmosphere," Abdul said.

"No they wouldn't," Jena said, "but nukes aren't the only way to obliterate all humans on a continent."

"True," Ryder said.

"They might have a bio-weapon worse than Ebola or botulism," Jena said.

"They used to say a worse danger from bio-weapons is mass panic, but there's just a few of us left to panic," Ryder said.

"We don't do panic, do we?" Abdul said.

"I think we should leave the third case in orbit."

"Jena, you are so predictable," Abdul said.

"I'm not saying we don't try and open it, but we've already listed why it shouldn't be opened near people, yet a human presence is needed."

"Only if it is like the first two," Ryder said. "They must know there are no humans in orbit and configured the case differently."

Abdul's hands twitched with anticipation of real astronaut work again. "The remote cam-grabber is fully charged now. Shall I go for the case and take it to the Return Vehicle?"

"Certainly not," Jena said, spilling her coffee as she rushed over.

"Yes," Ryder said. "At least go up for a good look. You're okay with that aren't you, Jena?"

"Yeah, as long as no attempt is made to move it. Suppose it's booby-trapped. Bang! There goes our ISS for ever."

"Point taken. Abdul, go for an inspection."

"And if I'm outvoted on the decision to bring it to Earth," said Jena, "I still want a say on where."

Ryder shook his head. "You'd want it in the middle of the ocean. How useful is that?"

"I suppose if it has to come Earthside, it might as well be

accessible by someone. But I doubt the French group of arty-farty students will be of any use."

"I'm disturbed at the thought of it going to Canada," Ryder said. "Not only does it risk our friends there, but Antonio could get hold of it and use it in some malevolent way. Or put it out of our reach."

Abdul, who was making final preparations for release of the remote cam grabber, said, "How about sending it to Charlotte in Australia? By the way, I've just completed the emissions sweep, and once again, the case is not radioactive, magnetic, nor emitting radio waves, although it is twenty-five degrees above background temperature."

"Does Charlotte have any friends with her yet?" Jena said.

"She's on her own."

Jena thought then said, "You know, Abdul, the Return Vehicle could land with its hatch in the sand, or in a river. Opening that capsule door, when upright, without a desperate passenger pushing from the inside, takes two people. And she's a comms expert, not a weightlifter."

"But she is closer than the rest," Abdul said, "assuming we might need to get our own hands on the case at some point."

Ryder looked at Abdul's fingers dancing in a blur on the keyboard and touchscreen. "How far, exactly?"

"I'll tell you," Jena said, activating her NoteCom and bringing up a route finder. "Five thousand, one hundred and thirty-six miles. Here to Calgary is five thousand, seven hundred and six, and to the Lyons area in France is a huge nine thousand, three hundred and fifty-six miles. Um, France is growing on me."

"You mean if the case is a deadly virus, it gives us greater distance," Ryder said. "Agreed."

"I can activate the number keypad lock on the Return Vehicle, so they can't open it until we give them the combination."

"Excellent idea," Jena said. "Okay, then. Although it's against my will to bring it to Earth, let the French have it and use it against the aliens in their precious domes."

"I think what we do with it has to be discussed again later," Ryder said, looking at her eyes trying to ascertain the level of seriousness in them. "Abdul, how are you progressing with the remote cam? Can we have it on the big screen?"

It was as if they were in space. The image scrolled by smoothly in black and white, but only because the velvet backdrop of space was interrupted by the silvery whiteness of the ISS.

Abdul's rusty steering skills created two minor collisions with struts.

"I'm not accepting complaints. You try steer a trashcan in a free-fall three-dimensional maze trying to guess where it will be after pressing GO two seconds before."

"Okay, hand it over," Ryder said, grinning, knowing Abdul would never let him.

Abdul wasn't steering by the visual input of the camera but from a computer screen split between a schematic showing the ISS infrastructure surrounding the remote and scrolling directional data telling him optimal movements. A red dot indicated the location of the case, but it was Ryder and Jena who first gasped at its sight.

Not that it looked different from the first two, apart from the triple chevron, but the sight of the enigmatic container sent joint shivers up their spines.

Something pressed against Ryder's back. His pulse quickened, but when he turned, he saw one of the women, who watched Bryce, breathlessly absorbed by the sight on the screen. The other two doing the same.

"At least one of you need to be watching Bryce, please."

The nearest, a young redhead whose peach shower gel residue lingered, reluctantly moved away. Ryder smiled after her, but she wasn't looking at him. However, Jena was, wearing a thunderous face. He returned to the screen, feeling her icy stare boiling inside him.

"I don't get it," Ryder said. "Nothing is securing it to that non-magnetic aluminium strut. We'd have to use bolts, straps, or superglue. None of them would work, because they couldn't relinquish their hold when a human is present. Why doesn't it drift away?"

"Because there is no wind out there," Jena said. "And there shouldn't be any sudden vibrations. The ISS is moving in its orbit but smoothly. All they had to do was stick some dollops of chewing gum on the struts."

Abdul shook his head. "It was a very special gum to be gooey when frozen to avoid being knocked off with a robotic arm but drift off when a human was nearby. No coincidence, not twice."

"I was coming to that," Jena said, as if her subordinate officer shouldn't have spoken. "We have to ask ourselves what a human hand inside an insulated glove has that a robotic metal arm doesn't."

Ryder shook his head.

Abdul never gave up on a challenge. "Even with a pressure suit, there will be a different electromagnetic spectrum signature from a human than a robotic arm. There would be static electricity differences, and there will be temperature differences, even if only a few degrees."

"Exactly," Jena said. "Those clever fuckers must have built tiny sensors into the chewing gum that releases the case at a threshold distance of, say, a few centimetres."

At that moment, the camera moved and the Earth peeped round the shaded, curved wall of the space station.

"Last time I saw her like that," Jena said, "it was with my own eyes."

Ryder swore he could see tears.

She continued. "It's beautiful. A shining blue and white gem, teeming with life and love. And what did we do?"

"It wasn't your fault," Ryder said, patting her hand, which she snatched away. "Everybody wanted it."

"*I* didn't."

"Because, my love, you were the only one blessed with hindsight before it happens. I suppose it's foresight. I'm not going to suggest there's such a thing as women's intuition."

Abdul dared a short laugh. "You like living dangerously, Ryder. Anyway, you two, I am as close as I want to get to the case before deploying the grab."

"Wait," Jena said. "If we take it to the Return Vehicle before it's been programmed for the exact landing coordinates, the aliens could make it land here."

"Jena, you're being paranoid and unusually illogical," Ryder said. "I bet they know about us here and could have blasted us to hell if they wanted to. It's possible this case has a cure for ARIA-1. The ARIA-2 only stopped the memory loss from getting worse. This could unlock lost memories—like the issue Julia and Teresa have been working on."

"If that was the situation, oh naïve one, why not take it straight to where it's needed?"

Abdul shook his head. "They're information gathering. They don't seem to be aware of us or they would have already eliminated us. They seem to use telepathy, so maybe they're not adept at picking up leaked radio signals. And there must be hundreds of isolated, uninfected groups in valleys and remote areas all over the planet. They can't be bothered to do a detailed global survey and will let us, or whoever is sufficiently resourceful, collect and use this third case."

"What a load of fucked-up reasoning," Jena said. "All wishful thinking. Sure, they wanted to get at whoever is the most resourceful, and bam, get rid of them. It's the space-age Trojan Horse."

"Or Pandora's Box," Ryder said, "inside the Trojan Horse. I don't share Abdul's outlook, but we might as well take a close look, see if it moves, and take it to the Return Vehicle."

"I can disable the launch ability of the Return Vehicle until we are ready," Abdul said, "but you knew that, Jena."

"I forgot."

Abdul joked. "Put her in quarantine."

Ryder knew that Jena hadn't forgotten. She could've programmed the Return Vehicle's launch herself. "How do you intend to grab the case?"

"See the grabber? It can operate like your hand but with telescopic fingers such that it could open more than the twenty centimetres necessary and then close on the edge of the case. It has rubbery slip-proof fingertips. I am going for it."

Jena batted her hands at the screen. "Adieu case, adieu communication links, adieu Hubble telescope link, because it's goodbye ISS when it blows up."

"Life's juggling its balls in the air," Abdul said. "Here goes."

Jena walked away to join the woman keeping watch on Bryce, but Ryder and the two other Bryce observers couldn't pull themselves away. Although it was happening in space while he was relatively safe, his stomach tightened.

Ryder watched the grabber inch closer to the case. He looked so hard, he swore he could see the case vibrating. He squeezed his eyes shut then opened wide. What if the case shook free because of some spring mechanism triggered by the presence of the incoming grabber? It might drift off into space. But, even so, it should be recoverable, because the remote grabber can fly without tethers. A pain though. He stared at the holographic image of the three chevrons. He'd seen nothing like it other than on the cases. Earth-based holograms didn't look solid like these. Each chevron had clear space between them. In his previous career in media, he would have sold his soul for that effect.

Abdul manipulated the grabbing hand to open, move around an edge of the case, and then gently closed on the silvery, smooth surface.

Ryder fought the urge to close his eyes again, realizing that in his need to see everything, he hadn't blinked for minutes. He forced himself to blink. On reopening, he saw the fingers, and their reflection, converge. The case shimmered.

"Is that an optical illusion or is it vibrating?" Ryder asked.

"Vibration. Damn, it's slipping."

"Squeeze harder to get a firm grip. No choice. We don't want to go chasing it all around the solar system."

"I'm not sure of my own strength with respect to the grabber."

Ryder's own hand clenched as Abdul made the grabber squeeze

the case. He saw the grabber fingertips indent into the case surface. "Enough!"

"Easy for you to say, don't forget there is a two-second time lag."

Ryder's eyes were stinging with perspiration. He looked at Abdul and saw that even this cool, composed, and unflappable Arab had a wet forehead. He searched his pocket for a non-existent paper tissue but had no need. Jena had returned unseen, gauged the situation, and wiped Abdul's forehead with a white cloth as if he was a heart surgeon.

"Thanks, Jena."

"You don't deserve it."

"I know."

The case, firmly in the grabber's hand, came away from the struts. No detonation. A chorus of applause and relief echoed round the room.

"Shush," Ryder said, amid his own laughter. "We don't want to alert the Dominiq clique."

"It will take me at least thirty minutes to manipulate the case to the Return Vehicle. Another twenty to seat it inside and do up its seat belt. Luckily, I can stop at any time and let it safely hang."

"Not like Heathrow baggage handlers then," Ryder said.

"You mean they'd throw it in from there or put it on the wrong plane?"

"Ha ha. I was thinking that now the tether is on the grabber, you could just wind it back to the Return Vehicle, but the case would batter the struts en route."

"Let me do it my way. You need to look at the map of the Rhône Valley to give me the exact grid reference of the landing site."

CHAPTER 22

FIFTEEN MINUTES LATER, Ryder and Jena "flew" over southern France. The enhanced aerial view stunned them, even though they thought they were immune to being awed. The images had been satellite updated and auto zipped to the ISS databases.

"Look at that," Ryder said, like a teenage boy seeing his first naked woman.

Jena laughed. "Hey, there are the three domes at La Voulte. Zoom in more. Maybe we can see the bozo Zadokians."

"They'd have to be the size of a car. I'm looking for a large, open area not too far away."

"That's no good. We don't want it too near the Zadokians. We know the French students have transport, so we should go farther. Also, if we land it out in the open, there's always a chance someone else will find it before they do. I know Abdul will run a thorough systems check, but those twenty-year-old Russian Return Vehicles have never been used."

"Hang on, Jena, I know all the Russian modules were upgraded two years ago. You're trying to pick fault."

"I consider my role to be a hazard tester. The upgrades were to the electronics for navigation and computers. As far as we know, the parachutes will tear apart. Imagine the case after it's bounced around the French Alps like in a pinball game."

"Speaking of French Alps, the Rhône glacier is not so far away. A large expanse of snow-covered ice. Hardly anyone around, yet there is a good network of roads in the area."

"Where have you been the last fifty years? Haven't you made multimedia programmes about global warming?"

"Ah. Yes, what's left of the glacier isn't much of a target. Okay, clever clogs. Have you a better plan?"

"Those Recovery Vehicles are made to fall onto water or land."

"You're not suggesting dumping it in the sea? They'd never find it. Anyway, a parachute-failed landing on the sea is as hard as landing on a field."

"True, though I'd expect drag from failed parachutes to keep the terminal velocity down, and hopefully, at least one of the three will open. But finding it is not as important as hiding it, and it's easy to do that underwater. The Return Vehicle doesn't need to be opened straight away as when it's carrying people."

"I thought they were designed to float if the hatch stays shut. Ah, you intend to blow the hatch? But that will make it too heavy for the students to lift."

"The case won't be damaged by water if it is safe to be exposed to the harsh radiation of space. As long as it is in shallow water, the tethered homing signal can be released when we tell it to. We give the frequency to the students when they are near it, and they dive in and rescue the case."

"Can't we arrange a device to send the case to the surface? A flotation collar to be activated on our signal?

"Excuse me, Ryder, if I knew you weren't in a hurry, I could spend the next few weeks designing and using the tricky remote grabber to build a fancy extraction system with hot and cold folding doors."

"I hear you. Hey, Lake Geneva is close to the La Voulte hideout. I'll show you on screen." Ryder punched in the name, and the view swung over the French-Swiss border before zooming in to the lake. A column of data displayed on the right.

"Useless. Far too small a target. Suppose the descent path deviates because of faulty parachute deployment or strong wind? And look at that depth—over three hundred metres. We're better off landing it in the sea, just off the south coast. Look." It was her turn to operate the game-like flight sim. In a northern bay of the Mediterranean Ocean, the Rhône flowed into the Gulf de Lion. For an area larger than Lake Geneva, the depth was under thirty metres yet far enough from the beach to be secure from prying eyes.

Ryder said. "If we land it in the sea, how long will it stay before being bashed by tides and dragged away by currents?"

"The capsule is strong, the case stronger if it's like the other two. If it drifts, we'll know where from the homing signal. I'll give you the coordinates for the Gulf of Lion."

"Right, as soon as you work out the appropriate launch window and ETA of the Return Vehicle, I'll brief the French."

"You'd better have a talk with Teresa and Gustav about how the students need to protect themselves from the case."

Ryder looked at her but knew she made sense. Gustav was Teresa's main bio-technician in London and responsible for keeping the case biohazards in perspective throughout the North Wales experience last year. But the look to Jena was one of resignation, not just because his conversations with his ex-fiancée, Teresa, were more fraught than being a tiger's dentist, but they knew the survival chances of the French group were low.

"MY ADVICE TO THEM IS CLEAR," said Gustav. He stood a hand's width taller than Ryder. His once-white lab coat had burn holes like a random map of Mars and coloured streaks where he'd wiped test stirrers on his sleeve. Rich brown from iodine, green copper, red iron, and tattered acid holes. His brown hair had been cut so short, Ryder could hardly see it.

"Raid a lab for biohazard suits. There should be plenty of factories, fire stations, ambulance stations, hospitals, nuclear power stations—oops. Then, store it like we did in a mine, cave, or bank vault until they are ready to investigate it under our instructions."

Ryder liked Gustav. He deconstructed the most complex problem into small steps. His Teutonic ancestors would have been proud of him. There was a flaw in Gustav's plan he needed to float.

"I suppose they will solve the problems of wearing biohazard suits under water when they dive for the case? But, if the case broke open as a result of a hard landing, the virus won't live long in water, will it? Especially seawater."

"Sorry, Ryder, I didn't know the Return Vehicle capsule was landing in water. We know so little of the two cases already arrived, it's too unpredictable to guess what the presence of water will do. Maybe nothing, probably nothing."

"Worst case scenario?"

Gustav laughed. "Ha ha, case. Sorry. I suppose contact with water could trigger a detonation, but like I said, we know too little. We have no idea what the case is made of, how it opens, the exact nature of the substrate or medium that the ARIA virus is held in, how it is released, how virulent it is—"

"Whoa, Gustav. Let me put it this way. What would you do to recover the case from the Return Vehicle underwater?"

"I'd get hold of a boat with facilities to lift or drag the Return Vehicle to shore. It doesn't have to be a naval submarine rescue craft or anything special, but I've been looking at the specs. If it is the modified X-38 Return Vehicle, then it weighs six tons. A trawler's net can haul that easily. In fact, a scuba diver could attach a hook and use the boat's winch to lift it."

"Sounds like a difficult mission for students. And they'd have to be looking out for infected, curious people."

"True, although those would be geriatrics struggling to survive with the memories of little children. I doubt they'd take much persuading to keep away. The Zadokians might take an interest though."

"Gustav, there's no perfect solution here, but better for the case to be lost in the sea than destroy us here."

"I'd rather it come here. It might be useful in our analysis of the second case."

"So, you are in agreement with Teresa that it is likely to be another ARIA-type virus, which might unlock lost memories in the infected?"

"Maybe. Don't you?"

"Not at all. What's the point? As you say, most of the world's population is dead. Why have a few geriatrics have their memories returned? It wouldn't make them the people they were before. Think about the traumas they've suffered witnessing their children and grandchildren die. They've probably killed to make it this far and live in appalling situations. They will be psychotic, paranoid, and grotesque."

"Maybe the third case has a virus that will wipe out all that and just give them their memories up to ARIA-1. No, that won't do, because all their families are no more. Maybe you're right, Ryder. Hey, suppose it's a virus that makes them into human servants."

"You mean slaves? No need, ARIA-2 did that, or rather in the presence of the Zadokians, the humans in Winnipeg seem to be in a trance while they are working. I don't think case three can be anything like that."

"You really think it is just an explosive device aimed at us here?"

"We are their biggest threat, Gustav. Okay, not an explosive device. It seems rather small for that, although I keep being told not to judge by human standards. But it could be a deadly virus that wipes out all humans within a set radius."

"Like fifty miles to ensure an island's humanity is exterminated?"

"Or a thousand miles to be sure."

"Ryder, France is nine thousand miles away. Our French friends are dispensable?"

Ryder spread his hands. "We're all dispensable. It's a question of how much effort and sacrifices might be necessary for human beings to have a future. I am assuming that it is worthwhile for humans to survive."

"The urge to survive is what keeps all species ticking, although having the ability to intellectualise existence instead of merely living it, gives us the opportunity to question whether humans are worthy of being perpetuated. I know great works of art and humanity were thought to be a legacy for the future, but did it outweigh the evil men do?"

"Oh dear, I forgot that Gustav, the pessimist, still lurks inside you. You have a point. Humans have been a dreadful species, with so much torture, murder, and war, but there's a lot of compassion, unselfishness, love, and empathy too. A paradox, I know, but let's not slit our throats just yet."

Gustav moved towards Ryder with his arms open. "Don't forget friendship. Let me give you a true European hug."

"Get off me, Gustav. I know we're friends, there's no need for—" Too late as Gustav hugged, laughing.

"Ah, the great British reserve."

"It's more to do with preservation than reservation. I don't want my breakfast squeezed out of me." Gustav placed Ryder back on his stool then stood still as a thought progressed.

"Ryder, it's a pity the Zadokians didn't produce a virus that stopped the evil in humans. Damn it, they've either made a huge mistake in an effort to help us, or they're more evil than humans."

"Sadly, it's the latter. The other reason I wanted the third case to be somewhere near the Zadokians is that somehow, I'd like you biologists to investigate the effect of the third case on the Zadokians. You know I am convinced by logic—*reductio ad absurdum*—that the third case contains a deadly virus to finish us off, but I am fermenting a plan to use it for our benefit."

"You mean, if we find that the virus also kills the aliens, you'd use it on them? Forget it. Too risky. If we think the case is that dangerous, we should keep it in space, like Jena wants."

"No way is it safe up there. Don't you see, Gustav? They put it there. They can remove and use it in a way that's out of our control. I know by retrieving it, we tell them we are still around and capable of such action, but they don't know for sure what we are, how many, or where."

"Then put it in the bottom of a deep ocean."

"Why? If they can zip around in airtight spaceships, they can surely nip underwater and fetch it, assuming they know how to find it."

"No, Ryder. You've been watching too many Thunderbirds episodes. The engineering required to stop a spaceship exploding in the vacuum of space is totally different to preventing it from imploding under the huge pressures beneath the waves. I'm certain the case would be out of reach on a deep-ocean floor."

"Perhaps, but I don't like the idea of it being out of our reach. It might represent our best chance to be rid of the buggers."

"Ryder, has your fermentation process bubbled up a plan? Assuming you're right about the case holding a deadly virus to kill us, I don't see how you are going to keep us alive, unless you build us the largest biohazard container."

"I'm not saying yet. People have a habit of knocking my plans down before they're ready."

"You keep so much inside, you're going to burst. My God, Ryder, perhaps that's what those domes are really for?"

"As biohazard containment shelters? I doubt it. You've seen the pictures, with the unlocked flimsy doors, simple air-in filters. They're merely clean air accommodations and greenhouses, with positive air pressure to keep pollutants out. Would they keep viruses out?"

"No way. But it wouldn't take much for them to be modified to be an effective containment space for, say, a few days. Anyway, I'll go and create a statement for our French friends. Teresa and I have been in touch with them regularly."

LATER, Ryder walked back to the school lab, doing his best to avoid being spied by Dominiq or one of his supporters.

"Hi, Abdul, how's it going? I'm so knackered. It must be all this brainwork."

"Go home, Ryder, and get some sleep. You only make mistakes when you're tired."

"I don't want to miss you launching the Return Vehicle. Wake me for the countdown, will you?"

"I'll wake you in four days. That's when we have a good window for landing in the Gulf of Lion."

"Clever clogs. I'll see you later."

CHAPTER 23

AFTER ENSURING THAT Abdul and Gustav were coordinating schedules, Ryder's weariness enveloped him like a heavy blanket. He fought the time-wasting quasi-hibernation of sleep, but he couldn't wait to reach their allocated holiday chalet and collapse on the bed for a mid-afternoon nap. The holiday village on the outskirts of Avarua should have disturbed him by its abnormally silent mode, but fatigue denied logic. His semi-conscious state managed to look up as an afternoon convection thunderstorm rumbled. He was used to the steady rain that soaked North Wales the previous year, but these short, intensive tropical storms took him by surprise every time.

Extra-large raindrops splattered the white paving like water bombs. Luckily, Ryder had just reached the final furlong although he didn't mind the warm, refreshing rain. Clothes dried in minutes in the clean, hot, dry air that followed.

Another shelter seeker had beaten him to his porch.

"If I were you, Tiddles, I'd scoot off. Hide under a parked car. There's a ferocious animal who lives here." He pointed at the door, while the ginger tabby looked at his finger. As he pushed the door open, the cat sat on Ryder's wicker chair that he never had time to sit on and licked a paw.

The darkened room had the sweet smell from sandalwood candles, but once Ryder saw the bed, he flung himself on it and gratefully closed his eyes. Part of his brain looked for reasons why the room was dark, conjecturing the clouds outside. Another on why candles were lit, but Jena often did, so maybe she was here and left them. Whatever, he was too tired to care. Sleep was prescribed, and he cashed in, crashing out.

Moments later, the thunder rumbled outside and rattled his Venetian blinds. Rain soaked through his T-shirt and dribbed on his face. He only put effort into opening his eyes when his nose detected a strong peachy aroma, which is not usual to the rain he knew.

"Stop pretending to be asleep, you bastard." The freshly showered Jena dripped from her glistening, naked body all over him.

"You'll get the bed wet."

"A little role reversal, eh? Your turn to have the wet T-shirt, ha ha."

"I know you'll find this incredible, sweetheart, but I really am tired." In spite of his reasonable plea, demonstrated by his shut eyelids, he detected his trousers being interfered with.

"I've never known you to be too tired, lover, and if it were true, why did you light the candles and send a message for me to come here?"

Some inconsistencies in her interrogation bothered him, but they couldn't successfully reach through his haze. In any case, his opened eyes devoured more of Jena's agitated breasts, and his morphing crotch anticipated more than sleep.

"Sex first, inquisition later," he said, at last reaching for her.

"All right, but first, let's try this massage oil you placed on the bed with the rose petals." She uncorked a green bottle and sniffed, resulting in a sly smile.

"I don't remember..." There were too many puzzles, so he surrendered to the moment. "I suppose it's your favourite Yling Ylang and Jasmine."

"Nonny, no, you've outclassed yourself this time. The label says it's ginger pheromone. I say it's my turn first. Move over. You know what to do."

Still in a daze, dozy Ryder poured a little of the green oil into the palm of his right hand to warm it. He brought it too close to his nose, making his head jerk back when it registered the powerfully sweet but sharp fragrance. "If this doesn't send the cat running, nothing will."

"On my back, moron, not my pussy."

"I wasn't... oh, never mind. Here we go, ready or not." Perhaps it was the blend of the morning's excitement, the crashing storm, and his tiredness, but adding this dollop of sensual olfactory experience sent a strange tingling through him. He circled his palms into the small of her back for a few minutes. Her moans, punctuated by lightning and deafening booms, encouraged his increasingly wakeful self to change strategy. After reapplying the slippery concoction into his hands, giving himself a mental note to wash his hands before making sandwiches later, he plied his fingers to her toes.

He loved her toes. Not that they were perfect. Some rough skin here and there, chipped nails, and two toes nearly crossed themselves. But he took immense sensual pleasure in manipulating the now-oily digits. One foot at a time, he rubbed her soles, playing her moans like a musical instrument. He stopped to listen. In the rare silences, he could hear real music. A music player must be turned on.

Jena noticed his lack of attention. "Keep going, you're doing fine."

A cacophony of acoustic booms, abetted by driving rain against complaining windows, drowned the music. The candles enabled Ryder to keep his hands on target.

"What's that music?"

"I was going to ask you when you came in. I assumed you put it on with the candles."

With his eager hands hovering over her perfect bottom, he paused. "But that's Joe Loss's band playing *For ever and ever*. How could you think I'd put that on? I am insulted. Take your punishment."

While straddling her legs on the bed, he slapped her right buttock, but his oiled hand, saying hello to her wet skin, slithered and slid off and onto the pink candlewick. His face smacked into her round rump.

"Harder."

"I can't, your tush is too slippery."

"Tush? How quaint. Just try harder, master. Some people like Joe Loss."

He regained his straddle posture, gathered composure, and slapped again using his left hand after wiping it drier on the insides of her upper thigh, making her groan loader than the sing-along-musak. "I would have put Roxy Music on. We both swing to *Avalon*."

At last, he massaged both buttocks simultaneously in counter rotation. Her flesh, though firm enough, travelled in a wave under the pressure of his enthusiastic fingers. His smile wavered as his nose was assaulted under the influence of disparate aromas. Peach shower gel and sandalwood candles made a volatile cocktail to the senses by the ginger in the massage oil.

He couldn't resist leaning forward, so his hands reached around and cupped her breasts. She protested by wriggling her rear, obliging him to renew his kneading.

In her huskiest voice, she finally gave permission. "Come on, lover. I'm ready."

His pre-encounter weariness waxed and waned, but like the moon, an appropriate simile that brought a smile, he was in danger of setting too soon. He knelt, so did she, and so rhythmic coupling commenced. How he had sufficient energy to complete concupiscent manoeuvres would have surprised him had he not succumbed to sleep within a few seconds. Even so, a fragment of consciousness informed him that an unimpressed Jena rolled him off.

"WAKE UP, YOU IDIOT."

For goodness sake, this woman was insatiable. Couldn't she tell he needed rest?

"I've let you recuperate, but damn it, Ryder, wake the fuck up."

"Can't you finish off yourself? Leave me be."

"What? Oh, my magic rabbit did that an hour ago, and a better job it made too. Listen to me. Are you for real when you said it wasn't you who lit the candles, did the awful music, and rose-petalled the bed? 'Cos it sure wasn't me."

"Why would someone else do it? And you said something about a message to come here. Right. Either we have romantic friends who thought we both needed rogering, and not just with your magic rabbit, or someone wanted us out of the way."

"Dominiq needed us here instead of the lab. But he'd already put a guard on there. So, he knows about the school backup systems."

"In turn, he must have a spy there. Maybe one of those women I set to observe Bryce."

"Which means Bryce is not being observed, or at least not at Aroa. Has he removed his tag?"

Ryder rubbed his eyes, wondering if an hour was sufficient for what looked like another twenty-three-hour day. "Let's get over to the school lab. Have you tried calling Abdul?"

"His phone appears to be switched off. There's coffee brewed in the kitchen. Cold now but swallow some before we throw ourselves out there."

"At least the rain's gone off," he said, peering through the kitchen window. The paths had already dried as if no storm had occurred. The cat, sitting smugly across the road, surely laughed at him.

Eager to verify their deductions, Ryder yanked open the front door. But he couldn't cross the threshold because the same huge guard, Sergeant Deal, fondled his MAG sub-machine gun and didn't look like stepping aside.

"Ah, Sergeant. Look, I'm sorry for the subterfuge earlier on, but we had a mission, just like you have missions. Nothing personal."

"I know that, Sir." In their first exchange, the sergeant's eyes looked straight ahead revealing nothing of the inner man. Now, they burned with vengeful anger. "Orders from the Security Council. You are under house arrest." His legs stiffened and fingers visibly tightened on the trigger.

Ryder and Jena couldn't stop laughing. They had to diminuendo rapidly when the realization hit them that Sergeant Deal didn't deal in humour. Jena gained acceptable speech first.

"Why are we under house arrest?"

"Don't bother asking him. He never knows anything."

"Oh, come on. Sergeant Deal looks like an intelligent man. He must know why he has to put two members of the Security Council under house arrest. Don't you?"

The guard shifted his feet as if slowly rehearsing an on-the-spot dance.

"See?" Ryder said. "Sergeant. You cannot put us under house arrest without a charge. So unless you tell us the charge, you have to go back to Mr Massey and ask for the charge document." Pleased with his bullshit, Ryder expected Deal to go off to Dominiq, but he stood, seemingly growing.

Jena smiled at the guard. "Sergeant, for how long are we under house arrest?"

"I've not been told, Ma'am."

"So you're going to prevent us leaving until told otherwise?"

"Yes, Ma'am."

"Are you going to be relieved at some point?"

His eyes twitched as his brain tried either to remember or work out the answer. "My superiors will have a schedule, Ma'am."

"But I'm worried about you, Sergeant. You will need your dinner and go to the toilet and sleep at night."

Deal stamped to attention. "We are trained to do our duty irrespective of personal needs, Ma'am."

Ryder thought better of making remarks about making puddles on his doorstep. "We'll bring you out a cup of tea." He shut the door. "That was cruel, Jena. Reminding him of a need to go to the toilet. He'll not be able to stop thinking of that now. I like it."

"I need a cup, now, to help me think this through."

As he walked to the kitchen, the situation hit Ryder. He'd coped with many difficult situations over the last eighteen months. Some, such as fighting savage dogs in a railway tunnel and being shot at by ARIA-infected youths, were potentially fatal. He had a reputation for being calm in a crisis, but his stomach rebelled by tightening. Deal looked as if he would riddle him with bullets. He'd had his military integrity abused and was in no forgiving mood. A striptease repeat wouldn't work this time. In any case, merely escaping from one situation to another didn't resolve the issue being created by Dominiq. Ryder called Abdul's mobile phone again.

"Abdul, stop faffing about and answer your phone."

Jena's cell phone bleeped. "It's a text from Abdul. He's at the backup backup site. VR auto launch Wednesday. Bryce still at Aroa, but so is Dominiq."

"That's no big surprise, although it's astonishing he'd let observers have his collusion with a quarantined patient be witnessed. Hey, we can use this information, Jena. In fact, we need it in order to extricate from this absurd situation."

"We can get out of this chalet without Deal noticing, unless he's running fast in circles." She went to the bedroom at the rear, and surreptitiously peeped through the blinds. "Just a cat."

"Assuming Deal doesn't speak cat, we can slip out, but then what? We need to contact people who agree with us that Dominiq has finished governing. We need what is left of the military on our side. Who can we trust?"

"There are several coast guard personnel, such as Tilley, but I wouldn't trust Bat."

"Ah, Jena, you have to understand the psychology of a gun-toting self-important clot like Bat. Look at the way he let off shots at Bryce. If we persuade him, with Tilley's connivance, that he can be temporary president of the whole of Rarotonga, or–why not?–The Cook Islands, he will not only be with us, he'll bully the rest of his cronies."

"Where do you think Emperor Bat will be now?"

"In the Yacht Club bar, such as it is, with its diminishing stock of malts and non-local alcoholic beverages."

"Ryder, do you want me to dress provocatively to help win him over?"

"You don't think it will. You just enjoy playing the tart, don't you? In fact, I think we should split up. I'll find Bat and work on him. If you like, I'll offer you as a treat. As for the real you, will you find our crew? Abdul, Gustav, and Teresa. Find them a safe place."

"And Bronwyn and Megan. We'll meet up–where?"

Ryder scratched his head. "I've noticed the cricket pitch is getting overgrown, so I guess the pavilion is unused and out of sight of the masses."

"I've no idea what or where the cricket pavilion is."

"Sorry, it's a Commonwealth legacy. Think of baseball but with more quaint rules. In fact, it's only a ten minute jog from where Tilley keeps her helicopter, which is another ten minute jog from the marina."

"Agreed. Give me your cell phone and NoteCom. I'll rapid charge them before we leave. Ryder, it's possible we won't be returning here. Backpacks with essentials?" While she plugged their mobile communications into the kitchen charger, he threw in some clothes, first aid, water, and concentrated food. He knew she'd add bathroom stuff and what medicines were viable. He fetched handguns and ammunition from under the bed, and a wallet of computer memory sticks. He discovered an MP3 recording of a talk show, and after putting it on a loop, set the volume to match their conversation before pressing play.

Jena re-inspected the bedroom window, opened it a little and checked again for observers. "I don't get it, Ryder. Deal might be a wooden top, but his training should've programmed him to secure all the exits."

"There is hardly any crime so less experience of control. Also, although Deal had a shock to his system when we conned him at the lab, he assumes that once we've been told to stay in the house, we'll do just that. Most of the islanders would do as they were told, especially when the teller has a weapon."

Ten minutes later, Jena unplugged their NoteComs and cell phones.

After checking that Sergeant Deal was still guarding their front door, Ryder slipped out through their ground-floor bedroom window. As soon as Ryder put his foot down, an ear-piercing sound shocked him so much, he staggered back. "Bugger, he's alarmed the place after all."

Jena leaned out of the window. "No, he hasn't, you idiot, look." A ginger cat ran faster than a bullet across the wet, unkempt lawn. The guard was bound to have heard. He needed to think they were still in the chalet.

"Go to the front door, quickly."

"What, and ask him what that racket was?"

"Yeah right. Ask him if he wants a cookie and hurry up about it."

CHAPTER 24

RYDER STOOD BY A BANANA PLANT, its huge leaves hiding him from the yacht clubhouse. He hesitated in his entry in search of Bat. It was likely that Dominiq's instructions to put him under house arrest would be known to the security personnel. On the other hand, maybe Dominiq had kept it as a covert operation since he wouldn't want anyone knowing of his visit to Bryce.

A residual raindrop dribbled onto him from an overhanging leaf, making him look up to greet a second drop in his face. While water was the least of his troubles, it spurred his decision to risk walking up the path and into the clubhouse.

The uniform was retired Colonel Marsh, immaculate in his white pressed trousers and navy-blue jacket with polished brass buttons. A New Zealand navy badge proudly announced itself on the breast pocket. The gold rope and crown, the silver anchor symbolising the past, and wishful thinking of the future.

"Colonel, have you seen Bat?"

"Flight Lieutenant Malise was in what you Americans call the John a few moments ago," he said, in between sipping his gin and tonic.

"I'm not an Amer— oh, never mind. Thanks." He saw Bat leaving the toilets, running fingers through his long, sandy-coloured hair.

"Bat, we need an urgent chat. Private."

"Okay, how about the function room down the corridor?" He led the way. "How's that temptress of yours? Quite a wildcat, ain't she?"

Ryder wondered if he should've let her work on Bat after all. Her work would have been half done by the sound of his adoration. "She's not far away." He waited until they were in the function room. Ryder hadn't explored the geography of the clubhouse so wondered what classed as functions here when all he saw were pool tables, dart boards and silent game machines. He ensured they were alone and the door shut.

"We have a problem with Dominiq and need your help."

"Welcome to the club, and I don't mean the Yacht Club. We've had trouble with him for years. Hey, hasn't he put you under arrest? I suppose that came and went with the wind too."

"He did and put Sergeant Deal on guard."

"Don't worry about Deal. Completely harmless. He enjoys playing soldiers."

"Are you sure? I didn't like the way his knuckles went white on the trigger."

"Really? Oh, I heard about Jena teasing him. Maybe you've riled him beyond his tolerance level. Um, unpredictable then."

"I'm more concerned about Dominiq's activities. You know that those two boat people are in quarantine for a very good reason, don't you?"

"The infectious amnesia bug? But I thought that was the point of the case being lowered to them. To cure them."

"We have no confirmation that it did, and more importantly, they might still be infectious. Yet, in spite of that, Dominiq has gone down to be with them."

"What? He's an even bigger idiot than I thought. Why would he do that?"

"I thought you knew that Dominiq and Bryce are related."

"Now that makes kinda sense. I was wondering why that Bryce would be so determined to reach us. His navigation system must have been radioed by Dominiq. Then, there's that hole in the fence." Bat looked as if he wanted to spit on the floor but hit his fist on the wall instead. "The stupid fucker. *He* might be infected now and losing his mind. I suppose that's that. We're done for!"

"Bat, we can't leave it there. He might bring them here and infect us. The only other person we know who was infected with ARIA-2 before having ARIA-1 went mental, killing his friends and colleagues."

"I'm getting what you're saying, Ryder. We have to expel them, or at least keep all three in quarantine for a few weeks. Right?"

"Sure, but can you see why Dominiq is making bizarre decisions on behalf of the Security Council to keep me and my group out of action?"

"I thought that was because you wanted to bring the third case back here and that was outvoted."

Ryder shuffled his feet, uncomfortable with having to lie. "No, that's been resolved. He's worried we'd tell everyone that Bryce is his relative."

"What do you want me to do about it? Tell the rest of the Security Council?"

Ryder took a deep breath. "That, of course, but also to gather some armed security people. They trust you. And ensure the quarantine integrity of Bryce, Benita and Dominiq before they come here and infect us all."

"Hang on, Ryder, this is sounding more like a military coup than a simple security manoeuvre."

"There's nothing simple in securing a cunning ex-colonel, who is so blinded by family ties, he's putting the safety of the whole island at risk. Nor is it simple to keep him under guard. Do you think you could manage that?"

"Are you kidding? I can rustle up a posse of armed-to-the-teeth team in no time."

Ryder smiled, but not too much. He'd finally caught Bat by his own pride. "Then go to it, Bat, like yesterday. And don't forget that Rarotonga will need a new leader. Could you manage that, too?"

"Gee, how did you know I'd had that dream. Boy, oh boy. Catch you later, Ryder. I've work to do."

"That's great, Bat. I hoped I could rely on you. One more thing. Can you arrange to have Dominiq's goons called off from my house and the others of my group? You could use them to guard him at Aroa."

There were loose ends, but Ryder had to get to the cricket pavilion, covertly. Sergeant Deal had yet to be apprised of the new situation.

Ryder gritted his teeth at the ignominy of having to sneak around taking cover behind walls and rubber trees. This island would be dying if it weren't for him and his escapee friends. He used to laugh at businessmen who'd say that their rivals were opponents but their enemies were standing right behind them. As he approached the cricket pavilion, he saw Teresa and Jena, along with Gustav and Abdul, already there.

Jena walked up and pointed behind him. "Your friend's here."

He turned and saw the ginger tomcat licking its paws. A young redheaded girl stopped running, picked up the cat then looked across at Ryder. He smiled at the thought of how similar they both were. The cat kept its nonchalant distain, but the girl smiled back and waved. Ryder returned the wave, pondering on how their manoeuvrings were for her generation, and the future, which made all this effort worthwhile.

CHAPTER 25

Wednesday July 13ᵗʰ 2016, Rarotonga.

SAVOURING THE LATEST STRATEGIC VICTORY, Ryder and Jena took breakfast at the yacht clubhouse veranda cafeteria. The rising sun chased away the morning dew, allowing Ryder to recall similar breakfasts of coffee and croissants at vacation apartments. The bittersweet coffee aroma was all the more pleasurable knowing he no longer needed to look over his shoulder for Dominiq's guards and that his decision to go for the third case to be retrieved was accepted by those around him.

Jena nudged his foot under the table. "This is what living on a vacation island should always be like."

Ryder was about to agree when his NoteCom beeped into life.

"Morning, Ryder. Charlotte has asked to be patched through to you. She's on your NoteCom."

"Hello, Charlotte. It's been a while since we had a chat, although I hear you and Abdul have a virtual love affair. What can I do for you? Is it morning there for you too?"

"Hi, Ryder. Yes, it's morning. It might be breakfast time for you, but it's four in the morning for me, tomorrow. I wanted to catch you. You do remember me?"

"Ah, Charlotte. You are often in our thoughts and not just because of your usefulness with regard to space communications and observations, believe me."

"I don't believe you intend to come and get me, in spite of your promises."

Ryder blushed even though he was five thousand miles away. "I'm sorry, Charlotte, it's not possible. Have you had any contact with other uninfected groups in Australia?"

"Don't you ever talk to Abdul and Teresa? I did have some radio contact six months ago from a Brisbane uninfected group, but they were surrounded by ARIA people. Nothing since. There's likely to be pockets of uninfected in ranches, mountain valleys, small coastal places, and out in the bush, but either their radios are down or they haven't tried my frequencies. I can't broadcast my location or use a frequency from which they can track me. Don't forget that the first cases of ARIA hit Australia within days of it reaching New York. That's over a year and three months ago. Many will have caught it within a week in all urban areas, losing sixty-five years of memory if they have enough life to lose that much. There's hardly a cattle ranch out here that doesn't get a visit every day from someone who's breathed in an aircraft or shook hands with someone who had. I'm scared witless, Ryder."

"I can imagine, Charlotte, sorry–again."

"I see smoke now and then from the south."

"Would that be from Perth? It's a big city so there might be fires from short circuits, lightning—"

"Ryder, Perth is five hundred miles away. I wouldn't see a nuclear mushroom cloud let alone bonfires. They might be from oldies fumbling around or, more likely, from younger people who'd only been infected in recent times. Either way, they're a danger to me."

"I've been told you've set up a good security system up there in the Carnarvon naval base? You've plenty of power, water, and food?"

"Are two navy ships counted as a naval base? Yeah. I raided the town supermarkets. I've enough to last three hundred years. But that's not the problem."

"Lonely, I guess. Must be tough."

"I thought I could cope, but the nightmares, loneliness, and the sheer turgid boredom makes watching paint dry exciting."

"We do appreciate the difficulty of your situation, Charlotte. We were in isolation at Anafon, but we had each other for company. I'm not sure what you expect us to do." Ryder knew what she expected him to do, but putting the lives of possible rescuers in danger wasn't a good option. "You're doing a great job for us."

"Ryder, most of what I do could be done anywhere with the appropriate receiver dishes, electronics, and computers."

Ryder shifted uneasily in his seat, threw a querying glance at Jena, who responded with a silent "whatever" fling of hands. "Decision made," he said, "I'm hesitant to suggest this, Charlotte, but have you considered commandeering a boat and coming here?"

"Yes, and no way. I'm a landlubber, Ryder. Surfboarding is the closest I've been to being in charge of a vessel. I could program the navigation systems, but I've no idea how much fuel to take, how to stop the boat turning in circles when I'm asleep, and the thought of repelling boarders and coping with stormy seas scares the shit out of me."

"Good. I wouldn't want you to try." Ryder had a fleeting thought of Bryce being able to sail, but over a relatively short distance, and with the assistance of Dominiq, but then Charlotte could have had similar guidance-system help. An incipient, devious plan niggled to be developed, but Charlotte threw another ingredient into the soup.

"I have a secret about the ISS and the aliens."

"Really? What's that?"

"It wouldn't be a secret if I told you."

Ryder could feel the edge she projected in her voice that said now come and get me. "I see you are indulging in playground games."

"You know I love you guys, but I have to look after myself too. If you want the information I have, the skills and equipment, then come and get me."

"I'll put it to the committee. In the meantime, I need some information. For instance–"

"I'm ahead of you, Ryder. If you arrive by air, there's thousands of gallons of aviation fuel and some aircraft here. Of course, the planes have been gathering dust for over a year, and looting took place in the early weeks. But if you–"

"Sorry, Charlotte, we won't be flying. We only have one aircraft capable of the distance, and with just enough fuel on the whole island to reach you. That means, with refuelling at your place, we'd result in no fuel at all after returning. We could hunt for more fuel en route, say in Fiji, or if we flew via New Zealand and South Australia, but we have no contacts there. Too risky."

"I thought that might be the case. At the docks here are huge stores of marine diesel in underground tanks. We'd have to manually extract the fuel. There are loads of barrels, hundreds, but I haven't done an inventory to see which are suitable. In any case, there's a flotilla of beautiful ships here, from pure sailing yachts to millionaire's floating playboy casinos. Two navy vessels."

"The navy vessels sound useful, though I doubt any of them can be jumped in and sailed straight away. Like the planes, they don't like being idle."

"Oh, a few extra barnacles and rust spots shouldn't be a problem, Ryder. Aren't you just being difficult?"

"Not at all. We all love you, Charlotte. I have to be practical, damn it, even if it makes me a beast. The batteries will be flat, including buffer backups for GPS systems. Bilge pumps will not have been working, probably in need of a thorough overhaul and pumping out before trusting to a five-thousand-mile journey. And you've had a couple of cyclones during the last year. Any damage?"

"Fair dues. Nothing much gets past you, does it? Yeah, we've had some big blows. Some boats are now dry docked in the car park, but the navy vessels are likely to be okay."

"As long as it's safe, you might as well look for something suitable for a return journey in case it's needed, or we help you bring one here on your own."

"Out of the question, Ryder. There's a reason why I haven't picked up sailing as a skill: I get gut-wrenching seasickness. I know I can dose myself, but then, I wouldn't be in a fit state to navigate and sail the bloody thing."

"Charlotte. I'm going to be too busy with Abdul flying the third case to France–so to speak–today, but can you wait a while longer?"

"Struth, I've been on my jack for over a year, what's another few weeks?"

"It would take three or four weeks for a fast boat to reach you, Charlotte, so take your time packing your bags. And I'm making no promises we can come for you at all."

"Bloody hell, I thought you couldn't resist rescuing fair maidens. Just to remind you, I am blonde with blue eyes, which are fluttering like crazy at you. I'll send you a self-portrait. There, that's yesterday's."

"Hah. Jena's looking daggers at me from across the breakfast table now. Keep in touch, Charlotte."

"There might be a break in comms soon, one of the secrets I referred to. But don't bust a gut, I'm working on a way round it."

"What do you mean, a break in comms? Damn, she's cut me off."

"About time someone did. So, you are going to rescue a damsel in undress distress? I thought you said you'd like to, but she and her satellite communications were too valuable where she is."

"Jena, situations change. In this case, her state of mind. Pity, she's gorgeous. I mean in her personality."

"Sure, let's see. Umm, look at those golden locks, squeaky-clean complexion and blue eyes. I wouldn't mind her myself."

"Hey, I saw her first."

"Not so fast. Let's have a closer look. What do you see behind her, Ryder?"

"The Indian Ocean. Ah, and what might be smoke. I'll send it to my computer for a better look. The zoom on this NoteCom isn't marvellous."

"There isn't any land out in that direction, is there? Madagascar's too far away. It could be a boat."

"Not unless it's on fire. According to my NoteCom gazetteer, there are a couple of islands just offshore. The smoke is possibly coming from Bernier Island. So, if we send rescuers, they might find company. Should I send her a warning, or is that needlessly worrying her?"

"Ask yourself, Ryder, if Charlotte was an ugly, fat, sweaty guy wearing a stained, tatty vest, would you devote valuable time and resources to rescue her–him?"

"No. But you haven't heard my deviously clever plan."

Ryder was about to elaborate when they heard running and doors slamming. Fearing a counter coup, he wished he'd armed himself. He exchanged concerned glances with Jena, who merely sipped at her coffee. Abdul burst onto the veranda. In spite of his lithe fitness, his words gushed out in short gasps. "The Space Station is down." He collapsed on a chair, staring wildly at the two of them.

Jena looked at him over her cup. "Do you mean the Return Vehicle is already down? It wasn't due to launch until fourteen hundred hours our time."

"No. Charlotte sent me a message overnight that we should launch as soon as possible, so I brought it forward. Sorry, I should've mentioned it. It's not landed yet. ETA thirty-two minutes. I've messaged the French and gave them a clue to crack the hatch-open code. But the ISS went offline ten minutes ago."

Ryder tapped his NoteCom a few times. "It must be online or we couldn't have just been nattering to Charlotte. The phones only work through the ISS?"

"It did, but there are several comms satellites she and I have been doubling up as relays. The ISS was used to synchronise data and boost signals, but if it went off air, we would be able to switch to the others."

Jena rapped the table. "So, she knew all along that the ISS was going offline. Was this her secret about the aliens and the ISS? Or did she remotely pull the plug on the ISS to make it look like the aliens?"

"No way," Abdul said. "I swear to you that she wouldn't jeopardize the ISS. It was too useful for her comms links."

"But you just said she's backed up the telecommunication facilities, so making the ISS less significant for her," Jena said.

Abdul sat heavily on a chair. "You don't understand, yet both of you should. The satellites drift both in orbit and calibration. They need to be kept in line to be online, so to speak. Charlotte and I have spent months so that the ISS did this automatically. Programming its robotic functions. We were working on making the ISS do the same for the telecommunication satellites within its range but hadn't finished. You may now find that the signals are much more erratic. She could program the Carnarvon satnav computers to assist, but the ISS was much better. Plus, she used it to monitor Hubble and other satellites for which we have no backups."

"Damn," Ryder said, "I forgot about Hubble. So, can we still talk to Manuel and the French group?"

"Not at the moment, I tried on the way here."

"I don't like it," Jena said. "How could she know the aliens were going to sabotage the ISS? I wonder what they did? Cut a few links to the transmitter dishes, zap it like they did the nukes, or flood it with a high-energy field?"

Abdul turned to her. "If they did the latter, maybe with a small nuke a few miles away so the electromagnetic pulse knocked out the electronics, we could be all right in a week or so as the electronics are purged and come online again."

"Don't get your hopes up," Jena said. "If the aliens wanted it out of action, why make it temporary, giving their enemies another opportunity to use the facilities against them?"

Ryder, cradling his chin with elbows on the table, said, "Suppose the Zadokians were hoping we sent a *Marimar* space vehicle up to the ISS to retrieve the case and so brought it back here or wherever we had a base. We didn't, and so now, they've temporarily knocked the ISS out. They assume we know there's a case up there and want it. So we assume there's a technical hitch and go up to try and fix it but return with the case. They then detonate the case with some superbug to wipe us out for good."

"Why do it after the case has left in the Return Vehicle?" Jena said.

"Maybe they don't know it has."

"How did Charlotte know any of this?"

"Jena, you are getting paranoid over her because she's pretty."

"But she used the ISS for the telescopes. She could've been monitoring the approach of one the alien ships."

Abdul looked out over the ocean. "I understand your logic even though they are huge assumptions. But I worry why my Australian girlfriend–and I saw her first by the way–didn't report any such Zadokian activity to me."

Ryder stood. "She had her reasons. You know she wants us to rescue her from her isolated base and was putting pressure on us, saying she knew a secret."

"Ah, she kept that a secret from me," Abdul said and laughed at Jena's pulled face. "But it's possible she detected something unusual without knowing what was about to happen. She's shrewd, you know."

Jena smiled at him. "My God, you men and pretty blondes."

Abdul looked at the ground.

Ryder tugged his arm. "Come on, we've work to do if we're going to try and see what comms are left to tell us where the third case is going to land."

Jena stood too. "I'm coming too, I want to see if Abdul's target practice is as good as he says it is."

Ryder hoped that Charlotte's re-routed uplinks, transfers and downlinks were ready in time for them to receive the telemetry from the Return Vehicle. They wouldn't have had any control over it, but it would have been useful to know whether it landed in the Gulf of Lion or missed the target and plopped in the middle of the Atlantic or crunched into the Vatican.

To his astonishment, a woman in the lab was monitoring the screen displaying an image of Bryce. Ryder rushed over to see Bryce and Dominiq on the computer.

"I thought the links were down. Is the ISS back online? Sorry, what's your name?"

"It's Tania, Mr Ryder, Sir. And the local networks work independently of satellites. We are using our mobile phone and landline network. Always have."

"Tania, keep up the monitoring, you are doing a grand job. Can I get you a coffee?"

"Cola, please."

Abdul called from the ISS-dedicated console. "Tea for me, Ryder. You might as well make yourself useful, there's nothing on here, yet."

Ryder brought the drinks over but stopped to stare at Abdul's monitor. "But you seem to have a normal screen."

Abdul reached for his drink while studying his monitor. "I didn't say our network wasn't working. We can still communicate around the island and with some of the satellites I have links to."

Ryder came forward to prevent Abdul's lunge for his drink becoming a disaster. "So, can we receive telemetry from the Return Vehicle?"

"Sadly, no."

"Damn. I hoped it could be received directly by one of our dishes."

"It could, but we haven't had the time to re-calibrate the hardware nor configure the software. Charlotte could have done it, but she's not here and still not online."

"I thought anything she could do, you could do better."

"Ryder. I am an astrophysicist, subordinate to Jena. I know enough comms to get by, and I am fast. Charlotte is a postgrad telecommunications engineer. I've been enormously impressed by what she zaps over to me, but this was unforeseen. It takes days, sometimes weeks, to make and test re-configurations. You've no idea."

"I wish I had a day's pay for every time someone says that to me. When will it be too late to get the telemetry?"

Abdul looked at his computer clock. "Two minutes ago. It should be down now."

"Bugger. Let's hope the French group got our message in time and pick up the case. Damn, I was hoping to give them detailed instructions on handling and the immediate future." He was about to bang the desk but had greater respect for the equipment: hard drives and earthquakes don't mix.

"Ryder, you need to relax. You have a tendency towards control freakery. Gustav, Teresa, and I have sent bilingual bulletins to the French group. Leave them to us while you focus on the danger from that quarantine group. They're our greatest danger, as you know."

CHAPTER 26

Wednesday July 13th 2016. Bryce Massey, thirty-eight, ARIA victim, has lost his memory back to when he was fourteen. Benita Eyes, mid-thirties, is Bryce's woman. Neither remember how or when they met. Both have been exposed to the ARIA-2 case before being ordered to a quarantine chalet at Aroa on the south of Rarotonga. They are watched by camera and armed guards are nearby.

THE THREE OF US LAUGH as we charge at the waves. Before we hit the water, I grab Kev's arm so I can get in front, but he falls and, shrieking, I tumble over him. Glen doubles over with hysterics. Miss Keebles shouts at us to stop horsing around and keep out of the water, but we take no notice. School trips are for getting away from being told what to do. She's already liberated the crabs we raced for dollars behind the Bondi Beach rock pool and screamed at us to match the cries of the seagulls we ran at. More for teasing her. Glen had pulled Kimberley's bikini top off, but it's less fun when she merely smiles.

"You three get back here."

"Or what?" shouts Kev, giggling like his sister. We join in. Yesterday's science exams receding happily, we kick sand at a small dog and run into the sea. Brrr, that's colder than I thought it'd be.

"Bryce. Bryce, it's me."

Is that Miss Keebles yelling at me, again? Tell her to bugger off.

"Bryce. You're getting another mug of water over you if you don't wake up."

I've just had a wet dream, so to speak. I look at the woman. Ben... Benita. Hey, I remember her name.

"Morning, Benita, thanks for the early bath. I dreamt of Bondi Beach, have you been there?"

"Yeah, full of fucking needles in the sand and idiots snatching at my top."

Funny how memories and dreams are so different. She's right about the needles.

"I remember your name. Did I remember it yesterday?"

"Dunno. Look, you oughta know summing."

"I remember last night. We had burgers and instant mash for

supper. Before that's a fog, or is it fug? Are we married? Do we have kids? How did we get here?"

"Bryce. Shut up. Someone's coming."

"So? Oh, we're supposed to be on our own. Infection quarrel? No."

"Quarantine. I read the notes to be sure. We had the amnesia infection, but they exposed us to what they hope is a cure. Sort of. Here, read it yourself."

"Benita, that explains why I remember you from yesterday but not before. Bugger, my head hurts. Do you have a jarring buzz in your head, right in the middle?"

"The beers we downed last night—hey, but you only had a couple. Maybe it's our memories, fighting their way back in. Those people have stopped."

She's looking out the window while I read stuff on my NoteCom, but some of it's hard words I don't know.

"Apart from yesterday and this ridiculous old body, my head tells me I'm still at school, and you're not there. Do you know those people coming?"

"I'm at school too. But it might be South Africa—dunno. Nah. Man and a woman. Look harmless enough. Maybe they're quacks."

"Pretty stupid if we're in quarantine, even if they are doctors." I stop reading and look out the window. A tall, thin man with blond hair looking familiar. Even as he brings his hands up like a megaphone, something tingles the back of my neck.

"Bryce, can you hear me?"

"Who wants to know?" I shout my usual childish rejoinder.

"Do I need to say?"

"Bryce," says Benita. "It's difficult to be sure, but if you shaved off your scraggy chin hair, that could be you out there."

"Can't be. My brother's a kid. What am I saying? He's just two years younger than me. It must be Dominiq. He must know what's happened to Mum and Dad." I go to the door and take a few steps out to be sure. Now, my stomach is boogieing to the weird noises in my head. "Dominiq, is that you?"

"You bet it is. Come here, brother." His flashing white teeth brightens his whole face. It is him. I run to him, and we hug like the long lost, which it is for him, even if not for me.

"Bryce, what's happened to your ear, there's a notch out of the lobe?"

I finger the sore ear. "I dunno, Dom. No idea, and nor does Benita."

"Most men put notches in their bedposts," says the woman, and then she laughs.

"Here, Bryce, you remember Nessa?"

I look at the woman behind him biting her nails and shuffling her feet. Her brown hair hides half her face like partly closed theatre curtains. I've no recollection of her. Is she your wife?"

"Oh, come on, Bryce, I know you've lost some memory, you came to our wedding in Wellington five years ago, and—" he lowers his voice. "It was after divorcing Rachel. You remember that firecracker?"

I shake my head. "Dominiq, my last memory of you is what feels like a couple of days ago at your thirteenth birthday party."

He grins at me, but the mouth muscles are fighting. He doesn't believe me. He glances at his notes then at Benita. "Is she your new wife? What's her name? Benita?"

"I don't know."

Poor Dominiq can't take in the reality of this ARIA problem. Nor can I. Until yesterday, I had only a day at a time to get used to it.

"You must know if you two are married. Have you wedding rings?"

Benita waves her hand at the pair of them. "We both have rings, but it doesn't mean we're married to each other. We might've been living in sinful ignorance for years."

"Or just a few days," I say. "Dominiq, why are you here? Isn't there a danger of infection from us?"

"I took that chance when I brought you here. Ah, yes. It wasn't coincidence that your navigation system brought you to Rarotonga on both occasions–the *Viking Moon* flotilla and this last one."

"I've no idea what *Viking Moon* is, and I don't remember coming here. You don't get it, do you? I have amnesia bad. All the last twenty-odd years has gone. Not even flashes or bits–all gone."

"Help me get my head around this," says Dominiq, clearly in a state of bewilderment while Nessa and Benita circled each other like two cats readying for a fight. "When you wake up in the mornings, do you remember the day before your memory disappears as clear as if it just happened?"

"Dominiq, you are just as big a prat as you always were. Let me see." I look at my NoteCom. "Do you remember what you did on Tuesday July 12, 1992?"

"What? Of course not. But it's different for you. I have twenty-four years of remembered events since then while you have none."

"I too have had those years for my brain to forget everyday events. They don't become fresher just because the intervening clutter is zapped."

"Tell him the rest," says Benita.

"What rest?" says Dominiq, looking worried.

"I guess she means the headaches, ringing in the ears..."

"You mean tinnitus?"

"I don't know. If that is a word for ringing in the ears that I've forgotten, then yes. Add to that the weird smell memories and dizziness. Other stuff too, I can't think of right now. Benita?"

"He means sex. We have adult hormones but child memories of what to do about it. But there's more related to hormones and sex, but I can't remember how I worked it out, if I did. I'm confused."

"There," I say. "I couldn't have put it better. And now you might have it too."

"Not likely. You've been exposed to the second case, so the ARIA-1 should be stopped and not infectious. We hope. Anyway, we couldn't carry on not knowing, nor without you. Why do you think I risked so much to bring you here?"

"I haven't had time to think about it. How's Mum and Dad taking it all?"

"Now it's your turn to be confused, Bryce. The ARIA effect started last year. Almost everyone would have lost around sixty years of memory. Most died from lack of medicine, food, warmth, feral dogs, clean water, and God knows what else. Mum and Dad would be fifty-eight now. Last I heard, they were in Perth. ARIA reached their city within days of it reaching New York. I'm afraid they must have passed away, brother."

He comes to me for a hug. My eyes fill. Why hadn't that inevitable idea come to me? Everyday I had to cope with surviving and filling my temporary memory with the absolute necessary information to get me through 'til bedtime. It never occurred to me to think Mum and Dad would've died. My knees give way, and I sink to the lush, grassy, unkempt lawn. Dominiq, also weeping, still in my embrace, sinks with me. The tinnitus is driven out by a red wave as logic fights emotional denial.

After minutes of mutual sobbing, I notice Benita on the ground convulsing with cries too. I don't know where her family is from. I might have asked every day, but not today or yesterday. They're probably gone too. And, of course, she wouldn't know where her parents had moved to since her teens, like I don't. Dominiq's right. We're all fucked up so much. I see Nessa hugs Benita. Group misery yet in mutual comfort.

After more minutes, we all lie looking at broken clouds skidding from the west. My back is damp from the dew to match my face.

"Bryce, do you know why you two were so late in catching ARIA? I'm glad, but by rights, you two should have lost more memory than you have life."

"Guess."

Benita throws grass at me. "Ignorant Bryce means that we can only guess we were on an island untouched by human hand until infected visitors called a few months ago."

"I can't get used to you two not knowing where you've been or your activities this last year, let alone the last twenty years. You won't remember where I found you."

I see Nessa give him a dirty look as if to shut him up. "Okay, Dominiq, how did you contact me? Ah, on this NoteCom. I never have time to read everything."

"My messages are likely still on it," says Dominiq, ignoring Nessa. "You've been working as an anthropology lecturer, researching in isolated communities on Samoa. Sorry, Benita, if I'd known your surname, I would have done a person trace on you too. It's probable you were with Bryce as his assistant."

"I might have been his professor," she says, sticking her nose in the air to emphasise his chauvinist assumptions.

"Maybe. Anyway, I sent an encrypted navigation homing signal to your NoteCom, so whenever you were close enough to the nav systems on a boat, it would lead you here. Unfortunately, you didn't come alone."

"Thanks a bunch."

"No, I don't mean you, Benita. You are welcome. Good company and that for Bryce." He coughs his embarrassment away as we laugh, including Nessa. "I mean you brought a whole fleet of infected pirates."

"I've no recollection of this at all, as you know. Are you sure we were with them?"

"The launch you sailed to this island, the *Second Mortgage III* is the same as in the flotilla with the car ferry, *Viking Moon*."

"And what happened?" says Benita before I can say it.

"I was against any violence," says Dominiq, looking me straight in the eye. "I wanted to protect you, but I couldn't tell the other islanders that you were my brother, could I? They'd be suspicious of everything I did. I'm afraid we have some new people with us, who are very aggressive and tried to take over. If it was up to them, you'd both be at the bottom of the sea by now."

"How come these new people aren't infected? Or are they immune?"

"They isolated themselves in Britain; their leader is Ryder. Watch out for him... he wants to take over. The others are from the space station. There doesn't seem to be anyone who's immune, although there's talk about a woman in Australia who might be."

164 | **ARIA: Returning Left Luggage**

"I still don't get why you've taken a life-threatening risk by coming down here. I thought our quarantine was for the benefit of the islanders, including you, but also for us."

"I don't get that one," says Dominiq. "How can you be in danger other than side effects from ARIA-2?"

"In my notes, it says some memory-loss people in Canada behave like zombies after catching ARIA-2 and others became killers. No one knows why. So, it was thought we shouldn't come into contact with non-ARIA people."

Benita waved her arm at the hills. "And there might be trigger-happy nutters out there, just looking for target practice. We're safer here, being guarded."

"We hope you don't mind," Nessa says, "but we'll be house guests for a while. I don't think they'll let us back in the town."

"There's several habitable chalets," says Benita, giving me a wide-eyed look saying no. But I kinda like the notion of being with my brother again.

"Or you can use the spare bedroom in our chalet." I stick my tongue out at Benita, and she retaliates in kind, making me realize how childish we two thirty-somethings are. Hopefully, Dominiq will interpret our behaviour as ARIA symptoms.

"A neighbouring chalet is fine," says Dominiq, as we stand then discover our damp backsides. He has a Jeep. He must have clothes and provisions. Has he brought any candy? There I go again.

Nessa, now alone with us, bites her knuckles. I guess she'd bite her nails but they'd spoil. I can't remember when I last saw emerald-green nail varnish. Her nervousness makes her take a few steps back. I ought to go hug her. After all, she's my sister-in-law. But Benita, bless her, beats me to the niceties.

"Come on, Nessa, let me show you your chalet and how stuff might work." She winks at me as if sharing my opinion that Nessa is one useless bitch.

CHAPTER 27

DOMINIQ SCREECHES TO A HALT, scattering beach gravel. Grinning, as if just about to start a well-earned vacation, he nods at the cartons in the back. I help unload.

"It looks like you've emptied a store, Dominiq. You know we can supplement our food from the land and sea?"

"There you go again. It's been years since, as kids, we used to live on fish we caught and bananas. I'm more used to *haute cuisine* these days. Hence, these packets of biscuits." We both laugh. Our merriment isn't equal, how can it be? I laugh with him and his silly joke, but it's disconcerting. That person pretending to take a caricature mighty bite out of a packet of biscuits—an item that must be rare on this island—is my last memory of my dad, when Dominiq was a stupid kid. So, I laugh out of embarrassment, mine, for not coping with emotions too well. He laughs because he's made a monumental error coming here. He must know it, and he's involved his wife. Awful situation. He should have waited. On the other hand, how will anyone know if we're infectious if no one visits? Maybe they were waiting a few weeks for our bodies to settle down with the new virus stuff in us and then send a prisoner or someone they hated. Nah. Okay, they wait until some drunk blunders into us and then play it by ear. Sure as hell, this Ryder leader man didn't plan to send Dominiq here, unless he wants rid of him.

IT MIGHT BE THE SUN WAKING ME UP. The split bamboo blinds allow the dawn rays to find my face. It might be the exquisite pleasure I am experiencing lying flat on my back with the first full erection I remember having. It's so hard, it hurts, but I don't want it to stop. I turn my face to the left but the hills in the pillow block our eyes meeting. I lift my head a smidgeon and lower again to flatten the white landscape, sending motes dancing in the sunlight and enabling us to smile at each other.

"Morning, Brycie."

"Hi, Bennie."

"It would be lovely if you'd do the same for me."

"Ah, so that is your hand, is it?"

"You mean you've lost contact with your own hands? Shame, I was hoping they might find me."

"Oh, all right then," I say, and my left hand travels under the sheet in exploratory mode. The notion that we must have already explored each other's body many times is pushed away. Maybe a benefit of amnesia is the novelty of sexual experience each time. However, when the amnesia erodes to puberty, brain and hormones become confused. ARIA-2 must be working if we have those feelings back again, or maybe our bodies are readjusting anyway. I feel very weird. I'm floating in a sea of emotions and fuzzy brain functions. It must be the aliens sneaking into my head, whether they mean to or not.

A large green beetle looks at me from above the window. What is it thinking about these humans?

"Brycie, are you going to sleep again? Oh, for fuck's sake, you're analysing again, aren't you?"

"Well..."

"Put your logic circuits on hold and let your hands free. Do you want to be the man with the best laid plan or plan to be the best laid man?"

I gasp. Has she always been this clever? If I'm not married to this woman, I want to be, although that's irrelevant in this post-ARIA world. I'm doing it again, using thinking instead of action. Oooh, but she's not stopped. My left hand extends and my fingers find warm, silky flesh that yields. Her stomach, I think. Up some and around the bulbous curves of her breasts tipped with erect, hard nipples. My fingers toy with them, and besides moaning, Benita squeezes me. I hurt, but without tears, so I think she isn't being passionate so much as exercising control. Does that mean she is afraid I'll pounce on her, or that I won't? My hands wander down across a smooth, undulating plain into furry domains. Into her oasis, and her moans sing higher. I hear chirping and wonder if my tinnitus is changing or whether the finches outside are joining in the chorus with our hormonal harmonics.

My ARIA-sensitised nose tells me she's musky moist, which means she's expecting me to be manly and do what should come naturally with two hot humans. I'm sure I'll be all right. Do what's expected. I might have forgotten all the sexual encounters I've ever had, but this is instinct, surely. I mustn't get worried, or my performance might be—no, I mustn't think about it.

I feel I ought to turn to her and initiate post-foreplay proceedings, but her grip remains. To be more accurate, my surging hormones are urging me to leap on her.

I whisper so as not to spoil the mood. "Hey, Benita, loosen your hand so I can come aboard?"

This is where I find if my ardour is a misdemeanour, a misconstruing of sad proportions.

"I might not want you on top."

"You're welcome to come here and play cowgirl." How do I remember that positional term? Is all this raised testosterone and other chemical cocktails enabling memory short circuiting? A revitalising up there as a by-product of reenergising down there?

I look into her deep brown eyes. Her eyebrows quiver with confusion. Oh cruel fate if my body has its readiness before hers. I start running the emotional programme leading to abort mission when I see her eyebrows steady and a lascivious smile spreads. The minx is teasing. Her hand slides up and down twice more before relinquishing its hold. She throws back the covers and swings herself over me.

"Hi ho, Silver."

"What? Careful!"

IN THE AFTERGLOW, the extra snooze, the relief that components have remembered their functions, my smile is so big my mouth aches. The beetle scuttles off in fear.

Turning to Benita, I find a crumpled sheet. A clatter in the kitchen tells me breakfast is on the way.

"Come on, Bryce. Looks like visitors on the way and lunch is ready."

"What happened to breakfast? Oh." I look through the window expecting to see Dominiq, but a humvee blocks our path. Biohazard suits point guns in our direction. "How long have they been there?"

"Dunno. Before I came into the kitchen. They copped a good eyeful before I realized and threw on my T-shirt."

"Why didn't you wake me?"

"You were exhausted, poor thing. And look, they're not threatening. Two of them walked over to Dominiq's chalet ages ago. Here, grab a coffee while I finish omeletting these eggs."

I do as I'm told while staring at our guards. With a flash, I remember that this chalet is bugged with cams, but I restrain myself from reminding Benita that our antics might have been a highlight feature on the island's fantasy channel this morning. I retrieve my NoteCom from the charger and check for messages from Dominiq. Nothing, so I call him.

"Hi, Dominiq, do you want me to come over to say hi to your friends?"

"Hang on for ten. They need to replace their air tanks, then we are conferencing in your chalet. Some interesting proposals are coming our way. See you then."

A shiver runs through me. Dominiq, being the younger, is always running away–the little squirt–because he's nicked my hat, kite, comic, sandwich...

The only memories I have of him being cunning is when he'd manipulate fights with his school enemies so I'd be the one battling in the dust on his behalf. The thought of him negotiating "interesting proposals" does not auger well.

I open the door to let Nessa and Dominiq in, followed by a biohazard suit, which I presume has a person inside.

"Please, take a seat," I say, but Dominiq's knitted eyebrows tell me he's in no mood for niceties.

"Bryce, this is Bat Malise, Commander of the air force on this island before the trouble. He's brought a proposal, originating from Ryder Nape, the unofficial leader here. I think we have to accept what they say."

"Hang on. Benita and I have gone through hell to get here. We might have the memories of kids, but we're adults, and not about to cast ourselves off again, if that's the plan."

Bat coughs, which isn't clever behind a facemask. His voice came through like a dog growling. "I don't give a shit about you two insurgents. You've compromised the health of everyone on this island, and though I know it wasn't entirely your doing—" His mask looks at Dominiq and then back at me. "I insist that you consider this proposal. It gives you an element of freedom while still in quarantine. The alternative is being guarded night and day here. And with the cameras running in every room. Savvy?"

Benita touches my arm and gasps as she realizes we provided X-rated TV this morning.

"What's wrong with us going to one of the small islands nearby? They have cabins like this but no one there. We could have provisions–"

"No, you might sneak back. It would be too difficult to monitor you all the time. Listen up. Now, the four of you are to be kept the hell away from this island until the medics say you are non-infectious. Maybe several months before they're one hundred per cent sure that Dominiq and Nessa haven't picked up nasties from you two."

Benita and I share glances of horror.

"Or we could send the four of you on a cruise. A mission of mercy that would keep you from contaminating us yet provide humanity with a service." Through the facemask, I can see Bat's eyes sparkle and laugh, surely sharing the joke with a big, unseen grin.

I say, "I've looked at our little boat, *Second Mortgage*–I don't know what that means–and I don't fancy a long journey squashed in it with four of us."

"It wouldn't be suitable for this mission," says Dominiq. "You were lucky not to be attacked by pirates. All right, there might not be any, but equally, there might be isolated people on islands like this, who are getting desperate for provisions. I don't mean to scare anyone, but we are taking one of the two coast guard cutters. It's armed with a gun as well as small-arms fire, rockets, flares, sonic weapons, you name it. Plenty of accommodation for four of us and for extra passengers on our return."

"Extra passengers?" Benita looks worried.

"Sonic weapons?" I say.

Bat laughs, which is too creepy when in a mask. "It emits a powerful subsonic boom that can rupture lungs. It's proved effective against pirates, sharks, and, hell, it might tame the weather for ya."

Dominiq turns to Benita. "There is an uninfected woman, Charlotte Teems, who is on her own in Carnarvon on the west coast of Australia. She's lonely and scared of getting infected."

I see he's speaking directly to Benita in an appeal to the soft-touch woman. I've a feeling it won't work on her. Dominiq has much to learn about Benita, but then, so have I.

Benita flutters her eyelashes at Dominiq. "Of course, we have to rush to any damsel in distress. I suppose you have a list? There must be many of them all over the southern hemisphere. I don't know the exact distance, but it must be at least three thousand miles away."

"Just over five," says Bat.

"So," continues Benita, "what's so special about Charlotte?"

"You're pretty smart for someone who's not right in the head," says Bat. "Okay, Charlotte is a real smart cookie, too. She's a telecommunications whiz whose expertise is space satellite comms, that sort of thing. We need her to solve some problems."

I have a feeling he's keeping vital information back from us. Is it his lowered eyes or the way he's pulling the cane strips out of a basket-weave place mat?

Nessa blurts it out. "She says she has a secret about the aliens but won't tell us unless we rescue her. The bitch."

Benita laughed. "Is that it? You're sending the four of us out on the wild ocean for weeks on end just on the ravings of a mad woman?"

"It's not that simple," growls Bat. "She really is a NASA-trained expert on comms. She's been known to Ryder's people and the astronauts from the Space Station over a year. And she's access to satellites and orbital telescopes that we don't. She's been running detection software on the remote sensing sats too. Lord knows what, but if there's anything to find about the aliens in space, Saturn, the moon, or on Earth, she's the most likely person to know it."

"I bet she's a cutie," says Benita, receiving a wry smile from Nessa. I didn't think these two women were going to get along. Now, they have a common adversary, however imagined, they might do just fine.

Bat turns back to Benita. "You shouldn't worry about the trip itself. The *Solar Sprint* is a beauty. Built for heavy seas yet fast and well equipped. You'll be in communication all the way, and you will have GPS." I see him flick his eyes to Dominiq. Now what? I test them out.

"Is the satellite communication and GPS satellites working then? I thought they needed ground servers and relays?"

Bat coughs again. Stupid man. "Okay, so the ISS has gone offline, and we were using it as the main orbital controller for comms, but we are working on getting other satellites online instead. There's dozens we can use."

"Let me get this straight," I say, getting closer to his faceplate. "At this moment, there is no GPS working and you wouldn't be able to keep in touch with the boat once it's over the horizon. Right?"

"Right."

"And presumably, you've lost contact with this Charlotte genius too?"

"Don't forget that Abdul and Jena, both skilled NASA-trained engineers too, are working flat out to rectify all this. It's not an 'if' situation but a 'when.'"

Benita says, "So, Bryce is right, you can't speak to Charlotte?"

"By the end of today we will. I expect. Even if, by some unlikely horrible circumstance, Charlotte isn't there, her notes and equipment would be invaluable to be brought back here."

Dominiq waves his hands. "You're thinking she might have been overcome by strangers who would've given her ARIA. Well, look at me and Nessa. We could stop it developing. We seem to be okay."

"So far," says Bat.

"Fair enough, and that's why we need a period of quarantine. But a voyage with a humanitarian purpose and a useful outcome is heaps better than being cooped up in here."

"I'd like to remind you," says Bat, "that you are not amateurs out for a joyride. You, Bryce, used to do a lot of offshore sailing in your twenties, according to your brother here. Okay, so you've forgotten, but it shows you have the ability. I dunno if muscles have memory. I'll leave that to the biologists, but seeing how you managed that little craft across open water to here while full ARIA infected is impressive. Also, you'll not remember this, but Dominiq was a colonel in the New Zealand army with special training in marine liaison."

"A desk job?" I say.

"Near the end, yes, but I have thousands of hours on board similar vessels to the *Solar Sprint*."

"We could do with time to mull over this," I say. "I presume you have plans we can see? Charts, provision lists?"

Bat blows as if to remove condensation inside his mask. "I've printed them out. They're on the *Solar Sprint*, which is sailing around from Avarua as we speak. But I've sent some of the crucial data to your NoteComs. You can think all you like about it, Bryce, but you don't have much choice. You're going."

I laugh at him. "You are in no position to force us, Bat. A few miles out, we could decide to head for Indonesia and try our luck for a better life there. We've nothing to fear from meeting ARIA-infected people even if you have."

Bat sneers back at me, although it comes out more like a cat in pain. "There's more than ARIA out there, you idiot. Plague, smallpox, and probably worse—with no antibiotics, no hospitals. Anyways, don't underestimate our determination and ability. What if I say *Viking Moon* to you? Eh, that's got you."

"*Viking Moon*? What are you blathering about?"

Dominiq steps forward. "Bat, you fool, these two won't remember anything about *Viking Moon*." He pulls at Bat's sleeve trying to take him to one side, whispering. I look at Nessa who shrugs, as does Benita. I switch on my NoteCom and do a text search in my old memory-aid notes.

"It's all right, Bryce," says Dominiq, clearly in an anxiety state. "You don't need to look for it. Irrelevant."

I find the brief entries about the ship and show it to Benita. I seethe, she gasps. "You sank the boat with people on it?"

"It's not as simple as that," says Dominiq, holding his hand up as if we are about to attack him.

"Did they all get off?" says Benita.

"You did," says Bat. "And we don't think there were many—"

"It's a fucking car ferry," says Benita reading on through tear-filled eyes.

"Even so, we don't think there were many on board."

I'm not convinced. "Then, why the need for additional boats, like the one I was on?"

"Look, Bryce," says Dominiq, "if it was just up to us islanders, we would have guided you to a nearby island, but it's this Ryder and his lot. They'd only just arrived and persuaded the Security Council that your flotilla had to be turned back. I didn't agree."

"I agreed," says Bat. "You represented a real danger to us here. There might have been hundreds of you. We'd have no chance of controlling all of you."

"But you had the case with ARIA-2," says Benita.

Bat is defiant. "It had only just arrived with Ryder's group. No one had studied it or made any contingency plans. Anyway, how do you expose one case to hundreds of people in several different boats? Anyhows, it's done. What would you have done, Bryce... in our position?"

"I'd like to say, 'I don't know.' I know it puts my feelings about undertaking a dangerous mission on behalf of the people of this island in another light."

"It might," says Bat, "but it shouldn't, because this island and the expertise on it are your only chance of surviving to old age on this stricken planet. And in that vein, I have to say that if we detect the *Solar Sprint* veering too far off the course we've set for you, we will come after you."

"Was the *Viking Moon* armed?" I say.

"Yes," says Bat, "but although your boat, as a coast guard cutter, is well armed as I've already itemised, we are better armed, so remember that."

A charged silence fills the chalet and spills out of the window where I see the coast guard cutter coming around the headland. I look at Benita, and she has tears cascading. I quiz her with my eyes, but she is crying for the loss of many. We don't remember the incident. Damn it, we can't recall the boat at all. Her family might have been in that ocean with bullet splashes being sent up by Bat and Dominiq, but we don't know. The tears are for what might have been. We know real people, who were as desperate as us, struggled in pain in their last moments. I am about to point at the *Solar Sprint* when I see Nessa whisper in Dominiq's ear.

He pulls again at Bat's sleeve and addresses us. "It's better for us if we want to go and perform this mission in spite of past tragedies. Partly, too, because of them, so others haven't died in vain."

I'm getting tired of the bullshit and about to tell him, but he floors me with a huge grin. "And there's always a possibility of finding our mum and dad."

What's this? He tells me yesterday they must be dead. Of course, he also said they were last seen in Perth.

Bat obviously doesn't like doubtful penalty shots. "I'm not sure it will be possible or safe to mount an extra mission..." He looks at Dominiq who is evil-eyeing him. "But I suppose we'll have to rely on your discretion when you arrive at Carnarvon and assess the situation."

BY THE TIME WE LOAD OUR MEAGRE POSSESSIONS on the *Solar Sprint*, learn how to help Dominiq with the Boeing 747-like controls in the cockpit, and the more complicated ones in the galley, the sun slips into the sea. The cowardly women wanted to wait until daybreak, but us macho men slip anchor, and so, here we are, at dusk, sensuously bobbing.

"This is ridiculous," says Nessa, moaning about setting sail at night. "I know we don't need to see the sea and the chances of hitting anything are infinitesimal with all our gadgets."

"And the lack of other boats," I say, although that's a bit weak considering what I did only last week.

Benita shouts down to us, excited. "Come up here you two, quick."

So we join her and Dominiq, who's using the topside steer controls. An explosion startles us, and we turn to see a flare that looks like it came from the mountain in the middle of Rarotonga. But in no time, I see it's a firework, then another, a coruscating display.

"They're giving us a grand send-off," says Dominiq.

I laugh and then can't help myself saying, "They must be celebrating our departure."

"Hey, they are hoping we're successful," says Dominiq. "Both in rescuing Charlotte and in proving us being with you ARIA-2 characters does us no harm."

"Yes, be grateful they're wishing us well, you ingrate," says Benita, giving me a dig in the ribs.

The display lasts less than two minutes, but it cheers us. "I suppose they haven't enough fireworks for a Sydney Harbour Bridge New Year event," says Benita.

"More likely, they don't want to attract too much attention from the aliens in orbit," says Dominiq.

"Or casual eyes from nearby islands," says Nessa.

My NoteCom bleeps, and I'm surprised to find Dominiq's archenemy, Ryder speaking to me. "Hi, Bryce. We haven't had an opportunity for a chat. I have to leave that to your brother, but I want you to know that we have a lot of trust in you. I've told Dominiq that if you get into *real* trouble, just head home, which is here. If you need rescue in an extreme emergency, we'll use our last drop of aviation fuel to fly as far as Northern Australia, but we'd need refuelling to get you back. The helicopters have a two-hundred-mile radius. Are you getting this?"

"Yes, I am, Ryder. Thanks for the vote of confidence. We'll do what we can to bring Charlotte back, along with the information and equipment you need."

"All of us need it, Bryce. We do have a long-term plan, even if it seems we're living day to day. Anyway, the best of luck from all of us. We'll keep in daily touch until we're out of range."

"I thought the satellite links would be fixed to enable us to contact you all the way?"

"Did Bat say that? No matter. We hope so, Bryce. Keep tuning in."

Everybody wants to know what he said, so in spite of the call lasting less than two minutes, it took fifteen to repeat it all with interpretations.

I leave the women to fuss in the galley while I see if Dominiq needs help at the upper cockpit.

"I'm going to get dizzy keeping an eye on all these screens," I say, noticing the radar shows nothing else moving.

"Most of it isn't needed unless it emits a warning buzz. Events like collision alerts, incoming missiles, and shallow-water advisements aren't likely to happen often unless Nessa's driving. Hey, she's not listening, is she?"

"If she isn't, I'll tell her what you said."

CHAPTER 28

Friday July 15ᵗʰ 2016, 23:00 hours.

I CAN'T SLEEP, so I take over the midnight watch an hour early. Dominiq grumbles about keeping to proper watch times and not to touch anything because it's all on auto. When and if the GPS satellites come on line again, we could be fully automatic. The computers will make all the navigation decisions and would get us to Carnarvon. But people prefer to be in charge and risk human error—and they get them. On auto at the moment means a fixed bearing of 220 at a slow twenty knots. I don't need to do anything. Electronics sound an alarm if we drift off course or if we are about to ram something big enough to make a dent. It would also do an emergency stop, which means taking seventy-five metres to come to a dead halt.

"Hi, Bryce," Nessa says, coming up behind me. "Can't you sleep either? I'm not surprised. It's quite an unusual adventure for all of us, isn't it?" She puts a warm hand on my right forearm as if I need comforting.

"Bryce, let's wander down to the gun deck."

"Why? Do you intend to make some parting shots at the island? Give them a firework show with real metal?"

"No, I have an intermittent pain in the neck."

"Yes, he was the same as a kid."

"Funny. I get spondylitis, so if I want to gaze at the stars, I need to lie down."

A couple of minutes later, we are lying on blankets on the soothing, undulating forward deck, while the computer keeps the boat pointing at Australia.

I wish I knew what those diamonds are. Their names and which are planets. With no light pollution, all those suns and worlds seem more real, closer.

"This is really terrific, Nessa, thanks."

"It's you who made me see all this, Bryce."

"Really? How do you mean? I'm sure Dom would know all these stars."

"He knows their names, but you brought their magic to me."

"That's hard to believe. I know nothing about all that up there, although I feel a sense of awe and wonder."

"Exactly."

"But, I don't remember you at all. Were you at the same school as us?" I look at her, but no matter how hard I struggle, I cannot recollect her in my first fourteen remembered years.

"No. You asked me out on an anthropology field trip in New Guinea. We were at uni together. Then you introduced me to your brother, and he and I clicked."

"Good grief, it's my fault? I am *so* sorry."

"You tease. Dominiq and I are like peas in a pod. Anyway, you found—"

"I can't believe you are as green a pea as he is." I laugh at my own feeble joke, but I am having trouble bringing my childhood impressions of the idiot brother up to date.

"Bryce, what do you see up there?"

"Apart from the stars? The moon of course."

"What can you tell me about the moon in the way of its phase?"

"Oh come on, Nessa, you know I'm pretty much fazed by all this stuff. I guess you mean it looks like a nearly full moon."

"Last time you enchanted me with star-talk, you would have been able to tell me that it is a gibbous waxing moon: one that's just three days from being full."

"You mean I was a real-live nerd? I'm not sure whether that's cool."

Her hand stroked my arm again. "Very cool, Bryce. Actually, it's a pity the moon is so bright; we can hardly see the Milky Way in the bright haze there. But overhead, look, there's Sagittarius, the Archer—although you told me it looked more like a teapot."

"I must have known a lot of things that have completely gone. Hey, look, one of them is moving. Now, when I was a kid, the chances are it would have been a jet plane."

"It could either be an alien vehicle or, more likely, one of our satellites, there's enough up there to cause traffic jams. With a bit of luck, one of the alien ships will bump into it."

"Can we see the system the Zadokians have come from?"

"Sirius? Not tonight, it's below the horizon."

"Good, I don't like the idea of them spying on me."

"Very funny."

"What? They might have a Super Hubble telescope."

"Yeah, but they're nearly nine light years away."

"So, I didn't like the idea of a Zadokian in nine years telling Dominiq I was lying on the deck with his wife." We both laugh, and she smacks my arm. She must like my arm. I hope she isn't developing a crush on me. I don't fancy her, I don't relish a battle with Dominiq, especially on a small boat on a mission, and I still want Benita, although I don't see us settling down. As if such a concept is valid any more.

"Nessa, just suppose those stars are closer than we think."

"You mean they're only, say, four light years away?"

"Physics has had to change theories before in the face of empirical evidence." I stood to scan the horizon.

"Come back down," she says, pawing at my legs. Luckily, I'd put long trousers on for night duty.

"I'm just looking to see if there are any lights from ships or islands. It's what the night watch is supposed to do." But the horizon is blacker than the sky, so I kneel beside her. I don't want to get into a compromising position where I might have to fend off her wandering hands. Listen to me. I would have loved feminine wandering hands yesterday, or what seems like yesterday.

"One night, Bryce, you pointed up there and whispered, *Te Whanau o Marama* to me. Do you remember? Of course you don't. It's Maori-speak for stars."

"Really? This brain of mine knows Maori?"

"It did, well it knew that Maori phrase for the family of light. You must have picked it up when you did a temporary job assignment in Alice. At the same time as—"

"As what? Come on, Nessa, you're keeping something back from me. What have I done in my middle-aged past? Murdered someone?"

"No, no. It's Dominiq who should be telling you, not me."

"All this pussy-footing around. I couldn't stand all the PC niceties as a kid, I bet I didn't as a young man, so don't give me all that crap now. Out with it."

"Maybe... I'll have a word with him in the morning."

"Yeah, sure. It's that tangled web when practising to deceive. Hey, I remember fragment of Walter Scott. We did him at school."

"What else do you remember? I love a man who knows poetry."

"I remember that you're about to tell me something big that I did."

"Oh, all right. You're married. There."

"Is that all? I didn't have a secret tryst with the first woman Secretary General of the United Nations?"

"You might have done. You are a good-looking guy, and I haven't been watching you for years."

I feel a large sway rocking the boat, reminding me I ought to return to duty. "Thanks for the chat, Nessa. I'll be telling Benita the good news over breakfast."

Another swell makes me stagger and grab for a handrail as I make for the steps.

"It's not Benita."

I stop with a foot hovering above the first step. I see a red light on the distant horizon. I need to study it through the binoculars and check the radar, maybe alert the others. I need to do the observations quickly, but I am stuck. So, Benita and I aren't married. No big deal. Two desperadoes thrown together by unique circumstances. She's fun, and I hope I'm good for her, but what is marriage today anyway? I don't think she'll be upset we're not hitched. It means when we get back, she can have the pick of the island. Not me though. I have a wife. I HAVE A WIFE!

I forget my maritime duties and turn to Nessa, who is standing, folding the blanket, ready to return to her bunk and resume sleep. "Who is she, Nessa?"

She waves a free hand out at the western horizon. "Does it matter any more? This is why I wanted Dominiq to be breaking it to you."

"What do you mean it doesn't matter? Maybe not to you…"

"I mean that you met her, married her–and all that–in the last ten years. So, you won't remember her. It's all so far away in time and distance. It might as well as never happened. It can't be a part of your future, can it?"

In the moonlight, I see her face is wet. I want more, but maybe she's right. Dominiq will be able to tell me more. I let her go off down to the cabins. I remember her words, "and all that." What does she mean? Just that my married self–an unknown self–and my wife had a house? Kids? Whoa, that must be what she meant. I go to the door, but she's locked it.

I have to go and observe that light. As I mount the steps, I can't stop thinking of being with this strange wife of mine. How many children? What sex, ages? Where did we live? What is her name, family, career, and appearance? There's so much a void in my life. And the biggie–where is my family now?

Maybe focussing on my tasks will help me get through the rest of the watch. I find the 10 by 60 binoculars and train them on the light bobbing on the western horizon. Maybe it's us that's jigging up and down and the light is on land. Are lighthouses working? Maybe they store solar energy by day so mains power isn't needed. It is in the right direction for Tonga. I twist the focus and see the light as a ruddy tiny disc. Even my bad memory tells me I'm looking at Mars.

I double-check the radar at different scales. We're in the middle of

ARIA TRILOGY

Geoff Nelder

£5 each or £10 all three.

nowhere and will be for hours. The only dangerous bit is the straight between the northern tip of Australia and New Guinea, but it seems that there's hardly anyone left to trouble us.

It is unsettling to know that you have a wife, a warm real being, who's been in your arms, and yet, you have no clue who she is. Was her fragrance of peaches, roses? Damned frustrating to have no scent memory to waft in. Nessa could have told me her name. There must be a reason why she didn't. It must be someone I already knew. No, she said I hadn't met her in my pre-memory-loss time. The only people I know of since those days I could count on the fingers of this left hand that's tapping the radio console.

I've been going through all the usual frequencies I remembered as a kid, and then some. Just static FM. Yeah, the only women I know are Nessa. Hey, maybe I was married to her! What a blast, but it didn't come out like that so I guess not. Jena, who is Ryder's bitch and an American astronaut. Can't see that either. I never got to meet or talk on the radio to any others besides Benita. Except I know about Charlotte–the reason for this little jaunt. Charlotte? Is she my wife?

Let's suppose she is. Why didn't Dominiq say so when trying to persuade me to sail to Australia? Maybe he was saving it for when I wavered. If the weather or meeting hostiles became too much and I looked like doing a mutiny, he would have told me that the gorgeous creature we're rescuing is none other than my wife. Super card-up-the-sleeve job.

How can I find out for sure? I could wake up my damn brother, but he always lied in our childhood. He got me in no end of scrapes at school.

The only other person is Ryder. I don't know him except by reputation as being hated by Dominiq. That's it. Ryder has no reason to lie to me. I know he's probably in bed, but can I rouse him? My NoteCom's out of range, but this ship has the latest satellite radio and the Inmarsat comms satellites are still active, even if the ISS isn't. I use the encrypted set channel we've been told to use but nothing comes back. It's one-thirty in the morning, and already, no one is listening out for us. Maybe the satellite isn't working. I know we're too far away for the line-of-sight ship-to-shore VHF radio. Hello, the GPS has come on, excellent. That Charlotte must be working through the night. I speculate if wedding vows is something we have in common. I'm trying the satellite radio again.

Ah, I'm sure that crackling and hissing is different this time. The incoming light's on, let's see if it has voice.

"—*Sprint*. Come in. Dog Catcher calling *Solar Sprint*. You must have someone looking out and listening in even at the mid-watch. Over."

I laugh at the name Dog Catcher. They argued for ages what to call themselves, so that if the aliens overheard, they wouldn't know, too easily, that it was them at Rarotonga. And Dog Catcher was to do with the Zadokians coming from Sirius, the Dog Star.

"*Solar Sprint* to Dog Catcher. Keep your hair on, your signal's only just come up to strength. Any news? Over."

"Yes, the GPS is on. It was our engineers that got the satellites and links working, not Charlotte. Still haven't heard from her, maybe tomorrow now the sats are working. Over."

"Can I know who's talking? I'd like to speak to Ryder. Over."

"It's Bat here, Bryce. Don't you recognise my voice? Over."

"Last time I heard you, it sounded like you were inside a whale's arse. Over."

"Oh, the biohazard suit. Anyway, what do you want Ryder for? He's not available. Over."

"Then wake him up, pull him off Jena or whoever. Tell him it's a crisis. Over."

"Have you seen another boat, a plane? Is there a problem with the *Sprint*? Over."

"I'm not speaking to anyone except Ryder. Out."

"Don't be stupid, Bryce. You can trust me. Come on... Bryce! I knew you'd fuck things up. Out."

I BETTER SCAN THE HORIZON. It wouldn't look good if I missed a hijacked super tanker creeping up on us. Now that Nessa has returned to her cabin, the only sounds are the constant throb of the diesel engines and the ocean sloughing against us. I would be worried if I heard anything else. Ah, I heard an extraneous gurgle and a singing in the wires. A splash from a flying fish, or it could've been a nosey cetacean. A shiver runs down then up my spine as the creepiness of this situation sneaks up on me.

An urge for my eyes to find something through the glasses to complain about takes over, but a three-sixty finds nothing to account for my unease. Then, the thought surfaces that someone might be boarding the ship, maybe from a dinghy alongside I hadn't noticed because I was looking at the bloody horizon. I let the glasses hang from my neck like a pendulum as I lean over the rail. The black water slaps the boat's sides, and in its frustration churns into froth in the long, straight wake. Even at twenty knots that white line would be visible from above, especially if their eyes had magnifiers at least as powerful as mine. I look up as if expecting to see an alien ship and its telescope with accompanying pointing finger shouting, "Got ya!"

Maybe because my neck is bent back, but I get a sudden buzz of ringing in my ears. Tinnitus. It's very irritating, and I understand why some ancient peoples drilled holes in their skulls to let out the demons.

"Bryce, it's Ryder here. What's the problem? Over." Ah, Bat did get Ryder out of bed. I'm impressed.

"Ryder, I have a question, and I want a non-pussy-footing-around answer. Over."

"Is that all, Bryce? Not being chased by pirates, spaceships, or your brother lost overboard? Listen, I've been working late and just crawled into bed. Oh well, I'm here now. What's this so-important question? Over."

He's making me feel guilty, but I'm past that. "Who is my wife, and where is she? Over."

I'm sure I heard a deep breath before his mike cut. Exasperation. He'd better not try and fob me off with any "don't have that information" type answers. I'd be astonished if they haven't downloaded the relevant databases for all the personnel on that island, especially those lording it at the top.

"Hello, Bryce. I deal with issues to do with the alien cases and what they are up to. People problems aren't really my bag. What has Dominiq told you? Over."

"My stupid brother hasn't told me a damn thing. But Nessa, whose heart is made of softer stuff, has at least told me I am married and it isn't Benita. Over."

"So, it would seem to me that Dominiq has a good reason for not telling you. Agreed? Over."

"If you know my brother, you'd know he enjoys playing mind games. At least he did as a kid. Has he changed? Over."

"Not much in that respect. Look, Bryce, I don't have the personnel files of your family in my head, but you guessed we have them on computer here. I'll get someone to dig them out while we chat. Okay? Over."

Here we go. He's cunning enough to know I'd guess they have the data on file but hoping I'll forget to ask about it again later. If it isn't enough for me to sort out whether I've got alien messages in my brain, I have to put up with wankers like Ryder and Dominiq trying to fuck with my head.

"Okay, Ryder. But I already know, don't I? Over."

"Sorry, you lost me there. You know who your wife is? Over."

"It's Charlotte, isn't it?"

"Is it? If Dominiq didn't tell you this, who did? Nessa?"

"You all think you're so clever. I worked it out for myself. Hey, we've stopped saying over. Over."

"Listen, Bryce, it would be a huge coincidence if it was Charlotte. I mean she is a doll, but..."

"I see, you want her for yourself. Over."

"Yes, that's it, Bryce. But wait, if you like. Bat is clicking away on the database..."

"Yes, as if I'm going to believe what you tell me now. Over."

"So if I tell you that Charlotte isn't your wife?"

"Then I won't believe you. Unless you can send me proof, but you can't can you? Over."

"As soon as the Internet satellite comes on line, I could e-mail to your NoteCom the relevant files, but I suppose you'd say they were forgeries. Over."

"Absolutely. I got you out of bed for nothing. Over."

"I hope you do go and get Charlotte, even if you find that she isn't your wife. We've a lot to benefit from her, and the equipment being here. Over."

"So I gather. I'll let you go back to sleep, Ryder. Out."

That was a waste of time, as it would waking that bastard brother of mine. But if Ryder's right, I'm still as much in the dark as this boat. I look up as a cloud obscures that bright moon. Now, I see the Milky Way in all her grandeur. Like a wide diamond river snaking through Sagittarius. I know Sirius is below the horizon, but it doesn't seem right that from such beauty has come a beast.

CHAPTER 29

July 15ᵗʰ 2016, Winnipeg.

ANTONIO ADMIRED HIMSELF IN THE MIRROR, and curling his upper lip, snarled like a threatened dog. Keeping his scowl, he checked around his reflected image, through to the kitchen behind. He didn't want Manuel or Julia to see him perfecting his Mr Nasty look. Then, he remembered they were in the neighbouring clinic Julia had transformed into a laboratory. The hand he'd sliced off a hapless Zadokian had her all a-buzz.

A few months ago, he wouldn't have had to pretend to be more evil than he was. What was happening to him?

Although the excitement in the dome had brought on the intense, swirling spotlights of a migraine, the memory of the adrenalin charge changed his snarl to a laugh. He'd hardly seen his housemates since they ran into their lab with the half-hand. They jabbered about cell structure, coppery blood, bendy bones and the absence of fingernails. None of that interested him. He burned to know the real reason why the aliens came to Earth. So, the new ones, including the one he mutilated on the run, were prisoners, but what had they done? He recalled last night's supper-table discussion.

"I suppose you think I'm *una idiota* for not being fascinated by what Zadokian biology you can extrapolate from one lacerated hand."

"Antonio," Manuel said, "before you went crazy, you were the finest physician NASA had. You would've shouldered us out of the way to stab a scalpel into that hand."

"I already did the stabbing bit."

"I could use your analytical skills in the chromo-separation studies," Julia said, smiling at Antonio.

"Not my bag any more. My interests lie higher up."

"You're not expecting to get into their heads, are you?" Julia said; her smile transformed to a grimace. "I know you think you pick up something that tells you what to do in the constructions, but that's not the same as being able to converse with them. They don't seem to talk, do they?"

"What do you know? Nothing. I'm surrounded by fools. *Si*, you are right that somehow the Zadokians project coded instructions, maybe in this intermittent tinnitus some of us get. But I'm convinced that I can get through to them...if only I can grab their attention for long enough. They see us as worker ants, no more. So, they haven't tried to communicate conversationally. I'm going to force it."

Manuel drained his bottled beer. "Haven't you caused enough trouble? I'm amazed we haven't been tracked down after you attacked that prisoner."

"They're too busy doing... whatever." Antonio's thoughts drifted into the various scenarios. "What do you think those prisoners must be guilty of to be transported all this way?"

"I've been wondering that too," Manuel said. "Must be something their home planet believes is so serious, they cannot bear their presence."

"As if they are a contaminant," Julia said, always the biologist.

"So, they can't have capital punishment, even though it would be a lot cheaper," Manuel said.

Julia banged her fist on the table. "They don't have the same scruples eliminating a whole planet's population."

"To be fair," Antonio said, "we don't know for sure they intended to end humanity. In fact, their planting of the second case, and a third, is indicative of a phased program. If they wanted to kill us all, they'd just leave the first, or a more deadly virus."

"No way," Julia said. "They wanted all of humanity out of the way, yet with a clean atmosphere for themselves. They threw us the second case to save a few lackeys for slave labour, and God knows what the third is. Probably a lethal virus to finish us all off."

"Paranoia," Antonio said, feeling uncomfortable that his pet theories had opposition. "Do either of you know what those Frenchies are doing?"

"Last we heard, they were preparing to retrieve the third case," Manuel said.

"Why didn't Ryder arrange for the case to drop here?" Antonio said. "It would've been interesting to experience its opening."

"Hey, it might well be fatal for everyone," Julia said. "The near certainty that you would open it is probably why Ryder sent it to France. Anyway, why don't you ask the Zadokians what's in the third case? Oh, but they aren't talking to you."

"You are such a scream. I'm going to ask the Oz *bella donna* what she knows. My God, it's so hot. Is it thirty already?"

"Hell, Antonio," Manuel said, "what's that in real money? Eighty-five?"

"Close enough and too hot," Julia said. "And you can't call Charlotte or Ryder."

"Who says I can't? You're in no position to order me around. Hah. You must be madder than I thought."

"Keep your diaper dry," Julia said. "Last I checked, the ISS was dead, so no signal."

Instead of experiencing foolishness for letting fly before checking the facts, Antonio was past self-incrimination. He grabbed a bottle of filtered water and after slamming the door, strolled to the Buick and climbed in. Slowly, because although his brain had instant access to all his memories—a near epileptic experience which needed control—he needed to think through his next step. He turned the air con full on while he plotted. Antonio's self-survival was the number one issue, but was it with the pathetic humans left grovelling around the planet? Or was it with these cunning Zadokians? They might believe they have ordinary humans sussed, but he was no ordinary man. Half a hand might be sufficient for Julia's biopsy work, but he needed more.

Antonio's mouth twisted as he switched on the ignition.

NIGHTS HAD BECOME PALPABLY THICKER since the power stations forgot how to make electricity. Antonio sat in the vehicle and wondered how the alien laser-like device was powered. His newly acquired but crude intuition informed him that no batteries were included. An urge grew to view the domes from a high vantage point. Instinct said find a nearby hill, but there were few Earthly places flatter than Winnipeg. He released a brief laugh at recalling local folklore tale that hills were banished by a spirit of the Cree so that white men couldn't hide. A tale from a drunken Winnatobian so maybe true. Hah! Artificial hills did exist.

Fifteen minutes and leg-aching flights of stairs later, he looked over the Winnipeg alien domes from a high airport building. He laughed at the incongruity of standing in the observation lounge, dark and echoing instead of the raucous bustle it was built for.

The ghosts of airplanes spiralled in their lofty queues. These days, mice-spotting hawks occupied the same role.

Looking over the city, a few pinpoints of yellow lights pricked the blackness. Winnipeg, the busiest city in Manitoba's grain prairie land, was the flattest city on the planet, relief from two-dimensional living offered only by the few phallic-tall buildings. But at eleven, the darkness blotted out the shopping malls, warehouse industry, apartments, and homes. He knew there were a few people, the dome-construction force, whose memories had stopped being retrograde after being infected with ARIA-2, but he doubted they possessed sufficient survival skills to last much longer. Most would succumb to illnesses. Others would consume contaminated food and water or catch tetanus from losing battles with each other and feral animals. But, for that night, the few lights showed the persistence of groups of people using candles, oil lamps, and battery lamps. Some might have persuaded diesel-operated generators to help them survive.

Antonio thought it might be worth tracking those down–they must have more initiative than most–and taking them under his command. Perhaps a willing woman fancied sharing his glory.

He looked hard at the black horizon across miles of suburban wasteland where weeds obeyed Nature's orders to reclaim its heritage. Just three lights, and one of those could be a fire. He'd often seen building fires since arriving in Canada. They were unlikely to be caused by electrical faults. Some might have been where sunlight focussed its incendiary power through glass ornaments, or where lightning licked with its thirty thousand-degree tongue. In the early days, the idiots would forget they've left burners on or bonfires took on a life of their own, and with no emergency fire services, the blazes happily became infernos.

Having satiated his curiosity of the post-ARIA Winnipeg, he turned to look at the dimly lit domes at the far end of the airfield. He didn't recall lights being installed; maybe they were integral to the fabric. Probably similar to the solar energy storage and release lights humans managed to scrape together before the Zads arrived. There must be so many tomorrow-gadgets he could use. Pity the economy nosedived into the ground before he could profit from the techie miracles he was about to plunder.

The absence of movement, vehicular or pedestrian, gave him confidence. No guards nor entrance lights at the domes. They were so complacent.

He toyed with the alien gun, if that was its purpose. He ought to test if it still worked, so pointed it at a picture of a scarlet combine harvester gobbling golden wheat in better days. He waved the weapon, urging it by thought to slice into the wall a millimetre deep full circle around the picture. A whiff of smoke and, with a crash of smashed glass, the harvester's image met the floor. Antonio laughed his embarrassment at creating sound where none should be. He peered out of the window, but of course, nothing moved. The nearest beings were unconscious in the domes. Nevertheless, he felt foolish even though he'd shown that the gadget worked well. Maybe its power source was his thought energy. Hah.

BACK AT THE BUICK, he shouldered a rucksack and walked around the outside of the main dome. He knew where the dormitories of the alien prisoners were. He had a feeling they were all asleep, including the non-prisoners. Guards was the wrong name, because although the prisoners moved on their command and didn't run away, there were no sentries. Maybe the guards used thought control on their prisoners, although they carried the type of weapon he'd purloined. He could go through the doorway, which now was a kind of airlock to keep the air pressure higher inside the dome than outside to keep the dirty Earth atmosphere out. However, he didn't want to risk coming across a stray guard wandering in the interior wondering about the real reason for being so far from home.

He picked his spot and thought doorway to the weapon as it sliced through the dome's plastic wall. He stepped inside the soft-lit gloom. Double bunk beds lined the small dormitory. He laughed at the familiar scene. It could have been a youth hostel, residential school— or a prison.

His tinnitus became excruciating as if sonic alarms tripped in his head. Maybe these hapless saps were screaming "Save me" at him in their own telepathic way. He hoped to find out by doing just that for one *bandito*. He flipped open his rucksack and jabbed a morphine auto-syringe into a coppery arm of the nearest alien. In spite of his pretence, he'd looked over Julia's analysis of the Zadokian blood and decided that morphine might not have had the same anaesthetic effect as it did on humans, but that if it killed it, he'd merely take the next victim without the jab. He waited ten seconds. The Zad remained alive but asleep. He had no trouble taping its arms and legs, nor in lifting it. Once outside, he put the Zadokian down on parched July grass while he resealed the doorway with their own weapon.

AN HOUR LATER, he had the Zadokian plastic-tagged to a bed in Julia's temporary clinic. Antonio swaggered to Julia and Manuel's bedroom and woke them by switching on their light.

"You'll like this. Never mind half a hand; I've got you a whole body."

CHAPTER 30

July 17ᵗʰ 2016, the southern suburbs of Montpellier, southern France.

FRANÇOISE, EXHAUSTED BY THE DRIVE south from La Voulte to Montpellier, looked to her left at Bono, who did the driving. His white teeth had grinned all the way. Only occasionally would a large tongue sneak out to wet his mouth. His black hands matched the colour of the cloth-covered steering wheel. It looked like they were joined.

"You actually enjoyed that journey, didn't you, Bono? I'm worn out being a passenger."

"That's because you don't have the faith, sister. You see abandoned vehicles and assume ambush. You think you hear gunfire and assume the Zads are overhead. Negativity is your speciality, not mine."

"You got something there. But, we still have some way to reach the Mediterranean and find a boat to get the case."

"Is Victor awake yet? He's not as pretty as Elodie, but the brute will come in handy for handling boats and winches. Have you seen his muscles? What am I saying, he's your squeeze, of course you've seen his muscles, caressed them, licked—"

"That's enough. He's still asleep. Most people cope with eight hours, but I'm lucky to have him conscious for as much. You need to come off the A9 onto the N112 and head for Agde. Lord knows how we're going to find the thing—Zut! They said it will transmit to my NoteCom when I tell them, but all the radio channels have been dead for days. *Oui*, Victor's in good shape, about as bright as a lump of coal, but strong. I used to think you were dumb until we took him on."

"I won't take offence. It's such a lovely day. Look, there's deer crossing the road. Isn't that sweet enough for you, Françoise?"

"Idiot. They're being chased by those savage hounds. Drive into them. Go on."

Bono steered the Renault at the lead dog. Oddly, it just stops and snarls at them. Bono braked sharply and steered left to avoid it. "What the hell?"

"They're not used to seeing moving vehicles any more. Or, they're so removed from domesticity, fear isn't on their agenda."

The minor coastal road leading to Agde should have been devoid of the horrendous scenes of decomposed corpses and burnt-out buildings they witnessed on the main north-to-south road parallel to the river Rhône. But they had no easy drive even though they had left the dogs behind. No road gave them a smooth ride. Every square metre had detritus from falling earth banks, walls, windblown debris, and abandoned vehicles. She looked forward to going out into the bay in a boat, just to experience travelling in a straight line once again.

She called out to Bono. "Now, it's left—the south road—to Port Ambonne. Just a couple of kilometres and we're there. We need to find a high building. Let's go for that hotel." She pointed at a pink monstrosity of a stepped building that used to be packed with pink and brown holidaymakers.

"As if we're going to see a blackened capsule that should have frightened the sharks days ago."

"Yesterday. It orbited for a few days to get to the correct entry window."

"Hey, I can enter a hotel without climbing through a window. That'll be a first."

Françoise shouted at Victor. "Wake up, you lazy sod."

She reinforced her request with the barrel of her rifle, resulting in startled gasps. In response to Bono's chortling at the unusual method of waking up her lover, she laughed back at him. Laughter relief had become an essential survival tool.

Walking into any building carried dangers for the uninfected. Françoise insisted they all wore surgical masks as a basic precaution. Whether the unpleasant odour of disinfectant would be effective carried a high unlikelihood factor, but it gave them the false confidence they needed to move quickly. Like all the other buildings they'd visited over the year, this had been ransacked—untidily and dangerously, with broken glass and unidentifiable furred ex-foodstuffs decorating the floor. Hardly stopping, they made it to the roof and peered through their rifle sights at the ocean.

"Was it supposed to release a buoy so we can find it?" said Victor, his long red hair getting in the way of the scope.

"That would alert the aliens to something interesting," said Françoise.

Bono laughed. "Look out there, lobster pot markers and shallow water buoys all over. Anyway, why would the aliens try to recover the case when it was them who planted it?"

"Good point," said Françoise. "Well, Victor, I brought you, not only for a hug and a jump, but to steal a boat and take us out there. Hopefully, the water's clear enough and the capsule is in shallow water."

"No problem. I suggest two stages. There will be glass-bottom tourist boats to look for it, and then a trawler to recover it. Let's get to the marina."

As the eager men ran down the stairs, Françoise had another stare inland. Smoke drifted from trees a few kilometres northwest. An immediate surge of adrenalin shook her. It could mean they'd have company. Would it be safer on the boats, or should they identify the source of the fire? It could take days to find the ERV underwater and then another day to recover it. They would be discovered if other people were around. She had to convince Bono and Victor to temporarily abandon the boat. They wouldn't like that.

SHE HAD TO RUN. The men, behaving like boys, had seen a collection of tourist trip boats and were eager to leap on them. They should be more cautious, but she supposed they assumed she did all the security-big-mother work. And she did. She kept stopping, stooping, and looking around. A flock of seagulls squawked into the air a hundred metres off. She didn't want to see what they were feeding on. Corpses on the road were dried-out carcases. Hardly enough food for animals and birds. The gulls were probably taking in the sunshine, hot on the quayside and disturbed by Bono and Victor. She hoped she was the only observer. She had to skirt carefully around a large puddle. A storm drain was blocked by debris, so the previous day's thunderstorm rain had flooded part of the town.

"Listen, guys, we have to leave the boats for the moment."

"No way." Bono said. "Look. *The Fifi Joly*. And it has fuel."

"And drinks," said Victor, brandishing a Cognac bottle. "Plus, a large, fluffy love bed for *us, chéri.*"

"*Fifi* will still be here when we return. There's smoke a little way inland. We must investigate it in case whoever made it investigates us."

"You're obsessed with ARIA people. There aren't any left, Françoise," said Victor, pouting. "Except with walking frames."

"It only takes one to surprise us close up. Then, it's the end. I want us to have a future."

Victor smiled. "I'll stop here while you and Bono explore. There's plenty of preparation work here. Stop pulling that pretty face,

Françoise, I'll keep a lookout. We can use our cell phones to keep in touch."

"They only work periodically since the ISS went out. I haven't been able to raise Ryder at all. I'd rather we stay together for safety, and you know what happens in movies once people split up?"

"One gets lucky?"

"Unlucky, and the others waste time looking for the ginger-nutted bastard."

"You're not my mother. I'll take my chances here."

FRANÇOISE HAD NO CHOICE. Bono accompanied her back to their vehicle.

"What's that terrible smell?" he said, pinching his nose.

Françoise crumpled her face, as if it helped. "It wasn't here when we arrived. Perhaps the sea breeze has blown it from those wharf buildings."

"There's a fish wholesalers, but if the rodents were too slow, any thawed foods would've rotted away by now."

In spite of the solid odour, they slid back the door. The rusty, squealing door worried Françoise with its noise but curiosity overrode her fears. "Ah, that recent storm brought down the roof. It smashed into the freezer unit, which must have contained fish, so the whole gooey mess is now all over the floor. Hey, watch out for the rats."

"There must be hundreds of them. Look at their size. Let's go."

BACK IN THEIR ESTATE CAR, Françoise navigated and rode shotgun. Bono meander-drove the car out of the port area, through the ghost-town suburbs, and into farmland. It wasn't difficult to see where to go. They headed for the source of the thin smoke drifting inland with the sea breeze. A herd of pigs crossing the road made Bono emergency brake.

"Those hogs look as mean as poked rhinos," said Bono.

"They probably reverted to defensive aggression to beat off the dogs."

"I'm glad we're not on foot. Have you noticed something about your smoke?"

"You mean it's not a single source? Oh well, there was a thunderstorm yesterday, so it's probably another forest fire. It looks like this farm lane terminates at that barn. We'll have to risk walking."

192 | **ARIA: Returning Left Luggage**

"I don't like that, Fran."

"Don't worry. We are well armed and have the disinfectant masks."

"No, I mean my new Brogues. Only liberated 'em last week. It'll be muddy, scratchy in those woods."

"I told you to bring appropriate apparel."

"Yes, my posh mademoiselle, but you also said we'd be on the sea and in it. So, scuba-diving gear is packed. Shall I put my frogman flippers on?"

"Sorry Bono, if your Brogues get irreparably damaged, I'll steal you a new pair, now grab your rucksack and weapon."

Françoise tried to phone first Victor then Rarotonga, but the links remained down. In spite of the mid-July heat, the dry former farmland transformed to sucking mud in the shade of the oak woodland.

"That's it. You owe me new shoes already, let's hope you don't have to plunder a black leather jacket store too."

"Put your face mask back on, the smoke is thicker in front." She noticed her hands, steadying her progress by leaning on tree trunks, were blackening. She sniffed her fingers even though logic told her they would wrinkle her nose with the whiff of wood ash.

Bono, keeping behind her, said, "Fran, it's not likely to be a campfire, is it? Unless it got out of hand. This is stupid getting all messed up, let's go back."

"Just a few more metres. Ah. I thought it might be. Come beside me, Bono, and tell me what you think."

"Fucking hell, it looks like a giant chainsaw swept through here then set it alight. Ah. At the end of this singed swathe through the trees will be our spaceship. Victor will be annoyed."

"He can play boats another time. Just wait 'til I tell Abdul he was off course with his programming. He could have set fire to the whole region if it hadn't been raining."

"I thought you told us that a slight increase in wind here or there would blow it off course."

"Let's find it." In spite of her outburst, she was elated at not having to search the depths of the Mediterranean. She eagerly but carefully stepped over charcoaled branches. After ten minutes, she could see the blackened Return Vehicle among smouldering trees. She looked behind to encourage Bono and laughed. "My God, Bono, I didn't think you could look more black."

"You should talk," he said, flashing brilliant teeth.

She joined in with the mirth but now eager to get to work.

"Fran, how the fuck are we going to get that beast out? It must weigh tons."

"It does. I was thinking we could use one of those lorries that carry skips. I saw one on the way here. But, we might have to use a farm vehicle to drag this thing out of the trees."

"But what then? Wait for a signal from a problem radio link? Why didn't they tell us the code for the door?"

"For security reasons, dolt. But they didn't know the ISS was going off line. I suppose we could look at the hatch. See if there's a way to open it in an emergency."

"Yeah, it might have forced open in the crash with luck."

They clambered on the fragile and charcoaled brush and finally reached the hatch. Apart from the burnt look, it was in perfect condition but no easy-to-open ring pull. She used her already blackened sleeve to clear soot off the number pad.

"We don't know the number," said Françoise, looking at Bono for inspiration. "So, we either try a million combinations or lug the whole thing out."

"I thought they gave us a clue. What was it? Something that an ARIA-infected person couldn't possibly know."

"A fine time for them to play Cluedo with us," said Françoise. "I think it's a four-figure number."

"Ah, then, it's easy. Two-oh-one-six. The date. Get it?"

"Surely not, though I suppose ARIA people finding a newspaper will think the date is two thousand and fifteen. Hey, that's quite clever."

"Let me."

"Will the hatch blow out with explosive bolts?"

"They'd never design it so the sucker punching the correct code would be sent flying hugging the door." Bono punched in 2016. Nothing happened.

"Do you think it's faulty? Or the batteries flat?" said Françoise.

"No, it would be designed for worse landings than this. We've got the code wrong. Maybe, there is more than four digits in the code. The numbers are zero to nine. Even with four digits, there's over six thousand possible numbers."

Françoise groaned, she could hardly bear the thought of having to organise removing the whole vehicle out of the woods, onto a lorry, and back to base in order to wait for communications to be restored. "How many combinations if just two, zero, one and six are used and not repeated?"

"Easy, twenty-four. Okay, I'll try it in reverse first and then methodically lowest to highest."

As soon as he punched in 6102, a soft hiss announced the hatch lifting and sliding. Françoise hugged and kissed Bono, but then had wobbles of panic. "My God, Bono, I was about to dive in there. We've precautions to take. Open your rucksack."

"Ah, *oui*, the case might open if you get near it with naked hands. Here's your thermal-insulation gloves. I better put mine on too."

"Stand clear. If it does go wrong, there's no point both of us frying."

"Fran, if that is a bomb to rid the planet of surviving humans, then standing behind a smouldering tree a few metres away isn't going to protect me. Come on, climb in, I promise not to leer at your derrière."

"Liar." But she wriggled in through the hatch anyway. As Abdul described, the case had been manipulated by the robotic grabber into a cargo cell, which had been filled with extruded polystyrene. All she could see of the case was the white box surrounding it. But it weighed little and wearing gloves–maybe unnecessarily with the polystyrene coat–she pushed it through the hatch.

WITH THE CASE SAFELY BOUNCING IN THE LUGGAGE COMPARTMENT of the estate car, they drove back to the marina. A typical Mediterranean sunset gave them a treat. Gentle incandescent pinks and apricots seeped from the west, painting the few ribbed clouds.

"Wow," said Bono. "Doesn't that make you glad to be alive, human, and an arts student?"

"Such beauty among vile evil. Speaking of vile, the rotten fish odour is still here. Let's tear Victor from his love boat and head back north."

"We'll park far from that smell. Oh." He braked sharply sending the unbelted Françoise battering against the windshield. "Aargh! Sorry, Fran. I stopped 'cos it looks like Victor has company."

"*Merde*, where's the glasses... It looks like an old man, at least eighty. He's standing on the gangplank waving his stick at Victor, who's only a metre away. Fuck, fuck."

"I could drive up and honk the horn to scare the oldie away, but that wouldn't change anything."

"You're right. Damn him. If he'd come with us like I said..."

"Like you're always bleating at me, it's what we do now that counts. Ah, the old chap's moving off. What shall we do?"

"I can't think clearly. We should drive away, but I can't just leave him. We're an item. Anyway, I'd like to know what they were talking about."

"Fran, the old chap thinks he's a kid. He was probably asking for a ride on the boat, or when the ice-cream kiosk was opening. What's the point in hanging around? It's stretching your misery and putting us at risk."

Françoise looked in the mirror in case a geriatric horde was creeping up on them. She couldn't believe how her emotions were driving muscle spasms in her stomach, and her face glowed. She knew Bono made sense, it was exactly how she'd trained him to react in these situations, but she hadn't factored in the emotional baggage that went with abandoning her best friend and paramour. She clutched at reasons to talk to Victor besides verbalizing her adieus. "It's possible the oldie was recently infected and knew something about the aliens we don't."

"You're giving me a laugh. We're probably the experts on aliens after what we've seen at La Voulte."

"Let's try the radio one more time." She used the car radiophone to call Victor's cell phone with zero expectation. "Fran calling Victor, are you hearing this?"

Anticipated crackles led her to stare at Victor in the distance. She could see him, but at 200 metres through the digiscope, and with his back turned, she had to guess at his actions. He appeared to be shaking his head then poking a finger in his ear. She recognised the classic symptoms of the onset of ARIA.

The speaker crackled again. "Hi, Fran, was it a barbeque gone out of control? Are you ready to test this beauty?"

"Oh my God, Victor. Are you all right?"

"Of course, *cheri*. Why shouldn't I be? Anyway the boat is ready as soon as you get here."

"Victor, we saw you talking to someone."

"Don't worry about him. He said this was his boat, but we could hire it for five francs. Can you believe that? His memory is pre-Euro. What a jerk. Anyway, he's gone to fetch his father. It's a joke, he must be a hundred."

"Victor, that old man probably thinks he's only a teenager. You were really close to him, weren't you?" She turned the radio off as she swore. "Stupid, stupid man. I can't believe he'd let anyone... *mon Dieu*. I can't talk..."

She handed the mike to Bono, who looked surprised until he saw her tears cascading down her face.

"Hi, Victor, it's me, Bono. You realize that old chap had ARIA, don't you?"

"Yeah right. He was just an old geriatric. They're all confused at that age."

"He behaved like someone who's lost fifty years of memory. How do you feel, Victor?"

Françoise shot him an evil eye, not wanting their fears confirmed.

"I'm fine. Really. I can't wait to get this tub out to sea. Come on down from wherever you're hiding."

Bono switched off the radio and put an arm around her. Liquid sore emotions looked into his steady deep brown eyes.

"He could be right," she said between sobs.

"You know he's not. Okay, while he's awake, alert, and stimulated by constant input of images, sounds, and tactile senses, the memory he's losing won't be noticeable for a while. According to Abdul, ARIA-infected people lose fifty-two hours per hour. Let's wait ten minutes and call him again. If he has it, he will have forgotten our call and the old man. Then, Fran, we will have to leave him."

"But we can't just abandon him." She fought her tears again. "I know he can't come with us, but we could make sure he's got some survival gear."

"Yeah, well, he's in a good spot for that. I noticed unopened cans among the trashed debris in the hotel, and the boat is provisioned for a few days."

"There is another option, Bono." She glanced behind her. He looked too, but frowned.

"There's no one creeping up on us, is there? Ah, I see. No, Fran, we're not opening the case. Not even breaking through the polystyrene. Forget it."

"Wait, Bono. The second case had an antidote? Well, suppose the aliens thought its spread wasn't fast enough and so sent this one as a duplicate."

"My, you are clutching at straws. More likely a super virus that will wipe out the rest of humankind—along with the other mammals. That's the considered opinion of the scientists Ryder's with. Too risky."

Françoise moaned. She brought up her knees and hugged them, rocking, as if they were her Victor. She'd run out of other options. She had sufficient logic to work through her emotional responses, which would have led to ignoring the global plight of humans. She knew Bono was right. The last chance was that, somehow, Victor hadn't breathed in the ARIA virus. Finally, she steeled herself to look through the scope at him.

"He's rubbing his head again. Damn, he's swigging from a bottle. Probably beer. Just when we need him with all faculties alert."

"If I thought I had ARIA, I'd hit the bottle."

"Fair enough. *D'accord*, ten minutes is up. Let's find out. I'm all right, I'll do it. Give me a sec." She put her wet paper handkerchief into the car's side pocket and pulled out a dry one, wondering how many years supply of such toiletries were left. She thought of the irony of children in a few years using the last ballpoint, can of cola, plastic sandals, and wondering at the images in faded magazines. It would be back to basics for real. *How many people do you need to sustain some kind of civilised existence?* She'd have to think about it later.

"Victor? Hello. It's Françoise."

"Hi, Fran, where you been? Bring some aspirin."

"Victor, what did the old man say?" She waited, listening to his breathing as he considered her question.

"I get it. A trick question?"

"See, Bono? He hasn't got ARIA."

Bono shook his head at her.

Victor's voice came over the speaker again. "You must mean that chap at the campus, who saw us off? Are you bringing some painkillers, my head's throbbing something awful. Hey, did you get that smell?"

"The dead fish?" she said.

"Naw, the peanut butter. Wow. There must be some around in the galley."

Bono gave her a knowing look, but she recognised the childhood aroma significance. She gave the radio back to Bono, unable to speak.

"Victor, it's Bono here. Listen man, I'm sorry to say that there is little doubt you have ARIA."

"Stop all that horsing, Bono. Come here, both of you. Don't we have a Return Vehicle to find?"

"Victor, in another hour or two, you will not remember coming down here or what for. Listen man, I'm going to feed some basic information on ARIA to your NoteCom. Always keep it with you."

"I don't believe I have ARIA. Not everyone with a headache...damn, something is happening, isn't it? I don't remember..."

Françoise took over the radio. "Victor, you really do have ARIA. But you will be okay for quite a long time if you keep making notes. Remember Manuel in Canada? No, we haven't met him, but Ryder and others have told us that he survived by keeping notes, as have others. Use your NoteCom, notepads, anything. Victor, are you listening?"

"Yeah. Is this for real then, *cheri*?"

"I'm afraid so, darling. There should be painkillers in the first aid box in the boat. Look for a notepad too."

"Found the first aid box. Actually, the headache's turned muzzy. I keep getting aroma memories flooding in. Weird. You know how raspberry sweets have a different smell from fresh raspberries? Hey, this is cool. You should both try it. Maybe we could help each other."

She looked at Bono with horror that her beau had ARIA, but tinged with relief it wasn't a totally awful experience for him.

Bono shrugged back.

"What are you going to do, Victor? You might be best finding others and share resources. It would be easier to protect each other from animals..."

"Sorry, Fran. I am staying on this boat. It's my home now. I'll get more water and provisions before casting off."

"Victor, that's too dangerous. You might forget where you came from. Oh, that wouldn't matter. What if you run out of fuel?"

"I'll hop around the coast. If I'm done for, I wanna be done for on a boat. You get that, don't you, sugar?"

"I am worried for you, Victor. You've got to keep your NoteCom charged and your cell phone as backup. I'll call you every day."

Bono leaned over and called into the radio. "I'm sending our radio frequency to your NoteCom, Victor, and that for the campus. Can you figure the frequency for the boat?"

"Oh, just use channel seven. Shouldn't really use the emergency channel, but no one else will interfere."

"Fine. But write it down too." Bono sat back to let Françoise say her goodbyes.

"I'm not saying goodbye, but *au revoir*, Victor."

"Suits me. Are you coming down now? Oh, you can't. We'll see each other on the radio."

"Do you want us to search for bottled water and food for you before we go? In fact, you can have some of the stuff we have. We'll leave it on the quayside, but stay in your boat."

"There's water and food on board, but I'll get more before casting off. Yeah, okay. Put the food near that phone box. Can you see it?"

Bono started the Megane Estate and stopped by the phone box on the concrete quayside. Victor could be seen in the cockpit of his tourist trip boat. The two of them unloaded a full six-litre container of water and boxes of food.

"He's remarkably calm," said Bono, as he climbed back in the driver's seat.

"Too calm. I wanted him to be as upset as me. It's as if he sees it as an adventure."

"Probably the best way. Say *adieu*. I want to make some distance before it gets dark."

"Victor, sweetheart."

"I'm listening. Oh, I see you now. And are those for me? Thanks. I'm on my way over."

"No. No, Victor, stay in the boat. Oh God, it's too late. He's jogging over."

The vehicle stalled. Bono swore at it to get the engine restarted, which it did but continued its protest by coughing and performing the slowest acceleration in its history. Victor, gasping, caught up and grabbed at Françoise's window just as she wound it up. Spittle splattered the glass from his gasps as he slipped back, his bewildered expression mixed with exhaustion from the unaccustomed sprinting.

As the car made headway up the hill, Françoise's last view of Victor was diminishing in the mirror. She contained herself no longer and cried great gulps in anguish as if he'd died already. After ten miles, her heart, having gone into meltdown, cooled, and then hardened. Thoughts turned to revenge, and she knew how to exact it.

CHAPTER 31

FRANÇOIS DREW A DEEP BREATH. She wasn't used to addressing a crowd, but she had to convince these ARIA-uninfected remnants of her college field trip they should take the threat seriously.

"Yes, it should work, but..." Bono drew a finger across his throat. Françoise tried to decide whether his gesture meant he was for or against her revenge scheme. Then she realized everyone at the impromptu meeting at the university campus smiled in agreement.

Françoise, confident her plan would work at several levels, glanced at the others: a mix of lecturers and students. Six, besides Bono, she could count on for action. Three preferred to think the whole ARIA thing was some diabolical mistake. The aliens are a figment of our imagination, and as long as they keep calm and hide in their homes, it will all blow over.

Three more continually pointed her at the Bible. Father Dubois, in hushed words she could hardly hear said, "There is no ultimate problem. They are not aliens; they are the hosts of the Lord Yhovah. It is in Exodus, Leviticus, and Kings. We are blessed to have the Glory of the Lord among us. The sickness is but a mighty plague. We are chosen to inherit a cleaner, sinless Earth. You do see this, don't you?"

"*Peut-être*, Father. So, the aliens are angels?"

"You see the light too?"

"I see a different light than you, Father." Françoise grabbed Bono's arm to drag him outside. "I'm glad we hid the case on the way here. These idiots would be opening it, thinking it's a new sacrament."

"Tonight then. We've obtained the hoses and we'll target the main dome."

"I hope Anton and his friends are sober enough to have gathered the right sort of vehicles. Bono, I only worry that we might be affecting innocents too."

"The beauty of this plan is that it will only damage the aliens."

"I mean their prisoners."

"We can't afford to be that fussy. We're fighting back while we can, right?"

"For Victor."

"And three billion others."

"Of course. That reminds me. You go prepare. I have a long-distance call to make."

"Give Abdul my regards."

FRANÇOISE LOCKED HERSELF into the campus computer room, and after another fruitless attempt to call Victor, tried Rarotonga.

"Fran, it's wonderful to hear from you. Abdul here. How are you?"

"You just want to know if we cracked your code and retrieved the case. Well we did."

"Excellent. Just a minute while I call Ryder."

"I haven't time, Abdul. Listen, we haven't brought the case here. There are too many possibilities for it to fall in the wrong hands. We hid it."

"Good plan. So where?"

"We found an abandoned strong room and put a code on the door. We used the same one you gave us to unravel."

"Okay, we still need to know where it is in case we either come over or send others. Fran, you're not holding out on us for some reason? Pique?"

"As if. It's *sur le pont*. Get that, Abdul? In case our visitors are listening, I don't want to say more."

"No need. In Qatar, we sang our French lessons at school. *On y danse*, correct? Now, rest and behave while we figure out your next mission."

"*Salut*, Abdul." She couldn't help laughing. If he only knew what she was about to do. But her laughter subsided in moments as Victor's image slid into her consciousness. The thought of him adrift at sea, dehydrated, confused, out of fuel, without any chance of rescue. Her helplessness in his situation froze her logic circuits, leaving only the vengeance targets burning.

THREE IN THE MORNING, yet all the assailants, revved up and eager to fight back, were not tired. Françoise suggested all eight wore dark clothes and black balaclavas. Observation of the domes over the past weeks showed no exterior guards in the early hours, but she had to assume they'd have sensor surveillance. And the freedom-fighter outfits lent them added righteous fervour. A few human workers were kept in one of the three domes, supplies in another, but the large dome housed most of the activity.

Once again, she lay on damp, coarse grass, this time under olive trees, examining the domes through an image-enhancing digital scope. An eerie green landscape filled the screen but nothing moved. She panned to the right to find the movement she wanted to see: Bono and two other students carrying three fireman's hoses up to the dome's pale wall. Switching to the left, another group pushed three more to the wall on that side.

She tapped her cell phone. "That's good work, Bono and Anton. Both groups are in position. Start cutting."

No replies were necessary as she saw both groups use sharp electric knives to cut slits into the walls.

While they pushed in the ends of the hoses and sealed them into position with duct tape, she again tapped and called. "Peter, push the van into position." Good, she saw a group pushing a van from the right. Slowly, but it gathered momentum when Bono's group added their muscles. They parked it in front of the dome's entrance and placed razor wire under the van to stop any escapes.

"Generators... switch on." She focussed on a building to the right from where three of the hoses snaked. Her Fine Art lecturer waved at her, then thumbed up. Over to the left, a student did the same.

"Right, everyone back here."

They retreated across the bridge, running bent over as if that gave them more cover. "It's tempting to stay, but we'll rely on our hidden camera to witness justice. In the bus, everyone."

Anton jabbered to Françoise. "I haven't been so exuberant since I streaked down the Champs-Elysée on Bastille Day. And, boy, what an idea. To pump in polluted air that would just make us cough but probably kills them. Excellent. I wish Elodie was alive to see it."

Françoise hugged him. "She would have appreciated the poetic justice of what we've done. However, we don't know it's worked yet. Possibly their air-conditioning filtering is better than we think. Excuse me, Anton, what do you and your group have there?" She pointed at a couple of bulging plastic bin bags they'd brought back from the dome.

"Carrie's idea. Somehow, she knew the smaller left dome had plants in there. She's a botanist. You know?"

Françoise's mouth gaped. "You went into the other dome and snaffled their plants? That could've jeopardized the whole mission."

"Fran," said Bono, switching her attention. "Look at the screen."

Assuming something had gone wrong, she stared at the green image of the dome. No activity, the hoses looked full, so the dirty gas from the specially tuned diesel engines must have been pumping as planned. "I can't see anything."

"Exactly. It's working great. If their filtering system increased its activity, I would've expected to see smoke being emitted from the upper vents, but there is nothing visible, yet the hoses are working."

She looked at her watch. "Twenty-five minutes. I'd be suffering in there now." She shivered, yet it was a warm July night. They shouldn't be celebrating at the choking to death of any creature, even those. Did it make her feel better about Victor's miserable demise? No.

"Fran, have a sniff in the plant bag," said Anton, bubbling with childlike excitement.

She shook her head then buried it in her hands for the rest of the journey to the campus.

"WAKE UP, FRAN." Reluctantly, she slit opened an eye at Bono. When she saw his serious face, she opened both wide. He thrust a cup of ready-blown coffee at her. "First, you need this."

After a few sips, she looked again at him. "So, it didn't work then. Shame, and yet..."

"Oh, I think we poisoned them all right. But listen. When Anton and his groupies showed those weeds to his dorm, they had a smoke."

"I'm not surprised. They looked like a cross between cannabis, bindweed and red cabbage. Their dormitory must smell awful."

"The plants are weird, alien but now growing in Earth atmosphere, so maybe altered to what the aliens expected–or not. I suppose the aliens might have hit on the perfect growing conditions for the galaxy's most potent weed. Our students got instant highs. Guess where they are now?"

"On the ceiling, flying off the roof? Let me get back to sleep."

"On their way back at the domes to collect the rest."

"Oh no." She leapt out of bed, visually treating Bono, because she only wore a camisole. He grinned while he turned for her to dress. "I presume you've been calling them. How many? Have they taken the minibus? When will they reach the domes? Oh my God, the workforce will be awake. We don't know if ARIA-2 is infectious. What time is it? Eight. Damn."

"Yes to most of those questions. They should reach the domes in fifteen minutes. Our car is waiting and is faster."

THEY HAD TO STOP ON THE OUTSKIRTS OF LIVRON, a small town on the east side of the Rhône. Françoise had been monitoring the camera they'd set up. Bono shared the horror with her as they saw Anton's group being attacked. A dozen humans slashing maniacally with kitchen hatchets overwhelmed them. The drugged students had no chance.

She opened the passenger door and threw up onto the road. Her sick engulfed the new groundsel and dandelions reclaiming the tarmac. Her hands were clammy but cold, so she massaged her griping stomach for a few minutes before staggering upright and walking down the dusty road. Life was rollercoastering for her. Mostly lows. Through her tears, she saw a Labrador dog on the pavement seemingly sunbathing. His eye watched her, so it wasn't asleep. Two years ago, she would have greeted it with a biscuit or a hand to sniff. Generally a friendly breed and good around children, these days, it could be looking at her hand as food.

"Fran, we've got an emergency call from Abdul."

She waved goodbye to the dog, and gratifyingly, its tail wagged. Not everything was malevolent.

"Hello, Abdul, we have some news for you, though you mightn't like it."

"Whatever you adventurers have done, it has stirred some hornets. Aircraft are in the skies heading towards your area."

"When you say aircraft..."

"The orbiting real-time radar only tells us that three flying objects at Mach three are buzzing, so that means the smaller alien ships. They're probably going to their domes, but from the north. They seem to be making a beeline for your campus. You haven't done anything to upset them, have you?"

"Bono here, Abdul, I prepared a report. Sending it to you now. We better alert our people. Over."

Françoise and Bono looked aghast at each other. What could get worse? She glanced again at the screen but could only see still shapes on the ground. "You call them to see if there are any survivors while I use my NoteCom to call the campus."

A minute later, they heard the sonic booms. Bono laughed. "They can't be going to the campus, they'd overshoot it." She laughed with relief too, but only until they saw the plume of black smoke mushrooming in the mirror. As they turned to see it properly, the low-frequency crump filled their ears.

CHAPTER 32

Daybreak July 16ᵗʰ 2016, approaching Fiji.

"THERE'S BREAKFAST IN THE GALLEY, BRYCE," says Dominiq, running up the steps to the top cockpit. "Sorry I'm late. Go eat and catch up on your sleep. How long have you been at full throttle? Twenty minutes?"

"Since I worked out that my wife must live on one of these islands. Unless you tell me which, we're stopping at each island between here and Australia." I'm playing a bluff, figuring he won't tell me.

"You've been pushing sixty knots in the dark?" He looks shocked, and I laugh at his open mouth. It's not difficult for him to verify our average speed with the positioning data.

"It's not really dangerous with no land and a radar that's singing to anything bigger than a seagull."

"We could've hit a whale or partially submerged boats."

"I hadn't thought of that." I spread my arms in mock apology.

"Nessa's got fried eggs for you down there." He avoids my question but looks aside at me, knowing I won't go away. "All right, yes, you are married, but don't work yourself up. She can't be alive now. She was in Oz but must've been on a plane with ARIA when she arrived in New Guinea last year. The infection arrived there damned fast. You were on an anthropology research job in Samoa. Not only did Samoa escape the early travels of ARIA victims, but you were out in the sticks. You and Benita must have caught it long after your wife."

"Now, we're getting somewhere. What's her name, besides being Mrs Massey?"

"Gabby, but it won't do you any good. She's thirty yet would've lost over fifty years of memory. Even if you found her alive, she wouldn't know how to talk. It would be like her being born every day only as an adult." He stops going on about it when he sees my fists clenching and unclenching. He was like this when we were kids. Always assuming the worst.

"Maybe you're right, but has anyone seen her body?"

He speaks softer, knowing he's gone too far, again. "No. I suppose there's the faintest possibility she avoided ARIA."

"Or immune. Plenty of people have strong immune systems. They never catch colds and other viruses."

"I understand you want to be hopeful, but look on the bright side. Your memory has no recollection of her. We don't even have her photograph. It's as if..."

He can't bring himself to say as if she never existed. He's right, but a bastard for nearly saying it.

"Sadly, Bryce, it seems everyone gets ARIA—no immunity, just avoidance."

Benita comes up the steps bringing my coffee. "What about babies born to ARIA mums?"

"Nope. They're not immune and so either catch the virus in the womb or as soon as they're born. No hope."

"There's always hope," Benita says. "Look at us."

"But there's no ARIA-2 outside a small area of Canada and Wales. And now you two, maybe me and Nessa."

"How are you and Nessa?" she asks, showing more concern than they deserve.

"Fuzzy heads, but our memories are intact. However, they are not enhanced like happened to the only other experiment, Antonio Menzies. He went berserk, but he was exposed to the first opening of the second case. An electromagnetic wave was emitted along with a presumed powerful dose of ARIA-2. It gave him access to all his memory. It sent him psychotic, although he seems to have it under control, according to him."

"You haven't told me where she is."

"Bryce, what's the point? We have a mission. Charlotte is alive and ARIA free. Surely?"

"Where?"

"Last I heard, Gabby was in Port Moresby on New Guinea. And yes, we are going close by. So, I suppose you will insist we jeopardize the whole mission and our lives."

"Set a course while I catch up on some sleep."

EITHER A FALLING-OUT-OF-A-TREE NIGHTMARE has returned or we've hit a storm. I stagger to the head and then up top. Windblown rain makes the top deck slippery. The ocean has transformed from millpond to choppy, white foam racing from south to north. Dominiq wears yellow waterproofs, sees me, points ahead and mutters incoherently. I peer, and where I think the sea merges with the grey sky, a darker smudge shows.

"New Guinea?"

"Fiji. At this rate, we won't reach New Guinea until tomorrow evening or Sunday. I've reduced speed to forty, so we won't get thrown around so much."

"Are we stopping at Fiji?"

"Not planned to. We've enough supplies to reach Australia. We should keep away from Fiji in case of pirates."

"I can picture it. Eighty-year-old swashbucklers swinging from their masts."

"Bryce, you were out there on a boat only a few days ago. The risk is still palpable."

"Maybe, but by now, I would have the memories of a thirteen year old. Hell, I still don't have any of my memories between teen and a few days ago. And I've no idea what a palpable is."

CHAPTER 33

Midday Monday July 18th 2016, outside the breakwater of Port Moresby, New Guinea.

IT'S A MESS. The harbour looks like a kid's bath after he's had a tantrum with his toy boats.

"The storm," says Nessa.

I'm looking through the glasses. "I can see algae on the decks of some of the boats where they must've been wrecked for months."

"My, look at those dogs. There's hundreds."

Many are snoozing on the dockside while others scamper around. Three are having a tug of war. Can't see what's being pulled apart. It might be another Fido. "It's a bit choppy out here. I'll sail into the harbour."

"I don't think Dominiq wants us in the harbour. There could be dangers."

"The wind's getting up again. The danger could be worse out here. But run along and tell him if you must." I wait for her to leave the upper bridge before inching the *Solar Sprint* into the harbour. By the time Dominiq bounds up the steps, we are passed the 10 MPH sign and we are heading to anchor in the middle of boat-wreck city.

"Damn you, Bryce. There could be wrecks just below the surface."

"Listen to grumpy Dom. The water's calmer here. Look, you can see the bottom, and it's easier to examine the dockside."

The women come up to referee. Nessa takes Dominiq to the left bridge rail while Benita slings an arm around my shoulders and plants a smoochy kiss on my cheek.

"Having a brothers' tiff?"

"Never mind him. I'm looking for the best way to get off."

"You're not seriously thinking of feeding yourself to those dogs? They might've been pets two years ago, but now..."

"It wouldn't be difficult to draw them off."

"Erm, hello, Brycie. I don't think throwing a stick features in their good things to do any more. Anyway, the chances of Gabby being around here is so remote."

"You mean she's probably become dog shit like the rest of the people here?"

"I was trying to be delicate."

"You? Don't bother. I'm a realist, apparently. Dead humans always became food whether it's maggots or bacteria. Looks like dogs will inherit the Earth. The aliens don't have a chance."

"You're making me shiver." We hug while I continue to look over her shoulder for any sign of human activity.

"Right, we've seen enough," says Dominiq. "We're wasting time. Let's go about and get on our way before some mad sailor thinks we're a soft target."

"I'm going ashore."

"I hadn't realized," says Dominiq, "that ARIA sent you bananas. You'd be eaten within minutes. Using the ship's megaphone to shout 'Stay' isn't going to work."

"Dom, the sonic device we have would scare them off, but it might be better to attract them to a focus point, so we know where they are."

"Bryce," says Nessa, walking over to me and placing her hand on my arm. "Even if Gabby is there, you don't know what she looks like or which hotel she might be in."

"I do know what she looks like." I take out a folded paper from my back pocket. "I persuaded Ryder to look her up. He found her on our family database on the mainframe at Rarotonga. They gathered personnel data before the main Internet servers went down."

Nessa took the print from me and showed Dominiq the picture of a black-haired woman. Benita doesn't want to see it. I think she's jealous, which is stupid since she has a wedding ring, so her feller's dead too. All we have is each other.

Dominiq coughed. "That was her, but..." He waves at the shore. "You can see beyond the docks. It's a ghost town. What's the point?"

"To satisfy myself. I dunno. To feel I tried. To pick up vibes of the last place of this woman, whom I had feelings for, yet I don't remember. I have to do it, that's all."

"I'm coming with you," says Benita.

"Hey, come on," says Dominiq. "Two suicides in one day is just ridiculous."

"I can understand it," says Nessa. "You'll have to go heavily armed, and take your cell phones."

Dominiq threw his hands up. "Take no unnecessary risks. What am I saying?"

"At least I can't catch ARIA again. If I do see victims, then they will catch ARIA-2 from us. That can only be a good thing. Yes?"

"This is an island. You're not likely to start a rescuing diffusion pattern from here," says Nessa. "But you never know."

"So, are you going to land here or round the coast away from the dogs?" says Dominiq.

"No point around the bay," I say. "The hotels are here, so I'd only have to make our way back to the dogs. No, we'll distract them first and land on that jetty to the right. No dogs there."

It's weird how my language is growing up all the time from that geeky teen only a day or so ago.

"How are we going to distract them? Blow up a building with the ship's gun?" At last, Dominiq's eyes light up with pleasure.

"That would cause confusion and might even send them in our direction."

"I know it's horrible," says Benita. "But if you shoot a few dogs over on the left dockside..."

Nessa pulls a disgusted face, but Dominiq grins. "It would work. I'll use the rifle. I'll kill them outright, don't worry about feeling bad. Without us, all those dogs will eat each other as they fall ill, injured, or old. Most will die being torn apart while alive. At least a few will die cleanly and quickly with bullets."

THE GRUESOME DISTRACTION PLAN WORKS.

Instead of using the noisy outboard motor on the dinghy, Benita and I paddle over and hear four shots, followed by silence then a canine orchestra. We tie up at an iron ladder. We have rucksacks, rifles, and holstered pistols like we're going to war.

From the boat, I'd targeted a tourist Novahotel for our first attempt. We run a hundred-metre dash to it seemingly undetected by the dogs. Benita slips on the wet marble steps and cries out. I help her up while looking up, but the nearest dogs are fighting on the other side of the harbour. I help her in and she rubs her right knee through her jeans. The overcast light outside makes the inside gloomy and foreboding.

A large cola-drinks cabinet has been pushed over. Its glass front is smashed and liberated cans are everywhere, mostly empty–stamped on. No bodies, but indistinguishable dark stains, furry faeces, and a coating of grit layers the otherwise white marble. Our trainers are silent on the once-smooth floor, and the muted barking makes the spacious reception hall an eerie place. I feel my stomach tightening and hairs doing their own dance on my neck. I look at Benita, and her pained expression goes beyond her wounded knee.

"So spooky in here," she says.

"Yeah, like it belongs to the Addams family."

"Are you saying I'm Wednesday?"

"Wrong colour, but hell, I like Christina Ricci. Wonder where or what she is now? Look out for cobwebs."

"Too late, I'm spitting it. And it's my new hair look and yours. We're not doing a room search are we?"

"I'm looking for the register, should be on the reception desk, but I'll have to search the drawers. I suppose you might as well look for unopened bottles and cans to take back."

The reception's desk is decorated by thick dust accompanied by dead flies and roaches. I open it where a ribbon marked the page. June 15th but that's last month. Ah, 2015 last year. Oh fuck, that's a year and four weeks, which means anyone catching ARIA here would have lost fifty-six years of memory. Fuck. That's assuming this last entry is the leaving day—everyone too confused to continue working here.

"Not much, but I got some bottled sauces and tinned fruit. There's flour and rice in the kitchen but crawling with weevils. Any luck?"

"No Gabby Massey or Gabby, Gabrielle anything. The last day was over a year ago."

"Really, they got it before Samoa then?"

"Apparently, the airfield on Samoa was out of action when all this climaxed, so we didn't get ARIA 'til the boats arrived. Let's get out of here."

"Back to the boat? I can hear dogs again—louder."

"If you want to go back, go. I want to try the other big hotels. Nessa says we were well off enough to use the expensive ones. The local Hilton is not far inland."

"I'm coming with you."

IN SPITE OF THE DOGS, the lack of humans makes the place disturbingly quiet, which makes sudden, unnatural noises more scary. Benita grabs me when we pass under the sun canopies of glass-fronted stores and a crash inside scares us both.

"Dogs?"

"There are other creatures hunting for food. Rats, cats, and hogs. There may be people, and I don't mean ancients or those, who like us, coped by keeping notes for ages. I think there will be people who are survivalists: aggressive, tough individuals who are immune to most diseases."

Benita steps carefully around a festering heap that leaks dark liquid into a nearby drain. It's not possible to see what animal it used to be. "A cunning back-to-nature human can't survive once his memory's all gone."

"Why not? His stomach will tell him to eat. Instinct keeps him running from danger or after food. He'll not freeze to death here in the tropics. He'd be like a wild animal. And *that* could nearly have been us, Benita."

"I dunno about that. It takes skill to avoid trouble and know which foods are edible. Animals learn survival skills and remember them. If your survivor lost their memory down to day one, they'd be vulnerable as soon as they woke up. They'd know they were hungry but wouldn't know what to eat. They might get lucky and not eat poisonous leaves or rotting fruit but maybe not the next day when it starts over. Does he know to avoid snakes?"

"Wow, Benita, that was some speech."

She giggles. "So it was. And not prepared, although I have been thinking about it since we had ARIA-2."

"What job did they say you had on Samoa?"

"Apparently, a teacher. Figures, huh?"

"Yeah, randy, mischievous, always wanting to spank me and put me in detention."

She laughs again. "Hey, Bryce, we're here. The Port Moresby Hilton's door's shut. They don't want our business."

She's right. Most of the doors in the street are wide open, some smashed in. This is an all-glass door, but it's been boarded. "Look where you're going, Benita, there's broken pots and glass everywhere. They must have had some rock bands staying."

"I've a bad feeling about this; let's go for that fancy one up the road."

"What's to be scared of? This must have been done months ago. There's an unbroken window here we can smash to get in. Stand right back while I throw this chair at it."

"Look out!"

A blur passes my right peripheral vision as a large plant pot smashes on the road. I leap back. I should go forward under the narrow doorway overhang, but I want to see who bombed me.

"Did you see what happened?"

"No, I just saw it falling and shouted at you."

The five-floor hotel looked normal except for a couple of broken windows. No one appears, but they're watching us for sure. I try communicating. "Hello up there! We're friends!"

A woman shrieks, "Bugger off!"

"Bryce, directly above the front entrance. I saw a man's face in the top-floor window—the open one."

"We can help you," I shout again. This time, a wizened old man appears. A ragged white beard contrasts with his bald brown head.

Someone behind him seems to be handing him a book. No, it's a brick. "Benita, get in the back of that grocery van."

"There might be rats eating stale crumbs. Oh, all right. You be careful."

The brick lands a metre away to my right. It's then I notice a dog at the harbour end of the road. It seems to be waiting. Damn.

"We don't want no help. Fuck off, or it'll be bullets next."

"Come on, Bryce. You could spend all day and get nowhere with them."

"But if we got close enough for them to catch ARIA-2, it could start a recovery."

"Hardly. This is an island, and only idiots come here. Hey, will this vehicle go?" She peers through the narrow window to the cab.

"The tyres are flat and the battery will be." I glance down the road to see the dog has salivating reinforcements. I push logic away. "It is an old engine, before electronic systems constantly drained the battery."

I climb in and turn the key. The van lurches forward and stalls. I'm embarrassed. "Hah. I've forgotten how to drive. Oh yes. The clutch has to be in." I push down the left pedal and turn the key again while gently pumping the gas pedal. The starter motor coughs, and the vehicle kangaroo hops up the road away from the dogs. The right wheel climbs hotel debris, but once past, I find second and accelerate to a dizzy fifteen miles per hour. At the top of the hill, I turn left and emergency brake.

"What? Hey, stay put while I climb out of this grubby hellhole and join you in front... That's better, that's a great view. Look at that horizon. It looks like a bath of mercury. The *Solar Sprint* is lost among all that jumble of boats in the harbour. And there's another grey coast guard vessel in the next harbour. Looks like a yacht's mast has fallen over it. You're not saying much, Brycie. Still miffed at not making friends with the inhabitants? What are you looking at through those glasses?"

"A very interesting hotel sign."

"Why interesting? Is it flashing?"

"In a way. When Dominiq and I were kids, we used to holiday with an aunt in Sydney. She took us to the Janolan Caves. Bloody marvellous. I loved those caves."

"And the point is?"

"I can't imagine romancing without taking my fiancée to the honeymoon hotel there."

"Ah, penny's dropped. If she saw that name, she would want to stay there because of the name association. Can you tell if it was a four star or a dump?"

"One way to find out. Hold tight."

WE PARK BEHIND AN ABANDONED POLICE CAR.

"The doors of the Janolan Hotel are open," I say.

"Open? They're missing. But, I suppose it's less likely the place is occupied by mad barricaders ready to rain furniture on our heads."

We are cautious as we leave the van, partly because the area is so quiet. Almost normal if we disregard the blowing plastic carrier bag. Strange. I would've expected human garbage to be blown to their resting places by now. The sea is the planet's largest dustbin, and once there, plastic and paper doesn't like to return. Maybe a land disposal site is being mined by animals releasing debris to the air.

Benita screams right into my ear, sending me sideways, followed immediately by a horn blast from somewhere far away. "Struth, what the hell did you do that for? And you've set something off–listen to that."

"Sorry, Bryce," she says, hugging me so tight I can't breathe in again. "It's the body. It took me by surprise."

I look around then see a decomposed corpse in the back of the police car. The poor sod has his wrist handcuffed to the door handle.

The deep sound of a horn resonated over the town to us once more. "Bryce, it's the *Sprint*. We've forgotten to switch our cell phones on."

We share an embarrassed laugh as I switch mine on. "Hello, Dom, having a blast?"

"Stop buggering about and come back."

"Nearly done. We're trying one more hotel."

"We've seen more dogs and other creatures we couldn't see properly. I don't know if the same trick will work when you come back."

"Why not?"

"The dogs are milling around where you were. They've picked up your scent I suppose. I can't use the sonar gun without being sure you won't be deafened too."

"Okay. We've got transport, so we'll go to the next harbour. I can see a road to it that avoids going close to the marina we came in. I'll give you a call when we're ready."

"Now, Bryce. I–Nessa's getting edgy waiting around here, especially now we've had to announce our presence. We'll sail around and make sure there's a boat for you to reach us. Be ready in ten."

"What's the rush—? Oh, charming. He's signed off. He can wait.

Wonder why he doesn't want us to search properly?"

"Concerned for our health—your health?"

"Yeah right. More like he doesn't want us to find something or someone, Gabby. But he knows I know we're not going to find her alive. Weird. Let's find the register."

The rubbish condition of the once-smart reception hall doesn't surprise us. More faeces, broken glass, and scurrying of rats.

"I hope the vermin don't take a chance on us for dinner," says Benita, as she heads off for the kitchen again.

"Have your gun ready," I call, as I find the dusty register on the counter. A plaintive meow surprises me. Behind the reception desk is a cat basket complete with a ginger cat and kittens. It looked as natural as if nothing has happened.

"Hello, puss. Have you been busy catching mice?"

"Who are you talking to, Bryce?" she says from the diner.

"No one. Keep on to the kitchen." I didn't want her falling in love with the moggies. I find the last used page in the Janolan's register:

June 16 2015 Lt Col Morrison dble full 214
June 16 2015 Mrs G Massey fam full 322
June 16 2015 Ms E Fenney sngle half 117

Three twenty-two. I look for the room key, but it isn't there. She's either in there or took the keys with her when she left for the day. I hear Benita run back, her trainers crunching glass.

"A few cans, candles, and matches. Found her?"

"She was here on June sixteen last year." My eyes dribble stupid tears. I don't know this ghost, and yet, we were together, as one. Part of her must still be in me, surely? I peer mistily at Benita, who looks agonised.

"Hey, look, the clock's working. Amazing. How's that?"

I turn to see the reception digital clock that must be running on last-minute batteries. She is employing distraction psychology. "Come on. Up the stairs."

"Oh no. Bryce. What if you find her body half eaten?"

"I've got to know. To feel something. Stay here if you want." She comes with me.

"What's her room number?"

"Three twenty-two." I halt on the stairs and look at her. "It's a family room. Why would she want that?"

"You said she had money, so why not have plenty of room. I hate tiny hotel rooms. Come on, don't read too much into it."

We find her door locked. I look at Benita and find myself trembling. She hugs me.

"It doesn't mean she's in there. She could've left the hotel that day and took the key with her. Look, we can leave."

"No way. I know she's unlikely to be in there, but she could be. She won't be alive if she is or very unlikely to be—unless she barricaded herself in with a ton of provisions and water. But, Benita, she—like the others—had to die somewhere. I know I joke about the dogs, but it's like where do dead birds go? There's millions of them, but we only see the occasional corpse, but... let's get on with it.

"It looks like a solid door. I'm not going to bust my shoulder, give me a hand with that coffee table."

We run down the corridor to a low table, knock off the vase with its neglected roses, and walked back. In true castle-assaulting style, we batter-ram the door until it gives way. Apart from a layer of dust and a few dead flies, the room could be lived in today. A white cardigan lay on the bed coverlet. I finger it as if some sensory magic will tell me what's happened.

"Bryce, the bathroom is normal. Quite clean. If the taps work, I'll have a shower. Ugh! It's brown."

"Accumulated rust. I expect the hot water taps will run until the header tank is empty. Have a shower if you like, but don't come near me."

The desk has a pale green folder with a corner of a white sheet of paper showing. Again, I merely touch it with my finger and need Benita to say Open Sesame.

"Open it or take it with us," she says, getting impatient with my weakness.

I pick up the folder by the bottom corners and tip out the contents. Receipts and invoices for this trip. I hardly dare look. I can't see properly for the stupid tears for a woman I knew but don't. I pull back the dusty dust coverlet and lie on the King-size bed. Benita lies beside me. Before long, her hand wanders over to me.

"No. It's not right."

"Okay, but it's real luxury, this. When was the last time you laid in a big, soft bed?"

"I don't remember, and neither do you. It could be months in real time too.

"Benita, my wife, Gabby—wherever you are now—lay in this bed. She was the last person to occupy this space. I feel a tingle as if her spirit is here."

We lie in silence. I know Benita thinks I'm nuts. Maybe this ARIA stuff has affected my emotions.

Benita's cell phone jumps to life. "It's Dominiq wanting to go while the tide is on the way out."

I groan but sit up and look around. A pink zipped sports bag is hiding under the desk. Benita sees it too and goes for it while I visit the bathroom. I might as well use proper facilities instead of a tree.

As Benita says, the bath is remarkably clean, all but a house spider. As I wash my hands, the water clears, and I stare at the middle-aged grizzled stranger in the mirror. I freeze. Two toothbrushes keep each other company in a dusty glass. One is medium-bristled with a yellow handle; the other is pink, junior size with Mini-Mouse on the handle. I pick them up and turn to face Benita, who is holding a Barbie doll.

"Snap," she says. Her face, with the absence of a smile, says, oh dear.

"I have a daughter."

She tilts her head, not correcting me.

Before leaving, we search for more clues, but they seem to have packed all but the items we've already found. I stuff the folder, toothbrushes and cardigan into the sports bag and stop at the ruined door, looking back.

"They knew. They must've known about my daughter. That's why he's been hurrying us out, hoping we won't find this hotel or any evidence." I want to burst out in rage but can't. Not yet. And it won't be fair on Benita. Incongruously, I turn to her. "Maybe you have family, Ben. Have you asked?"

"Last night, while you slept, Ryder did a data search. He found a contract tag that I was a biology teacher on Samoa. Probably why we were together. Nothing else."

We hug. "So, you might have but..."

"Will never find out." She looks up at my wet face and uses her sleeve on it. "Which is worse, lover?"

We hug more for a long while before, holding hands, we leave the unlabelled memorial.

CHAPTER 34

AFTER A DIFFICULT FEW DAYS, ploughing through frightened waves at full speed, we had Western Australia's coastline on our port bow. Nessa tearfully reveals that my daughter's name is Annie, and three years old last New Year's Day. Dominiq is made to murmur apologies for not telling me everything, but he clearly believes I was better off not knowing. Probably doesn't want me distracted from the Charlotte mission.

"Still no peep from Charlotte?" I ask Nessa after she'd been on the radio for a long while nattering to other women at Rarotonga.

"No. It's worrying Teresa, especially, and Abdul. They'd built up a bond. The satellite links for our Internet and radios have been cobbled together by Abdul with earlier instructions Charlotte had sent. He said that he can ping her computer, which indicates it's on and working, but her NoteCom's not working, nor her phone, nor radio console."

"She must have been got at by the people who made the smoke we saw on the picture. Shame. Hopefully, we can get to her before her memory is lost too far."

Dominiq comes up onto the bridge. I descend, not enjoying his company since New Guinea.

"Bryce, we need to talk tactics. We're going to reach Carnarvon tomorrow late afternoon. Shall we go in under cover of the setting sun and following darkness, or wait for dawn?"

I don't mind talking strategies as long as I don't have to look into his supercilious eyes. "Pre-dawn's better. If there are others, they'll probably be dozy until mid-morning, and we'll have daylight to look for her."

"And the gear, code books, and other stuff we've come for in her comms room will be better looked for without putting lights on."

"Okay. Which comes first, looking for Charlotte or gathering the satellite gear? I know the answer, don't I?"

"You might think I'm heartless, Bryce, but we need that stuff whether Charlotte comes with us or not."

"I would say 'heartless bastard,' but that's a slur on my own parents too. Right, I'll look for Charlotte, you gather stuff. When you've loaded it aboard, you can help me. What about the women?"

"Yes, I've been wondering about them. Nessa will be happy enough to mind the ship. She knows how to operate everything, including the weaponry. Benita will probably want to come with you. How do you feel about that?"

What's this? I'm being consulted about a relationship issue by Dominiq? Wow. He's not asking the person who matters, but it's progress.

"Do we have maps or a description of where you are to look for the comms room?"

"We've been there, Bryce. Oh, you won't recall. Remember, I told you I was stationed in Perth in the army? I had to do some courses at Carnarvon. Also, when we get closer, you'll see the antennae. They're on the roof of Charlotte's lab and comms room. To the left, you'll see a large satellite dish too, but that's part of the Apollo space race. Used to relay the moon landing. Charlotte uses a smaller, newer one. I didn't know where her living quarters were. Presumably, she moved into her lab building in recent months. I brought you along a few years ago."

"It'll be a new personal adventure, but it helps if one of us knows where to go."

03:00 July 25th 2016 off Australian west coast. Two hundred metres offshore from Carnarvon.

A PRE-DAWN, mid-winter forty-five Fahrenheit greets our sleepy faces. Dominiq insists we wear flak jackets, so we should be warm. If only memories could be kept in as easily.

The coast guard boat's radar sees nothing moving for its range of twelve miles. Abdul tells us the most recent satellite infrared pass shows nothing, but ironically, he needs Charlotte's expertise to use the better-quality data to see small vessels.

We tie up at a small jetty away from the port. We check our cell phones and jog up the coast road towards Charlotte's lab complex.

"This is definitely her lab," says Dominiq.

"Yes, we can read," says Benita. "Australian Space Agency. Carnarvon Research Laboratory."

I'm surprised to see it's so new. All smoked glass and stainless steel. It must cost a fortune in air conditioning.

"At the top of these steps is the main entrance," says Dominiq. "I can't see any broken glass, so my guess is the door is unlocked. Do you want to come up and see or carry on round to the living quarters round the back?"

Benita and I share glances, reading suspicion. "We'll come up with you," I say. "Just to keep you company for now."

The double doors are locked. "We could break in," Dominiq says. "We're not going to be using this facility again, are we?"

"Probably not, but there might be some equipment we can leave running, such as receiving and transmitting. I assume there's solar power. We should find another way in or find Charlotte and her keys."

"No need," Dominiq says. He has a button-shaped key ring fob and swipes it over a red LED on the door, which unlocks.

Benita is about to go at him, but I hold up a finger and whispers, "Later, it's more important to find Charlotte." I, too, would like to know what's going on, but I remember Dominiq had several hidden agendas in the playground, so why should he be different now?

We follow Dominiq up the stairs to the top third floor where the laboratory and communications office occupy the biggest rooms.

Benita is the first to make observations. "There's nothing here to suggest a problem. No mess, apart from a couple of dirty coffee mugs. The systems are all on and lights are green."

"Agreed," says Dominiq. "And, as promised, she's packed hardware in several boxes. There's circuit boards, chips, memory sticks by the score. Also, YAGI aerials here dismantled and packed, ready to go."

"Is that all we need from here?" I say, pointing at the boxes.

"I'd like to send some test messages to Rarotonga and the French people. Then make some backups of the systems just in case she was waiting until we arrived to do last-minute saves. Maybe an hour, tops."

"Okay. We'll go look for her while you do that. Are there accommodation units in this building?"

"Not when I knew it. All in that building you can see at the rear, but she could be anywhere."

There's a graphics workbench near the door. "Are these images part of Charlotte's secret?" As I hold up a glossy colour laser print, Dominiq charges over as if it was on fire. As he goes to grab it, I snatch it with my other hand and pass it to Benita.

"Boys, stop arsing around. It's just pictures of endless fields."

"Here, have one," I say as I flip one in the air to Dominiq. He must've have thought they'd show something so wonderful or bizarre that he had to be the only one to know about it. He hasn't changed from the information control freak he was as a kid.

"My dear Benita, look carefully. Those are the Prairies, probably not far from Winnipeg where—"

"Julia and Manuel?"

"And the alien domes," I say. "Where Ryder says interesting

plants are being cultivated. So our keen-eyed Charlotte saw them spreading beyond into nearby ranch land?"

Benita laughs. "How could she possibly tell what the plants are? They're probably weeds."

Dominiq laughs too. "They most certainly are weed, of the hallucinogenic variety. She'd be able to tell they aren't wheat or the usual wild plants by their infrared signature. This image is a false-colour from a Landsat satellite."

I place a few in one of the boxes. "I hope we still find Charlotte somewhere. Hiding out."

As Benita and I carry a box each to the reception area, she says, "Do you want my theory? You are getting it anyway. She left to go home to bed and then was too scared by some intruders to return. Hey, should we prop the door open, we don't have that fob to get back in."

"Better not. We can phone him if we need to get back in. Let's see if there's a back door. I don't think Charlotte would spend several weeks hiding in her room, do you?"

We find a rear door, push it open, and although dawn is happily throwing itself at the buildings, we can see a window lit up in the dormitory.

"It must be her room," she says. We jog over then stumble over debris strewn around the accommodation-block entrance. DVDs, scattered magazines, crumpled boxes point to at least a burglary. Charlotte's apartment door lay in splinters on her floor.

"Is that blood?" Benita says, pointing at a brown streak on a wall.

"I've checked the bathroom and bedroom. She must have left alive," I say. "No one would bother carrying out a body, and there's not sufficient blood, if that's what it is, for her to have bled to death."

"Are we going to look for her? She could've been taken anywhere."

"True, but we have to look around the vicinity. I wouldn't feel right abandoning her. I would feel really excellent if we found her and gave her ARIA-2. She deserves it."

"I can't tell if you are being sarcastic, Bryce. I know the islanders haven't welcomed us, but we are alive, and when we go back, we will have some sort of life."

"You don't see me arguing, do you? Right, we better check out her bathroom cabinet."

"Why? Want her deodorants? Not a bad idea, come to think..."

"Drugs, idiot. No, not recreational, unless she has them."

"Oh, her medicines. Good grief, you can think deep."

We collect the analgesics and tubes, and I fill a holdall with gadgets, memory sticks, and her battery-flat NoteCom. We leave her light on and a note to say who we are and why we took her stuff. I have a rethink as we leave and rush back to replace some of the medicines. She might return and be really pissed off at a second burglary.

"We'll keep an eye out for any signs of her while we go shoplifting," says Benita, obviously looking forward to a spell of retail therapy after a long abstinence.

Daylight is firmly established at nine o'clock as we wander towards Carnarvon town centre. We find the widest street in Australia, according to a plaque. Made wide for camel trains to turn but none of them hang around these days. Thanks to a convenience store, I add batteries and torches to drinks and candy.

"I heard a noise from the pharmacy," Benita says, gripping my arm as if I need a tourniquet.

"Get your gun ready. Look, I have mine. You never know if a rabid dog or idiot is going to leap at us." In true FBI style, we flatten ourselves on either side of the open doorway. I hear glass break–maybe a small bottle fell. "I'm going in and keep to the right. You stay here as backup."

"No. Look, if you stand on that seat, you'll be able to see through the window."

She's right.

"It's Dominiq. He said nothing about leaving the lab. He's put some pink boxes in a rucksack. Let's surprise him."

"Bryce, are you thinking, like me, that he's been acting sus since we arrived here?"

"Ten out of ten. Maybe only seven. He's been acting suspicious since he conned us into going on this mission. You sneakily find out what the pink boxes are. He took them from the green cabinet behind the counter on the right." As I enter, I deliberately fake laryngitis so he doesn't shoot first.

"I might've guessed. You nearly got your head blown off. It's okay, Bryce, you find a food store. I'm collecting medicines we're running out of on the island."

I ignore his beseeching to go away and decide to get in his face instead. It's what brothers are for. I point at a shelf behind him. "What's in that red box?"

While he turns to retrieve it, I pull at his rucksack, but I only draw out a box of vials.

"Hey, leave my fucking rucksack alone." Dominiq drops the red box and lunges for his bag. I swing it behind me and hold out a restraining hand. I am bigger, so he stops. "That's just vials of Ketamine. I got it from the vets next door."

"Special-K? I remember this stuff. We used to fly on it at parties."

"Idiot. It's needed as an anaesthetic on the island. We also need entonox, which is why I'm lugging around that blue and white cylinder."

"Hey, Dom," says Benita, "there's an ambulance up the road. There might be more portable entonox kits inside."

"I'll come with you," I say. "With a bit of luck, the engine will start."

"Actually, that would be excellent. We could probably add to whatever's inside from this gear, and..."

"And what?" Benita says, looking at me as if she's worked out what he filched.

"Just something Nessa particularly asked me to look for."

"Such as? We might see it ourselves."

"Probably not in here. All right, she is partial to custard cream biscuits, but there were none."

We both laugh, but Dominiq doesn't see the funny side. Benita consoles him with a hug. "Actually, I saw some packets of diabetic custard creams in the case by the till. Better than nothing, eh?"

As anticipated, the ambulance had been plundered, but plenty of plasters, wipes, and ambulance first aid kits, along with water bottles will come in handy. After fetching a replacement battery from a nearby garage, I get the engine going and reverse it on flat tyres to the pharmacy.

As we load the ambulance to bursting, Dominiq interrogates us over the condition of Charlotte's flat, seeking assurance we removed any computer bits that might be useful. He doesn't seem surprised that we didn't find her.

"I'm astonished to find you in town, Dominiq, I thought you'd be too busy."

"Charlotte had already packed."

"Yeah, but you were supposed to find the fuel we need to get back."

"She'd done that too. I found a note from her. It led me to a warehouse on a quay farther out of town. I'm going to need help. In fact, we need to bring the *Solar Sprint* to the dock. Do you think it's safe enough?"

I pull Benita into a stationers on the pretension of snaffling boxes of copier paper.

"Hey, this is sweet of you, Brycie, but do we have time for fooling around?"

224 | ARIA: Returning Left Luggage

"No, but time for you to tell me about those pink boxes."

"Contraceptive pills."

"But won't they have expired?"

"We've collected lots of medical stuff that's expired, including the Entonox."

"I suppose the use-by-date has a wide safety margin and most analgesics will still work, but surely, gases in cylinders will last for ever?"

"You know nothing, Brycie. Under pressure and over time, the gases separate. We did it in school science–only last month. He he."

"Okay, let's get back to those pills. Surely, Nessa doesn't need them at her age?"

"What are you saying?"

"He's obviously having an affair."

"For God's sake, Bryce, did you eat conspiracy theory cornflakes for breakfast again?"

"I've a good mind to tell Nessa. He's got another woman or two. And if he has, they shouldn't be taking contraceptives; we need as many babies as possible."

"Idiot. They could be hers. There are other reasons why women need hormone treatments. Now, take those two boxes of eighty-gram paper. I'll bring another one."

CHAPTER 35

THE SUN HAD GIVEN UP its look-at-me game by the time we'd loaded enough fuel for our return. We are all on the foredeck securing satellite equipment, mostly in crates apart from a couple of three-metre dishes.

"That's too bad," says Nessa, "not finding Charlotte. What are we going to do? Can't we sail farther south and look for her?"

"We are going south, remember?" says Dominiq. "We promised Bryce we'd go to Perth, where our parents lived two years ago."

I see him look at his watch. "Okay, Dom, I know it would take an extra two days just to get there and back. A few days looking, being disappointed, devastated, and maybe eaten by dogs. Hey, why haven't we seen many dogs in Carnarvon?"

"Poisoned," says Dominiq. "I saw dog skeletons, but the vet clinic had broken boxes and spilt rat-poison powder. Did Charlotte become a poisoner to protect herself?"

Nessa covers her mouth with her hand as if to suppress the noxious notion. "I don't think it's what she'd do."

"From what little I know of Charlotte, I doubt she'd kill them either, not deliberately," I say. "But in survival situations, people act desperately."

"So, can we go back to Rarotonga now?" says Dominiq. "I'm a hundred per cent certain we'll never locate our parents in Perth, and being a huge city, it would be much more dangerous than here or Port Moresby."

"I'm not so sure. I know we need to get back, and I'm aware of the dangers, but this could be our last chance to find them."

"Bryce," Nessa says, "they'd planned a trip to the United States, leaving while we were away. Didn't you tell him, Dominiq?"

"Oh, come on," I say. "Who's kidding who now?" But my bones tell me to believe her over him.

"All right," Dominiq says, flushing. "You needed extra persuasion to come out here. It's not a real lie in that when the ARIA news broke, I'm sure Dad would've called off their vacation. Alas, we didn't call each other during those crucial days, so we don't know for sure if they stayed in Perth, continued with their planned tour–or tried to– or whatever, wherever."

I FIND MYSELF DELAYING THE DEPARTURE. We have left the relative danger of the quayside and drifting a mile offshore while we double-check systems. I guess my indigestion, which hasn't subsided by taking the anti-acid tablets Benita gave me, is down to the nagging feeling we should look more for Charlotte. I gave up in Carnarvon too soon. Yet, how many buildings do you smash into, facing the risk of being attacked by dogs, emboldened rats, or crazy oldies? And I have qualms about abandoning the search in Perth. It's over five hundred miles away so probably not worth the risk, but I'm not likely to be back in this region, ever.

"Smoke," says Benita.

"No thanks," I say then see she is pointing back at Carnarvon. "Probably another high sun event." We noticed several blackened buildings and have developed many pyrotechnical theories. We postulate sunbeams focussed by glass bottles or ornaments overheating inflammables. Maybe rummaging animals knock bottles or cans over. Or methane from corpses and rotting vegetables combine with a spark from the afternoon thunderstorms that crop up. Sometimes, we see a whole row of stores remain only as charcoal. No fire brigades to show off their muscles and hoses.

Like the others, similarly reluctant to leave, I lean on the rail and watch the black tendrils snake into the hot air.

"Does it remind you of a photograph?" says Benita. I think for a moment and then walk round to the opposite rail and raise the binoculars.

"It's difficult to be sure, but I believe it is there." I pass the glasses to her and beckon the others. "The last image we have of Charlotte. Do you recall it?"

Dominiq shakes his head.

Nessa says, "It was an outside shot of her at the Carnarvon lab. Drop dead gorgeous."

"We saw smoke in the background and wondered then if she might be in danger. We thought it could be a ship or the next island."

"Bernier Island is twenty miles away. It would have to be a huge fire for you to see that. If it was a ship, then after five weeks, it could be in Africa by now. We're wasting time. Let's return to Rarotonga. I'll inform them we're on our way."

"Without Charlotte," says Nessa.

"Or a serious look for her," says Benita.

"Twenty miles is nothing for this turbo-charged cutter. Let's satisfy ourselves. We can't feel good, but let's have a feel-better factor."

"If there is a community on Bernier Island and they have snatched Charlotte, it means they are rapidly losing it and dangerous."

"But you said the smoke must have been from a big fire if from Bernier. Something like a moorland fire. So, why should that imply a large community of no-gooders? They could be do-gooders who are mixed up. My vote is for investigating. Show of hands?" I win the argument with a forest of three hands.

ON A REMARKABLY CALM SEA, we charge along at forty knots, leaving the dolphins that initially appear alongside laughing at us in our wake.

"What do they know that we don't?" says Dominiq, in a sulk at being outvoted, or the notion that we consider it necessary to enforce democracy.

"They're wishing us luck," Benita says, smiling and waving at a new group of cetaceans.

"Dolphins are gay sharks," he says. We crease up at the old joke, but more at Dominiq for saying it.

Nessa calls from the controls. "Radar is blipping at two-fifty degrees."

We peer through our binoculars and agree on a speck in that direction. It could be a boat. "Hey, it is producing smoke," I say, as a new plume of black appears.

"The blip is now returning a transponder label. Cee-Gee-fourteen. Anyone? Any ideas what it means?"

Without taking his eyes off the target, Dominiq says, "Of course, we are in the Carnarvon Gas field. It's a gas rig. I'd forgotten about them."

"Oops," I say.

"I can't be expected to remember every geographical detail. It doesn't mean I have ARIA. Oh, you're winding me up."

"I have a radio frequency that should work on them, shall I?"

"No, Nessa," Dominiq says, and I agree.

"We have to work out a plan," I say. "Cut the engine. In fact, go about and go just out of radar range while we consider the situation."

"What is there to consider?" says Benita, "Either they have her or not. We have a bigger gun. End of story."

I reach for a chart. "It's unlikely but possible they have weapons. More importantly, they, if there are 'theys' on that rig, might have Charlotte. I don't want to risk hitting her with a round from our gun, nor do I want to see them lock her up, so we can't find her."

"So, your plan is to wait until dark, get close enough to climb the ladder and look for her while they're asleep?" says Dominiq.

"Have you a better plan?" I say. "Suppose we follow Nessa's instincts and throw a radio call at them. Will they panic and do unpredictable things to Charlotte, or be calm because we are not mounting a surprise attack? But if they thought about it, we could call first, pretend to be friendly and then attack. No win for them, so I say let's go in unannounced under cover of darkness."

"Won't it depend if they have ARIA or not?" says Benita. "I think there's a good chance they haven't. They might be riggers who have escaped contact by working when it all kicked off. When TV and other communications told them there were problems, they chose to stay. They probably have provisions for a long stay or can go to the abandoned islands around and raid the tourist chalets. In which case, they might welcome us and a chance to return with us."

"A cosy scenario," says Dominiq, with an undisguised sneer.

I feel like strangling him when he treats us like this, especially when he's so bloody condescending to Benita.

Dominiq continues. "If they haven't ARIA, then they would be able to use their comms specialist on the rig. It's not likely that they hadn't found our cobbled Internet connections via the ISS and discovered Charlotte's role in it. She would have found them too and told us."

"To be fair," Nessa says, avoiding Dominiq's hateful eyes, "Charlotte has said several times that there are others pinging and downloading information off the web we created with the ISS before it went down. And that she didn't know, or wouldn't say, where they were located."

"Probably the aliens," says Dominiq. "In my opinion, if there are people on that rig, they have ARIA but not for too long. Maybe they stayed isolated until they became desperate for food."

"They might have tired of eating fish every day," I say, instantly regretting lightening the topic.

WE KEEP RADIO SILENCE but send an e-mail to Rarotonga to ask for any evidence of movement, smoke, or radio traffic at the rig and vicinity. Nothing, but they have limited vision until Charlotte's skills can be applied. Vicious circles are our speciality.

AT TWO IN THE MORNING, we approach the rig and turn off our radar and transponder in case they are monitoring. I'm in the small boat rather than the rubber dinghy, which would submarine quicker if bullet-holed. Dominiq comes with me, while the women stand guard a hundred metres off. This gives them a good view and would let their infrared-sighted weapons reach the platform that overhangs the ladder up from the water.

We have light rucksacks, flash-bang stun grenades, and the usual raid equipment. We wear night-vision goggles that auto-revert in brightness. Dominiq is above me, and I repress an irreverent snigger at the look of his SAS gear, complete with holster, ammo belt, knives, flak jacket, helmet, and handcuffs. I wear the same and laugh silently at myself. The mirth helps calm the raging butterfly storm in my guts. Adrenalin is supposed to hype you into battle, but I have knee-wobbling stage fright.

After a long climb, the metal ladder takes us to the platform's wide veranda where more ladders lead to two floors of buildings. The derrick is on the other side of these buildings, which must be the office and accommodation. We lean against the thin, plastic-coated steel wall, but hear nothing except the breeze whistling through gantries and cables. The slough and slap of the waves seem a long way off. I look to sea and just make out the darker shape of the lights-out *Solar Sprint*.

Like a kid, I wave, knowing they are watching. I imagine their tut-tutting.

The platform is remarkably ordered. Rope and hoses are coiled, there's no litter and all the doors are shut. It points to Benita's optimistic view that we have a non-ARIA group. I let Dominiq lead the way. He digs out a mini-periscope and looks in the nearest room. We creep along three rooms like this until his peeping-Tom activity makes him stop, turn to me, and raise two fingers.

I return two, but of course, I know he means there are two people in there, neither being Charlotte. He mocks sleep. He takes a small gun from his multi-tool belt and squirts superglue along the door crack. Clever. We sneak further. The last is unoccupied, so we need to climb the ladder. Our rubber soles silently take us up.

The first cabin he shows me a thumb up followed by giving me the finger. Ignoring his ambiguous crudity, I look. A woman is in the left bunk while a man occupies the lower right. I didn't telescope the periscope to examine the top bunks, accepting Dominiq's observation. I reckon the woman is Charlotte. Her hair looks fair, and I see a handcuff. He prepares a flash-bang while I squirt a fine lubricant on the door hinges and lock area. After inserting earplugs, I am to go for Charlotte while he ensures the other occupant stays put. I am ready.

He slowly opens the door, and without entering, flashes a low-set torchlight at Charlotte's face. Initially, we hope she'll quietly waken and we take her out without a fracas. He closes the door again. A twirling hand signal at his brain indicates his opinion that she is too asleep, maybe drunk or drugged, to waken easily.

He shows me the primed flash-bang. I kneel beside the window. Even through my earplugs, the detonation shocks me, and the white light bursts through the window and out across the sea. I feel the wall bulge, making me think he's used a fragmentation grenade by mistake, but he pulls at me. I take out my earplugs, rush in, and use my bolt cutter on the chain tethering Charlotte's ankle to the metal bunk.

"What... what? My ears. I can't see."

"Don't worry, you'll be all right. We're your rescue mission," I say this even though I know she won't hear anything for half an hour. I throw off the sheet and check her hands are free before lifting her and carrying her out of the room.

"Wait, wait, my coat... stuff." I risk laying her under the window and nip back in. Dominiq has taped the man, who has wide, wild eyes, but he probably can't see or hear anything either. Near Charlotte's bunk, I find a large shoulder bag and a waterproof jacket. I wasn't going to bother with her day clothes, because we have spares on the boat, but maybe, she has crucial stuff in the pockets.

Back outside, I put her jacket around her shoulders to give her some comfort we aren't the baddies, hopefully. We follow Dominiq, who has a short muzzle Koch waving at dark places. The glued door makes a noisy percussion drum as we pass. The two in there are wasting time on the glued door instead of throwing a chair through the window, but who are we to argue?

Within six minutes, we have Charlotte, sipping hot chocolate, in a comfy chair. Her ears remain silent, but her vision hazes back into action.

Nessa starts the engine to take the *Solar Sprint* a mile away from the rig.

Benita writes on a card to show Charlotte: *Hello, Charlotte, we've come from Rarotonga to rescue you.*

"I needed rescuing..." She starts sobbing. "But I don't know who you are..." Crying again. "Why Rarotonga?"

I exchange glances with the others. She has ARIA.

Benita has been writing again: *You have amnesia, but you will be all right now. We are friends. Best for you to sleep now, and you can hear better when you wake up.*

"THEY'RE NOT COMING AFTER US," says Nessa, on the upper bridge at daybreak.

"They've probably forgotten the incident but will know something odd has happened," says Dominiq. "Such as being handcuffed to his bed and two finding their door stuck or broken from forcing it. Hey, Bryce, do you think they will remember Charlotte?"

"Difficult to say. I made notes of important stuff, and we wore name badges. I think ARIA works slower if you keep your memory refreshed."

Benita calls us to meet again with Charlotte. She's been chatting to her. The ARIA has stopped now she's been infected by our ARIA-2, and she's ready to meet us all.

"Hi, Charlotte," I say and go to give her a hug, but she holds one hand up to stop me and the other covers her mouth.

"Whoa, Bryce, you big lug," says Benita. "What do you think's been happening to her over there?"

"Sorry, Charlotte, I'm just a big lug, apparently."

"No, sorry... Bryce? I don't know exactly what's been happening to me."

"Well, I do," says Benita, and before I can stop her, she says, "She was kidnapped, raped, and kept prisoner."

Charlotte erupts with a wail.

"Benita," I say, grabbing her hand and dragging her outside. "One of the few advantages of amnesia is that bad stuff is obliterated. It's bad enough she was brutalised without you reminding her all the time. And, no doubt, you made sure she knew it was men who did the bad things to her?"

"It *was* men, idiot."

"Not all men behave like that. What do you want her to believe? No answer? Benita, I think that you have taken on Charlotte's horrendous experience, reliving it in your vivid imagination, as she cannot."

"You pompous prick."

"Tell me something I don't know." We both stress-release a quick smile and then hug.

"Seriously, Benita, is Charlotte okay, physically? We both know the traumas and angst she's yet to go through, let alone the headaches, tinnitus, and funny smells."

"Her breasts have been bitten, and besides the cuts from handcuffs, she is bruised all around her back and genitals. She's torn too."

"Bloody hell, the animals."

"Animals don't behave like that. We've administered analgesics, and Nessa has some rapid bruise-reducing lotions. She should recover, physically, in a few days. By the way, after some searching, I haven't found any contraceptives or HRT treatment in Nessa's stuff. My guess is that, sadly, you are correct, and the fart we know as Dominiq is having an affair."

"Damn, at least he could be adding to the population not preventing pregnancies."

"Oh, so we are just baby-making machines for the post-apocalyptic world?"

"Yes. I must do my duty and impregnate as many women as possible." I wink at her, and we laugh.

We return, arm in arm. Charlotte smiles tearfully at us.

"Now the tantrums have settled," says Dominiq, "let's try to settle the facts. Charlotte, when you woke this morning, where did you think you were?"

"I thought I was in my Houston postgrad student apartment. I'm on a mission-control secondment with NASA from the University of New South Wales in Sydney."

Benita started to clarify, but Dominiq stopped her. "Charlotte, how old are you?"

"Benita's told me I'm twenty-seven, which is ridiculous as I'm only twenty-two."

"Has she told you how you've been helping the survivors of this ARIA attack by the use of your work in Carnarvon maintaining the Internet and satellite telecommunications? Apparently, you have a real flair."

"Yeah, and I guess I can still do some of that, given time to study what I've been doing."

"More importantly, Charlotte," says Nessa, pushing Dominiq's raised hand away, "you have many admirers–some say they are really fond of you–getting to know you over the speakers. Not only in Rarotonga, but you've touched hearts in Canada and France. They all want you to know their best wishes are urging your recovery. Look." She pulls out a double sheet of e-mail prints.

Dominiq scowls at the waste of paper.

Charlotte takes the goodwill messages, and tears fill her eyes again.

"I know what you're looking for," says Benita. "I hadn't gotten round to it at breakfast. I'm afraid there's no messages there from your parents or other relatives."

It hit me in the stomach too. It's awful to find out that one moment you have a family and then wake to find you haven't. Is she's going to find out she has another family, like mine, of which she has no memory? A gorgeous and clever woman like her must have had a string of men friends. I say quietly to Nessa, "Does Ryder know if she was married, kids and that?"

"Abdul had most talks with her, and he says not. Her parents and sister were in Sydney. He's sent a bio as much as he could remember it. I'll give her a copy later."

Dominiq stands. "Charlotte, you have a double first-class degree, top of your year, awards that make the rest of us blithering idiots. But I hadn't realized what a personable young woman you are."

Wow, is this the same Dominiq?

"But, before we leave for Rarotonga, we need to make a decision about the people on the rig..."

She is clearly overcome with emotion over her parents and the whole traumatic experience. "I'm... sorry. Can I have some time on my own please?"

"I'd rather you wait until..."

"Go, Charlotte. We can wait," I say, as I push Dominiq up the stairs to the top cockpit. I don't bother with a lecture. We look at the rig through binoculars and see three men looking at us.

"They might be wondering why we aren't moving," I say. "Let's suppose they've only lost the same memory as Charlotte, okay, a bit more. From a close look at that one, they've lost between seven and ten years' memory and in a state of confusion. I bet they use that motor-launch fettered to the rig, to go to Bernier and Dorre Islands, to restock fresh water, but why back to the rig?"

"I suppose at least one dominant man has worked that rig for ten years, then it's a safe haven. But that's dangerous once they forget about the islands or Carnarvon. Just a moment, they would have stopped forgetting. Stupid me."

"That's interesting; we might have started a diffusion of ARIA-2 for the Antipodes. Or they might stay here forever," I say. "I hope they don't find other defenceless females."

"She must have been surprised in her bed. If she's like most Oz women, she would've fought those bastards off and made 'em run. But they're tough riggers. We might find them useful on the island."

"No thanks. I don't mind leading them to Carnarvon, but not back to Rarotonga. They've obviously got back-to-basics fever. Luckily, Charlotte won't have any fond attachments to them and won't remember them nor have revenge urges. Leave them here." I look at my brother. "Dominiq, I know I treat you like a prick. And I think I have good reason, but what you did on that rig blew me away. You were a veritable James Bond. That trick with the superglue was a stroke of genius. I am so impressed."

"I am a colonel in the army, you know." He smiled for the first time since I re-remembered, clearly pleased to have impressed his elder, wise-aleck brother.

"Let's go then," he says, "I'll go tell Nessa and the others. I'll get onto Ryder and tell them our ETA."

CHAPTER 36

July 17ᵗʰ 2016, Winnipeg.

MANUEL FOUGHT HIS FEAR of the unknown to look over Julia's shoulder at the strapped-down, sleeping alien.

"He's not going to bite," she said.

"You're used to being up to your elbows in biological specimens. I did meetings and media presentations."

"I was a virologist, not a butcher. I've taken fresh blood and tissue samples. If only we had an MRI-scanning machine. Ah, just look at his dermis; astonishing."

"Speak English, Julia."

"His skin. The layer just beneath the coppery surface, where we have layers of fat, hair follicles, and sweat glands, he has a layer we don't. Where have I seen it before?"

"What are you looking at? Hey, that magnifying screen is amazing."

"Those bronze-coloured cells. They look just like chloroplasts."

"Come again?"

"Chloroplasts. You said you had a greenhouse when you were a teenager. So, you know about chlorophyll. Yes?"

"Yeah, the green stuff that leaves use to convert sunlight to food."

"Exactly. In advanced plants, the chlorophyll is in cells that can move to optimise energy production or away from too much harmful UV."

"And these Zadokians have plant cells in their skin? Why aren't they green? Little green men."

"Chlorophyll is green, at least the Earth variety is, although we have copper beeches. The green is masked by other chemicals. In this Zadokian case, it might be blood. But, you see the significance?"

"We can use a weed-killer to eradicate them?"

"Pay attention, Manuel. The Zads get their food, or some of it, from light. Just think what an advantage that is if you're stuck on a desert island. Even at night, you'd be able to keep starvation off by switching on a light."

"I suppose that explains why their mouths are so small too,"

Manuel said. "And we know they use telepathy, so why have a mouth at all?"

"To supplement their food. Just over one square metre of skin won't make sufficient energy for an active being. They still have to drink, and I expect they can talk if they have to."

"They don't take up water through their feet?" Manuel said, walking round to the dozing alien's small feet.

"In most anatomical details, they are remarkably similar to humans—five toes, no—there's only four! Two legs, two arms, five or four fingers... Not that similar then.

"It's logical to have a thumb acting at right-angles to fingers in order to grip," she continued, "but, I have work to do if I'm to get this data to Teresa and Gustav on Rarotonga and work on alien blood to see if it's carrying any ARIA-type viruses."

Manuel was left alone with the Zadokian as Julia scuttled off to her makeshift lab in another room. The usurped, abandoned medical centre in Winnipeg's suburbs had become their temporary home. Antonio had gone off to bed and left them to examine and restrain the drugged alien. Julia had hooked it up to monitors, so Manuel could hear the slow heartbeat. Besides blood, skin, inside-mouth swabs, and key-holed tissue samples, she had snipped some of the Zadokian's short, curled, orangey hair.

He knew it was silly, but he bent down to look with the magnifier at the soles of the alien's feet, risking tickling him awake. If its skin was plant-like, maybe it really did take in water by osmosis. They looked disappointingly human, but maybe, if he cleaned a spot, he might see larger pores. He dampened a cotton-wool ball and rubbed in circles on the ball of the Zad's left foot. With his applied pressure, he could see the coppery skin did have tinges of green, which changed slightly depending how hard he pressed. No pores different from human skin, but then, what did plant stomata look like?

His mouth downturned in disappointment that there were no thread-like root hairs to absorb water. He concentrated so much, he was slow to notice the heart monitor's bleep accelerating. Manuel's head filled with a burst of activity, hurting his skull from the inside. He fell back onto the floor, thinking he'd been shot. All his headaches had come at once, but then as quickly, passed. He lay on his back, holding his head as if to stop it shaking apart, but now, his head throbbed with a dull, fuzzy echo.

"What the hell was that?" He sat up and saw the alien struggling with his restraining belts. "It's just as well belts have no brains or they'd be apart by now," Manuel said, as he staggered to his feet. The alien stopped struggling and looked at him with tiny green eyes. A feeling of warmth came over Manuel, and small tinnitus-like sounds fluttered in and out of his head, as if the alien was pinging him, like testing the connections to a computer. Manuel smiled at the alien, and said, "Howdy, little man. I don't suppose your burst of anger was directed at me, was it?"

The Zadokian's face remained impassive, the mouth stayed closed, all one inch of it. Only the eyes darted around but always returning to Manuel's in what was obviously an effort to communicate.

"Well, Antonio says he can understand you guys, but all you're doing to me is blast my head with a garage-sale full of headaches."

The alien opened and shut his mouth a few times. Manuel assumed he was attempting speech, so he put his ear closer to listen. All he could detect were sucking sounds. "Ah, you're thirsty?" Manuel made drinking motions with his hand holding an invisible cup. His head received a warm velvet colour. Reaching for a paper cup, filling it with water and adding a straw, Manuel realized they'd had a successful communication. He held the cup and placed the end of the straw in the Zad's mouth while the alien sucked. When the cup was dry, Manuel's head received a peach glow.

The warm colour invaded him, making him mellow and contented. Manuel needed a nap. He aimed for an armchair, but as he slowly walked there, a spike of blue light in his head stopped him. He turned to look at the alien whose eyes loomed darker, bigger— probably an optical illusion. A wave of peachy yellow filled Manuel's head, drawing him closer. "Hey, I hear you, fellah. It seems criminal, you being all tied up an' all. You were a prisoner of those damn Zadokian guards, so why should you be ours too? You are on our side, right?" The pleasant tingle through his body increased in proportion to the closeness to the alien. Inching a little nearer, Manuel wore an inane smile and knew it but was too exhilarated to care. Anyway, there was no one to see. He touched the couch with his knees. The Zadokian's eyes deepened to black liquid pools emanating friendship, love, understanding, anxiety, and a need to be released.

In a trance, Manuel undid the straps allowing the alien to sit up. The peach and apricot colours in Manuel's head abruptly kaleidoscoped with spikes of blue and white. He took a couple of steps back, shaking his head. The tinnitus crescendoed, making his knees buckle. Through the rapidly developing headache, Manuel saw the alien slide off the bed and shuffle to the door.

The door squeaked shut behind the Zadokian, but Manuel's head continued buzzing as if a swarm of bees had taken up residence, so he remained on his knees. His hands clutched at his face as tears escaped. "What have I done?" he wailed to himself. "He'll get back to the dome, and we'll be attacked." His self-incrimination stopped as the door reopened and in walked the alien.

"Thank God," Manuel said, sticking his fingers in his ears, hoping that would stop the telepathic mind control. But then, he saw Antonio following the alien.

"Hi, Manuel. Don't worry. I've told him to stop interfering with your head. I picked up some of the extreme thought waves when I arrived. This helped to change his mind about his *arrivederci*."

Manuel saw that Antonio waved the alien weapon in his hand. Slowly, he returned to his feet as the alien lay on the couch again. "I've given him a thought command such that he now cannot try to undo the straps himself or make someone else do it."

"It would have been handy if you'd done that earlier. Oh, he was unconscious, wasn't he?"

"I could have planted the command even so, but to be honest, I didn't think he'd survive the overdosed morphine shot I gave him at the dome."

Manuel could have smashed his fist into Antonio's smug face. He had such disregard for life, any life. "It wasn't this Zad that planted the virus or him taking over the planet."

"Don't be naïve, Manuel. I wouldn't be surprised if the prisoners are up to some scam with their guards. I still have a theory about a group consciousness, which some stronger individuals manipulate."

"I'm going for some coffee; this head banging has knocked the stuffing out of me."

"Not for me, thanks. I'm going to interrogate our friend. Don't worry, I won't use splinters under his fingernails."

"You'd have a job, he has none. No physical torture though. Right?"

"Of course not, Manny. Go help Julia with her microscopes and Petri dishes."

Manuel decided he would do that, but he'd return. He didn't trust Antonio as far as he could throw their truck.

ANTONIO RELISHED THE OPPORTUNITY to communicate with this Zadokian. The only telepathic exchanges he'd had were with guards, who refrained from anything except orders, which came as bursts of feeling in his head. No words as such, but understandings as if the concept attached to the word triggered the correct synapses. Now, not only did he have a captive Zadokian, but one who might be glad to be out of the clutches of the guards.

A spate of coughing stirred him to throw a more concerned look at the alien. Of course, the domes kept the air clean. He mentally thanked Manuel for rigging up the diesel generator. He switched on the air conditioning, setting it to maximum filter. He needed to keep this one alive, at least for a while, and wondered if his own physician's skills might be needed. The brassier colour instead of copper must have significance.

Sit up, Antonio thought at the alien, who, with another cough, struggled to sit up. Antonio helped him while thinking, *You should be breathing better soon.*

The alien's skin returned to its coppery hue as his respiration improved.

Antonio's impatience to start led him to bring up a chair in front of the Zadokian. He played with the alien weapon for effect. *Do you have a name?*

I don't understand.

Antonio groaned, although he anticipated the similar response as given by the guards. They appeared to identify each other by thought patterns combined with colours, or they used thought, sound, or electromagnetic spectrum frequencies beyond him. He recalled the guards he acquainted as Zad-1 and Zad-2.

I will refer to you as Zad-3. You already know I am Antonio. Why are you on this planet?

The alien became agitated once more, shaking and trying to get off the couch.

Antonio waved the weapon. *What's the matter with you?*

I am outside the dome.

I told you the air conditioning will improve the air.

We are protected inside the dome.

You mean from us, but your guards seem to control humans who get close.

No. We must stay in the dome until a signal that outside is safe.

Antonio logged the issue, wondering if it had to do with the third case, but wanted to move on. *I asked you why you are on this planet.*

I did not choose to be here.

Why did your planet choose to send you here?

I was not allowed to stay.

Interrogation of aliens presented more difficulties than he anticipated. He came from another angle. *Can the guards detect you are here?*

I cannot detect other Zadokians nearby.

Can you detect any Zadokians far away?

No.

When they know you are missing, will they look for you?

Why should they?

You are a prisoner, are you not?

Yes.

Why are you a prisoner?

You took me and have a weapon.

Before that, you were a prisoner of the guards.

The Zadokian remained with silent thoughts.

Antonio wondered if he was thinking of an appropriate response or going to sleep. *Why don't you answer?*

You haven't asked a question.

It was like having a conversation with an autistic robot. *Were you a prisoner of the guards before I took you?*

Yes.

Why were you a prisoner of the guards? At last was he getting somewhere.

They were commanded to be our guards.

Antonio knuckled his own head.

Who commanded the guards? And don't say their commanders.

The Elders.

Hooray, thought Antonio. *What had you done to upset the Elders?*

I didn't upset them.

Si, tell me which of the following apply. One, you killed a Zadokian. Two, you stole property belonging to another. Three, you badly hurt another Zadokian. Four, you conspired, with your friends, to overthrow the Elders. As soon as his list finished, the Zadokian's skin colour rippled a red-tinge wave before settling.

All are abhorrent.

Antonio slowly shook his head, smiling. Surely the whole planet can't be devoid of crime. And no murder at all? It wouldn't be human, but it wasn't, was it?

Zad, your people have murdered billions of humans, and yet, the thought of killing your own upsets you?

Yes.

Yes, what?

Yes, the thought of killing our own is not available.

But killing other beings is all right?

If it suits our needs.

But isn't that immoral?

I don't understand. May I ask a question?

You just have, but ask another.

We understood that ending lives prematurely was the norm on this planet. Was that not the case?

Only in war or personal problems.

Silence followed, until Antonio realized he hadn't ended with a question. *Why did your planet think we killed each other?*

We saw from electronic-wave broadcasts that many millions are killed in fighting or allowed to die from starvation. Billions more are captured, tortured, and put to death for pleasure reasons. We assessed humans had no culture of respect for life.

It was Antonio's turn to be silent as he mulled the alien's observations. Eventually... *Oh, you mean the way we rear livestock and slaughter them for food.* Capisco. *That doesn't count; they're not people. They're animals. All right, we are animals too, but they are not of our species. They're not intelligent.* Si, *they have intelligence but not nearly as much as ours. Don't you eat non-Zadokians?*

Why should we? Why do you?

Because our bodies need... no, scrub that. Va bene, *because they taste nice. Arrgh, that sounds immoral.* Si, *because it is part of nature. A food web. Not that all humans eat animals. None of this is relevant, anyway, is it?*

Yes.

It is relevant? You mean our population would not have been obliterated if we didn't eat meat? Oh, you saw all the TV about wars and murders. I have to tell you that most of that was fiction. Also, what wars happened tended to have a lot of repeated broadcasts. I'm getting side tracked. Zad, did your people intend to harm us with the ARIA virus or help us and it went wrong?

I don't know.

Si, *you're a prisoner. I still don't know why you are a prisoner. What did you do wrong on Zadok?*

It was a group of us that inadvertently hurt a protocol.

The group that came with you here?

Yes.

What sort of protocol?

We started to think of improvements to how the planet's administration could be run. It is a thought crime.

Un momento, do you have democracy on Zadok?

I don't understand.

Do you have elections to decide who should run the country?

No. Elders are born to do that.

So, your group are political exiles. You've been deported. Is that the situation?

I think you are right.

Why didn't your group go underground? I mean, why didn't you hide?

There is nowhere to hide on Zadok.

Ah, they'd be able to detect your thought patterns. How about off world? Are there other habitable planets in your system?

Many.

Are they are all ruled by the Elders?

Yes.

So, from their point of view, there is no crime on the Zadok planets?

No. There is crime.

What activity is counted as criminal on Zadok?

Distributing contraband substances.

What else?

Nothing else. There is no need for what you call laws except for growing and distributing toxic or hallucinogenic substances. These can affect the mind and so thought. It could lead to unpredictable behaviour.

Si, that's why we take them. You are forgetting the law you broke, aren't you?

No.

You broke that protocol and so were sent here.

Antonio was losing patience. He poured himself a malt and water while waiting for Zad-3 to come up with an answer. Then, he realized he hadn't asked a question.

You broke a protocol law with the others?

I said we hurt the protocol. It isn't a law, and we didn't do anything except have thoughts about a different protocol.

This might be a revolutionary idea, Zad, but did your group consider fighting for your right to have an opinion?

I do not understand. We do not fight.

You might not need to have a physical fight, but have your group tried to influence the opinion of others?

No.

Why not?

It wouldn't occur to us to attempt influencing other's opinions.

Ah, I've got you. One of you must have had the idea to change the protocol that determines how Zadok is run and then sought to influence others, including you?

I don't know. The alien's skin colour plunged into deeper purples around his head. Antonio offered him more water.

How did it happen? Is your group a coherent body such as a workforce, a society, or hobby group?

We were an exploratory team on Zadik, one of our moons. It is uninhabited but has breathable atmosphere. We were investigating why the moon is much colder than the other moons even though the astro-geometry suggests it should have the same climate.

Maybe the geology has a feature that takes heat from the atmosphere. Did you test for that?

I cannot discuss it with an alien.

Me, an alien? Si. Did your team think rebellious thoughts? Antonio warmed to his interrogation and rubbed his hands.

It occurred to us, as a collective whole, that something was wrong.

We know there are other domes on this planet. Do they all have prisoners like you from Zadok's moon?

I don't know.

Maybe not for sure. Zad, is it likely that your team on that moon is split? How many were you?

We were many. It is likely the other landing areas have members of my team.

Going back to when you said your group thought it wrong. Zad, it isn't wrong to think of alternatives to an existing system. Is it?

It is to us. We think that possibly a trace gas in Zadik's atmosphere might be responsible for our corruption.

You are not going to believe a mere human, like me, but thinking of new ideas is not a corruption. How did the Zadok authorities find out?

When we realized we were not thinking properly, we informed the Elders.

Good grief, Zad. You have a lot to learn about rebellion.

Antonio passed from amazement, through derision, to a plan. *I have a proposal for you, Zad. I might release you soon on some conditions. If I did, where would you go? I imagine it would be back to the dome?*

Of course.

Because of some misguided sense of loyalty?

The air is cleaner in the dome.

So it is. Before I decide, I want you to think how your group might formulate a plan to bring about a fairer society on Zadok. How about it?

I don't understand.

Your team was exiled for having the germ of ideas for an alternative way to run the planet. Right?

It could be put like that.

Do you think it's fair to be punished for thinking? Even when that thinking is about improving society?

I don't understand fair. I don't know that our muddled thinking would improve life on Zadok.

Antonio's frustration showed in his fists clenching.

When you are released, you are not to reveal our presence, and I want you to think with your team about how a different protocol might improve life on Zadok.

That is not possible. It is against the existing protocol.

So, what would the Elders do? Deport you to another planet?

I don't know. It's never happened before.

I'm going to report our conversation to my friends now. In the meantime, you are to think over what I said. You are not permitted to leave this room unless I say so. Understand?

Understood. The deepening purple shades in the copper made him look like heated brass, showing he was under stress. Antonio was about to tell him that he and his friends had better learn to control their colouring since it gave away their emotions but realized his face, too, was often an angry red.

CHAPTER 37

MANUEL PACED THE LAB, his coffee lapping over the cup's rim with each turn. Apparently, Julia had given up calming him, focussing instead on the microscope screen. She'd told him she'd found signatures of the ARIA virus in the biopsy sample extracted from Zad-3's cerebrospinal fluid.

"What do you think of Ryder's plan?" he said after putting down the cup and licking his scalded hand.

"Which one, sending us out and about more to spread ARIA-2?"

"No, the one to use the hundreds of unused communication satellites to broadcast messages and old TV to confuse the Zadokians into thinking life's carrying on, and so they might as well give up."

"Nonsense, the Zadokians aren't idiots, and I told him so. It's just one of many ideas he's floating."

"Granted, they're not fools, but they could be fooled. They appear to be overconfident. Look at the way Antonio was able to kidnap one and the French to poison a dome?"

"We don't know for sure if any were killed in the dome, and they retaliated, didn't they? To be honest, I've been expecting a posse here. It can't be difficult to find the only building with lights and using radio transmissions. Maybe they're clever but not as devious as they need to be. Look out, trouble's coming."

"*Buon giorno*, when's lunch?"

"Whenever you make some, Antonio," Julia said.

"I'll have whatever you're having," he said. "I've had a breakthrough with Zad. They've been brought here for thought crimes. Can you believe it? All they did was think there might be a better way to govern Zadok. They must have that planet so tied up, all it would take is one pair of scissors and pop, it will all come apart. I've got him thinking about how to get his team to rebel, but it isn't easy convincing him. I'll write up my interrogation report so everyone can have it. Some interesting properties of one of their moons, Zadik. Maybe we can use it. Something in the atmosphere there allowed our Zad and his team to break their mental conditioning."

"Wow, Antonio," Manuel said, "you could be useful after all. Why can't we telepath a conversation with him? All I get is headaches, tinnitus, and damn-near blacking out."

"I told you, I'm special."

Julia laughed. "Only because you got the first blast with the opening of the second case. Though, it could be your weird brain."

"You're only jealous. After a few more sessions, I think his whole approach to rebellion will change; the concept wasn't in their vocabulary. Amazing. Then, I'll send him back in with a mission to work on the others and bring them out."

"Oh my God, you're serious," Julia said. "What about the guards?"

"They can come too if they want," he said, grinning.

"No, idiot. The guards might not be what they seem."

"What? How can you find out anything about them? Oh, the French?"

"Françoise has told Ryder that the plants the students liberated from the dome had powerful hallucinogenic properties."

"It's weed? You mean the guards might be using their prisoners as horticultural workers to grow plants illicit in their system?"

"I know. We must have it wrong."

Antonio poured himself an instant coffee. "Not necessarily, the guards are certainly genuine but may be looking for a way to improve their remuneration. Mind-altering substance would definitely be illegal on a planet where keeping a tidy, untangled mind is paramount. In fact, Zad-3 told me distributing contraband drugs concerned their only law. What better cover could there be for the guards to cultivate their weed in giant cloches where the prisoners therefore have something to do?"

"It's a ridiculous distance to go unless they're growing it for themselves," Julia said. "It goes way beyond Kevin the student growing cannabis in the attic under UV lamps."

"We shouldn't underestimate the reach of, and obsession with, mind control on Zadok, and more importantly, they turn themselves in, running to the Elders to confess. They kamikaze themselves as soon as they think they've done something wrong."

"Even so," Julia said, "it's literally too farfetched. Zadok is nearly nine light years away. So, even if their ships achieve the impossible and do light speed, it would take nearly twenty years for a round trip."

Manuel shook his head. "I believe that was one of the secrets Charlotte used to force Ryder to rescue her. I bet her data will reveal a much closer Zadokian base. Maybe the prisoners have come from Zadok, under some hibernation technique, but the guards will be flitting back and to a hotel not far away."

"That could explain why I've seen the guards nipping around in smaller blue ships while the prisoners came in a larger silver fuzz-ball."

July 20th 2016, Inkster Boulevard, three miles from the Airport Dome, Winnipeg.

MANUEL'S HATRED FOR HIS FORAGING TRIPS increased in proportion to the distance he was obliged to travel. The actual breaking into potentially rewarding stores carried excitement, but as he neared Winnipeg, he discovered more rotted corpses, snarling dogs, and once, a black bear.

He drove down the wide Inkster Boulevard on the northern outskirts of Winnipeg. He'd raided or dismissed the outermost stores and warehouses in earlier weeks, preferring to keep away from the potential dangers of the city centre. The Chevy truck held all the essential burglary tools and a shotgun to complement the holstered handgun. Julia had ordered he wasn't to take any chances with crazies: man, beast, or alien.

He drew into the parking lot of a Mac's Superstore he'd yet to plunder. The dozen vehicles, mostly neatly parked, gathered dust, guano, and moss. He didn't clean his own vehicles: mud was the in colour. He shouldered two big rucksacks and carried the shotgun.

The automatic sliding doors had been forced, but he preferred to find the delivery entrance, make one if necessary, and keep the front for emergencies. He had a recurring nightmare of being trapped in a store by a pack of wolves that snarled between him and the one door.

A wagon partially blocked the raised side entrance, but Manuel was able to squeeze in while reminding himself that he'd have to abandon full rucksacks if he needed to use that way for an emergency exit. He changed his mind, turning to leave when the noxious stink hit his nostrils. He leant against the doorway holding his nose and with eyes smarting. It could be bodies, or one body, freezer food, excrement not dried out in the damp atmosphere. Damn. He'd forgotten to bring a facemask. It had a charcoal filter that would both protect and deodorise. No. He could find another store, hotel, hospital, or homes, but he shouldn't let his offended olfactory sense interfere. There should be worthwhile provisions in sealed containers, especially his favourite, peanut butter.

Trying to breathe only through his mouth and with a forced smile to counteract a gag reflex, he ventured to the edge of broad steps leading down into the store. Skylights and the doors let in sufficient sunlight to illuminate the stacks and tills at the far end near the front entrance. Flies flitted around in the crepuscular light beams like motes. From his vantage point, he could make out the avoidance zones: butchery, fresh fruit, and the bakery. He should have added alcohol to the prohibited list, but man cannot live on baked beans alone.

He stopped to listen, hoping the dreadful odour hadn't affected his ears. He knew it shouldn't, but when one sense was overwhelmed, his others recoiled in terror too. A breeze flapped a plastic blind near a high window. He'd often see birds and bats among roof girders, but the odour here revolted them too. There was no movement below, so he headed down to reach the tinned food section.

"Aargh, what...?" His ankles told him the ground floor was flooded. He peered in the gloom, only then seeing ripples from his paddling. He was already wet, so he sloshed over to the canned meat. Empty. Cursing, he splashed around to the grocery-products section. Good, there were cans on one shelf—extra hot curry. He shuddered but put the four-pack in a rucksack along with a jar of pickled eggs.

Behind him, a man's voice said, "What the hell are you doing in our store?" Manuel kept still, thinking the man would see him reaching for the shotgun slung behind his back. He slowly reached for his holstered gun while saying, "No harm intended. It looks like—"

"Leave your weapon alone and turn round."

"—you've already taken most..." Manuel fell silent when he saw three silhouettes in the front doorway. Was this his last and most ignominious hour? Up to his ankles in filthy water, his nose so pinched it wouldn't be able to open for days, and a miserable failure at snaffling any more than a drunk's supper. He couldn't see if they had a weapon. Hey, they wouldn't see him clearly either. The speaker had bluffed. This meant he had not lost too many marbles so probably had his ARIA stopped by meeting either Antonio or one of the dome workforce. Maybe a cheery greeting would stave off violence.

"My name is Manuel, who are you guys?"

The man in the middle spoke with a southern accent. "This is our store."

"Of course it is. Hey, I only have four cans and a bottle. It wasn't me who emptied this place."

"Don't matter none. You shouldn't be in here."

"Nah," said the friend on his right.

Manuel knew he had to do some quick thinking. They would have suffered the ARIA as he had, endured the headaches and infernal buzzing. Maybe he could bluff them, so as soon as they reached outside, he'd make for his truck. He still wondered if they'd see him unholstering his gun, but didn't want a bullet in the guts to let him know. He ought to offer his pilferings.

"I have some stuff you might want."

"Yeah?"

"Can I come up there? It's wet down here."

"Sure."

Manuel created new ripples, but these died out as the floor sloped up towards the entrance. He worried about his weapons. Was he their prisoner, or, if unarmed, were they his?

The two either side of the main talker showed teeth as they grinned at Manuel, arriving into daylight. His shotgun remained slung around his back, but they should be able to tell he had one from the ammunition belt. They'd also see his holstered handgun. He could see now that they were only in their middle thirties. Maybe they'd escaped the initial ARIA by being on one of the huge isolated prairie farms. He had to stifle a laugh at their dungarees and check hillbilly shirts. Were they grinning in their glee of finding a victim with weapons to loot?

"Do you wanna use the men's room?" said the main man.

"Sorry?"

"That's what we use this place for now it's empty."

"But..." Surely there were plenty of houses with toilets they'd use, using a bucket for flushing if they had overpowering urges to be hygienic. He'd have thought they'd be using walls and gardens anyway.

"It flushes. There."

Sure enough, to Manuel's right were the Men's, Ladies', and Disabled bathrooms. One of the men pushed open the door. Old toilet papers stuck to the floor, though it was dry. Manuel didn't want to go, because he'd have to unsling his rucksacks and shotgun just to get through the door.

"So it flushes, huh?"

The main man signalled to the one not holding the door. He hurried in and proudly pressed the flush button. His grin broadened with the cascade. Anyone would think this activity had replaced TV for Winnipeg's entertainment. It beat waiting for traffic lights to change, but only because they didn't any more.

"There must be a rain-collecting header tank on the roof," Manuel said. Then realized where it flushed to, and in despair looked at his shoes. He'd have to find new ones quickly.

"Dunno." The three looked puzzled, as if wondering why would anyone try to figure it out. They'd definitely reverted to school age, maybe earlier.

"Where is it?" said the tallest one, who spoke and thought for the others.

Manuel offered them the jar of pickled eggs.

"Nah—fowl."

"Foul, no, they should be fi—ah, you said fowl, hens. Right, how about these?"

The cans of curried vegetables didn't broaden their grins either. One of the men pulled at the rucksack to look inside, but the taller man pulled him back.

"That's it?"

"I'm afraid so, you caught me too early." He laughed, but they stopped grinning.

"You eat it."

Manuel couldn't tell if that was a command or a thanks-but-no-thanks.

"We got grub if you want."

At last, Manuel had the clue he needed. They saw him as a fellow victim. "Okay. Is it far?"

"Not in your pickup it ain't."

And he thought the camouflage was clever. "All right, but I'm driving."

To Manuel's relief, they didn't argue but leapt in the back, while the main man joined Manuel and waved navigational arms.

"My name is Manuel, what's yours?" He'd been directed south towards the centre of Winnipeg. He'd avoided it out of fear. His forehead was wet from fear perspiration in addition to the midday heat.

"Chilton." He held his right hand across to Manuel, who felt obliged to risk a quick shake, grabbed the wheel again to correct the vehicle after a tyre met a wayward trashcan in the road.

"Hi, Chilton, good name. Have any of your group worked in the domes with the Zadokians?"

"Zad—what?"

"The aliens are from the planet Zadok. Did you work in the domes?" It was like climbing a down escalator.

"Nah, but those two idjits, back there, did. Had a calling or somat. There I was porking Mavis, fell asleep. Woke up to an empty house. Everyone in the Blocks had gone. They strolled back at night crying for food and sleep."

"What's the Blocks? An apartment block?"

"What else?"

"What were they doing in the dome?"

"Dunno."

"Didn't they say?"

"Didn't ask. Just saw their dirty fingers."

"Ah, cultivating the weed."

"That must be it. Marie had some stuck in her shoes. Her Hollis rolled and smoked it. Sent him haywire."

"Is Hollis okay now?"

"Dunno. Not seen him since. He took off."

"What do you do for leisure these days, Chilton?"

"Ass-kicking contests."

"Ha ha, very funny. Oh, you're not joking." He stayed silent. Manuel hoped he hadn't flipped him with his flippant laugh. He was not looking forward to the next question he had to ask. "Chilton, some of the aliens in the dome are prisoners. What would you do if we managed to get them out?"

"Kill 'em."

"No, no, we don't want that. They're innocent of any wrong doing."

"Roast 'em alive. Look what they done to us."

"Not them, the guards. Actually, not the guards, their Elders on Zadok."

"Impale them on sharp stakes in Global Park, only it's a pity there'd only be a hundred of us instead of thousands."

"You're not listening, Chilton."

"Sure I am. You've been brainwashed like the others. The zombie workers."

"Try and think beyond the obvious. Not all aliens are alike just like not all humans are."

"They belong to the same race who's raped our planet of people. Just look at it." He waved his finger, loaded with gold rings like his others.

Chilton's logic crashed in on Manuel. Déjà vu á la Antonio.

"I believe we have to accept what exists then shape the future. We have aliens. Fact. We could be stupid and set ourselves against them. We could be smart by sorting the wheat from the chaff." He hoped a prairie farming metaphor might help.

Chilton opened his mouth as if willing a thought process to come out in words, but instead, he let Manuel continue.

"We captured one of the alien prisoners. He didn't plan on spending time here on Earth. We could turn some of this grimness around by working with these alien prisoners. What do you think of that?"

"Do what you like. The way we feel in the Blocks, if we see 'em, we kill 'em."

Manuel groaned, but maybe, he'd seeded the germ of an idea.

The boulevard led over several roundabouts. Debris on the road, made worse by ferocious storms with no one clearing up, meant he had to cross the central reservation. A felled sycamore had brought down power lines making progress slow. Dogs roamed wild and ragged. Some of them chased cats, but most slept in doorways or in the middle of the road.

"Over there." Clinton pointed at a warehouse. Again, Manuel parked among four-by-fours, estates, and vans, all resting on flat tyres.

"We keep the dogs out of here," he said, putting his weight behind a steel roller door ten feet wide and twice as high. "But we have to share with a few rats. You're welcome to whatever you can carry."

Manuel was about to suggest rat poison, but words wouldn't come. Sunlight shafting through the glass skylights and the door revealed a golden Aladdin's Cave. Rack on rack of unopened cans, bottles, and boxes. Millions of them, making him wish he'd brought a bigger vehicle.

CHAPTER 38

July 27ᵗʰ 2016, Valence, France; a few miles north of the domes.

THE DAWN GAINED ENTRY through the ancient, narrow windows of the Music Academy. Françoise had earned a violin scholarship at the gawky age of thirteen and spent five years in melodious bliss. School friends tripled and the tremulant matured. Tears splashed onto the desk at which she'd theorised all those years ago, in this very classroom. Her blurred vision made out the old-fashioned blackboard with its white-painted staves. A chalked fragment of a Brahms violin scherzo played silently at her, increasing the tear cascade. She shuddered at the thought that there would be no more composers, no orchestras or throngs of applauding enthusiasts.

On her right, Elodie used to sit and doodle in her theory books– the dippy but talented Elodie who died on the bridge at La Voulte with a bullet in her back. The classroom remained empty but for the echoes. An open window flapped somewhere, inviting in the wind, whispering down corridors. In each chair sat ghosts of her former school friends, and they smiled at her. Hallucination cruelly impinged, but the message she received crescendoed loud and clear. She had to justify her survival. Her tears dried as she stood and called out their names and that of their professor, Madame Barros. No more sweet Françoise.

THREE DAYS LATER, Françoise and Bono stood behind the open rear door of their Volkswagen dormobile. They'd had an arduous day travelling, but now, they were back at the university campus outside the only building left intact after the aliens blasted away their friends a few weeks ago. That was retaliation for their cunning act of poisoning the aliens, but the cycle of retaliation hadn't finished and wouldn't until there was no more in her to give.

They both wore head torches. Hers illuminated their shiny prize in the vehicle, his on her.

Like a maniac with round, bloodshot eyes, Françoise stared at the case. Ryder had given her the idea a long time ago when they debated where the third case should be landed. One of his abandoned options was to plant it on a prisoner-carrying ship on its empty return journey. It would have to be supplemented with an explosive, but Bono knew how to build booby-trap devices. She recalled last night's conversation and admired how cool she'd been.

"No, Françoise," Ryder said, "as far as we know, it needs a human contact for the case to open. It could be that it'd arrive on Zadok, you set off an almighty explosion, and obliterate the ship but leave the case shiny and untouched."

"It's a risk I'm prepared to take. I can't experiment with it to see if tying up a Zadokian so that he falls on the case will open it, can I?"

"We know that Zadokian skin and blood are different to humans. Anyway, he'd be dead by the time he reached Zadok."

"I've been thinking about that. Has Antonio quizzed his Zadokian on how they survived their journey? They must have needed a lot of food and water, unless light can keep them alive without any food at all."

"That might be possible, because they wouldn't need to expend a lot of energy sitting around for over eight years. Antonio has had little luck figuring out more. Probably because his prisoner is largely clueless as to what happened between getting strapped in the craft and landing on Earth. We suspect they must be put in some kind of suspended animation.

"Françoise, how are you going to detonate the explosives once the craft reaches Zadok? We have no idea how long it takes, at least nine years, so you can't use a timing device."

"There's a—what do you English call it? A whiz kid on campus—or there was. He thought about this and designed a device with two mechanisms working together. One works when rapid deceleration occurs until zero velocity is achieved. The other is a gravity sensor that works when it detects gravity after it had become zero, set to normal give or take fifty percent."

"They both seem dodgy to me, especially if high gee slingshots are done around other suns and planets. Maybe you should wait for our guys to come up with something foolproof."

Françoise seethed with another delaying tactic but ignored him. "You told me this third case is probably the ultimate human killer, to mop up survivors?"

"We believe so. Some think it might contain a non-lethal virus to turn us all into zombies, but that idea has fewer supporters. The aliens must prefer the absence of humans to an unpredictable danger. We assume there is something about the domes that would give them protection."

"What makes you say that? Have your scientists found ARIA in the alien body? Could they be vulnerable to the virus in another form, such as might be in the third case?"

"I'm not sure I should tell you too much, Françoise. I'd rather you wait a while to get through your grieving for Elodie and the other students."

"Fuck you, Ryder." She'd kept her anger under control in the hope of sweet talking him, but the wily man had seen through her. Her steam was up and the safety valve to stop her had flipped. "It's all right for you, lying on a deckchair, soaking up tropical sunshine in complete isolation. We're incredibly vulnerable here, surrounded by festering bodies, feral animals, aliens, and their controlled geriatric lunatic humans. It's Dante's *Inferno*. We'll be lucky to survive another week, so we're going to send their poison back to them."

"But, it might not be–" She cut off the connection and wanted to throw the NoteCom on the ground in case a future conversation with Ryder changed her mind. But she pocketed it. She needed to record her retribution and let others know. She was livid, not stupid.

On reflection, she realized her cool start waned badly. Ryder would understand. A good man, and although she ragged him about being secure, she knew he wasn't. The aliens probably had a good idea where the island was, and they'd demonstrated ruthlessness, although they would interpret their actions as expediency. Maybe they underestimated Ryder's resourcefulness. Her destructive distractions would strengthen his arm.

Bono nudged her elbow. "I said let's get on with it."

ONCE MORE, Françoise preceded action by keeping still. Bono lay beside her looking at his watch while she studied the domes through the infrared digiscope on her rifle. She knew they had a poor chance of planting the case on the grey ship they saw land yesterday. But she had to try, and maybe the optimistic Bono had their improved odds correct. He'd convinced her that their previous success in poisoning the dome was due to the alien's appalling disregard for their own security. Maybe on Zadok, the government's control was so absolute, there was little need for Earth-style security.

"Bono, I am agonising over whether we need a distraction. Astonishingly, they seem to have assumed they've wiped out all opposition and have posted no guards. Detonating a firebomb in that warehouse might wake them up and we'd be worse off."

"*Non*, I'm ready to send the signal. It took a risk to set up, you know. I had to dodge some crazy people and give my lunch to a dog."

"Your febrile state is clouding your judgement. For once, it's not the quality of your preparations that's important but the best course of action."

"So you think we can pull this trolley, with our makeshift bomb and the case, over to the dome they seem to use for storage, and through to the landing area between the domes? Get access to the ship and plant the thing, hoping it won't take off while we're aboard, and sneak off? All while they dream of frolicking on Zadok?"

"I'm so pleased you agree. As a concession, but a worthy plan too, you can bring the remote detonator for the incendiary bomb in case we need a distraction at any time." When she said this, Bono's teeth flashed in the dark. Boys and their toys.

"Let's go then," he said, tugging at the handle of the garden trolley. He'd oiled the axles so it rolled silently. "Remember, there's a chance there's no guards because they've set up a security system."

Françoise shushed him while peering at likely camera-installation sites. Wasted. She wondered what alien technology might've been used to sense them—no doubt an extension to their telepathic powers. Maybe they had telepathic transmission boosters disguised as blades of grass.

Their observations told them the dome on the right should hold stores but no aliens. They pulled the trolley to the entrance, pushed the flaps out of the way, and used their headset night sights to make their way through a narrow box-free path to the other side. She switched on the mpeg recorder integrated into her headset.

Yesterday, she'd pushed three coins together to aid her imaginings of the curved, triangular, central gap. The large silvery ship in the middle spoilt the anticipation of seeing the space in three dimensions. She sighed but then marvelled at the engineering. The surface of the ship had a metallic feel, had no joins, and like the beaten ground beneath, had no scorch marks. The silvery, fuzzy ball image they'd seen on their NoteCom sent from Ryder had changed to this equally beautiful but different view. They pulled the trolley to a ramp leading up to where there should be a hatch. But they saw no joins or marks.

"Damn, I bet they just think at it to open," said Bono. "Now what?"

"I've already tried urging it to open. Maybe there's an embedded pressure and heat sensing pad, but I doubt it." As Françoise walked up the ramp, a noise behind made her stop. Her heart pounded as she expected to find a bloody hole appear in her chest. Hearing wordless grunts, her knees buckled. She put out her hand on the ship to support her only to find a doorway appear, and she fell in. Finally, an adrenalin surge enabled her to roll over onto her back and ready her rifle. She saw Bono standing over a crumpled alien. Bono stooped, touched its neck and shook his head.

"Dead. He came out of the dormitory and horticultural dome carrying this." He tossed a banana-shaped grey stick. "What now?"

She stayed in the doorway, hoping that would keep it open. Stunned by yet another death, even one of an alien. But she had to get on with her mission: her blow on behalf of Mankind. "Damn. We have two choices. Take him back with us and give him an unchristian burial. Or we hide him in here."

"Good thinking. If the bomb doesn't open the case, it would send a message to Zadok that we don't want them."

"I wish I could talk to Ryder about this."

"Why? I thought you weren't bothered about his opinions."

She opened her mouth as if to reply but changed it to, "To do the opposite. Bring the body up to block the door, and I'll help with the trolley."

Moments later, Françoise gawked at the soft-blue-lit interior of the Zadokian ship. Inclined seats were arranged in random order, not rows. She placed her hand on one and smiled as the soft grey material absorbed it, making an impression when she withdrew. Bono had brought up the trolley, blocked the door with it and hid the alien's body under a couch inside a box-like structure. They put on metallic oven gloves to place the case and the detonating device in what might have been a locker at the rear.

"I'll fetch the nasty bits," Françoise said, as she returned to the trolley and brought back containers. "I hope these body parts will trigger the case if the explosives don't."

"When this device blows, the remains of this man will be everywhere."

"Ironic that the old man died on Earth, as a result of Zadokians actions, but will end up on their planet. Are you sure the blood phials will not be frozen by then?"

"No, but I doubt the Zadokians would let this craft's internal temperature drop to freezing even returning unmanned. The explosion might thaw the blood anyway. It's a chance, just like the rest."

He found a heavy box, which he clipped onto lugs in the floor blocking the locker in the hope it would deter prying fingers before take off.

Before leaving, Bono pulled a plastic bag stuffed with alien weed out of the trolley.

"Just a minute," said Françoise. "What are you doing?"

"I thought it would be ironic for the Zadokian authorities to see what's being grown back here."

"But it won't survive the blast."

"If things go wrong with the gravity sensor or the explosives, I'd like to think we've done something. At least the guards back here would get their marching orders when their drug scam is revealed."

She couldn't disagree with poetic justice and busied herself, ensuring the images being saved were good enough in the low light. Movement told her Bono hadn't gone out of the ship as she expected. Panic troubled her stomach butterflies as she realized he'd headed for the pilot's cabin.

"Hey, Bono, come on. Where are you going?" Fearing his boyish pranks, she followed him to the nose of the ship. "No, Bono, you are not going into the cockpit. We mustn't give ourselves away."

"I reckon this might be easier to fly than driving our Volkswagen."

She pulled him out and then hauled their trolley out of the ship but looked back when they reached the entrance to the storage dome. The ship's doorway remained open.

"I wonder if I have to press my hand against the side of the doorway again?" But as she spoke, the door materialised, making the ship look as if nothing had happened.

After creeping back across the bridge and in the relative safety of their vehicle, they looked back at the dome's moonlit surface showing above the poplar trees.

Francoise tapped her fingers on the window. "I wish I knew when this one was due to take off. The others left within a day of landing, including yesterday's."

"Yeah, the longer it stays there..."

"Exactly. I've uploaded part of the mpeg of the ship and us planting the case. Ryder's group and the Canadian lot can see what we've done and be inspired. Hopefully, they can derive some useful data."

"I'd hate to think what that lunatic Antonio might do with it. Hey, I wish you'd let me have a go at flying that ship."

"It's not the same as a PlayStation." She pointed at the silvery banana he took out of his backpack.

CHAPTER 39

July 29ᵗʰ 2016, Rarotonga Communications lab.

"RYDER, YOU BASTARD," Antonio said through the speakers, enabling the crowded lab to hear. "I hold you personally responsible, but it won't work. You see. Your nasty plan will backfire. Blast you."

Ryder opened his mouth to respond, but Antonio had cut the connection.

"What have you done this time?" Teresa said, looking at the last still of Antonio's twisted face.

"Nothing."

"Typical. You did nothing when you should've persuaded the loony French group to hold back. Now look what your nothing has done. 'Nothing comes of nothing', isn't that what King Lear says?"

"Yes, but Antonio is no sweet Cordelia, and he, like you, have blundered to the wrong conclusions." He was tired of correcting the twisted interpretations of others. He preferred to watch again the video images Françoise had treated them to. "Her notes are too brief."

Abdul, resting his head in his hands, said, "Isn't it obvious what they've done?"

"I'm not so sure, Abdul. Have you a headache?"

"It's throbbing. Stress. I thought I had a good rapport with Françoise."

"You are the heart throb of Charlotte, too. I call it greedy. Did Françoise give you any clues to this melodrama?"

"I'd told her everything I knew about the tests we'd done on the second case, what kind of human contact opened it, and I sent her the files Julia had on the tests she'd done on the Zad's blood and tissue. I didn't think she was planning anything like this. I just passed the data on as a way of disseminating our information to everyone's benefit."

"Don't blame yourself, Abdul, but I have a sneaky feeling that we've only got part of the story. For instance, that looks like an alien body Bono is bundling under the couches on the ship. We don't know anything about what happened there, do we?"

"I thought it was a bag containing more explosives. Let's enhance the image. You're right, we can see its hand. There's nothing in her notes. Do they think an alien body blown apart in an explosion will trigger the case?"

"Maybe, but they have human parts from a few-days-old corpse."

"Gruesome."

"She thinks the alien's biology has enough similarities with ours, in spite of the chlorophyll in their skin, for the ARIA-3 virus or whatever is in the third case to do the trick. I wouldn't confirm what I know from the lab reports, which is why she's sore at me."

"Ah, it could be my fault then. I told her Julia found the Zadokian's DNA to be ninety-seven percent identical with ours. It sounds a lot, and not a lot different between us and chimps or dogs. It doesn't mean we and Zadokians have a common ancestry. Even yeast and human cells have a lot in common."

"Thanks, Abdul. You mean I am more related to a pint of beer than I thought? But it gives credence to Françoise's notion that the aliens might be adversely affected by an ARIA-3 event."

"When you two have stopped absolving each other of blame," Teresa said, "Antonio's connection is live again."

"By the prophet, could his face appear any more evil?" Abdul said. He turned off the microphone. "Ah, what's stopping him telling the Zads what the French have done?"

"Nothing," Ryder said. "Hopefully, they'll not believe him, or..."

Jena wagged her finger. "He'll have a reason for not telling them."

Antonio's shouts vibrated the speakers. "I'm trying to stop evil, you *bastardi*!"

"Antonio," Ryder said, "try to remember that it is humans who are the victims here."

The Italian looked confused for a second. "That's open to interpretation. You don't know if they are the logical successor and necessary inhabitants of this planet. Anyway, your feeble attempts to thwart history will soon be over."

"Oh my God," Teresa said. "I thought we'd kept our location from that lunatic."

"We have," Abdul said. "I have a filter preventing the name of this island, regional geography, GPS data, IP addresses, and other tags leaving the console. He must mean something else."

"You fools, it wouldn't take the Zadokians long to find you, but it seems you are too insignificant to be worth the effort. The French were too close and an annoying wasp nest."

Ryder took the others to one side. "I would've thought the same months ago, but he's bluffing. I truly believe they don't know where we are. They are not experienced with this kind of warfare and surveillance."

"Even so, we ought to create some distraction strategies," Jena said. "Maybe set up solar cell-powered lights and activity in other parts of the world. Damn, we should have instructed Dominiq to do that in Australia before he left."

Abdul grinned. "There are four solar-powered Internet hub servers ticking in Seattle, San Diego, Buenos Aires, and Rome. I believe I can make them ping each other as if they are talking. We have a blackout in operation, but you'd be surprised how many lights shine. There's garden and path lights powered by solar cells, and street lamps illuminating mice and cats as we speak."

"*Attenzione!*" yelled Antonio. "You fuckers gone to sleep? I haven't told you the best news yet."

"Get on with it," Ryder said. "We're busy."

"Busy? You don't understand the word. This'll set you chasing your tails. I'm going to tell the local Zadokian commander what that French bitch has done. Hah. Out."

"Quick, Abdul, get Manuel or Julia on to stop him leaving."

"It's all right, I've been talking to Julia all the time," Teresa said. "What do you want to say? Kill Antonio?"

Ryder shot her an annoyed look as he took over the microphone. "Hi, Julia, I'm sorry to ask you to do this, but—"

"You're asking us to kill him? I'm not sure, Ryder, he might detect extreme thoughts like that."

"I know it's difficult. We had this problem when he started shooting us in Wales, but you must try and stop him. Maybe you can lock him in or maim him."

"They've logged out," Abdul said.

Teresa frowned at Ryder. "You've gone mad. How dare you command two elderly people to try and kill Antonio. Granted, he seems to have gone off the rails again and might hurt them, but that's like signing their death warrant."

"I had to think on my feet. And it wasn't because Antonio was generally getting worse, it was his specific intention to tell the aliens about what the French had done."

Teresa stood, hands on her hips. "So, they stop the ship taking off? Big deal."

"No, it puts the case back into their hands to do with as those local guards see fit, as opposed to what the Zadokians who planted it intended. My guess is that the Earth-based Zadokian guards are renegades, or they wouldn't be usurping their position to grow contraband. They might decide to open the case out of curiosity."

"Ah. That might be bad," she said, "especially if there is an electromagnetic wave circulating the planet from it like with the second case. Do you think the domes would protect the aliens? Antonio's report of his interrogation revealed his prisoner's horror that he was outside the dome."

"Maybe the fabric of the dome has some cellular filter to stop the ARIA virus getting through. But we don't know where or if the case would be opened. Damn Françoise and Antonio."

Abdul slapped him on the back. "It's no use crying over what you cannot help. I've sent a message to the French, but they're not logged on."

"Good idea, Abdul, they're now in more danger. If I were them, I'd be across the Alps by now, but they're probably on a nearby hill to watch the take off."

"Can we see the French domes?"

"Of course, with the next Landsat orbit, assuming clouds aren't in the way."

"I'm sure we used to be able to keep the image over a single spot and get a real-time view."

"Yes, Ryder, that was clever Charlotte's doing when we had the power and functions of the ISS. When is she due back? We could do with those magic fingers now."

"They are due back tonight or tomorrow. Made good time in calm weather. We could have her perfecting things pretty soon."

"You morons," Jena said. "That woman has gone through unspeakable traumas. I know she was a genius at uni, but she's had ARIA. She'll need bucketfuls of TLC."

"And before you ask," Teresa said, "Nessa, quite rightly, has enforced bed rest on her. So she hasn't been revising with her technical manuals en route. I know you told Dominiq to suggest that to her."

Ryder held up his hands. "All right, I give up. Only trying to save our necks. Positives are that Dominiq and Nessa haven't caught ARIA or its variants; Bryce and Benita have stopped forgetting and started learning."

TWO HOURS LATER, Ryder paced the lab. The image of the French dome had looked no different from a few days previous. No radio contact from Canada worried him further. At least they had contact with Dominiq on schedule for a midnight ETA. He'd considered sending a chopper out to pick up Charlotte but knew he'd be set upon by the women Rottweilers here.

Besides Ryder, only two technicians hadn't gone to bed early. He was too agitated to consider sleeping but drank strong coffee, just short of giving him the jitters.

A technician called him over. Manuel had sent a text, something he only did in weak signal areas or if he needed to stay silent.

Dunno if I dun rite thing.

Took Zad wiv me—thot it mite help turn Ant. Zad unnerstand most my words.

Cant find Ant. Hes in dome.

I sent Zad in. I wait.

Ryder shook his head, wondering how to respond. There were too many unknowns, and he wanted, needed his old friend to be safe.

'Ryder here. Maybe better to get away.'

CHAPTER 40

MANUEL AGREED WITH RYDER, so why did he stay at the construction shed when his running-away muscles were eager to see action? He could make himself understood at a simple level even though the Zad couldn't make words form in Manuel's head like it could with Antonio. However, something along those telepathic lines was developing. He could be kidding himself, like when people think they understand their dogs when they communicate with tails wagging that they need a walk. Manuel grew colours and warmth in parts of his brain as feedback.

He'd only tried to involve Julia in a joint "talk" effort once. She was uncomfortable talking with one of her vivisection victims. Academic now. Keeping the large shed between him and the dome, he examined the western section of the airfield. Once, international jumbo jets landed there, circling in a giant helix to touch down.

A ghost landscape stretched out before him. Less debris than in the city, but enough windblown boxes, shrubs, and objects he couldn't identify to make a pilot attempting to land scream obscenities. But there was no screaming. No noise at all, wait, he heard the *tsee-tsi-tsi-tsit* of a pair of American goldfinches chasing each other in their rollercoaster flight. He liked to see mountains on horizons, but this was like looking out to sea. A calm vista stretching his soul into the distance. It instilled peace, or would do if he could have ignored the worry machine boiling inside him.

He took a step towards that inviting horizon, tearing himself away from the conscience-magnetic pull of the dome and then left towards his pickup. A noise behind sent his pulse racing. He turned to see Zad wave a kind of "Hi" to him. It looked pleased to see him, if that was possible with Manuel's increased awareness of alien facial expressions: hairless eyebrow dancing, the small mouth upturning, and eyes shining brighter. The greeting was reinforced by a rosy glow in Manuel's chest. To his amazement, following the Zadokian was another and then more until three stood there emanating caution, fear, and yet excitement that Manuel had no doubt he could detect. It was obvious they wanted him to take them with him in the pickup, so he led the way. Manuel smiled at how they each had variations of grey tunics and carried matching shoulder bags. The renegade escapees looked like an alien school trip. He had no choice but to take them back to the clinic, but he knew they couldn't stay, nor he and Julia. Antonio would lead any Zadokian posse straight for them.

AN HOUR LATER, Manuel drove a campervan with three Zadokians wearing filter-masks, while a fuming Julia followed in the pickup with the other two. He recollected her reaction.

"Tell me you're joking, Manuel? I should've expected it. I'll have to take my research data and equipment, while you throw our stuff together, and food, bottled water–and, and everything. Eeeeek!"

"You shouldn't need to take equipment we can find in any hospital. And Kelseyville has clinics, stores, and it should be safe."

"But why so far? California for God's sake? We might not always find fuel. I could throttle you."

His words stumbled. "I'm sorry, Julia, but what else could I do? This could be a breakthrough for us as well as them. Just think of the authorities on Zadok, if they thought returning prisoners, instead of being cleansed, have moved onto a new form of revolution.

"The other reason is that Kelseyville had the cleanest air I've ever breathed even before industrial and vehicle air pollution stuttered to a halt. We could restart a lab with positive air pressure if the Zads needed it, but my bet is they'll get used to the natural clean air."

Manuel got agitated, because she was blaming him. Circumstances led him into these scrapes, not deliberation to hurtle them down deeper holes. He didn't argue, preferring to let her rant. He'd become her pressure valve. His spectacles steamed on both sides: from his discomfort and her hot breath.

He continued talking while carrying a box of dried food. "I know of a tucked-away medical convalescence home at Clear Lake. The California climate won't give us survival issues in winter, and the lake is fresh water. More importantly, there are no domes for thousands of miles."

"Are we telling Ryder? Only maybe we should keep our destination off the airways."

"Good thinking. It's possible all their calls are monitored."

That Julia accepted the situation showed itself in a note she wrote for Antonio: "Taking the Zads back to Banff." He hadn't thought of a bluff going-away letter. Nice one.

He assumed Antonio remained in the dome. Manuel regretted that he couldn't stop him, but he had other things to concentrate on, like navigating this beast along the debris-littered, but otherwise empty, highways. He smiled at the bizarre thought of being pulled over by the Highway Patrol at the US border.

"Passports please, sir? Any other ID? No? In that case, I'll have to report you to Illegal Alien Immigration Control." Manuel laughed out loud. He realized the Zad next to him was looking worried. "Don't worry, they're always running alien amnesties."

He glanced up at the loaded shotgun clipped above the windshield. It was like going back in history when the early pioneers had needed them on wagon trains to shoot game or fend off bears and cougars. He and Julia sported holstered guns too, and Zad-3 turned a delightful pink to be given the silvery stick.

CHAPTER 41

August 1st 2016, Rarotonga.

RYDER KNEW HE WAS IN FOR A ROUGH RIDE. He had the promise of backup from Dominiq, Bryce, and especially Abdul, who'd wrung his hands and prayed to Allah.

"She's only had two days to recuperate, leave the poor girl in peace," Teresa said, putting herself between Charlotte's bed and the men at the clinic door.

"You don't understand the gravity of the situation," Ryder said.

"Abdul has smuggled a NoteCom to her."

Instead of showing remorse, Abdul lit up a smile. "Did she use it, especially the updates page?"

"I don't know how far she got before she fell asleep again, and it hit the floor. Here, have it back." She thrust it at him, accompanied by a contemptuous glare. Then reluctantly took it back when Abdul's little-boy-lost eyes worked on her. "All right, but only if she is up for it."

Abdul's NoteCom buzzed in his earpiece. His smiling expression remained inscrutable. "Teresa, I'm being called away, but Bryce here wants to buy you a coffee and tell you all about his experiences."

"I do? Oh, I do."

Ryder could see Abdul's fingers walking, signalling him to leave. He guessed that he'd some news urgently needing attention but puzzled over the need to detain Teresa. But, he knew her better than Abdul did.

"Okay, what's going on? Ah..." She walked briskly to Charlotte's screened bed before calling out, "Where is she? What a stupid question. Ryder, you bastard."

Ryder accepted the blame even though he had no idea how Abdul and his technician friends had smuggled Charlotte out of the clinic while it was guarded by Commandant Teresa. He couldn't help smiling at her fury as he rushed to the comms lab.

ABDUL BURST INFORMATION ON RYDER as soon as he arrived. "We've had a message from Françoise. Another alien prisoner ship is circling the dome."

"Which means?"

"They're waiting for the booby-trapped ship to take off. Need a vacant landing spot assuming they still insist on landing between the domes."

Ryder frowned. "Why don't they land nearby? Surely they can guard it?"

"Don't forget it appears as an indistinct sphere to us when it is flying. Françoise's images show a solid, clean surface. It could be they hope we haven't seen it like that. Maybe they prefer the wind shelter, relative security, and ease of being right between the domes– especially for escorting prisoners off the ship. By Allah, how many prisoners are they bringing? There couldn't have been thousands on the Zadok moon exploration team."

"Once they concocted a system for transporting criminals, they probably widened the categories eligible for deportation. They can't have had feedback yet on the first batch, unless they've invented a faster-than-light communication system."

"I don't see Charlotte," Ryder said, knowing that Teresa would be along any time to drag her away.

"Back room, being briefed by my techies. We're hoping she's retained her expertise for tweaking the satellite systems for getting real-time images. One of my bright sparks has worked out a useful bunch of stuff from Charlotte's data."

"So, we don't really need her in person? Getting Teresa off our backs would be a bonus."

"She's a natural genius at this stuff. Go and see for yourself. I'll stall Teresa."

In a smaller side lab, in a scrum around a console, Ryder saw a crowd, like students who'd discovered an addictive game. He could see a shock of platinum blond hair nearest the large screen and guessed it was Charlotte. He didn't want to interrupt even though he had an urge to introduce himself as that crazy Brit she'd been listening to for over a year. Damn, she'd not remember any of their conversations and only know his name since her rescue. He hovered in the background as she and the technicians swapped code.

One of the onlookers cried out. "There! Movement from the dome."

"That's it," said Charlotte's Australian accent. "Now, we track it via this gizmo here. It pulls in two other sats, and we sync it with the Doppler merger."

Ryder scratched his head at the jargon, although most was familiar from his media career two years ago. He couldn't do what she'd done without a hundred hours of research, trial, and error. A chorused cheer rose as they witnessed in real time the launch of the tampered-with Zadokian ship.

"Off you go with our blessing," Charlotte said.

The door barged into him from behind.

"Hi, Teresa, see what a good job you made of looking after Charlotte. She's in her element."

Teresa looked gazumped. "Take care of her, she'll be going through ups and downs. Is that the alien ship taking off?"

The image changed as the ship left the range of one satellite to be caught by another. Charlotte tutted as she fiddled with more pressure buttons. "Damn not being able to access the ISS scopes. In other minute, we'll lose visual, go for plain trajectory. It'll be too close for Hubble until it's beyond the moon, our moon."

A technician called out a warning. "There's a blip on an intersect course. Looks like one of their smaller ships."

Ten seconds later, the booby-trapped ship detonated. The group suffered their shock in silence, although Charlotte and two technicians busied themselves with data gathering.

Ryder held his breath. When the second case opened, a mystery pulse emanated from it and travelled round the world. If that happened, he should expect it anytime. Nothing. "How far from the surface was it?" He'd passed the worry stage about the electromagnetic-or-whatever pulse and turned to the possibility of the case returning to Earth and continuing its probable deadly mission.

"Over a hundred k," said Charlotte, turning to face the speaker. "Are you Ryder?"

"Hi, Charlotte, I'm so pleased to see you alive and as well as you appear to be."

"I believe it's largely thanks to you. Hugs and kisses later, yeah?"

Ryder's face reddened as five smiling faces leered at him and more so as Teresa added, "I'm sure Jena will be pleased to hear that too."

Charlotte looked puzzled but returned to the question. "The way the ship exploded, the case would probably be in bits, burning up in the atmosphere as we speak."

"NASA found the first case to be resistant to everything they used on it except human presence."

"The French had placed human remains with the case," Abdul said, "so it should have opened. What we see there is probably the combined detonations of whatever the alien attack ship used and the explosives planted in the ship."

Ryder pointed at the explosion. "I'm sure you clever lot can analyse the images, including infrared, to determine the detonation timings. Let's suppose the case remained intact..."

"Really?" Charlotte eyes opened wide.

"You have to learn," Abdul said, "that our Ryder leaves no alien stone unturned."

"Fair enough," she said and smiled at Ryder, adding to his colour once more. Surely these gestures couldn't be more than gratitude? If Jena had a whiff of Ryder playing away, his limbs would be in serious danger, so he worried at all these knowing smiles in the room. Each had a tongue that would be playfully gossiping. The problem with island life was that rumour-mongering became the best entertainment activity since TV lost global sports coverage.

"Any surviving debris would be landing in the North Atlantic in ten minutes give or take local winds. That's good isn't it?"

"I'd imagine the case would sink if closed," Ryder said.

"If it's the same as the second case we have here," Abdul said, "it would sink. But it would've endured over two thousand degrees from friction in addition to the heat acquired from the explosion. And then the speed of impact must damage it. I'd say that piece of luggage is definitely lost and non-returnable."

"Good," Ryder said, "that it can't hurt us, but a shame in some ways that the French plan went awry."

"Yes," Abdul said. "Striking back has made me warm inside, even if it didn't work."

"What worries me," Ryder said, "is that it won't only be the French group that are hunted down. They've revealed flaws in their security they can't ignore. And I have a feeling it's the end of naïve aliens here on Earth. They might send a fourth, more devastating, case that doesn't depend on human handling."

"If the third was the final case, it would take at least nine years to put another one together and fly it here," Abdul said.

"Unless they have spares at Cassini."

"Oh great, I'd rather like to think they haven't put such dangerous stuff in the hands of their own corrupt guards."

"We have an incoming call from Antonio," said a technician.

"Your blundering has come to nothing, Ryder. I told them about the French sending back the case, ha ha. They were very impressed with me. I'm going to benefit so much."

Ryder made sure Antonio couldn't hear, then said: "Abdul, I don't suppose we know whether the call is from Winnipeg? I'd like to know if he's on Manuel's trail."

"He's using an Internet connection to the one we set up for Manuel, so he's probably at the house or the next-door clinic."

"Okay, I suppose I better speak to the insufferable psycho.

"Hello, Antonio. What makes you think we're interested in what you say to the enemy?"

"The enemy? Get real, Ryder. Hah. Be a real easy rider, Ryder. When the enemy is in control and occupy your land, they aren't your enemy any more. Well, maybe to you and your renegade friends. And perhaps you should ask your NASA buddy if he thinks all Zadokians are enemies."

Ryder would have relished teasing Antonio on whether the Zadokians were delighted at his housemates helping prisoners escape, but he didn't want him to know about the communication links. He wondered if he knew about the ship and case being destroyed.

"And what are your new friends going to do about the case? Wish it bon voyage?"

"You haven't heard? *We* blew it to bits."

"You are one of them now, Antonio?"

"I believe I am, in a way. I am special, as you must realize. I expect you think of me as delusional, but I know better. I feel more in tune with the Zadokian psyche than the pitiful remnants of humankind. Hah. *Mama Mia*, I feel deliriously fulfilled, Ryder. It wouldn't have happened, I suspect, without exposure to the various Zadokian-engineered viruses. And it is a shame that it couldn't have worked out better for all humans rather than me alone."

"Is that what you believe? The death of billions was an accident? That ARIA was meant to enrich us and not obliterate us by reducing our memories to nothing?"

"Quite possibly."

Ryder had momentarily thought Antonio had received original purpose information from the Zadokians, but it appeared he distorted the facts to suit his ego once again. "Just keep out of our way, Antonio. I don't think we want you in our species any more. Goodbye." He pushed the microphone away.

"Harsh?" Abdul said.

"Maybe, but I get nightmares from the way he killed our friends in Wales."

"Me too, but it wasn't the real Antonio. He was transforming too quickly after the case exposure. I think he's a lonely and desperate man."

"You're right, Abdul. It seems he finds it too difficult to relate to humans, so maybe, he'll find true love and happiness with a Zad." They both smiled but shared both an element of truth and sadness.

JENA HAULED RYDER OUT OF THE LAB. She said it was to share the sunset and tequilas on their chalet balcony.

"Where is it?" he said looking at black cumulonimbus clouds and then at the local beer she'd thrust into his hand.

"Would you have come out for murky skies and ale?"

"It depends who asked," he said, at the risk of discovering the efficacy of the local brew as a shampoo. But she surprised him by pulling aside her freshly-washed black hair to reveal a smile.

"I am so lucky to have a lover who is so amusing."

Ryder leaned over and kissed her. Their beers wobbled and tipped when their embrace became riotous. He could taste fruit in her lipstick, only momentarily because her tongue, and his, pirouetted. But with effort, he succeeded in wet lipping in order to identify the fragrance. A pre-ARIA fashion he enjoyed was to taste flavoured lipsticks. His favourite fruit was redcurrant, and he had the urge to discover if she'd remembered. She had. She disengaged sufficiently to whisper, "My nipples have redcurrant on one and strawberry on the other. Would you care to investigate?"

"May I supplement with cream?"

"I have it ready. Damn. Is that your NoteCom? Turn it off."

They wrestled over it a little until he saw it was a relayed text message from France.

"I have to take this, Françoise might have something urgent."

"Oh my God, another of your harem." Tugging a cord, she pulled apart her blouse and walked back towards the bedroom. "Don't be long. It's fresh cream."

He hesitated reading the message. Jena could be extraordinarily passionate, but rarely. His bones remembered each occasion. Was he going to regret not following her? He played with the NoteCom, turning it over without reading the message. Damn. He had to read it.

"Need speak private–Fran."

That meant going to the comms lab and using a radio-Internet link they can encrypt. He looked through the mosquito nets draping the doorway to the bedroom. Damn. Hopefully, his erection wouldn't be so obvious by the time he reached the lab.

ABDUL SET UP THE RADIO LINK and left along with Charlotte and the others to leave Ryder alone. And he urgently hoped it would be quick.

"Hi, Françoise. Are you and Bono safe?"

"*Oui*, for the time being. I have something important to tell you that I don't want Antonio, and thus the aliens, to know."

"I know what you're going to say, and we are gutted at the shooting down of the ship."

"We saw it take off but not any explosion."

"It would've been too far out unless you knew exactly where to look with binoculars."

"Was that today?"

Ryder had to look at a separate clock in the lab for current time in France, while thinking they could abolish time zones now. France was twelve hours ahead of Avarua. "Today for you."

"Good, but don't tell anyone," she said, followed by what Ryder assumed to be her telling Bono and the both of them whooping with joy. Perhaps they've flipped with all the pressure they'd been under.

"Why is it good?"

"Because they blew up the wrong ship. The one with the case took off two days before. We planted a dummy booby trap last night with a similar case from a posh department store." He heard hysterical laughter at the other end. Her message took a while to sink in, as if his neurons decided to take some side roads and drive slowly just to be sure. Once the dawn of realization hit full beam, Ryder smiled. A vibration in his chest reverberated upwards resulting in a chuckle that promoted itself to raucous laughter.

"Françoise, I assume you loaded the real case with a human remains bomb?"

"Yes, last night's had to be a convincing attempt. If anything, we did the first one better, but we didn't need to dispose of a guard that time."

"His disappearance and your bombing activities means it's too dangerous for you to stay. Where are you going to run to?"

"This is a safe line?"

"Encrypted."

"Before the domes, we'd heard of a group like ours near Geneva. The Alps make a good barrier between us and the aliens here."

"Sounds good. Eventually, it should be safer. It seems we uninfected are in no danger from those with memory losses who have met ARIA-2. But be careful, you might come across people who have only just met other ARIA-1 people."

"We understand. We were going to ask you to come and fetch us."

"I thought you might, and that's a maybe if you can get far away from the flight paths of alien ships, whether or not they are carrying suitcase bombs, but not for months. In the meantime, keep in touch. *Bon voyage*, Françoise and Bono."

"*Au revoir*, Ryder."

RYDER'S PULSE RACED FASTER THAN A HAMSTER'S WHEEL, but he couldn't decide whether to keep the news to himself. One danger was the aliens destroying it before it reached Zadok. He had a niggling worry that the aliens might decide to retaliate big time and destroy all life on the planet. He pushed that to one side. Antonio would tell them, but his credibility would shatter, so maybe he'd keep quiet. Manuel's new buddies might go back and reveal the secret, so Manuel and Julia had better not be told. But could he keep this huge secret for at least nine years? No. He'd have to tell at least one trustee or he'd go mad.

Technically, he should tell Charlotte so she'd know where to point telescopes and spectroscopic sensors, but she'd probably do that anyway, especially with a few hints. But she'd probably be so much more focussed and invent and employ techniques if she knew why.

Sentimentally, and for survival, he should confide in Jena, or she'd rip his head off when she eventually discovered he'd been keeping such a huge news event from her.

If there was only one person he should confide in, Charlotte was so obviously that one.

"WHY ON EARTH DID YOU TELL *ME*?" Jena said. "It is great news, wonderful if it pays off, but it's too big a deal, too heavy a burden for me to carry. Okay, I can do some astronomy with Hubble, Webb, and other satellites out there, but Charlotte will want to know why I'm using particular modules. After more recuperation and catching up with her brain, she would be better placed to know this news. Ryder, I love you, but you are an idiot." She gave him a hug. "You should know you can't expect a woman to keep a secret this big to herself. Let's go tell Charlotte."

"CLEVER, BUT NOT FOOLPROOF," Charlotte said.

"What, no whoops of delirious joy?" Ryder said. "Something in your beautiful but composed face tells me you already knew."

"I was eighty per cent sure the real case wasn't on the exploded ship but knew nothing of what happened to the real one."

"You ran spectral analysis on the explosion and not found evidence of unusual spikes from what should've been in the case. Right?" Jena said.

"Clever. We're gonna work well together," said Charlotte. "But that accounted for only ten per cent since we don't know what the ARIA blocks in the first two cases are made of and have no idea at all about the third. Just look at the image of the case Françoise sent us."

She enlarged and enhanced the image of the silver suitcase the French had planted on the ship. "They'd removed the suitcase handles and were very careful which sides to show to camera. Now, look at our image of the first two cases."

Ryder pointed. "The holographic chevrons are on the first two but not on the French one. But the chevrons only appear on one side, they could've had it upside down. Ah, you can see a seam on the French one. Okay, that's more hundred per cent to me. How come Antonio and his Zadokian masters were fooled?"

"He, like you, saw what your brains wanted to see. Without enlarging and enhancing, it is convincing. And it is still only eighty per cent to me, because I have not seen the third case from when the French found it."

"Oh, it is on file. It is seamless and identical to the other two except with three chevrons," Jena said. "Then, they sealed it in a polystyrene casing. So if the aliens analyse the spectra and image data, they will come to the same conclusion."

"Is Antonio bright enough to think a hoax might have happened?" said Charlotte.

"Absolutely," Jena said. "It's the sort of stunt *he'd* pull. The aliens might remain under the illusion they've destroyed the real case. But if Antonio has an idle moment, in between screwing helpless women and preening himself, I wouldn't be surprised if he takes a more careful look at those images."

"Why would he think of doing that?" Ryder said. "He's already seen them and acted on the information to ingratiate himself with the Zadokians."

"Yes, but if you were him, isn't there a nagging question?"

"Erm, you mean why did the French make it easy for him to see the footage? They wanted him to see it but hoped that he'd think they'd merely made a mistake not to send it to us with encryption."

"Exactly, so anytime now, Antonio will realize he's been duped."

Ryder couldn't help smiling alternately between frowning seriousness. "He can't really tell the Zadokians that they, through him, have been fooled. He'd lose his credibility. Excellent."

"Also," said Charlotte, "he doesn't know that the real case is on its way to Zadok. The Zads might if they have sensors on board, but we would have detected another explosion."

"Would we?" Jena said. "We detected incredible speeds by the Zadokian ship when we were in orbit. Maybe eighty per cent light speed within the solar system. That ship left over two days ago." She tapped a calculator. "It's already twenty-six-billion miles away, seven times farther away than Pluto. Abdul's had Hubble and a radio telescope pointing at the Sirius system, on alert, for months. So we can be fairly certain that ship is intact. So far."

CHAPTER 42

IN THE WAITING ALIEN SHIP, Antonio examined his hands. His fingernails had been bitten to the quick months before this latest disaster. Why hadn't he seen the red danger flags flapping hard when the French let him see their scam? His sneer transformed to a sly grin. He had the last laugh, he'd call it the *coup de grâce* in honour of the French bastards. His epiphany moment flashed to him with the realization of how easy it was for Françoise to walk through the domes to the ship.

Strapped in the couch, he allowed an extra laugh as he reflected that unlike her, he could think the hatch to open and close. He knew this otherwise empty silver ship was to take off momentarily. Just time for him to induce a meditative trance. He'd ascertained from the Zadokian prisoner that sensors in the couch would detect his presence and maintain life support along with liquid nourishment into his arm. His rifling of Julia's notes and his own research enabled him to mimic sufficient alien physiology for a high probability of survival.

His time on Earth was suspended temporarily. What joy for his new friends when they greet him on Zadok. And what a shock for Ryder when he finds out.

Book Three of
The ARIA Trilogy

ARIA:
ABANDONING LUGGAGE

Antonio arrives on Zadok. The ARIA-3 bomb had reached there two days previously, causing havoc. Surviving Zadokians consider a mass-migration to Earth to escape the effects of ARIA-3. Antonio's madness grows, and he makes disturbing discoveries in their laboratories.

Ryder's relationship with Jena is unstable and others have coruscating infatuations in tune with the increasingly desperate situation. When their island becomes unsustainable and the alien-Earth hybrid weed gets out of control, where should they go?

What was the Zadokian's real purpose with the ARIA viruses, and how does it all end?

About the Author

Geoff Nelder escaped from his roots in the south of England and now lives in the north. He would do most things for a laugh but had to pay the mortgage so he taught I.T. and Geography in the local high school. After thirty years in the education business, he nearly became good at it. A post-war baby boomer, he has postgrad researched, written about climatic change, ran computer clubs, and was editor of a Computer User Group magazine for eleven years. Geoff lives in Chester with his long-suffering wife and has two grown-up children whose sense and high intelligence persist in being a mystery to him.

Visit Geoff's website - www.geoffnelder.com

Other books by LL-Publications

Oops!
By Darrell Bain
ISBN: 978-1-905091-72-0 (print) / 978-1-905091-73-7 (ebook)

Oops! is the third collection of stories by Darrell Bain. When Cupid and a Gremlin bump heads, the sparks fly in a rare fantasy story by the author. Other stories in the collection include *A Simple Idea,* an almost ludicrously simple method of eliminating corruption and idiocy from the political process, one that has been around for centuries but gone unrecognized. *Cure for an Ailing Alien* finds a nurse who must come up with a cure for an alien, one whose bodily processes are completely unknown. You'll be amazed at her cure! *Retribution* is the story of unexpected consequences when alien meets human. *Robyn's Rock* is partially based on a happening in the author's life during a walk with his granddaughter.

There are many more stories in this collection, all written in the individual style that has kept Bain's readers coming back for more for the past twenty years. This a book to add to your collection, stories by a notable, multi-award winning author.

Bark!
By Darrell Bain
ISBN: 978-1-905091-15-7 (print)

Find out what happens when Tonto, a little, ADHD affected, one-testicled weenie dog, turns out to be the only thing standing between the Earth and accidental alien invasion!

Pure comic genius from multiple award-winning author Darrell Bain. Also includes the autobiography of the real Tonto, the little dog who inspired the story!

Lightning Source UK Ltd.
Milton Keynes UK
UKOW050426160713

213862UK00001B/44/P